DEL RIO

THE PACIFIC FRONTIER • BOOK ONE

DEL RIO

THE PACIFIC FRONTIER · BOOK ONE

MICHAEL LEE

TIREE
PRESS
an imprint of
THE OGHMA PRESS

OGHMA
CREATIVE MEDIA

Bentonville, Arkansas • Los Angeles, California
www.oghmacreative.com

Library of Congress Cataloging-in-Publication Data

Names: Lee, Michael, author.
Title: Del Rio/Michael Lee. | The Pacific Frontier #1
Description: First Edition. | Bentonville: Tiree, 2022.
Identifiers: LCCN: 2022935247 | ISBN: 978-1-63373-656-6 (trade paperback) | ISBN: 978-1-63373-657-3 (eBook)
Subjects: BISAC: FICTION/Historical | FICTION/Action & Adventure | FICTION/Westerns
LC record available at: https://lccn.loc.gov/2022935247

Tiree Press trade paperback edition June, 2022

Jacket & Interior Design by Casey W. Cowan
Cover art by Albert Bierstadt (1830-1902)
Emigrants Crossing the Plains or *The Oregon Trail*, Oil on canvas (1869)
Editing by George "Clay" Mitchell, Dennis Doty, & Bob Giel

Published by Tiree Press, an imprint of The Oghma Press, a subsidiary of The Oghma Book Group.

A remembrance to all the valiant souls that roamed this great country, native and foreign. Their interactions created what became known as "The American Spirit."

We are forever indebted and should hold to that standard unfailingly, raising that beacon for all who follow.

ACKNOWLEDGMENTS

NO ONE WRITES A BOOK alone, though it is a satisfyingly lonely place to be.

I am deeply indebted to a wonderful lady. Opal Viola transcribed my handwritten words into the typed manuscript, breathing life into *Del Rio*. She grew to love the story, urging me to keep creating storyline and character. I owe her from the bottom of my heart for her work and encouragement.

My son Adam, and daughter Abigail Lee, were always there with an encouraging word and support. They are always with me and in my every thought.

Another special person, I owe heartfelt love and affection to is Gertrude Thibodeaux. She read the work back to me, giving a new perspective, always a warm, loving friend, ready for an adventure and able to dance my legs off. She will be in my heart forever.

My first writing mentor was Paul Colt. A gifted and wonderful writer, always ready with a good word and encouragement, and a believer in *Del Rio*.

None of this would have been possible with out the friendship of the late Dusty Richards. His generosity to any writer seeking advice, was boundless. He introduced me to my publisher, Casey Cowan, of Oghma Creative Media, who signed me up and gave me leadership and direction. Editors, George 'Clay' Mitchel, Dennis Doty, and my buddy Bob Giel all have my deepest gratitude.

To all of the above, I could not have done this without your guidance every step of the way.

DEL RIO

1

DELAINO CLUNG TO THE MANE of the fleeing horse as it galloped down the street, his black cloak billowing around him. The iron-clad hooves sent reverberating crescendos echoing against the walls and cobbles of the buildings and streets, sounding as blacksmith's hammers forging new steel.

He looked behind him. No one followed. The tenseness of his body eased, but his stomach rebelled, and he vomited to the side of the road wiping his face with the sleeve of his shirt.

"Whoa, Raj. That's enough. Let's walk for a bit, shall we?" Steam rose from the flanks of the big stallion.

"I'm going to find you, Daniel Riodan, if it's the last thing I ever do. You're out there someplace and I'm going to find you. I can't stay here anymore." Del's breath came in short gasping intervals, filling his nose with the smell of his retching. Gulping cold air, he sucked in deep lungsful, calming his beating heart. He ran for his life from the house of his grandfather, where his uncle had just tried to kill him.

"Raj, we are on our own now. Uncle Beaux meant it when he said he would kill me. I saw that insane look in his eyes."

Christmas Eve, 1846, and Baltimore was festooned in reds and greens. Candles sparkled in windows, beckoning with food, warmth, and the closeness of family. Carolers' songs faintly drifted from the churches as he passed. Sweet and savory smells wafted to him as kitchens prepared their family feasts on this holiday. None of this would be for him.

Cold wind numbed his face as he slipped through the lanes vanishing into the night. He had fled from family, warm food, and bed back on his grandfather's estate.

What family have I ever had? My grandfather has always been cold and distant. My uncle treats me like a servant. Tucker has been my family for most of my life, and now, maybe, my father waits for me in Indiana. Knots twisted his stomach again, and he spat to the side of the road. Delaino's mind whirled with possibilities. He must get out of Baltimore tonight.

He was born Delaino Daniel Riodan, son of Daniel and Rebecca Riodan. His only friend and semblance of family had been his mother's Negro slave, Tucker, who had raised him from childhood.

"Tucker told me about my pa, Raj. I thought he was dead. Told me he waited till I was old enough to leave and go find him. He's in Indianapolis someplace, and that's where we're going. All my life I have been told my father abandoned me and died. Damn them to hell for the dirty liars and cheats they are. I hope to never lay eyes on them again." Del patted the big horse's shoulder.

"Let's get going."

Learning his father was alive left a resentful anger in his gut. Tucker had sat him down and told him the entire story a few days before Christmas.

"Your father is alive, Delaino. Your mother died of fever when you were five years old, and when your daddy came to fetch you, your grandfather told him that both of you were dead. When Daniel wanted to see the graves, Major Conlon had him thrown in jail and Beaux had some thugs beat him up, threatening to drown him in the river if he ever came back. The Major said that all Daniel wanted was money. That was the excuse they used to deny your father the right of ever having anything to do with you, or ever see your mama's grave. They are cold cruel men, Delaino. Don't ever trust a word they tell you."

"Daniel Riodan is alive? We never heard from him."

"Oh, he wrote. Wrote often. Major hid his letters. He stowed them away in his library someplace. I know he sent money too. When Daniel received no reply to none of his letters wanting to know when you and Becky would return home, he came looking for his family. Major Conlon, your grandpa, told him you was both dead of fever."

"They had him thrown in jail and beaten?" Del asked.

"Yes, they did. Locked me in my room so's I couldn't tell him nothin'."

"I lived with your ma and pa in Indiana when they first got married. Your pa didn't know what to do with me. He had never owned another person. So, he taught me his ways and how to live in the woods. Introduced me to living like the natives. I even lived with a local tribe for a few months. I was your ma's slave, you know, though she never treated me like a slave.

"Only ten years old, I was, when you were born. They loved you with all their hearts.

"Rebecca taught me to read and write. Gave me books on herbs and medicines. My most prized possession was Culpepper's Herbal. Daniel was my friend. First white man dat ever treated me right."

"You lived with my parents in Indiana?" Del's eyes never left Tucker's face.

"That's where they met. You daddy was a fine architect. Laid out the first capitol of Indiana in Corydon. Major Conlon traveled there with Becky, looking for investments for his bank. They met at the ball and fell in love. The Major resented Daniel's heritage—none. Daniel Riodan was a self-made man and your granddaddy hated him. Becky married him, anyway.

"You was almost six years old when we came back to Baltimore. Supposed to be just a short visit. Daniel built a new home for you in Indianapolis. He had accepted a job with L'Enfant, the architect of Washington D.C., designing a new capitol in Indiana along the National Road. Your ma caught a fever from a friend she had gone to nurse and passed. I been lookin' after you ever since. I doctored the slaves on the estate as well. 'Cept for the mean times."

"Mean times?"

"Well, worse dan most. That's not why I am telling you this story now. Maybe we'll talk, another time, if there is another time. Right now, you's got to get out of this house. You will be eighteen on your next birthday. You'll be of legal age."

"What's that got to do with my father?"

"Delaino, you will own the estate when you come of age. It came down through your mother's family. The Major and Beaux have no claim. Rebecca gave me all her papers on her death bed. Made me promise to take care of you and to get you to Daniel. That time is now. If you stay here, Beaux will kill you, sure enough. A copy of the will is recorded in the courthouse. It cannot be overturned. They tried, but your ma's family fought them and won. The only way for them to get it, is if you die."

"My father is alive? I own the estate? Somehow, all this is not making sense to me." Del stared at Tucker for a long time, his mind racing in dizzying circles and possibilities.

"Wake up, boy." Tucker slapped his face. "You's got to get out of here. I got it worked out. Da Major will be at the bank's Christmas party like they does every Christmas Eve. Beaux will be out drinkin' like he does every night. Go find your daddy's letters and read them for yourself. I'll have everything waiting for you in the kitchen that you'll need. Christmas Eve is the night to do it. You has to sneak out of town. They'll have men looking for ya everywhere, and they will kill you!"

"You're right, Tuck. I hate them and they sure enough despise me. We'll leave and go find my pa. I don't know for sure, how we'll do it. Maybe catch a coach to another town. keep switching coaches, using false names to throw then off. I'll think of something."

"There is no we."

"But Tucker, they'll punish you for telling me. You know they will."

"I only know that a boy with a black slave will draw attention. That will get us both caught and killed for sure. Somehow, someway, I will gets out of here and go to Indianapolis. You watch for me. I'll be comin' one of these days."

Taking advantage of a quiet house, on the Eve of Christmas, with Beaux and the Major out for the evening, Del searched his grandfather's desk. It took a while, but he found the packet of letters bound with string hidden between the Major's account books. He traced his father's signature with a finger in wonderment, feeling he had discovered a living ghost. Time seemed to stand still as he stood reading his father's words of love and his urging for his wife and child to return.

He also found ten gold sovereigns in a hidden compartment of the desk. Del had discovered this space as a child, while playing in the Major's library. These he took, feeling they were owed to him as much as his father's letters.

Stuffing the letters in his shirt and the leather bag of coins in his belt, he looked up to find Beaux standing at the door.

"I always took you for a thief." Beaux stoood in the doorway as he removed his hat and cloak. "I'm going to give you the beating you deserve." Flipping his riding crop out with his left hand in Del's eyes, he punched him in the face with his right, knocking Del to the floor.

"You are a coward, uncle. I am not the little boy you have pushed around till now." Del had been in many rough and tumbles down by the docks and on the streets. Mad with pent up anger, Del launched himself at Beaux, pummeling him in the stomach with both fists, doubling him over before he crumpled to the floor.

"You never thought I'd strike you back, did you?"

Beaux gasped for breath as he lay on the floor.

"I'll kill you for that." Beaux struggled to his feet, grabbed the iron poker from its stand and swung the iron, barely missing Del's face.

"You missed, Uncle. Has the brandy dulled your senses?" Del stepped back from Beaux's attack, tripped and fell across his grandfather's broad desk.

"I have you now, cur." Beaux swung the poker wildly, shattering the desktop, and missing Del's ribs by inches as he rolled to the side.

"You are a mongrel dog that should have been drowned in the river when you were a puppy." Beaux lunged again, aiming for Del's eyes. Del grabbed the poker with both hands, wrestling it away from his uncle.

"I've been fighting on the docks and streets ever since I was ten, Uncle Beaux. I'm not your servant and not a slave. My mother wouldn't believe the way I have been treated by her own family," Del said.

"Your mother—my sister—married a dirty, ill-bred frontiersman, against her father's wishes, and birthed a woodrat." Beaux slipped a knife from his boot, slashing across Del's belly, cutting his shirt and nicking his arm.

Del parried the knife with the poker and struck Beaux across the cheek bone, laying open a wound from temple to cheek. Beaux clasped his oozing face in shock and ran shrieking from the room. It was over in an instant.

"Here, here. Beaux. What goes on?" Major Conlon came through the library door, hat and cloak in hand. "I could hear you two fighting from the vestibule." Beaux pushed him out of his way, swearing and bleeding.

"What have you done, boy?" The Major stared at Del, accusation written across his face.

"Dear, kind, Grandpa," Del said, throwing the poker at his feet. "I'm taking what's mine and leaving." Del waved the packet of letters in his face.

"I'm taking the first ship out of the harbor in the morning. I'll be rid of you, and you'll be rid of me! Loving Grandfather. Major. *Liar!*"

"Rot in hell, Beaux!" He strode through the foyer after spying Beaux on the staircase glaring at him.

"I'll kill you for this! Frontier bastard that you are!" Beaux descended the staircase, waving his blood-soaked rag at him, stopping out of reach. His hand gripped the stair rail with a white knuckled intensity.

Del turned and threw the doors of the estate wide open letting in the cold night air and walked out. Pausing, he turned back and stood in the middle of the vestibule as gusty breezes swirled in and around the foyer curtains, blowing the candles of the heavy crystal chandeliers and wall sconces. He looked at his uncle with cold disdain.

"Daniel Riodan is a better man than you'll ever be." He turned and left the house.

"Delaino. *Delaino!* You have to come back and answer for what you have done." Major Conlon ran out of the house, stopping Del by grabbing his left shoulder. He saw his servant standing there with the reins in his hand, transfixed by all the commotion.

"Natty! I told you to walk Raj. Cool him down. Take him to the stable."

Raj, the Major's favorite stallion was standing by the portico, reins held by a wide-eyed groom. Inspired by this good fortune, Del looked back at the Major full in his face. Slowly, he pulled the hand away from his shoulder with a strong grip and didn't release it until his grandfather's face paled. Snapping to attention in his best British style, he saluted the Major and vaulted onto the waiting horse's back.

"I wish you all a Merry Christmas." Leaning over, he snatched the reins from the groom and kicked Raj away.

Tucker called to him as he passed the kitchen. Del pulled to a sliding stop. Tossing Del a cloak and a satchel of food, Tucker passed him his favorite cap, then grasped the young man's hand with a firm warm grip.

"Ride hard, Master Delaino. God be with you. Your mother did the best she knew to do for me, a gift I still cherish. Your pa did the best he could do for me as well. Tell Daniel, when you find him, I done my best for you, my boy."

"Tucker! I'll never forget you. I regret I can't take you with me. I will tell him about you. Never fear. Farewell, old friend. Perhaps, we'll meet again." Delaino looked into Tucker's strong face, hesitating for a brief moment before leaving, realizing he was still clinging to his friend's hand.

"Go. Go now. This is your chance." Tucker whacked Raj on the rump and sent them off. "Run! Run for your life!"

Speeding away, Del looked back at the forlorn figure, his only friend standing in the dark lane, waving to him.

That image would haunt him in his dreams.

ONCE THEY HAD RIDDEN THROUGH the city, Del turned Raj down the lane to the docks. He wanted to be seen and heard asking about ships leaving with the tide, hoping to lay a false trail, so he stopped in a familiar place where he was known.

"I'm looking for a ship, Rooney. Know of any leaving on Christmas morning?" Del asked the tavern keeper. Appearing drunk and confused, he sloshed his tankard of ale over the bar, cursing his family and Beaux Conlon. It was a common tale of a family fight, told often by boys running off to sea and away from unhappy homes.

"Let's see, Del, me boy. I know the *Chanticleer* is signing on men to set sail in the morning. *Olivia Lee* is out of dry dock a fortnight now and should be sailing with the tide. HMS *Vigilant* is in port, so be careful nosing around. Put down that tankard and keep a civil look about you. If the British troops catch ya and shanghai ya, you'll wake up with nothing and a sore head at that. Your back will be flailed raw by the time you make any port with that mouth. I think the *Olivia Lee* is your best bet, if you're runnin' away—as it looks you are. Try her. She's headed around the horn and over to the Hawaii Islands, I hear."

"The *Olivia Lee*. Hawaii Islands?' Del asked. He shook his head as if confused and pushed his tankard away from him. "Sounds good to me. Where is she berthed?'

"She's down by the Dingle Bay whiskey warehouses, on Porter Street. You be careful now. Come see me, if ever you return. Damn Beaux Conlon. I never did take a liking to him."

Satisfied his false trail was established, Del turned Raj's nose west on the National Road and began his journey to find his father, determined to leave the bright lights of Baltimore behind him forever.

"Raj, I'm afraid there's one more duty I must perform before I take leave of this place."

Christmas Day offered the promise of rebirth and renewal to all living things. The clocks struck midnight as Del knelt next to Rebecca Riodan's gravesite praying for her guidance before saying his last goodbyes.

They loped through the frosty night lit by a watchful full moon, kicking up the new snow into sparkle-filled fairy dust. Was this an omen of blessing for their new life?

After several miles, Del walked the big stallion. Raj was up for a journey. He wasn't tired and was ready to go when Del touched him with his heels again. The stallion moved to the boy's silent commands from his knees and hands as he had when Del put him through his paces on the estate. Many hours of travel later, they stole into someone's stable.

"Here we go. Here's a few oats and a bite of hay. If anyone objects, I'll try to talk my way out of it in the morning. At least we're in a nice warm barn." Del settled himself under his woolen cloak in the hay, soon fast asleep.

2

EL STARTLED AWAKE THE NEXT morning, when a door banged on the nearby house. A man stared at him, from the open door of the barn. Del rose, still muddled by sleep, looking up to the man who stood scowling at him.

"Thank you kindly for the stable last night. It was late when we passed and a haybed was too tempting. I'd be happy to pay you for the night and maybe breakfast and a few oats for me old horse." Del could slip into the jargon of the streets when it suited him.

"Hmm. Boy, I could have you arrested." Then looking at him, the man smiled. "All right, lad. It is Christmas, isn't it? Give a bait of feed and hay to your horse. I'll tell Ma to set another place for breakfast. You're in luck. Ma's a fine cook."

These good folks were the Claireys. Ma and Pa had come from Ireland the year before because of the potato famine.

"Sit down here, lad. I'll have you a plate in just a moment. I used to feed me boys when we were back home in Ireland. They'll be joinin' us in a few months, they will." She fed him several rashers of bacon, a corn pudding sweetened with maple syrup and three eggs scrambled on slabs of hot, toasted, fresh-baked bread slathered with her good butter. A pot of homemade strawberry jam was set alongside his plate. Del ate hungrily until he could hold no more. Ma filled a flagon with hot tea and pushed it into his hand as he got up to leave.

"Drop the flagon off, if you ever get back this way," she said. "I'll fix something to take with you."

Del told them his name was Jim and he was traveling to his grandmother's house down the way. He'd simply been too tired to continue last night. While he felt guilty lying to these good folks, if Beaux followed, he needed to throw him off his track.

They wished him luck and Merry Christmas. Del gathered his goods, making ready to be off.

Pa was standing in the door of the stable as he left.

"Nice old horse you got there, young fella." He raised a knowing eyebrow at Del. "None of my business, though. You seem a nice enough young fella. Stay out of trouble. Hope you reach your people by this afternoon. It's a-goin' ta snow."

Down the road, Del decided he'd better check the saddlebags to see what the Major may have left in there. He had seen the set of Howdah pistols the old man treasured and always carried. They were neatly secure in the saddle holsters in front of the riding saddle.

They were two large double-barreled .56 caliber pistols that the Major kept for defense. In India, where the Major had been stationed, it was common to keep such weapons in the Howdah—the large platform the men hunted from on an elephant. The British tiger hunters never knew when the tiger would sneak through the tall grass unseen and climb the side of the elephant, intent on mauling the hunter.

"What is the last thing a tiger ever sees?" was a common phrase used by the British Army hunters. The answer was the Howdah pistols. Two to four barrels staring at them at point blank range. The last resort. These two beauties, stamped with the name Purdy, were some of the finest guns made for this type of hunting. Del found extra powder, balls, and some leather gloves, a bit of cord, a section of canvas, a piston match and pipe tobacco in the saddle bags.

"Let's see what Tucker put in my haversack." He found a side of bacon, an old pot, a cup, a spoon, some coffee, beans, flour, salt, dried meat, and a butcher knife, along with the cloak and his old news cap.

What was this? Del untied a small parcel wrapped in linen cloth. Tucker had sent the small portrait of his mother he kept by his bed. He also found an oil skin packet for his father's letters.

Tucker had thought of everything. With the Claireys' poke, Del felt well provisioned for a few days. He distributed his goods in the saddle bags making certain the precious portrait and letters were safe, then secured the satchel, seeing the pistols were loaded and ready. Pausing a moment in reflection, he stepped back and looked at Raj.

"You look pretty good for a stolen horse." Of all the items he packed, perhaps the most important asset he had was Raj.

Major Conlon raised the finest horses, known throughout the Eastern seaboard. Raj was bred from the finest stock and had been trained for military fighting in the Spanish style. These trained war horses were a terror in battle, fighting with hooves and teeth. They could kick with any leg and could leap into the air striking assailants with their powerful hind legs. Raj could be ridden with the rider only guiding him with his knees as he went through his gaits and performance routines. The only thing his grandfather had shared with him was his horses. An expert rider, Del had ridden Raj many times, learning the marching cadence and gaits and complex war strategies as well as the stallion.

"Raj! We're headed for Indianapolis to look for a man named Riodan. He's my father. He's all I've got if he's still alive. I don't know anything about him. Tucker says he was a good man, a smart man. The Conlons were cruel to him when my mother died. They've put a roof over my head and food in my mouth, but they have been no family to me. Let's find out what kind of man Riodan is. If he's as good as Tucker remembers, maybe he'll take us in. If not ... we'll just make out on our own. We'll set out, Raj." He patted the neck of his friend.

Before they set off, Del realized his horse would draw attention. Getting to work, he rubbed dirt in his tail and mane, knotting them to look raggedy and unkempt. He darkened the stallion's stockings, so they wouldn't be as noticeable.

"There, Raj, don't look so gloomy. I'll fix you back, handsome as you were once we find Riodan." He re-saddled the stallion, covering Raj's back with the piece of canvas. "That will hide you a little and keep you warm."

So, on Christmas morning, Del and Raj headed west, to find

what dreams might unfold before them. Del remembered what an old sea captain had once told him.

"There are no promises, no guarantees in living a life. You learn what you can, then make up the rest as you go along. Truth today may not be your truth tomorrow."

He wasn't sure what that meant entirely, but he would learn its meaning. There were no promises. Nothing was guaranteed. If he went back to Baltimore, his future was death. Only by not knowing his future, could he continue. Del was surprisingly content with his present.

"There are no promises. We make our own future." He patted the horse's neck. The big horse's muscles trembled under Del's legs.

THE SUN WARMED HIS BACK as it climbed into the day. Del day-dreamed of the warriors of ancient myth he had read about as they prepared for battle. His stomach ached in excitement. His mouth and throat grew dry, his eyes and senses sharper. Unknown destiny lay before him. He tasted the air on his tongue and throat, as he took a deep breath on that Christmas morning, bringing a sensation that steeled his resolve. He burst with enthusiasm from the joy of being alive. It seemed as if the universe had opened the gleaming road ahead just for him.

A trick of fate? Del sat looking at the road before him. There is no fate. There is only the present.

They traveled as obscurely as possible. Del changed his gold, one coin at a time into smaller amounts at banks in the towns he passed.

"Where did you get a gold sovereign, young man?" tellers asked when he tried changing them at banks along the road.

"A Christmas gift from my Grandfather," he said simply. That way, he didn't have to change the coins at inns and taverns, nor worry with being cheated by innkeepers who claimed they couldn't change the larger sovereigns. Del and Raj kept to themselves, camping and sheltering at night with the canvas blocking the wind and warmed by a small fire.

Del watched his fellow travelers from a distance, remaining vigilant, absorbing useful information. People, goods, and services followed this busy, crowded artery from West to East and East to West, the life blood of the young country. They only stayed at an inn if the weather forced them to. Most often, Del slept in a barn with the horses. He didn't want Raj stolen. Raj was well trained and would not tolerate any rider. Only Major Conlon and Del had ever ridden him. A whistle from Del and Raj would toss an errant thief sprawling in the dust before he could get settled in the saddle.

Good weather and bad, they rode on. Del remained alert to any news from back home or of any news ahead of him. They overheard talk of a banking crisis back East as they crossed over into Virginia. Several banks had gone under. The funding for the National Road was at stake. It might not get finished, due to loss of funding from the collapse of the banks.

The days and nights grew colder. Snow sometimes trapped them in a barn or inn for a day or two until it cleared. Del worried there would not be feed for Raj along the way as most of the fields were covered in snow. Fortunately, enough businesses had grown up along the road that stocked feed and stored hay, and it wasn't a concern. The greatest concerns were thieves and highwaymen who would rob or kill a traveler alone and unaware. Del kept the Howdahs covered on the saddle. The butt of the pistol on his right was always exposed, so it could be quickly grabbed.

Late one evening, close to the western Virginia border, Raj and he came upon a buggy stopped in the roadway ahead. Two women sat trapped in the buggy surrounded by three men. One held the horses, one searched the wagon and one stood guard.

"Keep moving, sonny. This is not your affair," the guard said as they rode up.

The older woman looked up at Del. "They are robbers and thieves, boy. Ride on and bring back some men from the inn up ahead."

Del pulled the Howdah with his right hand and reined Raj to a stop, so he could cover all three men.

"Gentlemen, do I have your attention? Ladies, ride on quickly!

Send some men back for these scoundrels." The woman driving the buggy twitched her whip in the guard's face and snapped it over the horses' backs driving them forward, knocking the guard out of her way before the men could react.

"Now, don't that just beat all, Waylon? This kid comes up and off they go, and we don't get nothing. Nothing! I'm pretty sore. How about you? Kid, that pea shooter only has two barrels. You can't get all three of us, if you can shoot the thing in the first place. Let's get him, boys." They started to move.

Del pulled back the cover and produced the second pistol. "How about four barrels, mister? Do you want the first?" Del nudged his horse a few steps forward bearing down on the speaker.

"Not so chatty now, are you?" Del held both pistols aimed at the three men. "Just sit tight. Someone will be coming for you soon."

For a long ten minutes, Del kept his standoff. The thieves weren't sure what he'd do, so they stood for the time being. Though Del's guns were well balanced, they began to weigh heavy in his hands.

The talker began again, "Your hands are trembling. Boy, you'd better give it up. You'll miss the first shot and we'll be on you before you can pull the trigger a second time. Won't we, boys?" They stepped closer.

Hoofbeats sounded, approaching from over the rise.

"Get him, boys!" The mouthy talker lunged at Raj.

Del fired the pistols simultaneously. He had never shot the guns either standing, or on horseback. The double recoil somersaulted him over Raj's back end, and he ended up face down, in the cold mud.

Scattered by the sudden gunfire, the three men scrambled for their horses, mounted and escaped before the rescuers arrived.

"There they go! Sam, Pete, quick, go get 'em!"

"Tarnation Sam, they got away. They won't do that for a while. We'll be watchin' fer em if they try to do that again." Eager hands helped pull Del to a sitting position. He was covered in mud and filled with shame. Some hero he had been.

The rescue posse insisted that Del and Raj get cleaned up and have supper with them at their inn, a short distance away where the ladies in the buggy waited.

"Those men stopped you on the off side of the hill, Maudie, out of sight and hearing. They planned it that way. We'll have to be alert for them."

"I heard tell they was robbers about, Pete. I never expected it to happen to me and Sissy. Where is the law when you need them, I say? That young man saved our lives."

Del was embarrassed, having fallen off his horse in a ridiculous manner. The ladies washed his face and brushed his clothes. Raj got a ration of grain and green hay.

"That was a fine meal. I think I'll just sit over here by the fire and warm up, before Ned and me take to the road again."

This was the first group of people Del had associated with since the Claireys on Christmas Day. The human smiling faces and support surprised him as to how much he had missed talking to other folks. He enjoyed the attention and camaraderie. Pete insisted they stay the night in the inn and set them off the next morning fed and with clean clothes.

Del and Raj crossed into Ohio at the river, taking a ferry across. They kept moving, spending many cold nights protected only by the canvas to break the wind and a fire to warm them. Three feet of snow caught them in a small town in Ohio. They holed up in a tiny inn with a stable until the roads were safe to travel.

"How ya doing, Raj? Your hooves still look good. We'll rest up a bit here and get some good grub into the both of us. This snow will be gone in a few days." Del rubbed his horse down, checking his condition and his legs. "Got to keep you in good shape. You're all I got."

———

SEVERAL WEEKS LATER, THE TWO weary travelers reached the outskirts of Indianapolis. Since fleeing Baltimore, they had been on the road for two months, sometimes making only a few miles a day due to the ravages of the cold and weather.

Del found a warm, clean room outside the city limits. He hadn't been more than two miles from the National Road the entire way. He was exhausted. Raj was still strong, but much leaner. They needed rest. He would look for Daniel Riodan in the morning. After seeing that Raj was stabled and fed, Delaino fell asleep as soon as his head touched the pillow.

3

TUCKER STOOD IN THE SHADOWS as Delaino rode away. "God go with you, my boy."

"So, you helped him get away. The thief! That makes you a thief as well, doesn't it?" Beaux stood at the kitchen door, a blood-stained rag held to his face.

He grabbed Tucker by his collar. "I'll thrash you within an inch of your life. You babied that boy. Now, he can't protect you." Dragging him by the shirt to the smokehouse, Beaux bound Tucker's wrists together and secured them to a meat hook on a rafter.

"I'm going to slice your back like a side of bacon!" Beaux raged, ripping Tucker's vest and shirt to his waist.

Tucker never thought to resist. Submission was ingrained. Fighting back meant more fervent punishment. The Conlons weren't cruel to their slaves, but they were strict disciplinarians and punished disobedience. Now, Beaux was going to punish him for his loyalty to Delaino and for the ripped flesh of his disfigured face.

Sliding his belt from around his waist, Beaux wrapped the leather around his right hand. His left still held the rag staunching the wound on his face. He left the brass buckle dangling, clicking in anticipation. A look of madness flushed Beaux's face.

"Ya!" Beaux screamed and slashed the brass buckle across Tucker's exposed back. Tucker screamed. Three more strikes cut and tore into Tucker's back and shoulders. The brass bit cruelly into the tender flesh and deep to the bone, leaving Tucker hanging from his wrists at Beaux's mercy, weak and helpless with pain.

"Here now, stop!" said Major Conlon at the door. He had come, summoned by the loud curses from Beaux and the insistence of the house slaves. Major Conlon rushed to Tucker, supporting him, as he freed his bound hands from the meat hook. "My God, Beaux, what have you done?"

Beaux's belt slashed across the Major's back causing him to cringe in pain. "Stop, I tell you!" he said and grabbed Beaux around the chest dragging him across the room and out the door.

"Who is this? I'll kill you!" Beaux cursed, fighting his father's arms.

Major Conlon threw Beaux against the fence. "Beaux! You must stop this."

Beaux raised the belt to strike again when the blood cleared from his eyes.

"Oh, it's you, Major!" Beaux regained his composure and gestured toward Tucker. "He helped that brat escape, the little thief. Look what your grandson did to me! I caught Del going through your desk. He had some letters and a purse of coins. This slave has gone too far."

"Give me that belt, Beaux!" Major Conlon tore it from his hand. "We've got a lot to discuss this evening. Delaino won't go far. He's run away before. Raj is well known in town. We'll track him down in the morning. What were you fighting about this time?" He examined Beaux's mutilated face.

"I told you, I caught him stealing from your desk in the library. He knew about his father, and the only person who could have told him is Tucker. When I confronted him, the brat hit me across the face with a poker. Major, I'm maimed. I'll have the hide off Tucker's back if it's the last thing I ever do. He's as much a thief as your bastard grandson."

"Come, I'll send for a doctor to mend your face. You're going to need sewing up." He hid his thoughts from his son. The wound was deeper than he first suspected. He had pulled the bloody rag from Beaux's face. The left side was cut deeply into the soft flesh to the bone, from cheek to temple. There most certainly would be a scar. "Go into the kitchen. Tell Flora to get a clean compress. I'll be right there."

Inside the smokehouse, a chagrined Major Conlon sat Tucker on a wooden box and cut the bonds around his wrists. "Tucker, I don't know what happened here tonight, but I will find out. I'll send Flora to clean your back and bring you food, a shirt and some blankets. I'm locking you in here, so Beaux can't get to you. I have the only key. Light the fire in the stove. There's matches and oil by the door. Stay out of his way, Tucker. There was madness in his eyes. Did you tell the boy about his father?"

Tucker nodded.

Major Conlon looked at him worriedly, "You may have set off a firestorm that will destroy us all." He turned and left, closing the door behind him and leaving Tucker alone in the cold building.

Calling for a servant to fetch the doctor, Major Conlon said, "Tell him it's an emergency. Beaux has been hurt." The Major tried to calm Beaux down as his son erratically paced the floor repeating the events of the night over and over again.

"He has disfigured me for life!" Beaux ranted on with a wild unbalanced look in his eyes. His manic behavior disturbed the Major.

Dr. Hobson came in through the kitchen. "Major, this man of yours insisted I leave my home on this cold night. I am here. I hope your emergency warrants leaving my family on Christmas Eve!" Seeing Beaux's bloody face, he exclaimed, "Dear God! Beaux, what have you done?"

The Major spoke quickly, "An unfortunate accident, Dr. Hobson. Thank you for coming. We will be in your debt. Is it serious?"

"The bleeding has stopped. There are no major arteries involved, thank God, but it will scar," the doctor said. "This is going to hurt. I must sew the sides of your face closed so it will heal. If not, it will leave a hideous scar. Can you tolerate it, Beaux?"

"Go ahead!" Beaux gripped the chair back in front of him and stared off, lost deep in his own thoughts, never flinching as the stitches sewed his face back together again.

WHEN HE WAS FINISHED, DR. Hobson had to nudge him to regain his attention. "Okay, that's done. Forty-seven stitches, Beaux,
from temple to just above your mouth. You didn't jump once. I've
only seen that one other time, but he was dead drunk. Keep it clean
and dry. Change that dressing several times a day. If it festers, come
to the office at once. I will return on Tuesday to have a look at you.
I don't want you to talk or eat much for three days. It should start to
heal if you don't overwork the muscles and pull the stitches. There
will be a distinguishing scar. No rum or spirits, they will slow the
healing." He closed his bag. "I wish you both a happy Christmas."
Looking dubiously at them each, he closed the door.

"Beaux, sit here, will you? I have unfortunate news. This is not
about Delaino. He'll come back. He always does. Where would he
go? The bank is going under. It's failing! The board met for its last
meeting of the year. This is usually more of a party than meeting,
but several auditors were present, and their report put a dour note
on the proceedings. Misadvised investments... investments I cham-
pioned, have gone bad. Lost! White belly up, like dead mackerel.
The board voted me out! The yellow varlets ganged up on me and
axed me. Some voted out of malice. I could see the smirks on their
lips when the vote was called. There is a smattering of smaller banks
going under. The auditors predict a bank crisis in the coming year.
We're the first major bank in Baltimore to start wobbling. Like a
stack of dominoes, they will fall, the damn auditors said. My ac-
counts were seized by the bank. I still hold the estate, but it was in
Rebecca's name, through her mother's family. Delaino gets the estate
when he is of age. That and what money I've kept here is all I've got.
That's it, Beaux. I'm finished."

Beaux questioned the Major long into the night until they were
exhausted trying to figure a way out of their crisis but coming up
with nothing tangible.

"It can't be. The estate belongs to Delaino?" Beaux sat back face
drained of expression.

Major Conlon sat stone-faced, staring at the fire. "It's all lost."

"I'm left with nothing?"

"There's the horses and the slaves of course, but the house and property belong to Delaino, when he comes of age. The only way it would fall your way is if something were to happen to him. You could make a strong case for being next of kin, I suppose."

Beaux got up and left the room, stunned with the knowledge that he was penniless. He sat in his room drinking brandy, nursing a hatred for Delaino, blaming him for his loss of fortune and the disfigurement of his face. One thought was prevalent on his mind when he passed out,

Next of kin.

4

A FEW DAYS LATER, FLORA brought Tucker some more healing ointments and bandages. He was the unofficial doctor to the estate's slaves. That early hunger for the outdoors learned in Indiana had never died. With Culpepper's book and what information he could glean from the older slaves who knew a bit of plant lore, he had continued adding to his growing expertise.

"Slave, heal thyself!" He mused as Flora dressed his wounds with the ointment Tucker had prepared that Spring. He sat and fretted and planned. Beaux was sure to carry out his threats. He must leave as soon as possible. Flora offered to bring him food and clothes and help him run away, but Tucker would not allow that.

"I don't want you involved in my mess, girl. Just let me know when the Major and Beaux both leave the house." The slave information network had learned of the bank's failure and the Major's dismissal. There were few secrets the masters of the house could keep from them. Naturally, they were worried for themselves. Their fate rested with the estate.

"Nobody has seen nor heard from Delaino for days. Rumor is, he was gone to sea because of dat rift with Beaux. Whispers all about town. Street gossip mostly. She has not been seen boarding a ship, nor is his name on any ship's roster. Three schooners sailed Christmas morning is all anybody knows. Whether Master Del was aboard any of them, remains a mysterious mystery," Flora said as she brought Tucker breakfast on New Year's Day. "Nobody has seen that horse, either. It's like the haints swallered dem up into thin air."

"Flora, where is the Major? And Beaux?"

"Why, the Major's fixing to leave this afternoon in a carriage for Washington D.C. He gots to be dar by the firs of the week. Some Congressmen is concerned about several bank failures, and he's got ta testify before a committee. The Major is plumb nervous, that's for sure. Beaux leaves and doesn't come back till late morning, most days."

"This afternoon then? Thank you. Oh, would you bring my supper, after Beaux leaves this evening? I'm going to want to know what you can find out about this. I'm worried for Del. Thank you, my girl. I'm much obliged."

Tucker sat and made his plans. Tonight? This early after the holiday, there would not be many people on the streets. Flora brought his food that evening. He ate nervously. He did not know when he would have another meal. She asked him where he was going, but he did not share his plans with her. He planned to leave under cover of the night. He ate his supper, thanked Flora for her help, then took her key and tied her to a bench.

"This is so they won't blame you." He slapped her on her cheeks several times, causing the blood to rise to the surface and tears to her eyes. "I'm sorry to have to do that, girl. Tell them, the house servants too, that I hit you and took the key. Tell everyone that. No one can repeat anything they don't know. Thank you, Flora." He kissed her on the cheek.

"Take care, Tucker. Don' get caught!"

Tucker sneaked out of the smokehouse and up to his room. He quickly and quietly packed. He didn't have many clothes and little money. His sole prized possession was a rolled canvas sailcloth bag in which he kept dried herbs, tinctures and ointments he had prepared and the worn Culpepper primer. Leaving the key on the bureau, so it would be found in his room, he took food from the kitchen and nothing else. Slipping into the night, Tucker stole his own freedom and set out to find his friends Daniel and Delaino, traveling any way he could. With a large hat and the collar of his cloak turned up, he sought the streets. In the dark, he looked like any man hurrying about his business. He knew Del was headed to Indianapolis on the National Road to find his father. He was going to follow.

Tucker had little interference on that cold night as he walked along. He kept to the shadows, stepping out of the light whenever a carriage passed. There were several encampments along the highway. Tucker made his way past them slipping through the shadows. Many wagons gathered together at night for safety. This part of the National Road was frequently called the Cumberland Road as it crossed the Cumberland Gap in Kentucky. Wayfarers traveled east and west. It carried the wealth of the nation and was the main artery plunging into the heart of Washington.

Tucker hoped to join a group traveling west. He stayed to the shadows, but kept moving, until he came to some wagons circled around a campfire where he heard a woman sobbing.

"How's the child, Mary Beth?"

"She is burning up with fever, Brother James. She doesn't move. I've done everything I know to do. I can only pray more. She is so tiny. I can only trust in the Lord God's grace, that she will live."

Mormons. They were always moving west. Maybe this is a way. *My* way. He walked to the edge of the firelight.

"Brother, perhaps I can be of service," Tucker said from the darkness. "I have some knowledge of herbs and healing remedies." He drew nearer the fire. "If I can approach the camp? I come with respect. I have no weapons. I come in peace and maybe, hope to prayers unanswered."

"Come forward, stranger. You will be covered by our men. If you come in peace, you're welcome."

Tucker stepped into the light. He held his arms down, palms up. "I am known as a healer to my people." He turned to Mary Beth. "I overheard what you said to Brother James. I have treated many children. I may be able to help her. Might I see the child?" He spoke bravely, but his knees were shaking.

"A black man!" Surprised conversation broke out.

"I'll bring her no harm. I'm peaceful. My word." He held up his hand. "I am sort of a healer. I have read books and have learned God's gift of healing plants from the fields and forests. I have herbs in my pack that might break a child's fever gently."

Mary Beth looked at him in desperation. "I lost my first baby. If you can help this child, I'd be forever grateful. Maybe God has brought a stranger into our midst to aid us in our time of need."

Brother James sighed. "We would all be grateful. We don't know who else to turn to. Mormons are not welcome in Baltimore. We would be thankful for any help you may render. If it is all right with the mother?" After a moment, she nodded in agreement.

Tucker knelt beside the grief-stricken mother with her baby wrapped tightly on her lap. "May I?" He gestured to the baby clutched in her arms. Mary Beth's pleading eyes never left his face. Hesitantly, she placed her baby in Tucker's arms "There now." He cooed as he took the swaddled child and opened the tightly wound bundle, "Let's see here, little one." He brought her closer to the fire so he could see, as well as for the warmth. Gently, he examined the child. There was no swelling that he could feel with his fingertips as he pressed her stomach. A hardness in her lower left abdomen causing the infant to flinch brought concern to his face. She was very warm. "When was the last time she had a movement or passed water, ma'am?"

"Why, it's been since yesterday morning that I changed her. She won't nurse. She just lies there, listless."

"Let's see?" Tucker took out his rolled canvas containing packets of herbs. "I would like to make her a tea to stimulate the bowels and increase urine flow, helping cool down the body some. It's very gentle. Would that be all right, ma'am?'

"You can try, if you can get her to take it."

"It's some valerian root, passiflower, and chamomile with a touch of licorice and black tea, very soothing, ma'am, and with a mite of honey to entice the baby to swallow."

Someone brought hot water from the fire. Tea slowly steeped and brewed, turning the liquid into a golden amber smelling of pine and honey. Tucker brushed a soaked rag against the baby's lips, "What's her name, ma'am?"

"It's Sara Ann, sir. What's your name?"

"I'm Tucker, ma'am, just Tucker. That's all I've ever been called. It's enough."

He squeezed a few drops between Sara Ann's lips. She twitched, startled by the taste on her lips. Tucker tried a few more drops and they trickled down her throat. She whimpered.

"That's it, Sara Ann." Tucker crooned softly. "Just a little at a time. It's gonna make you better. That's it, baby." He began working the little legs up and down gently massaging the tiny tummy in a circular manner. "Now, just a little more." He squeezed a few drops in her mouth. This time the child swallowed it.

Tucker worked her arms and legs, massaged her tummy and her cramped little toes and hands. He tickled her throat with his fingers and she swallowed more.

"Come on, Sara Ann. Get well for your mama, Get well for ol' Tuck, too, will you?"

The group had gathered around the little child and mother. This black man working diligently in the flickering firelight intrigued them. All eyes were wide with hope, and prayers formed on every lip. No one spoke as they watched Tucker and the baby.

A loud flatulence caused everyone to jump and step back from the gaseous fumes that formed.

Tucker beamed, "That's what little Sara Ann needed, wasn't it? She passed gas, ma'am, as you can tell. The tea relaxed her insides letting it pass. Change her. She'll be fine by morning. Give her some more tea every now and then. You'll need to change her often, but once the ague has passed, she'll be fine."

Tucker smiled as he passed Sara Ann back into the arms of a surprised Mary Beth. She burst into tearful laughter, as she looked at Sara Ann's face. She seemed to ask, "What's all this about, Mother? Who is this man?" Mary Beth cooed at her good baby as Sara Ann filled her diaper and fell asleep.

Brother James sat down next to Tucker offering him food and drink. "Tell me how you came to be here, friend Tucker?"

Tucker told him he was a runaway. "I got beat for helping my master, a young boy I have raised since his mother passed away. He ran away from his grandfather last Christmas Eve. I gave him food and a cloak. For that, I was beaten. Major Conlon had no love for the boy. He did his duty by him and no more. He has been mistreated and ignored by the Conlons, since his mother died. Master Del is running away to Indianapolis to find his father. I knew the father. He is a good man. I am running away to Indianapolis, hoping I'll find them both." Tucker spoke earnestly. He wanted no secrets between himself and these folks. If they were going to risk taking him along with them, they deserved to know the truth. He spoke silent prayers under his breath as well.

Brother James nodded thoughtfully. "I've heard of this Conlon. He is not thought well of, by any of whom I know. A greedy man, whose heart is closed. You may sleep by the fire, friend Tucker. I need to discuss this with the others. We are headed for Independence, Missouri. Sleep, rest and we will not be ungrateful. Thank you, Tucker. You have performed a small miracle. Perhaps God has placed you with us for just this healing. Mary Beth's prayers have been answered. Rest. No one will disturb you this night."

Morning broke clear and bright. After breakfast, four elders of the Mormons approached him. They were willing to take Tucker with their group and hide him when needed. He would work like one of them, eat and drink as one of them. If anyone approached and demanded an explanation, they would say he was their slave. It was not unheard of for Mormons to own slaves. They would call him Jacob.

However, they would board a steamboat to St. Louis when they reached the Ohio River and continue to Independence, Missouri. They weren't traveling through Indianapolis.

Tucker was caught off guard, but he had to agree. It was the only safe way of travel available to him. He reluctantly changed his plans. Maybe he and Del would meet again, but now, his path lay with this family of Mormons seeking as new a life as he sought for himself. Fate sets no certain destinations, so he placed his fate in the hands of Mary Beth, Brother James, and the others as long as he was with them. West? He had never considered venturing further west than Indiana. It was something to stop and ponder. He had heard the West was very big.

5

EL SAT ON A STONE studying a sign commemorating the architect L'Enfant and his crew of surveyors, designers, and builders. They were the ones who had labored and planned the newly laid out streets of Indianapolis. Daniel Riodan's name was, indeed, printed on the sign. Del traced the words with his fingers. At last, solid proof that the man existed. He looked up and gave a start. People were watching him. Del stood and turned toward them, smiling sheepishly, a little embarrassed. Putting his hands in his pockets, he pondered. Where can I find Daniel Riodan?

"Excuse me, sir." Del turned toward the nearest friendly face. "I am looking for one of the men listed on the plaque. I understand he lives in the city. Do you have any idea how I would locate him?"

"Well, boy, you could try the Capital building, but the post office is right around the corner. That is where I'd try, lad. Who are you looking for if you don't mind my asking?"

"Daniel Riodan, sir."

"Hmm, seems I have heard of him. Worked under L'Enfant designing the streets of Indianapolis. Hmm. Daniel Riodan? Name is familiar, but I can't place him. Try the post office, that'll be your ticket. Good day and good luck, lad." He touched the brim of his beaver hat and passed by.

Del turned toward the post office.

"Daniel Riodan?" queried the clerk, wearing a stiff-brimmed postal cap. "Sounds familiar. Let's see, he used to live over by the river. Ran a couple of mills, a sawmill and a grist mill, I believe. Haven't seen him for a while. Here we are! We are to forward all mail for Daniel Riodan to the post office in Independence, Missouri. Seems your man is headed west."

"How long ago was that notice given, mister?"

"A few weeks or so is my guess. Lots of folks headed west these days. Sorry, I'm not much help. Next!"

Del turned to leave.

"Hey, young man!" Del turned to an older fellow with a beard and a pipe cocked in his teeth. "I can give you a word on Daniel Riodan, son. I worked in one of his mills by the river. Nice fella, he be, too. Daniel had wagons made to his specifications. He bought teams of oxen, packed the wagons himself, and set off for Oregon. He seemed restless of late. Kinda felt like he needed a change of scenery. Anyway, he sold his mills and headed for a wagon train in Independence, Missouri. If you seek him, you gotta go to Missouri. He left about three weeks ago, he did."

Missouri? Independence? Del had felt his journey was at end. Now, it seemed it was just beginning. Riodan was not here. It confounded him.

"Well, mister, I traveled all this way to find him. I guess I'm in for a longer journey than expected. You've saved me a lot of time, I think. Thank you. Best of luck to you." Del touched his hat brim and turned to go.

A hand stopped him. "Please tell Daniel, if you ever find him, Tom Reed spoke well of him. Will you do that for me, son?"

Del grasped his hand. "I surely will, Tom Reed. I surely will. I am indebted to you, sir." He dropped some coins in the man's hand.

Del sat on the marble steps of the post office. He was tired, bone weary of travel. This was to be the end of the journey. He wasn't prepared to go further and didn't want to think about it. He could stay here. He was far enough away from Baltimore. The Conlons wouldn't know where to look for him. He'd be fine right here. What work? There were no docks or ships. He could do physical labor of any kind. He could read and write. Not many had those skills, though Del had little used them lately. He needed to think. How far was it to Missouri? These last few weeks had been a whirl-wind. Del shivered. He was cold. The wind had a fearful bite.

He found a tavern close by. Sitting at the fire, he ordered hot cider. It was nice here— friendly people, a growing city. A man could do much here. He stretched his legs. The warmth of the fire slowly made him feel lazy and content. Facing cold weather and more trav-el seemed far off. He wondered how Tucker was doing. He missed Tucker. He wondered where his father was now. Would he be in Independence yet? Probably not. It's a long way to Independence.

"Well, look who we have here, Waylon!" A hand grasped his neck. "The kid who cost us the job in Virginia before he went head over backsides off his horse. Learn to shoot your popguns yet, son-ny?" A broad hand spun him around. The three highway men stood over him, hemming him in.

"It seems you owe us for that one. It got so hot for us in Virginia, we had to come west looking for easy marks, and we found you, me Bucko. Got any money on you? Where's that fancy horse? I can tell horses. He was a fine one. Where did you get such a horse?"

"Thieves!" Del shouted loudly. "Help, thieves!" The only response was a rap of knuckles in the face, swelling and bloodying his lip.

"Quiet, you!" The dark-eyed leader scowled and shook him to silence. "It's all right, everyone. It's just a little family reunion, we got here. Everything is all right. We'll just take our business outside."

Lifting Del by his shoulders, they dragged him from the tavern. The cold wind bit into their faces on the frozen streets. Del shook loose from his captor in front of the post office and pushed the near-est assailant over a low post and chain fence bordering the yard sur-rounding the building. He kicked the leader in the knee, hyperex-tending it. Both, yelped, and fell on their back sides. Waylon grabbed at Del but only came away with an arm full of empty cloak.

"Help. Thief!" Del yelled, slipping to his knees on the cold street. He landed on all fours at someone's feet.

"Here, you. Stop! Officer! Officer. Over here quickly. What goes on?" It was the gentleman who had told Del to go to the post office.

"They're trying to rob me," Del gasped as he pointed to the fleeing bandits. He retrieved his cloak and threw it over his shoulders, watching as the thieves scrambled around the corner of the tavern. "They're robbers I met in Virginia. I stopped them from robbing some women there."

The gentleman beckoned for the police again. Someone blew a whistle. The three thieves had hot footed it down an alley, not looking back.

"Are you all right, young man?" The gentleman helped to steady him on the slippery street and wrapped the cloak more securely around Del's shoulders.

"I'm fine, thank you. I'm indebted to you again it seems. Thank you. They were going to take revenge for spoiling their robbery in Virginia. I never thought I'd see them again. Thank you, Mister... May I have your name?"

"Of course," he extended his hand. "I am Randolph Randazzo, counselor at law. I'm late of Boston and have only been in Indianapolis for a few months. I'm moving my law practice right down the road there on Meridian Avenue. I'll be a partner with the Harrison law firm." He presented his card.

"Err, thanks Mister Randazzo. I'm Delaino Riodan, but I'm called Del. The man I asked about earlier was Daniel Riodan, my father. I'm looking for him."

"Sorry, Mister Randazzo, sir, we couldn't catch them. We'll be on the lookout for 'em, that's a fact. Are you all right, boy?" A policeman walked up, his feet crunching in the snow, puffing and rubbing his hands together, obviously winded from the chase.

"Yes, officer. Thanks for your help," replied Del. He shook the policeman's hand and then Mr. Randazzo shook the policeman's hand, and both watched him walk away, cautiously sliding on the slippery streets.

"You have found him then?" asked Mr. Randazzo.

"Huh!" Del was lost in his thoughts, wondering if he'd ever see those thieves again. "My father? Oh, no, he left three weeks ago. He's moving west to Independence and then on to Oregon."

"A rich, virgin land, Oregon. I've read reports from the Astoria and the American Fur Companies, who trade out there. Rich lands of grass, plenty of game, forests, water, some even talk of gold—everything a young man would want in seeking his future. Are you going to follow?"

"I didn't know until this very minute, sir. I think Oregon sounds like a wonderful place for the likes of me. You've helped me three times now. I am in your debt. May I offer you an ale? A hot cider on a cold day, perhaps?"

"Thank you, Del. I think I'll take you up on that. I'd like to hear your story."

Delaino and Randolph Randazzo sat for several hours enjoying each other's company. Randolph was an excellent listener and sat entranced by the tale Del told him. This was the first time Del had spoken of it to anyone. He emptied his heart to the attentive lawyer.

Randolph had had an exciting life, as well. "I was a United States Naval officer for several years, a graduate of the Academy. A cannon barrage put a splinter in my leg, and that ended my career. I am castaway to this island of America." Randolph smiled. He still walked with a pronounced limp.

Encouraging Del in his quest, he spoke candidly, "It is a large country, Delaino, and growing larger. Write to me when you get yourself and your pa settled in your new home. I'd like to know you made it. Oregon would be a fine country to start a new life. I envy you. I envy your father. He doesn't know what a quality lad he has begat." Warmed by the spirit of adventure, the two soon bonded. Aided by a few pots of ale and warm food, they became friends in a few hours.

Del had taken the horse trolley to the city to give his travelling companion a rest. Returning to his inn, he checked on Raj who was happily munching hay and oats, enjoying the warm straw-filled stable. Grooming the horse, Del told him of the friend he met and where they were headed next. Raj shook his newly combed mane. "We're going to a great land, this Oregon, Raj. My friend, Mister Randazzo, has told me about it. Seems my pa has set his mind on going there, too. So once again, we're going to set out to find him. We've got to move quickly, before his wagon train leaves from Independence, Missouri. He's going overland and he's three weeks ahead of us. Get your rest. We leave at daybreak." He curried the coat to a lustrous shine. "I know I'll have to disguise you later, but I want you to look beautiful when we leave in the morning."

Del was determined he would continue now. There was no doubt. He was on Daniel's trail. He turned in early, his spirit refreshed by a new friend and dreams of a beautiful and bounteous Oregon.

6

THEY LEFT INDIANAPOLIS FRESH AND early the next morning. Del bought new provisions in town including food, caps, powder and ball and another length of sailcloth to protect them at night. They were not pilgrims any longer. Del knew the road and how to handle himself. He had made mistakes, but more importantly, he had an eye for the other travelers and knew when to stay clear of what looked like trouble to him. He had learned to trust his gut. It was usually right.

The road through town was called Washington Street. On the way west out of town, it became the National Road again. He paused on a bluff, known as Mars Hill, overlooking the country spread out before him. The air was crisp, cool with a mild whiff of smoke mingled with new grass and thawing earth. It was a living breeze. This air, inhaled deep within him, was air never breathed before. It was cleansing, rejuvenating him, making him eager to continue the search for his father whose trail always beckoned just beyond his grasp.

Daniel Riodan, I'm coming for you, hell or high water. I will not quit, even if I have to chase you into the sea.

Patting Raj on his shoulder, Del kicked Raj's flanks and set off again not knowing where the road would take them or what fate would greet them. There were no promises, no guarantees. He and Raj took each day as they came and dealt with what was given. They left no harm. They caused no trouble to anyone. The vortex of this adventure that began back in Baltimore swept them forward again.

SPRING WAS BREAKING. THE WEATHER turned cold, then hot, then cold again, but mostly it was wet and muddy. Sometimes, they travelled a finished road. Mainly, though, it was a sloppy mire filled with trudging bodies and horses. Del helped push wagons out of holes. He helped feed families with his meager supplies. If asked, he called himself Jim. His horse was Ned. He attempted to be a grey man, blending into the surrounding countryside doing nothing to distinguish himself from any one of the emigrants on the National Road. They helped when needed and drifted away. Heavy snows and treacherous roads forced them to hole up, often for several days at a time. He slept in the stable with Raj. On a fresh clear day, horseman and horse took a ferry and crossed over the Mississippi into St. Louis.

St. Louis was situated below the confluence where the Illinois and the Missouri Rivers flooded into the Mississippi. Giant stern wheelers plied the waters of the Mississippi. Smaller ones ventured up the Missouri River. They were the express route up or down any of the great rivers. This was the epicenter for commerce in the United States. St. Louis was fed by the great rivers and the National Road.

If Del had to describe St. Louis, his first thought would have been that it stunk. Literally.

People swarmed all over like a pulsing human ant hill. Whites, Blacks, Reds, Europeans, and Africans co-mingled in a festering sore of a birthing city with whistles, horns, steel hammers and untold languages screaming as it took its first breaths.

Del needed to reach Independence before Riodan set out on the trail west. The fastest way he knew was a steamboat, pushing upriver. They headed for the docks led by their noses and the sight of small sailing sloops and stern wheeled steamboats anchored at wharves with men shouting as they labored, filling the hungry bellies of their ships with cargo. He felt comfortable there. He would gain a berth by working his way up the river. Del hoarded his money. He did not know when he would see more.

Del tried to make the big stallion appear as run down as possible. He had knotted his mane, darkened his coat again, and dusted him with road dirt. It was hard to hide Raj's breeding, though, and Del didn't want to lose the magnificent horse to a thief. They had come this far together. He would be wary, especially down by the wharves. Thievery was a way of life there. They set off to find a boat bound for Independence.

Several of the riverboats were loading, their wheels glistening in the sun as the cold water dripped off their giant paddles. Whistles blew, men cursed, engines chugged, steam whistles shrieked. Del felt at home.

"Hey, there! Know of any boats making way for Independence, matey?" Del asked several hands as they worked their lines.

"That there boat, up ahead. The one flying the green flag. Charlie O'Riley is the captain's name. Says he's Irish, but he's a scoundrel, is what he is. Tough lot works on that boat. He might take you. He'll make you work for it, that's for sure. He might take that horse, too! Keep your eye on him, matey. Tell him One-Eyed Joe sent you. It may help. It may not. Keep a weather eye, boy, you'll need it with that lot."

Del approached the green-flagged, boat. He had been around rough hands before and had taken blows and given a few himself. He knew how to work and the ways of men who earned their living with the back-breaking labor it takes to work any vessel on the water.

He decided to downplay any experience he had had, but still appear eager and willing. It was hard work on a stern-wheeler moving cargo about. It was harder still, finding someone who wanted that kind of work.

"Are you headed to Independence, sir?" Del asked the first man he saw on the Irish boat.

"Just as soon as we get loaded, sonny." The man was strong with a shock of curly, brown hair. The sun shone off his skin and the sweat on his face, even in the cold breezes.

"One-Eyed Joe said you might take me and my horse to Independence. I can work for passage. I'm eighteen," he said. "I see you're carrying some stock already. Do you need another strong back, mister?"

"One-Eyed Joe, heh?" replied the other man. "Yeah, we leave soon, I reckon. You look strong. It's back-breaking work on a boat. Not much fun for a young fella. You'll have to pay for the feed your horse'll eat. You got it?"

"I think so, mister! How much will it take, you think?"

"Couple dollars, I reckon. That's a good-looking horse, sonny, how'd you come by him?"

"My granddaddy left him to me," said Del. "Are you Captain O'Riley, by chance?"

"No, I'm Curley Joe Benton. That varmint with the pipe in his mouth is O'Riley. Hey, Captain! Over here!" Curley Joe waved the captain over.

Charlie O'Riley stepped over some cargo still on the deck and lurched their way. He walked like the seafaring men Del had known in Baltimore. He ambled side to side. He would be more comfortable once he felt water under his bow again.

"What do you want, Curley Joe?"

"This here young fella wants to go to Independence with us. Says he's willing to work and pay for the hay and oats his horse will eat on the trip. One-Eye sent him over. We do need another fella or two, Mister Cook was telling me."

O'Riley's eyes flickered to Raj. "What's yer name, boy?"

"I'm called Jim, sir." Del doffed his cap to the captain.

Del could see the captain sizing him up. He was strong and did not doubt that the captain could see he was capable of the manual work of moving heavy cargo. "You got a horse, you say?" He looked at Raj again. "My God, lad, that is a horse! How'd you come by him, son?"

"He's just an old horse me grandfather gave me for Christmas, sir. I call him, Ned, sir."

"We Irish love a good horse! You got the money for the feed? You'll not get wages. Your labor is payment for the trip. I'll feed you twice a day and work you hard, but you'll get to Independence faster than overland, that's for a certainty. I need an extra pair of legs and a strong back. You'll be responsible for settling your own hash with the men. I'll not take sides in a fight unless it concerns my boat. We're hauling stock and lumber to Independence and, of course, passengers. You'll stay below with the cargo. You'll not be mixing with the paying folks. You up for it, boy? Mind if I look at your animal?" He didn't wait for an answer but stepped over the gunnel onto the dock, fondled Raj's neck and looked in his mouth. "Aw, boy," he said to Raj, "the lad has left your mane in a fine mess, he has."

"Lad, you need to take better care of this animal." O'Riley stroked Raj's flank with admiration.

"Yes, sir, I will. I've been in a terrible hurry to get to Independence and haven't had the time to treat him right."

"Okay." O'Riley looked up, "It'll be five dollars for feed and oats."

"Five dollars!" Del exclaimed. "Curley Joe said it would only a couple of dollars."

"Curley Joe ain't the captain of this steamboat, boy. Its five dollars. You can't be feeding this animal trash, now, can you?"

"Oh, no," Del said.

"Ok, five dollars. Hand it over. Your horse will be well cared for. I don't put up with any sass or lip either, lad. As soon as you step foot on this boat, you're mine. I settle my hash with the crew sure enough until you step off in Independence. Me and Mister Cook are in charge. I'm hard, but I'm a fair man. Give me a good day's work and I'll give you your grub. Cross me and I'll thrash you as I would a black-hearted lubber!! Agreed?" He held out his hand to Del.

"Agreed, sir. When do we start?" He shook O'Riley's hand, not really sure what he was getting into, but nonetheless determined to go.

"Get your horse aboard and stow your stuff inside. Curley Joe will show you where. Every hand has a locker. No one will bother your chest. It's sacred. I'll thrash any man who violates that trust or steals from any of my crew. Any man. We're leaving as soon as we're loaded."

The hiss of the boilers and boom of the giant pistons turning the massive wheel were almost deafening. "You'll get used to it," said Curley Joe as he helped Del gather his gear. "After a while, you won't be able to sleep without it."

Del led Raj on board and into a stout stall. He filled the manger with good hay. The boat's sturdy stables held mules, horses and a few goats. Crates of chickens and pigs were stacked out of the way and lumber filled the rest of the hold. Curley Joe introduced him to Mr. Cook, an old black man with eyes as golden as any Del had ever seen.

"I'm the engineer. I'm boss on deck. You get two meals a day, no complaints. Any complaints and I'll make sure you get the runnin' shits. You got that, boy?"

"Err, sure. I'm Del." He offered his hand.

"Don't make no difference to me, just another mouth to feed and back to bend. Follow my orders, boy. What you don't know, Curley Joe will show you."

"Yes, sir."

Del stowed his saddle and gear in his designated locker. The cloak covered his guns. It was only a box with a lid and a clasp for a lock. It might have been painted blue at one time, but now, was so chipped and faded it was hard to say. Del didn't have a lock so he tied a piece of stout leather through the clasp with a knot he had learned long ago on the oyster boats.

"You know knots, do you?" observed Curley Joe. "You'll do all right." He looked at him quizzically, and Del knew he had glimpsed the guns.

The first deck carried the freight. Crates and boxes, bales of hides lay piled on the lumber, and sacks hung from the rafters overhead. The entire stern wheeler was laden with cargo bound for Independence and towns and farms along the way, but most of the cargo was bound for Independence, a growing town needing everything for the wagons and freight trains moving west.

On deck, he helped Curley Joe coil rope and secure some crates. "O'Riley's an okay captain. Cook's okay, too. Stay on their good side. On their bad side, they're mean as snakes." Curley Joe spoke quickly as he worked. "The other men are river men, sober on deck and drunk when ashore. Keep your mouth shut and listen to what you're told, and you'll be all right."

Men were the working muscles of a stern wheeler. They lifted the loads. They balanced the ship. They stowed cargo and carried it down the gangway to shore. The heavy loads were picked up by the gantry and swung over to the wharves. Most of it was loaded, carted or carried by the crew.

"Cook is first mate," Curley Joe said. "Captain is up in the pilot house. We sleep on the crates and bins and bales. We eat what they bring us. Most of the time, food is okay and enough. Mess up, and your food will be laced with something that will give you the runnin' trots. I made that mistake once. I was sick for three days."

"Curley Joe!" Captain O'Riley leaned over the rail calling

"Aye, Captain."

"Unleash the bow lines! Del, help him on the stern lines."

"Aye, aye, Captain," replied Del, jumping to his task over the cacophony and clatter of the ship as she was about to make way. He was now part of the crew.

She was the *Irish Queen*. She flew a bright, Irish green flag with a golden crown on the green field. She was painted white, though trimmed in green and gold. The big wheel, too, was green trimmed in gold. When the sunlight caught her at a certain angle, the gold glistened like flashing nuggets. The engines revved up and the *Irish Queen* shuddered like a living entity just touched by the hand of God and drawing her first breath. As the thick black smoke belched from the twin brass smokestacks, her bow trembled and pointed downstream. She moved with the current into the flow of the river. Two tugs pushed her around so her bow was soon against the current. Tooting their whistles, the tugs pulled away.

The *Irish Queen* found her sea legs and moved up the Mississippi, fighting the current to the mouth of the Missouri River. The boat quivered under Del's feet as the river beat against the bottom. It would be upriver the entire way to Independence. O'Riley pulled the steam whistle.

They were underway!

"We don't make as good a time moving upriver as we do down," Curley Joe said. "We make about five knots up and seven on the way down. Of course, that doesn't count for frequent stops, taking folks on or dropping them off or unloading freight at the towns and farms or tying up along the riverbank at night."

The men on board were a stripe of every nation. Most of the

work consisted of keeping the freight in balance, so the boat sailed with a level keel. As they dropped freight or added it below, it had to be evenly stowed. That was Mr. Cook's job. He was the mastermind of what was unloaded and where the new cargo was to be stowed. He gave the orders as to what was to be prepared to leave the hold next and in what order. The *Queen* was a hundred twenty-five feet, stern to bow and twenty-five feet abeam. She drew a shallow draft of only sixteen inches. She wasn't as big as the Mississippi boats, but she was queen of the narrower and shallower Missouri. They made their money by shipping freight and passengers. The more freight taken on or unloaded was money filling the pockets of the captain and board of directors. If they missed delivering a bale or lumber at a stop, Mr. Cook would hear it from the captain and the crew would feel the anger of Mr. Cook. It was hard, dangerous work.

The biggest danger was not from Cook, snags, or Indians shooting at them from the bank, but the boilers blowing up. The average life of a riverboat was five years. Cook pointed out several broken hulks washed up against the riverbanks from such disasters.

"That's the *Washington*. I was on her when she blew. Lucky to be alive, I am. That's why I've got my eye on these boiler gauges day and night. Some fella fell asleep on the Washington and she blew up. Killed thirty-five people that night. Most died in their beds. Not going to happen on my watch."

All day, the men pushed and strained, moving freight about, getting the next load ready to offload at the next landing. Cook conducted this symphony of stink and sweat, accented by curses and threats, like they were relish to a good meal. They worked through the smoke and steam of the boilers, sometimes not able to see each other, just shadowy forms going about their work. They kept the boilers fed and steam up under the watchful eye of Mr. Cook. Marching freight on and freight off was the only thing these men had in common, the work and the sweat on their backs.

At night they tied up along the riverbank as it was dangerous to navigate the moving sand bars and floating logs that might damage the hull. Del fell asleep on one of the bales close to the boilers, where it was warmer. He could hear the activity above him as people strolled the deck, laughing and talking. A piano played in the salon until midnight, most nights.

"It's a different world up there, mateys," Mr. Cook said one night while the crew was eating. Pointing his spoon upwards, "It's pretty posh in the rooms the well-off folks are paying for. Red velvet coverlets, carpets on the floors, nice meals in the salon, cost a pretty penny."

Del nodded in agreement looking at the deck over his head. He sucked down his stew and went to check on Raj. The horse was enjoying his rest. Del observed that Raj was getting good green hay and oats every day and clean water. His coat was shiny. Someone had brushed the knots out of his mane. His tail was bushy and full. Raj was having a lazy trip while Del worked hard. The irony that he was working while Raj rested was not lost on Del. He returned to his spot by the boiler, falling into an exhausted sleep.

Every day it was the same—coffee, molasses and biscuit in the morning, stew or beans and bacon at night. Mr. Cook never seemed to sleep. At least, Del never saw him sleep. The men worked, they ate together, and they drank from the same ladle, out of the same water barrel. Cook kept his eyes on them and the boiler's gauges. Del's shoulders and legs ached the first few days. This was different work for his muscles. He began to enjoy the feeling of strength building in his arms and shoulders. He did the work of any of the men, including the burly Curley Joe.

No one talked much except Mr. Cook issuing orders. Sometimes someone would start a song as they moved the freight around. Curley Joe had a fine tenor voice. The river ran strong with the winter melt, but they had to be careful of shifting sandbars and trees torn loose from the swollen banks. Captain O'Riley was a knowing man who had plied his trade on this river for many years. Even experienced captains got bogged on an unseen sandbar now and then.

The sudden impact jarred everyone on board, knocking them off their feet, leaving bruised knees and a few busted heads. Crates and barrels fell helter skelter. The *Queen's* shrill whistle blew her distress. A fuming Captain O'Riley appeared red-faced, his pipe rolling in his mouth from side to side. He and Cook looked over the side to determine the best course of action to back off the sand bar, now visible a few inches below the keel.

"We aren't holed, thank the spirits. but we're stuck on a damned bar. Move the freight back toward the stern to lighten the bow and then the wheel can pull us off," Cook instructed the men.

It took several hours, several shifts of the heavy freight and several attempts before the *Queen* was right again.

"That wasn't too bad," said Curley Joe. "Happens about once a trip."

Del visited Raj once a day, usually at night. The horse was always well fed and brushed. Someone had even taken care of his hooves. He had seen the captain looking at Raj occasionally, but he turned and walked away whenever Del approached.

Curley Joe had observed Captain O'Riley's attention to the big horse, as well. "The Irish do like their horses, boy, theirs and anybody else's. Even water lovin' old cranks like O'Riley there. Be wary, boy. he may not be able to hold his rightful course when it comes to that horse of yours. He can be avaricious in his covetousness."

Del was shocked, not by what Curley Joe had said, but he had no idea that Curley Joe knew any words like avaricious. Suspicion was growing within him as well concerning the captain.

Curley Joe saw the look of surprise in Del's eyes, "What's the matter with you? I've got some schooling too, boy, and I can read the Bible. I'm not as ignorant as I look." Del started laughing and soon the other man joined in.

"Thanks, Joe, I've been keeping my eye on the captain. He has been spending a lot of time with Raj—er Ned. More than I'm comfortable with. I'll watch out."

Curley Joe looked at Del briefly, a half-formed question in his eyes.

O'Riley was occupying Del's mind more often lately. The closer they got to the Independence landing, the more he worried. Who would take the word of a seventeen-year-old over that of a well-known riverboat captain? O'Riley surely would have friends in Independence who would vouch for him over an unknown boy. This would be especially true, regarding such a horse as Raj.

Curley Joe might speak up for him, but not if it threatened his job. He couldn't count on any of the rest of the crew. They had pretty much kept to themselves. No one else had made an attempt at being friendly. He would need more than the voice of one man to convince anyone that Raj was his. Watching O'Riley's care of the horse triggered that gut reaction he had learned to count on. He did appreciate the captain's attention to Raj, but he knew there was an attachment growing in O'Riley's behavior by the way he stroked and curried the horse. His hand lingering on his shoulder as he combed Raj's mane. Raj had not looked as well-groomed since they started the trip west. Even Del had begun to think of Raj as Ned. It was confusing to him. He'd be glad when they used their proper names and stopped the charade. Heeding the warning signs that were growing stronger in his gut, he began to formulate a plan. If he timed it right, it might work, too.

Quietly, Del set about devising his and Raj's escape. They would land in Independence in three days. That night, he thought through his plans and felt they were sound. He fell asleep on his bale, next to the boilers, satisfied. Cook was at his position on watch in his usual spot, a chair next to the boilers. Those golden eyes studied the valves and gauges intently.

Del woke from sleep with a jerk. It was unusually hot. The boilers were hissing and steaming with more ferocity than normal for this time of night. He studied the gauges. The needles were jumping to the end of the manometer's gauge on the main boilers. With alarm, he looked for Cook and found him slumped in his chair. He was asleep.

"Mister Cook! The boilers, Mister Cook!" The engineer awoke, startled and in terror when he realized what Del was saying. They both raced to the valves and began releasing steam from the throbbing lines. With an exhausted sigh, he sagged back against a bale after he was satisfied the danger had passed.

"You've saved us, boy. Another few minutes and she would have blown, sure as hell! I couldn't live through that again. Thank you." He reached down and clutched Del's hand in earnest gratitude.

"Mister Cook, why don't you finish your sleep? The danger's over. I know what to do. I can keep watch." Reluctantly, Cook agreed and lay back on a bale and was immediately asleep. He was that worn out. Del spent the remainder of the night alongside the boilers, watching intently. Before the rest of the crew awoke, Cook insisted he relieve Del.

"If you don't mind, Jim, I would take it right kindly, if you didn't mention this to anyone, especially the captain."

"This never happened, Mister Cook. I just woke up myself. When are they going to bring breakfast? I'm hungry. How about you?"

"To tell you the truth, I could go for some strong coffee." He smiled, golden eyes bloodshot but full of appreciation.

Early on the morning of their arrival in Independence, Del moved his saddle and gear, hiding them in the hay close to Raj's stall. He bridled Raj and saw that he had plenty to eat. It was going to be a full day.

He had a little surprise for Captain O'Riley, as well.

The morning was crisp and clear as they approached the wharf for Independence town. The morning colors seemed brighter, sharper than any other morning on their voyage. His blood was up. Del's eyes were shining and his skin prickled with anticipation, like he had been energized, by a lightning bolt. Excited to have this leg of his journey at end, he put his plan into action.

Water lapped against the bow of the *Irish Queen* as she squalled and rolled against the current. They had picked up a head wind rounding the bend in the river pushing at her hull and wheelhouse. The forces of water, wind and wood straining against each other, the splash, splash, splash of the wheel sounded in cadence, like a military march. Slowly the *Queen* made way against the current and the wind. Word was given to ready the gangway.

Del had been working as usual. He tripped, making a scene. He indicated to Mister Cook that he had hurt himself and limped over to Raj's stable, rubbing his leg. Cook looked at him briefly, his golden eyes holding that ever-present question, then he went back to directing the unloading.

As soon as the engineer turned away. Del saddled Raj with all his gear. He went to the side and dropped the poles on the side of the boat. With a loud, "Hurrah!" over the side they leaped. Briefly, horse and rider were submerged beneath the dark green waters of the Missouri. Del waved his cap when they rose again and another loud "Hurrah!" escaped his lips.

The men ran to the side of the boat. The escape had caused instant panic among the men thinking that a man was lost overboard. The panic was genuine. Most of them could not swim. Cook looked at Del calmly, then ordered his men back to work.

A crowd had formed on shore as Raj swam out of the water. The Queen's shrill whistle screamed and Captain O'Riley gestured frantically from the pilothouse. Many applauded, when Del and Raj ended their swim and climbed up the landing's grassy bank. Del jumped off, brushed the water from his face and clothes, and donned the ever-present news cap. He almost looked presentable.

It would have to do.

Combing Raj's mane and tail, he announced to the crowd that they should stay awhile, for he and Raj had a surprise for them. In the background, the city band from Independence began to play, welcoming the Irish Queen as her gangway crunched into the landing's gravel.

Raj was perking up after shaking himself free of the river water. Del was ready to put the second part of his plan into action. He hoped Raj had not forgotten his old routines. Del led Raj on a long lead in a circle, allowing him to prance and flex his muscles after being confined in the stable on the deck for so long. His coat caught the rays of the sun causing it to shine with luster. Raj knew something was about to happen and he looked ready for it. The busy crowd and music in the air caused his nostrils to flare.

A growing audience watched curiously, as Del mounted and rode Raj in a circle then reversed the circle. He rode with his arms up and palms out, using only his knees to guide the horse. Del watched as Captain O'Riley, Mr. Cook, and the rest of the crew pushed their way through the crowd.

Del stopped and faced the captain. O'Riley burst forward in a fine Irish temper, fist in the air.

"You've got my horse, you young scallywag! I'll have you in jail."

In reply, Del galloped Raj toward O'Riley, stopping mere feet short of his outstretched fist.

"Top of the morning to you, Captain O'Riley!" Del said so all could hear.

O'Riley gestured for the police to arrest Del. They moved to do so, when Mr. Cook and Curley Joe, gathered the rest of the crew around the two constables, hemming them in with strong shoulders and scowls. Curley Joe gestured for Del to continue.

"You may recall, good sir, that this horse and I boarded your gallant boat, the *Irish Queen,* in St. Louis." Del spoke like the circus announcers he had seen in the big tents in Baltimore. "Every one of the crew saw us. Mister Cook saw me stable him. You have helped feed and groom him, but that does not make him your horse. He is *my* horse, Captain O'Riley! You know that. This is my horse, trained by my grandfather, Major James Delaino Conlon of Baltimore, given to me on Christmas Eve, last.

"What do you call your horse, Captain?"

"Huh? I call him Ned."

"Call your Ned, Captain!"

Del moved Raj backwards about twenty paces from the captain. He held his arms out and took his feet out of the stirrups and held them out as well for all to see he was not controlling the horse. "Call him!"

"Ned, come here, boy. Come to me, Ned." Then he whistled for him. Raj stood his ground, not flinching a muscle. O'Riley called again, "Here, Ned. Here, boy!" Raj stood at rigid attention attuned to only Del's commanding presence.

In triumph, Del said, "Ned? You sound like you are calling a dog!" The crowd roared. Del rode Raj in a tight circle and stopped in front of the embarrassed captain. O'Riley blanched in the morning sun, his intent stymied.

Del began to ride Raj in wider circles, as he spoke. "Ladies and Gentlemen, it is my esteemed pleasure to present to you and the great city of Independence, recently from Baltimore, that incredible wonder horse, I give you, Raj!" He reared the stallion and waved his cap.

Del sat on Raj before the crowd and began to clap his hands in rhythm. The band joined in with a familiar marching tune. The crowd began to clap along to the music. Raj began to high step to the rhythm of the music, his head held high. His mane and tail, fully dry in the crisp breeze, flowed and jumped like tassels on the dress of an East Indian dancer's gown. The music picked up and Raj side stepped across the field. Then, he pranced back, knees high, as the crowd clapped louder in appreciation.

Del raced Raj in figure eights. He charged the crowd stopping inches from their shrieking laughter. They performed this several times, each time winning the respect and trust of the crowd. They loved it! They loved Raj. They applauded in amazement and appreciation. Del used only his knees to nudge Raj into action, demonstrating all his gaits, commanding him to back and kneel, wheel and stop, and then wheel back the other way. Raj held his head high, legs fully extended when he jumped, knees high as he danced and kicked down the field.

Del marched him across the field and then charged back to stop squarely in front of a befuddled Captain O'Riley who stepped back, awed and white faced. Del gestured for the crowd to quiet. Speaking again, very loudly for the crowd. "Raj! Bow to the captain." The chestnut stallion bowed extending his white-stockinged foot. His nose touched the ground. "Captain O'Riley, I thank you for the safe voyage up the Missouri. Raj, my horse, thanks you for the kind treatment you gave voluntarily to him on this voyage. Now, Captain, do you still claim that this mighty horse is yours?" Del signaled Raj to rise, "Or the Christmas gift my grandfather gave me?" It was a small lie. "Choose carefully, Captain. Your horse or my horse?" The crowd drew near. Not a whisper was heard, just the wind rustling the leaves of trees.

Defeated, O'Riley said, "He's yours."

"What? What now, Captain? Raise that strong Irish voice and tell this lively crowd who Raj belongs to!"

In a stronger voice, Captain O'Riley turned to the crowd. "The horse belongs to the lad! I swear on it!"

The crowd cheered and applauded. The band struck up "Camp Town Races" and Curley Joe came forward and shook his hand. "I knew there was something that didn't add up with you, boy. You played that hand well."

Mr. Cook drew the captain aside and spoke briefly in his ear. Captain O'Riley pulled back in shock.

Del dismounted and walked over to the captain. "Thank you, sir. I knew you had goodness in your heart."

They shook hands.

Captain O'Riley smiled. "After that performance, what else could I say? I told you we Irish could spot good horseflesh. Ned, er, Raj is a champion if ever I saw one. You ride like a champion yourself. That is a fine horse. I am envious. Congratulations, Jim. If that is, indeed, your name?"

"Delaino Daniel Riodan, recently of Baltimore, at your service, sir." Del grinned a toothy smile and bowed doffing his cap. He reined Raj to go.

"Oh, Jim? I beg your pardon. Delaino. There is one more thing. Mister Cook informs me, we owe you our lives, for waking him, before the boilers blew." He offered his hand, pressing two golden sovereigns into Del's palm. "You've got a great animal there, Delaino. You are more than you seem. If I ever can be of service to you, you can count on Captain Charlie O'Riley. Good luck and God speed you on your journey."

Del mounted Raj and reared the stallion, waving his cap again to the crowd and shouted "Hurrah!" as they loped away. After several miles, Del pulled Raj to a skidding stop. They were in sight of Independence! He could see several wagon trains in the distance. Their cottony tops billowed in the afternoon breeze. With a shout, he kicked Raj's flanks and set off for the nearest one.

7

"ANYONE HERE, KNOW A FELLA named Riodan? From Indiana? I hear he's looking for a driver?"

Looking up from his harness, the teamster smiled quizzically as his fingers worked the traces. "No, don't say as I do. You might ask on down the line or at the next train over. Ben Grubbs is the scout on this train. That's him there, with the beaver on his head. He might know if that fella's with us. Captain Nightingale will have him listed, if'n he's with this train. Ol' Ben should know, though. We just got hooked up with this train yesterday." He smiled and went back to his work.

Ben Grubbs looked up at the sound of his name. "I'm Grubbs. What can I do for ya, young fellow? What kind of guns in all blazes is them?"

Del tipped his hat. "I'm looking for a Riodan, supposed to be with a train going to Oregon. You know him, or if he's with this train?" Del ignored the question about his guns. They were his business.

"Riodan? Why, yes, he's here. Just keep on going down the line. Look for his two wagons, light blue is his colors, big Conestoga's he's got and oxen. What'cha want with him?"

Del's stomach lurched. His father was here!

"That's my business, mister."

"Whoa, now, fella! On this train, everything is my business. Me and James Nightingale, the master of this train and I'm the head scout. We don't want no trouble and no troublemakers."

Del pulled Raj up short. "Er... sorry, Mister Grubbs. Don't mean any disrespect. I heard this Riodan needs a teamster. I want to go to Oregon on this train, and I need a job or a wagon to join up with."

"That's better, sonny. Many men are looking to do the same thing. I would, too, if I was full of young blood and sassy as once I was. I'm still sassy, just not as young. Been over the mountains with Fremont and Carson."

"The Riodan wagon, sir?" interrupted Del.

"Er... of course. Down about six or seven wagons. Hope he still has that job open. Didn't know he did. Like I said, many men and boys are looking to go to Oregon. You know how to drive a team of oxen, Sonny? You look pretty green to me. 'Cept for those damn guns you got there, what are those things?"

"Mister Grubbs, if I get a job, I'll let you shoot my granddaddy's tiger guns. But, right now, I need to find those wagons." Del kicked his heels into Raj's sides and trotted behind the line of wagons looking for Riodan. He was anxious and had butterflies in his stomach. Maybe this wasn't such a good idea. He reined Raj to a walk, his stomach alarm churning like fresh buttermilk. Do I really know what I'm doing?

"Tiger gun! What in hell's tarnation is a tiger gun? I never heard of no tiger, in this part of the country anyway?" said Ben as he watched the young man ride away.

Del's anxiety dimmed, as he became aware of the prevailing buzz that surrounded him. Life reverberated from the wagon train. People talking, shouting, animals bawling, shouts of alarm, peals of laughter, jangling chains, smells of cook fires and laundry pots, mud sucking at the men's boots as they went about in preparation for the big day of leaving. Women turned their faces west and prayed silent prayers in the warming sun as they went about their chores. They were caught up in the melody of a train set and bound for the trail. A trail that would take them to Oregon, beyond the Rocky Mountains.

Raj crow-hopped nervously down the row of wagons, as Del searched for the light blue wagons of Riodan. Wagons were blue, red, yellow, and green with the billowing white canvas tops lined up in states of readiness. They reminded Del of brightly colored pastries with white meringue tops he had seen in the bakeries of Baltimore. He could use a sweet bun now to settle his stomach. That was for sure. His stomach knotted. His mouth was dry and his mind a vacant place. He did not know what he would say.

As he approached two neatly-painted blue Conestogas, he heard loud angry voices on the other side of the wagons.

"Hey, I told you never to touch the animals with your whip again. I've told you, Adonis, more than once."

"Well, it kicked me! I'm just paying it back, that's all."

"I don't care. He kicked you because he doesn't like the way you treat him. As a matter of fact, I've had it with you. You're fired! I've told you too many times. You're stubborn as hell and don't respect nothing, man nor beast. Here's what I owe you, now get out."

Del rounded the farthest end of the second wagon. He saw a slim man in buckskins walking away from a taller one, a mountain of a man, in wool pants and shirt. His face was bearded and his eyes full of malcontent and heat. He held a coiled whip in his right hand.

"You can't fire me like that, you skunk!"

The big man let the whip uncoil from his hand. Stretching his arm back, he flicked the tip of the whip behind him. It was evident in a moment he knew how to handle a whip and was about to unleash its fury on the slim man's back. Del, a few paces to the side of this angry conflict, sitting his horse said evenly. "Hold it, mister!"

Del pulled one of the pistols and cocked both barrels. "Do you know what my granddaddy would say that this is?" He spoke with conviction, leaving not a doubt that he knew what he was doing. He lifted the Howdah's .56-caliber double barrels up to eye level of the huge angry bear of a man.

"What the hell! Boy, do you want to get thrashed, too?"

Del repeated firmly. "I was wondering if you know what my granddaddy would say about this pistol I have pointed at your nose, mister?"

The other man in buckskins, had spun around. He held a Bowie knife in his right hand. His eyes beheld a boy on a horse with a big gun and the whip in Adonis's hand snaked out, ready to be used.

"I don't know your gol'danged gran'daddy, boy. I do know I'll skin you alive for interferin'." He glanced over at the other man, then back to Del. His eyes flickered with indecision. He knew he was caught now. He could have lied about what happened with the whip, claiming self-defense maybe, but not now.

Anger had a different resonance to it and people were already noticing. Their attention being drawn to the disturbance in the melody of the camp. Men and women moved closer, alert to any threat, ready to help if there was danger to any of the members on the train.

"Mister, I'm waiting here!" Del now had a kind of bemused tolerance in his voice.

The mule skinner's arm, still outstretched with the whip in his hand, glanced back in a snarling reproach at Riodan as he came closer.

Del repeated, "What would my granddaddy call this here tiger gun, mister?"

"Tiger gun! What the hell?" Adonis's eyes looked around the crowd then darted back to the Howdah. The anger was sinking in his eyes that now filled with embarrassment.

"Okay, okay... what the hell would your granddaddy say about that damn gun you're so proud of?"

"Glad you asked, mister," Del bent over in his saddle and pointed it closer to the mountain's sweating face. "My granddaddy would say this is the last thing a tiger ever saw!"

Adonis visibly blanched. He nodded his head, coiled the big whip, fastened it to his belt, and wiped the sweat from his face. The crowd that had gathered quieted.

There was silence. No one knew what to say. Only the wind whooshing around the billowy white canvas sails spoke. A coolness, ruffling the caps, aprons and hair in the crowd put a calm on the confrontation.

Ben Grubbs, with gun in hand, drawn to the hubbub, croaked from behind Del's horse. "Well, I guess so!" and the crowd broke into relieved laughter. Several of the men repeating "I guess so" and nodding their heads as they held their pipes and walked back to their wagons. "I guess so" became a hallmark of the train after that, bringing a smile to the faces of those who said it and to those who heard it.

Adonis's eyes stared into the big-bore barrels pointing in his face and he swallowed mightily. His huge hands smoothed down the front of his shirt, until they got caught on a button and he looked down. He looked at Del then over at the other man like someone who had got caught with his hands in a dead man's pocket. He spat on the ground and started to shoulder his way past the crowd around Del's horse.

"Leave the whip, Adonis. It belongs to me," Daniel said.

"This ain't over yet, Daniel. I won't forget."

"Anytime you want to meet face to face, man to man, just whistle. Get your gear and clear out. I don't want to see you around my wagons anymore."

Adonis threw the whip on the ground and walked away glowering at the dispersing crowd. Climbing into the second wagon, he threw his gear out the back, jumped down, gathered it in his arms and stomped off.

Del quirked an eyebrow. "Adonis?"

"He has said he was a beautiful baby and his parents named him Adonis because of it. My name is Riodan. I owe you a thanks for saving my beautiful skin a while ago. Thank you."

He reached up to shake Del's hand.

Del was taken aback. He had been caught up in the drama and wasn't prepared to shake hands with the man he thought to be the father he had been searching for. What was he like? Was he what Major Conlon thought of him? Was he as bad as the Conlons? He had to know first, before he told this stranger who he was. As these thoughts flashed through his head, he remained sitting on his horse looking vacant eyed and aloof, ignoring the proffered hand.

Riodan's welcoming smile faded as his hand dropped. He looked puzzled. "Well, er, how about showing me this gun which I am indebted to. What's your name?"

Del was embarrassed. He blushed and dropped his eyes, his mind flashing on a name to say. It's a... they call me...think... think... think of something! My name is Del. Err. Del Riodan... no-o-o. not that. Del. Del what? Yeah! Del, Del Rio. That's it. Whew!

"Del Rio, at your service." He said the words quietly.

Riodan looked questioning at this kid. "How about that gun?" he asked again. Del handed it to him, butt-end first.

Riodan looked admiringly. "A British Howdah. I haven't seen one of these in years. A beauty of a gun."

"Had it long?" Riodan watched Del's eyes. A question was forming in his mind, but he didn't ask it.

"No, not very." Del was trying to be evasive without lying outright.

"Your granddaddy, was it?" He studied Del's face.

"Yep."

"Well, interesting. Here." Riodan handed the gun back to Del, butt first. "Were you passing by when you heard this ruckus or looking for something?" Again, the tall man intently watched Del's eyes.

"I was looking for a job, mister... Riodan, isn't it? I'm good with horses and animals. I'd never beat them. I've never driven oxen, but I can learn. I'm a fast learner. I want to go to Oregon, and I need a train to get there. What do you say? Don't you need another driver?" Del's enthusiasm bubbled. "I can learn anything you teach me. I got a horse and a gun and a strong back. I worked on the docks." Baltimore almost slipped out, but he choked back the words.

"Docks, huh? Where did you work on the docks?'

"St. Louis. I worked on the docks in St. Louis and worked my way upriver on the *Irish Queen*, so I could get to Independence. I sold papers on the streets, and I can fight, too. Been fighting someone or something my whole life."

"Really. I'll bet Adonis could say the same thing. You going to grow up like him?"

"Well, no, mister. That big thug isn't like me at all." He grinned. "Besides, I grew up handsome and beautiful!" He laughed. "How about it?"

Caught off guard by the young man's humor, Riodan felt a slow smile spread across his face. "It's a deal. I'll teach you what you need to know." He held up his hand again and Del Rio shook it firmly, this time.

A smile beamed on his face, his eyes on his father's face for the first time in his remembrance. Del felt like he was going to burst with excitement. This was where he was meant to be.

Riodan stepped back looking at the boy and horse. "Good horse! Where'd you get him? St. Louis, too?" He looked at the horse again, a fine horse with good breeding. He looked back at the boy with a question he didn't ask in his eyes.

Del patted Raj's neck. "Yeah, we came from St. Louis."

"St. Louis, huh?" He walked around the horse, eyeing the steed's condition. "English saddle won't do here. You'll need a saddle with a horn and a rope. You got money? You need a Mexican pommel saddle, like the Mexican *vaqueros* use, some clothes." He laughed. "Some boots, too! Folks are running out of money and are selling anything extra, they don't need. You might be able to pick up some of the things you need, by asking around. I know someone who will sell you a good rifle reasonable. The rest you can get in town."

"A rifle? I'd like that." Del slid down off Raj and began taking off his saddle. "My friend deserves a rest. He's taken me a long way." Del dropped the saddle over a wagon tongue.

"I hope you know what you're getting yourself in for. This is a long, hard, mud sucking at your boots, bone dry at times, hot sun in your face every step of the way, kind of journey. It won't be easy. Months of back-breaking toil, walking, pushing, pulling, fever and swollen rivers. Those that make it, have got to watch out for savages who will pluck them like a roosting chicken when they are at their weakest. I'm not talking about the red Indians. I'm talking about the white men who suck the life out of the weak and unwary. Men who would stomp on your back just so they could steal the pennies off their own mother's eyes. The west is filled with black-hearted men as well as the good honest ones. You got the backbone for that, Del Rio?" Riodan looked at this young man standing by his horse, following the words intently.

"I'll take whatever comes, mister, you can be sure of that. There are no guarantees for anyone." Del could feel his father's eyes searching him, assessing his answers.

Riodan smiled. "I'll bet you will at that, Del Rio. I'll bet you will. What about your folks? Where are they?"

"Haven't had any folks, Mister Riodan. I've been on my own for some time now."

"How about that granddaddy you talked about?"

"Oh, I made him up."

"You made him up? Well, okay then," Daniel said, looking surprised by the sudden answer. "Do you have cash money, or did you spend all of your money on that horse and fancy guns?"

Del felt a tingle of alarm run up his spine, as Daniel questioned Raj and his guns.

"I can advance you some on your wages if you've a need. I've got plenty of food."

"No, I'm fine with money for now. Thanks, Mister Riodan," Del replied. He knew Riodan wasn't satisfied with the answers to his questions, but that would have to wait.

"If we can't find what you need on the train, we can go into town in a few days and get it. We'll be leaving in ten days to two weeks, I reckon. Give a few more wagons time to catch on. The grass needs to grow green, and the rivers to sink back within their banks, before it's time to travel. I'll put out the word on what you need. Let's see … You got any more clothes? No, I guess not. Looks like you left in a hurry. That cloak will be okay for a while. Wool is better to sleep under. You'll need more blankets when we get to the mountains. Best to wait on that. Might shoot us a grizzly and make a coat out of an ol' bear. You may be able to trade along the trail for items you may need. The Indians have been pretty good at trading when they don't decide to steal it from you first."

"I've read about the Indians. The papers say they're blood thirsty and vicious. Is that so?" Del let Raj drink from a bucket hanging on the side of the wagon.

"The ones I've known were decent people, despite being lied to and cheated and forced off ancestral lands the government stole from them. I don't think the Indians west of here have been exposed to whites long enough yet, but they'll catch on quick. Right now, most of them are curious about our ways and happy to trade for metal knives, axes, and cloth. I'll warn you that once they've seen more and more of us and watch their people die of our diseases and are pushed off their lands, then you'll see vicious Indians just like you and I would be. I saw it happen back in Indiana.

"All right, let's get started! You can stow your stuff in this second wagon. That's the team you'll be driving. This is a walking job. You won't ride the wagon much. All the way to Oregon you'll walk, four to six months depending on weather, water, sickness, and what befalls us on the trail.

"You'll be driving eight oxen with a milk cow tied behind and a coop of chickens on the side. You're to take care of them and guard 'em. I've got eight oxen per wagon because these Conestogas are heavy. Most of the other wagons are prairie schooners as you can see. They're a lighter wagon. I plan on building a sawmill and a grain mill and freight what I grind or cut to the cities and towns. The towns will be growing and needing the lumber, flour, and meal. I'll be trading for gold, furs, and other stuff that I'll need to live. That's how I've made my living so far, plus some surveying thrown in. Just got too crowded in Indianapolis. With all those people and bad memories smothering me, I couldn't breathe. Oregon sounded clean and fresh, so I decided to up and go. Took years of saving, but I did it. What are you planning to do in Oregon, son?"

Son! Was that a falter he had heard in Riodan's voice? Surely, he had meant it in a general use sort of way, but the word had seemed to catch on his lips. Del noticed a hot blush that hadn't been there before.

"I... I don't know yet. I know I didn't want to be where I was." He looked away. "I heard that wagon trains were heading into Oregon, California, and all points west. Sounded like a good place to start my life."

He walked Raj around and tied him to the back of the second wagon, tossed his cloak and gear in the back and walked to the front of it. "Where's my team?" The moment had passed as quickly as it had presented itself.

"They're grazing over in the meadow. I want them full and fat when we start. We'll begin your training tomorrow. Do you know Gee and Haw?"

"Everyone knows that, Mister Riodan. I've been around horses and mules my whole life. I'm not just a city boy, you know. I worked. I got schooling too. I know how to read and write, know my numbers, enjoy reading. Not much time for it lately."

"By the way, how old are you?"

Del was big for his age. He lied and said he was twenty. He wanted to be sure of this man, before he told him the truth. That is, if he was his father. Though, it seemed to him, this was the man he had been looking for.

"Twenty? Hmm." Riodan looked skeptical. "Hey, Del, why don't you just mosey around. Introduce yourself to the train. Find Captain Nightingale. Sign the register. Get the feel of the place and I'll see you in time for supper. I usually have supper with the Kincaids, a few wagons back."

Del felt like he'd just been pushed away. "I guess I'll let folks know who I am, what wagons I'm with and what I'll need. Thanks for the job, sir. I won't let you down.'

"Yeah, do that. We'll get the rest in town tomorrow. Make a list." Daniel looked at Del, expectantly, "Okay, see you at supper." Riodan seemed to study Del's face as though looking for something, then turned rather quickly and walked away, as if he were embarrassed. Deep emotions were welling up inside him over this stranger and he couldn't figure out why.

Del watched the man walk away, a slump to his shoulders he hadn't noticed before. Had his father sensed some familiar connection? Daniel walked over and sat on a stump, leaned his head against the front wheel of the first wagon and stared at his hands. They were folding and unfolding of their own accord as he stared out onto the sloping meadow before him.

Not sure what to do with himself now. That uncomfortable feeling was back. Del mounted Raj bareback and looked over at the lonely figure. Should he say something? What could he say? Deciding there would be a better time later, he pulled on Raj's bridle. Giving his father one last look, he turned away to explore the train, his thoughts whirling.

He saw about twenty wagons strung off for a half a mile behind the Riodan wagons. Not a large train by anyone's standards, but it would grow. To his right, he could see the stock grazing on a green hill sprinkled with yellow, blue, and pink specks of spring flowers as he headed for the front of the train. A few drovers milling about the herd were silhouetted in the background by white fluffy clouds set against a robin's egg blue sky. Up high a fluttering V beat its way to the north, lifted by warming winds and driven by ancient memories of a home far to the north. He only heard their calls when they were almost out of sight. He smiled at that phenomenon. Every sound, sight, smell, touch was so vivid it almost hurt.

He met Captain Nightingale and introduced himself and who he was working for, before signing the register. This document laid out who was in charge and what each man and their wagon's duties were to the entire train. Del pulled on his gloves after he had signed and walked back to Raj. He had made it. His gut felt good, and his spirit soared with a sense of accomplishment. Mounting Raj, they rode off to explore.

Del took a deep breath and looked about him. God, he felt good! Yet he was also conflicted. What was he supposed to feel? He didn't ever remember feeling so alive, so confused. He could feel the blood pumping through his body. The wind caressed his face and arms. Wafts of smoke tinged with cooking odors, manure, sweat, perfume, horse, cattle, and people smell whirled around him. The weariness of his journey suddenly overwhelmed him in the realization that he had made it. He dismounted and ground hitched Raj, so he could graze. Del let his body crumble against a fallen log. An expectant promise lingered in the air as he faced the west's horizons, shimmering under a white yellow sun. It was so beautiful. He caught himself choking back tears in his shirt sleeve. He had come a long way. Raj and he had found their way. Was this man, this Riodan, the man whom he sought? Was he home? He thought of Raj and what they had been through and blew his nose. Tucker's face popped into his mind. I wonder what Tucker is doing right now.

"Well, young fella!" A cheery voice erupted behind him, and a strong hand clasped him on his shoulder. "So that was a tiger gun. I would have never known. It was just a gol' dern big 'un if you asked me. Big enough to back Ol' Adonis down, didn't it? Hee! Hee! I never saw blood drained out of a man's face so fast. Ha! Ha! Ha! Ha!" Ben Grubbs bent over laughing. "Looking around, are you? Lots to see. I've been out west, clear over the Rocky Mountains and tasted the salty seas that lap Oregon's sandy shores. I was with Bonneville with the first wagons that went through the South Pass in 1832. We'll come to the Sweetwater and follow her to the headwaters, cross over to the Green River, drink up, rest a mite, then head south for Fort Bridger to stock up. South Pass is the new gateway to Oregon if you want to get your goods there by wagon."

Del looked at the old scout. Out of impulse, he replied rather loudly, "Well, I guess so!"

Ben stood open eyed, his mouth twitching at the corners then broke down in a guffaw so strong he bent over grabbing his stomach, "Well, I guess so!" he said cackling.

Ben supported himself with his hands on his knees, looking up with one eye closed. He said soberly, "You'll have to watch yourself around that man from now on. Likely, he'll land with another wagon. Bad pennies always turn up, more than likely with other bad pennies. You'll find that most men, Indians, too, are decent, but all folks' societies have monsters living among 'em. I knew a fella, a trapper he was. White man so mean and ornery and dead in his mind, that he once set fire to a man's barn 'cause the fella wouldn't let him sleep there for the night. Indians raid other villages for horses and women. It isn't considered mean, just natural Indian to Indian. Like the Indians don't consider a wolf evil. It's just the natural way of mother earth and nature. It's the white way that is the only way to most white folks. They see evil if it isn't their way. It's conflicted between the two, how they think of themselves in the world and how the Injuns see it for themselves. Hard to say right or wrong, but then there's folks like Adonis where you can only see the dead in their eyes. Their brains are tumbled about. You watch out for him.

"Matter of fact, young fella, watch out for everything out here. You can be dead so fast you don't even know you're dead. Knew a fella once. Him and me was scouting for ol' Bonneville. This fella was up in the mountains and got shot with Indian arrows in his back and was sitting his horse straight as you please when he rode into camp. We figured he had been dead for two days. Never fell out of his saddle, eyes as blank as canvas, reins tight in his hands. Mostly folks die by accidents out here. Fall off a wagon, shoot themselves, such as that. Keep your head on a swivel, watch how things move, what patterns they be. When something doesn't match the pattern, watch out. Listen for sounds. Birds are the first to notice mostly. If you hear their alarms or they go quiet, duck down and watch!"

"Birds give alarms?" Del asked.

"You've only heard city birds, boy. Listen to the bird sounds out here in the west. Study them when it's quiet and you'll be able to tell the difference when they've seen a snake or an owl or a man. They'll let everyone know just by their alarm calls. Each one is different. You mind if I take a look at that there tiger gun?'

Ben held Del's attention for hours that afternoon and Ben was pleased Del remembered his promise to let him shoot the tiger gun. Del's mind wouldn't think about Riodan now that they had met face to face. He wasn't sure how he should feel or what to do, but he knew he was in for the full ride. His gut alarm had not gone off. No one had made any promises.

8

CAPTAIN NIGHTINGALE GALLOPED UP. "Hey, Ben, would you see that the privies are moved and covered? We don't want Independence to think we're leaving our mess here for them to clean up!"

"Yes, sir. I'd rather be out scouting though. What's your prognostication of us startin' out, Captain?" Ben asked.

"A week or so, I guess. River is still high. I want more grass for grazing. Can't get caught on the prairie with no graze for the stock. Sorry about the privies, Ben, but right now, we're just stewing around waiting and they need to be moved. Get a few men to help you. I'll have you back scouting in three days' time. Then we'll see what's doing when you get back. I want to be first across the river ahead of the big train forming up south of us."

Ben introduced Del. "Captain, this here is Del Rio. Del just ran ol' Adonis off and saved Riodan's back from a lashing. He signed on with Riodan's wagons. He'll be a good man for the trip."

"We met. Glad you're with us, Rio. I heard about Adonis," said Captain Nightingale. "Stick with Riodan, he'll teach ya what you need to know. Ol' Ben can teach ya a lot too when he's not yarning you. Maybe he'll let you scout with him. Learn ya a lot."

"Well, shucks, Cap'n, all my tales are my true-life adventures," said Ben. "You know that."

"Yeah, if you say so." Nightingale chuckled. "I hear there's a community supper tomorrow night. I hope to see you there, Del. You'll meet everyone. There'll be some singing and dancing if you've a mind for it. Enjoy yourself now. In a few weeks your feet will be sore from walking, and you'll fall exhausted into your bedroll every night."

"Nice meeting you, sir. If I can lend a hand to anything you need, let me know. I feel Riodan's a fair man as well. I'm looking forward to working for him."

"Just stick to your wagons, pay attention, and follow your division leader's orders. That'll do. Oh, and don't be running all the men off with that gun, will you?" Touching the brim of his hat, he grinned and wheeled away.

"Must like ya, Rio," said Ben. "Captain doesn't joke much—too much on his mind. Here's the layout of the camp." Ben swept his arm across the meadow they were camped on. "You've seen where we graze. Going to have to push over to the next meadow soon. The privies are downwind from the camp. You familiar with them? The daisy sign is for the women, the bull for the men.

"Community dinner tomorrow is like a church social in the middle of camp. We've got some fine cooks in this camp. I'll tell you, I never ate so good as on this train. Every wagon brings a dish. Then everyone digs in, with music and dancing later. Maybe a speech by Captain Nightingale, but the one announcement everyone is waiting for is going to be awhile. I'm riding out to check the river levels and how the grass looks when he sends me scoutin' again. If we can keep up with the greening, we'll have good grass to the mountains. We'll see about the water. Water gets scarce in the summer when it's hot and dry. Well, we'll see. How about going with me? It'll open your eyes and larn you a thing or two about how big the west is."

"I'll see you tomorrow night at the dance and let you know. I've got to ask Mister Riodan first. He's the boss."

"All right then, tomorrow! Got my camp duties to go about." Ben marched off to follow Captain Nightingale's instructions, calling to the teamsters to come and lend him a hand with the privies.

Del walked Raj up the line of wagons counting as he went. There were twenty-three, he figured, and more coming. All wagons pointed west. It was real pretty, the line of wagons against the sky, and off in the east, the faint outline of the town. To the west and beyond, the majestic mountains stood unseen. He had been amazed at the Blue Ridge Mountains. He wondered if the Rockies would be like them.

Del made his way back to camp. He was beginning to feel at home here and started to relax, glad to have his journey end. Soon, he'd buy what items he needed for the rest of the trip and start learning how to drive his team of oxen and take to settling in to camp life. There was not one doubt in his mind that he had chosen well to seek out his father and go west. He had no regrets about the way he left or about the family he had cut ties with. There was a spring in his step and a wild curiosity about Riodan and the vastness of the West beckoning to him. Their future lay out there in Oregon. What promises might he discover there?

Del found Riodan in a better frame of mind. He had had his black moments. Now, he was bustling about the camp. "Hey, young fella. Did you look around? Meet Captain Nightingale? He's a good man. He and Ben have traveled the Oregon Trail before, but on horses, no wagons. They've ridden with Bonneville and Fremont through the south pass, that's why we're going on this train. My wagons are bigger than most. Need 'em to haul freight later on, so I'm taking the chance we can get through this south pass I've heard so much about, instead of horseback or mules.

"Feed those chickens, will ya? Then go check our stock in the meadow. Look in on them. Make sure they are fat, happy and healthy, all up and eating. Come back and get cleaned up. We're eating with the Kincaids tonight. Nancy is a fine cook and me and Thomas are part of the planning committee on the train. I'm a division leader. Good folks. I'm taking her some dried peaches, so she can make a pie. Not many thought to bring much fruit. It'll be welcome. Still, lots of daylight to get work done in. Tomorrow, you'll officially start. Can you crack a bull whip? You'll learn fast enough. You're young. All right, I'm off. See you in about an hour."

Del followed orders to the letter. He was still trying to get a feel for Riodan, but the man seemed more distant now, preoccupied with performing his work duties around the camp and for the train. His orders had been direct.

Riodan's oxen rolled their eyes as Del rubbed their backs. "Whoa, big fellow, watch those horns, will ya?" He didn't know if they had names or not. They would be on the trail a long time, and he knew how much would depend on the health of these animals. Riodan had a lot of oxen—eight to a wagon, sixteen in total, plus a cow and their horses. It seemed like a lot to Del. He knew the way was long and hard, the wagons heavy and cumbersome. Still, they were needed to haul the machinery Riodan was bringing for his mills. Oh, well, not Del's concern. Out here, feeding sixteen oxen was about the same as feeding eight. There was good grass here. Grass was greening up everywhere he could see west and beyond. Could it be that hard?

The Blue Ridge Mountains were wide, and it had taken tremendous effort to build the National Road through them, making it easier for the emigrants moving west. West, where they were going, there were no roads and barely a trail yet. There had been some trains ahead of them, of course. Nightingale and Ben were experienced guides and knew the trails and passes. Del continued puzzling on it. He realized that these early movers were like the earlier immigrant threads that had migrated west into the Appalachians. The movers went first. Slowly, roads followed, then the floods of people he had experienced on the National Road. He imagined this early Oregon route would eventually be another national highway continuing west, eventually to the Pacific coast. Del thought on that as he sat and chewed a clover blossom while studying the clouds as they swept in from the west. Sunset would be in a few hours. He felt like one of the stars up in the universe. Tiny in comparison, yet valuable and important, an intrinsic piece, caught up in a huge moving phenomenon and having a life of its own as never seen in human history.

"Well, come on, boy, shake a leg!" Riodan said later as he was combing his hair.

It was the first time he had taken stock of his appearance since he and Raj had climbed out of the river that morning. He hadn't realized what a mess he looked. Had it been only one day?

"Nancy's fixing everybody fried chicken tonight. Hers is the best I've eaten in a long while. When did you eat last, come to think on it?" Riodan asked.

"Last night I reckon. I am feeling a mite hungry at that. It's been a mighty exciting day. Peach pie and fried chicken. That sounds like a feast to me, Mister Riodan, let's go!'

Nancy Kincaid stood up wiping her hands on a towel after stirring a pot on the fire. She smiled as she saw them approach and waved over to her husband, Thomas. "Howdy, neighbors," she said, "I hope you're good and hungry. Is this the boy with the big gun?"

"He is, indeed. Saved my skin today."

"Daniel, welcome!" Thomas came out from around the wagon where he had been washing up. "Welcome to you, boy, as well."

"Nancy and Thomas Kincaid, this is my new teamster Del Rio, and yes he is the one who saved me from a whipping this afternoon. Nancy, I've been bragging on your cooking to Del. I know you won't let me down. Did you have enough peaches?"

"Sure did. Welcome, Del! Come sit." Nancy had been cooking all day for this dinner, a feast for men who were used to beans and salt meat. Her table was laden with crisp fried chicken, mashed potatoes and white gravy, cooked poke and dandelion greens with vinegar and bacon, decorated with slices of eggs. Fresh corn bread sitting on a blue and white platter was cut in thick wedges, topped with melting butter. The crowning glory was a golden-crusted peach pie with a pot of thick cream sitting right next to it. A glass pitcher of dark molasses was nearby to mix into their coffee.

Shushing her two young sons, Bart and Nate, Nancy nodded and motioned to Thomas, who offered a brief blessing, and they all tucked into a fine meal. The evening passed happily. The two boys fussed with each other, while they sparred with fat drumsticks. Del envied the boy's play realizing he had never experienced that type of camaraderie with anyone as a young child. He listened as the adults talked of the train's progress and when they thought they'd be leaving. They discussed the possible hazards on the road, hoping they were prepared. Thomas thought they had too much weight for the trip. Nancy told him that if it came time to throw out furniture, she could do it, but wanted to wait until the last moment before she would.

Dan Riodan said that he only had the metal fittings and equipment needed to build his mills along with personal possessions and basic food supplies. They carried no furniture. He had heard the Indians had been friendly so far, mainly more curious than contentious. Indians came to trade for metal knife blades, guns and axes, beads and blankets. Exchanging hides and meat, moccasins, herbs and roots they had gathered in return trade.

"Ben says the Indians look at the wagons with wonder and laugh at the white men's stupidity. They think we'll all die soon, and the they'll get all out possessions, anyway. Then, they'll go their own way, no longer bothered by our stupidity," Daniel told them. "Ben is probably of the same mind as the Indians. He's been out here a long time. We need to listen to him."

The men smoked while Nancy and the children cleaned up. Del felt grown-up. He was being treated like an adult, but he declined the offer of tobacco. It had never set well with him when he had tried it. Joining in the adult conversation was a new experience for him, and he listened more than he talked. It dawned on him. He had turned eighteen back in February. He really was eighteen. That was a shock, forgetting his own birthday.

It was now early April. He was a year older. He felt ten years older. Deep down, he felt a deep pride of accomplishing so much in the last few months. He had earned his place as an adult. There was much more to face, but he saw no reason that he, that they, couldn't handle anything. The more he listened to Thomas and Daniel talk, the more he learned to respect this tall man and started to think of him as his father. He'd give it more time before he approached him, but what he saw and heard, he liked.

Daniel said it would be good experience for him to see the country and learn from Ben, when he asked about scouting with Ben. "Keep your ears open when riding with Ben," Riodan said. "He is the canniest man I know on a trail or on how to keep your scalp from the Indians. He sounds daft sometimes, but he has wisdom only experience can teach."

The west was so much different than back east. This was raw, beautiful, untamed country, verdant with the smells of earth and animal and the primal forces of nature. It was almost shameful, an unforgivable sin to intrude, because eventually it would become civilized. Judging from his experiences back east, Del wasn't sure if he wanted any part of civilization anymore. It had only brought sorrow, deep regret, and bitter experiences. Experiences he had been powerless to change. In the west he could grow, unfettered by the fake moralities and restrictions of civilized society. There, he would help make the ways and means of living. He could and he would make his own life.

"Del. Del Rio, wake up, boy. Time to get home." Dan Riodan shook his shoulders. Del had dozed off into his own thoughts.

"Good night, Miz Nancy and Mister Thomas, sir. Thank you. Supper was the best I have had… ever…" said Del sleepily. "I guess I'll see all of you tomorrow. Good night."

He and Riodan made their way back to camp and bedded down under the wagons. The last thing Del remembered was a huge night sky lit up with millions of twinkling stars, a faint whiff of wood smoke in the air, and the sound of cowbells from far off on the meadow.

9

THE NEXT MORNING, DEL WOKE to the smell of a wood fire, bacon, and coffee cooking. Daniel Riodan was whistling a faint tune as he worked around the campfire. "Rise and shine, Del. Today is going to be a busy one!"

They breakfasted on bacon and biscuits, molasses syrup and hot, strong, sweet coffee. Daniel fried some of his hens' eggs for him—the first eggs Del had had in months. There was fresh milk for their coffee. Daniel said there was buttermilk, as well. He kept the milk in a spring nearby but gave most of it to the other people on the train. The Kincaids had offered to care for the cow, as their boys drank a lot of milk. Nancy had suggested it last night. It would teach their boys responsibility they felt. Del fed and watered the chickens, gathering a few eggs. He put them in a makeshift pen so they could dig for bugs and grass yet be protected from predators. Whistling "Old Rosin, the Beaux", an old song he remembered from the time he had worked the docks he walked the cow over to the Kincaids's wagon. Nancy promised to take good care of her. The boys were excited to have a cow. They walked around petting her sides and nose.

"What's her name?" Bart asked.

"I think I heard Riodan call her Flossie.' Del chuckled when Flossie flipped her tail at Bart.

Later, Riodan showed him how and in what order to yoke the

oxen together. Del soon had the long teamster's whip whistling in the air over the oxen's heads cracking commands, "You want to keep their attention," Riodan said. "The whip is not punishment. These animals work hard. You want to encourage them, not harm them. You both work as a team. Adonis couldn't figure that out. Oxen don't think like people. They don't reason. They're willing to go where you lead them." After a pause, Riodan said, "Most of the time that is. There are exceptions. You have to be ready for the exceptions."

They worked with the team all morning. Del's lead oxen were "Big" and "Bigger," second set, "Black" and "White," the third group was called "George" and "Jefferson," for Daniel's favorite presidents. The last two animals in line weren't oxen, but bulls about one year old. They were young and inexperienced animals not used to pulling. Daniel told him they would learn on the trail as they pulled through the grass lands. He also hoped they would be worn out by the end of the day so they wouldn't cause any of the orneriness bulls can get into. Each had a ring in his nose and could be led by it. The bulls were of good English stock. Daniel hoped they would either start his herd or he could sell them to someone who wanted to start a herd with prime beef. These cattle were both brick red Durham bulls. Daniel called them "Blood" and "Fire."

"It's a gamble taking bulls, but this whole venture is a gamble. We'll see how we do. If they don't work out, or we can't handle them, then we'll have beef to trade or eat. My team are all Linebacks, an old American breed used often for oxen."

Their midday meal consisted of beans, bacon, biscuits, molasses and coffee and that buttermilk Daniel had promised.

"You ready to go to town? Oh, I got a few things for you, from some of the other wagons. Here's a wool shirt, some long johns, you'll need those later for sure. The wool will itch but keep you warm. A few pair of socks. That's a start for clothes. Someone bought the rifle I told you about. I found a revolving pistol for you instead, a .36 caliber Paterson. I'll take it out of your wages. You'll need to find a holster for it in town. I'll keep the money while we are on the trail. When you need any, Del, draw it on account. I keep good records. That way you'll have money at the end of the trail when we get to Oregon.

"Let's see, you need a decent hat. Another shirt or two as well as a couple of pairs of pants. Some boots, of course. We'll try to pick up some moccasins on the trail from the Indians. You can get buckskins from them, too. More comfortable wearing buckskins. They're like your own skin. Moves with you. You'll blend into the woods and rocks when you're hunting.

"You'll need some bar lead and bullet molds for those cannons you got and the pistol. We better pick up some more powder and caps as well. Buy as good a rifle as you can afford. It'll last you. Can you shoot a rifle? You can practice on the trail. Have you ever hunted? Trapped? Shot your own game?"

Del had done some hunting. He had trapped a little using snares and traps the way Tucker had taught him. He didn't tell Daniel that he and Tucker had gone to the woods to hunt and fish when he should have been in school. Maybe, he would tell him about Tucker one of these days. They had been friends, from what Tucker had told him, and Tucker had taught him the craft of living in the wild. Craft Tucker had learned from Riodan and the Indians during his time with him in Indiana. Del smiled at the irony of it.

Raj whistled a greeting as Del went to retrieve him from his picket. Raj seemed rested. He had slept, eaten of the lush green grass in the meadow, and was ready to go.

"You'll need a saddle. Maybe the saddler will give some trade on that English outfit." Riodan told him, "That is a fine horse. You handle him good too. I hope he makes it the whole way to Oregon. He'll throw some beautiful colts."

Del hadn't mentioned any of the doings down at the wharf before he had found Riodan on the wagon train. He had left it alone, wanting to be as unrevealing as possible, wanting to blend in, not stand out.

As they rode into town, a lot of people noticed his horse. People appreciated good horse flesh and breeding. Riodan noticed it as well.

"Raj is quite the horse, here about. We'll have to keep an eye out or somebody is liable to steal him. You go into the store and get what you need. I'll sit out here and watch over the horses. You got enough money, Del, for what you need?"

"I think so, Mister Riodan." Del hadn't shown Riodan the gold pieces he had. He hoped he had enough.

"Anything we need for the camp?" Del asked Riodan before he went into the store.

"I've got enough food. You might pick up a blanket or two for yourself. You don't have much in the way of belongings, so any personals you need, razor, comb, those kinds of things. And a hat, buy a hat!" Riodan settled into a rocker against the store front, pulled his hat over his eyes and commenced to rocking.

The first thing Del looked at in the store was a hat. He settled for a broad-brimmed black hat that would keep the sun off his face, like the Amish in Pennsylvania wore. A woman clerk helped him with his list. He bought a bag of licorice, some cherry striped candy canes for the Kincaid boys and peppermint drops along with the clothes and personal items. A beaded leather hatband caught his eye and he bought it. "Indian trade," the clerk told him. The store was well supplied, and Independence bustled with activity and noise. St. Louis used to be the supply post, but Independence was becoming the supplier and outfitting capital for all travelers going west. The trails led to Santa Fe and Texas, then to Mexico, California, Oregon, the Rockies, and all points west.

U.S. Army units on their way to fight in Mexico were camped on the outskirts of town. There were at least four to five other trains camped in the area, supplying as well. The clerk told Del that one of the trains carried the nickname "The Big Train." It would have six hundred people, the biggest yet to leave for the western mountains, with over one hundred wagons.

One hundred wagons? Del couldn't imagine it. He tried several cap and ball rifles before deciding on the one that caught his fancy and felt right in his hands. He had everything bundled up and was turning to leave....

"May I help you with that load, mister?" Black hands reached for his bundles.

"Huh?" Del turned.

Tucker stood before him, a wide toothy grin spread across his face.

"Tucker!" Del dropped his packages in astonishment. The men

grabbed each other in excitement and then stepped back, remembering where they were. Both bent to pick up the bundles, broad smiles on their faces.

"Ah, sure you can help. Wait." Del looked through the blinds. He could see Riodan sitting on the porch out front through the window of the store still talking to some men. "Tucker, what in the world? How did you get here? What are you doing here?"

"I run away, Del. Beaux whipped me good for helping you, and I run away."

"Shh, come over here!" Gathering the packages, the two men went down to the far end of the counter.

"Yes, sir, Master Del, I run away. I hooked up with a nice Mormon family coming west. I worked my way to Independence with them. I been here two days wondering what I was going to do. It ain't been decided if Missouri is slave or free yet, so's I just acted like I was going about my business. I was coming to this store to see if I could get a job. Everybody's so busy in town. There's so many people of every nation here. No one paid me any mind. I even had a free lunch in a saloon. I bought a beer! I had a little money, so I bought a beer and ate a ham sandwich like a free man. I like being free, Master Del. I like it a lot. So's I was walking up these steps when I saws a man talking to some men about a horse. I couldn't believe it was Raj! Then, I saws it was Mister Dan with Raj. I almos' jumped for joy. Mister Del, I was so excited, I practically runs over some poor woman in a yellow dress getting myself in the door, looking for you. I knowed you was in dis store. Here I am and there you are, too. And here we both are. Oh, Del, I's so glad to see you!"

"Okay, okay Tucker, I am happy to see you too! So Riodan is my pa for sure?"

"Right as rain, Del. Right as rain! He ain't changed. That's your pa. Sure enough."

"Whew." Del dropped his head in thought. Tucker changes things. That's for sure. Riodan really is my pa. Tucker's confirmation began to sink in.

"First of all, my name here is Del Rio. Pa doesn't know who I am. No free man calls another master. I'm not your master, never was.

You're as free as you can be, right now. Just act like it. You've just got to start thinking on it. No more Master Del, its Del, Del Rio. You'll call attention to yourself, by calling me master."

"That's a right smart name Master Del. Del Rio. Gee, I like that," Tucker said softly yet excitedly. "When you gonna tell Master Daniel who you is?"

"Okay, again, cut out the master business. I don't know when I'll tell him. Sooner now, than later, I guess." Del started thinking fast. He and Tucker were about the same size.

"Tuck, you ever heard of Oregon?"

"Oregon, it's a long way from here, isn't it, M—Del Rio?"

"Yep, well, that's where Pa and I are going. You're going too! If you want to come with us. You can't stay here. The slave hunters will find you sooner or later. Your best bet is in Oregon with us. Ain't no laws west of here, save the ones we make ourselves. It'll be hard and you'll earn it every step of the way. What do you say?"

"I'm for it, Del. I needs to get my things from the Mormon wagons. They're not far from here."

Del told him where their train was located and described Riodan's wagons for him. Del would buy the supplies Tucker needed for the trip. They would meet up that evening at Riodan's two wagons. Del forgot to tell him about the pitch-in dinner.

Shaking hands, Tucker left unnoticed out the back door. Del got the clerk's attention and bought another set of what he had just bought and an extra pair of boots for Tucker. He guessed he had the right size.

"Whew!" Del thought, "Life goes fast out here on these plains!" His head was swarming with a million thoughts. What was he going to do now, and how was he going to sneak Tucker onto the train? When to tell Riodan? Would Riodan object? What would they do if he didn't want Tucker to go? Del figured the Conlons would be looking for Tucker sooner or later. They wouldn't let any slave escape them. They had their honor! On the porch, Del saw an excited group of men talking and gesticulating wildly with Riodan.

Riodan eyed him as he approached with his packages. "Appears to these gents that there horse of yours is a fancy trick horse."

Del saw Captain O'Riley, Curly Joe, and many others gathered around Riodan.

"I had a heck of a time convincing them that I was watching Raj for you, not stealing him!"

"Hello, Captain O'Riley, Curly Joe. I did a few tricks with Raj. Seems some people wanted to claim him as theirs and I had to prove he was my horse. No big falderal, actually. Curly Joe, would you show me where the saddler is? I need a saddle to go out west, it appears."

"And some saddlebags," said Riodan. "I like the hat."

"And some saddlebags," said Del.

O'Riley was not to be put off. "That is some horse, Del. If you ever want to sell him, I'm the one to see."

Del put his hand on the captain's shoulder and looked in his face. "I know he'd have a good home with you, O'Riley, except we're going west. I think Raj gets seasick. He prefers hard ground and green grass under his feet." Everyone laughed.

Del mounted Raj and followed Curly Joe down the street to the saddler. He bought a good used saddle, saddlebags, and a scabbard for his new rifle. He traded in the English saddle and paid the saddler with some of his gold.

"Pilgrim down on his luck, sold his outfit to me so he could go back to Illinois. He missed his family," the saddler said. "I'll give you a good price on the whole outfit." He threw in the rope attached to the saddle, as well. Curley Joe wished him well in the west as did the other rivermen.

It took Del a while to tie all his packages onto the back of Raj, but he got it all fitted into place on his new saddle. Right comfortable it was, too, as he squirmed around in the big saddle. "Roomy as a chair in the parlor," he said to Riodan as he settled in his own seat.

Riodan commented that they looked like a traveling peddler as they rode back to camp.

"There's other trains buying provisions and several Army units headed down the Santa Fe Trail, outfitting in town. A train, they're calling The Big Train is headed to Oregon, same as us."

"Hope we get out ahead of them. Not much grass left after a big train like that mows down everything in its path. Glad Captain

Nightingale's train is smaller," Riodan said. "I expect the captain's got his eye on the big train, so we can stay ahead of them."

"So, Raj is a trick horse?"

"We did a few little tricks to shake off Captain O'Riley, who had some idea he was going to steal him from me, and I had to show the crowd Raj was my horse, not O'Riley's. Got him to back down. I think he was a little ashamed at that. O'Riley's not a bad man. His Irish avariciousness fell in love with a good horse, and he tried to take advantage of the situation. I, er, me and Raj simply brought things back into focus for him, and I got the crowd on my side and forced O'Riley to back off. He's okay, just a few silly tricks running up and down a field, that's all. He's no fancy trick horse."

Riodan just nodded as if he were pondering something.

Del felt it best to keep his cards close to his vest. He wasn't ready to reveal all to Riodan as yet. He wanted the timing just right for that.

Back at camp, Riodan showed Del where to pack his stuff in the wagon. "You sure bought out the store, fella," Riodan said as Del unloaded his goods. "You've got enough for two people. I guess you had enough money. I'm not going to get a bill from some store, am I?" He helped Del try on his boots. "I see you bought two hats," Riodan said. "One for Sunday meeting?" Riodan asked, watching Del intently. "It's your money, you can do what you want with it, I guess."

"Yeah, guess so." replied Del nonchalantly. He had bought it for Tucker, of course. "Hey, how about that pistol you got for me. Would you show me how to load and fire it?" Del sought to change Riodan's questioning looks as he unpacked all his packages. He had bought a cross draw holster for the pistol.

"Is this holster okay for the pistol?"

"Uh, sure, sure enough." It was a good fit. The thong over the hammer held the pistol in place snuggly. "That cross draw should be more comfortable on horseback and easier to reach." He looked at Del with questions in his eyes.

That afternoon, Riodan showed him how to mold balls and load his guns. He advised keeping the spare cylinder loaded and close at hand in case it was needed in a hurry. Del learned to aim and fire slowly. Riodan stressed making his shots count the first time, so as not to waste powder and ammunition, but most importantly, to save his life.

"One good shot is better than twelve shots fired all over the place. An Indian, a grizzly, anything out here, can and will kill you. It sounds hard, but you must kill them first or, for sure, they will kill you. You might only get one shot at a deer or buffalo. That shot may mean food on the fire or your belly gnawing your backbone on a cold night. Take your time. Be deliberate. Make your first shot count. If not, be damn sure the second one does … That is, if'n you're lucky enough to have a second shot."

Del wasn't happy with his marksmanship. He came close but had a hard time hitting his mark dead on each time.

"Keep practicing, it'll come to you soon enough. Aim slowly, relax, and fire. Once your shot goes where your eyes see, you'll know. Speed will come as your reflexes become used to the pattern of aim, relax and fire. You're young and sharp eyed. It'll happen. See your target, line your sight, fire smoothly and with confidence. The rest will follow, like all things. Your body will learn with practice. The weight of the gun will fade, and it'll feel like shooting with your finger in time. All things take time."

Afterwards they cleaned up camp, tended to the livestock, and then washed up for the social that night. They could hear the fiddles tuning up already.

Riodan had a joint of antelope he had been saving for this night. It wouldn't do to show up empty handed. Even the bachelors brought something. He had spitted it earlier in the day and had it roasting over the coals.

Del changed into his new clothes. He had a red and white checkered shirt, brown leather vest, blue canvas pants, new boots and his new hat. The pants felt awkward and heavy. He'd get used to them soon, he hoped. He did like his hat.

He didn't remember the last time he had cared what anyone else thought of him. These people were becoming family in a way he had not expected. He wanted them to like him. He wanted to like them. He wanted to do well. Riodan was well known and well liked. He wanted Riodan to be glad he worked for him, to be proud of him. That thought just popped into his mind. He wanted his pa to be proud of him. This was a new beginning, and Del relished it as nothing he had felt before in his life. Maybe I'll dance with a pretty girl! He'd seen some girls his age about the train, bonnets thrown back on their necks, noses freckled by the sun, sweat wetting the fine hairs alongside their faces and necks as they worked, performing their various duties about their camps.

"I might at that," said Del. "If any are lucky enough to catch my eye!" He laughed at himself as he combed his hair in the mirror hanging on the wagon. He had forgotten about Tucker. He was in such a good mood.

Del bent to polish the dust off his new boots.

"Get a move on there, dandy!" Riodan hollered at him. "We can't spend all day getting prettied up!" Del looked up at a much-improved Riodan, a fresh white cotton shirt, black vest, black canvas pants, and a black hat such as he had.

Together they were a fine-looking pair as they walked laughing and joking with everyone they met on the way to the social. Both pitched in helping the others set up the tables, covering them with red and white tablecloths. Del helped Alice Hardy, the niece of Captain Nightingale. She was newly married to a handsome young man with a pleasant smile named Russell Laughing easily, the three soon had the tables covered with cloths and decorated with small candles and wildflowers that had been gathered nearby. An area was designated for the bandstand. Someone had a harmonium. Several played fiddles. There was a squeezebox, a washboard, and a trumpet. The camp was planning on a big ol' time in preparation for the day they would leave. Soon, they would have their full complement of thirty-two wagons as more wagons and pilgrims arrived daily. All were eager to be off.

"Oh, Del? Would you mind going back to camp and fetching that joint of meat?" Riodan asked as he helped some of the ladies placing the torches around the dance floor "I'm a little busy as you can see." He flashed the lady a toothy grin. "I've got my hands full!"

"I see you do, Mister Riodan," Del said and waved at him, then turned and started for camp.

Del took a shortcut that led through an oak thicket on his way to the wagons. He ducked under a branch, and someone grabbed him by his shoulder. Del shook him off, gave a quick roll away and came up fists clenched, teeth bared. His face was red with anger and fright.

"Oh, I didn't mean to scare you." Tucker stepped out from behind the tree. "I been hiding here, until dark."

"Damn Tuck, you scared the devil out of me! Gosh, Tucker, I am glad to see you!" They shook hands.

"Okay, okay, grab your satchel there and come with me. Wait, wait, I don't want anyone to see you, not until I've told Riodan anyway and so… so, here, wear my hat. Pull it over your face. Pull your sleeves down to cover your hands. I don't want to give you away yet or have somebody think you're a thief. I'll hide you in my wagon. We're having a social and I'll bring you something to eat later. Just stay in the wagon. We'll get this all sorted out tonight when we get back after the social."

Del placed his hat on Tuck's head and pulled it down. Tucker clutched his canvas bag to his chest, and they moved to the wagons. No one seemed to pay any attention as they passed through the train. All were looking forward to the festivities and paid the pair no mind as they ducked in between the wagons. Del helped Tucker climb into the back.

"Nice hat, mas—er, Del. Oh, sorry. I'll have to get used to just Del, I guess."

"Yes, you will. I'll take my hat. There's yours, the tan one and some clothes if you need them. Stay low, out of sight and keep quiet. We have a lot to talk about, and we'll do that tonight. Boy! Riodan didn't know what he bit off when he allowed me to join up, did he, Tucker?"

"Probably not. This is a nice hat, too. Is it really mine?

"It's yours. All that stuff next to it is. The rifle, too. Riodan will show you how to use it. My gift to you. Call it a homecoming gift. Now stay tight. Hopefully you won't need the privy. Stay in the wagon. I'll see you tonight … I'm glad you're here, Tucker. I've been thinking about you a lot. Now, hush."

Oh boy, oh boy, oh boy! The fat was in the fire now, for sure.

Stolen horses, guns, runaway slaves, trains to Oregon! I must be plumb out of my mind.

Oh boy, oh boy, oh boy!

Del started back. He forgot the joint of meat! Turning quickly, he ran back and grabbed the spit, wrapped the roast in some oil cloth Riodan had left for that purpose and ran off to the supper, dripping meat juices in the dust as he ran.

10

DEL COULD NOT RELAX. HE had been hungry when he helped set up for the party, but now, all he could think of was how to tell Riodan about Tucker. He tried to eat a few bites, and it was like dust in his mouth. A few of the girls acted like they wanted to dance and tried to catch his eye only to be rebuffed by him staring off into the night sky. He stayed in the shadows watching Riodan cheerfully greeting the different families, complimenting the women on the wonderful food, joking and laughing with the men. Daniel danced a waltz with a cheerful lady in a blue checkered dress as Del sat on a wagon tongue and watched. He spent a miserable evening as he tried to work out the story he needed to tell Dan.

"What're you doing back here by the wagons?" Ben asked as he passed by Del. "Get out there and have some fun, boy! You're all dressed up. A few of these gals would love to dance."

"Thanks, Ben. I'm all right, thanks."

"Okay, Del Rio. Can't make ya dance if'n ya don't want to," he replied. "You a-going trackin' with me tomorrow?"

"What? Oh, a... yeah. Riodan felt I should go. Sorry, Ben, got something on my mind."

"I could tell you're a frettin' about something. See ya in the morning."

So, the time passed enlivened by the fiddles, washboard, and organ. One family sang "Barbara Allan," then the mother and daughter sang

"Greensleeves" and the son and father finished with "The Girl I left Behind." Families ate, danced and sang old tunes they all knew. "Old Dan Tucker," "Camptown Races," "I'll Meet You at the River," and finally, "Good Night Ladies." Del was oblivious to all the frivolity, until someone asked him to move so they could pass by with the organ.

The crowd slowly dispersed, saying good night and "God bless" to everyone. Captain Nightingale had given a speech, saying they would be leaving soon. He wanted to leave ahead of the big train before they got all the graze and fresh water. He would send Ben out to see how the grass and water were looking.

Del caught up to Riodan as he was giving bidding good night to the Kincaids.

"Oh, Del, there you are! I looked for you. Thought I'd see you dancing. It's been a long time since I last danced. Danced last time with my wife." He grew silent. Riodan was a little drunk. "Whew, anyway, I expect I'll sleep good tonight."

"Mister Riodan? We've got to talk."

"What's the matter? You… You ain't leaving already, are you?"

"No. I'm not going anywhere… unless you change your mind."

"Change my mind?" Riodan said, not comprehending. "I haven't changed my mind about anything." He dropped his hat and wobbled a little as he bent to pick it up.

"Yeah. Here, I got something to show you." Del took his arm and steadied him.

"Okay, show me what?"

As they neared the wagons, they could see there was a commotion near Riodan's wagons. Several men were holding a struggling man.

"Must be a thief! I saw him sneak into Riodan's wagon. What's he doing here?"

Riodan was suddenly alert. He ran forward and spun the struggling man around.

"What are you doing in my wagon?" Riodan asked loudly. Tucker turned to face Riodan, fear written on his face.

Riodan's anger turned cold in an instant. "Tucker? Tucker, is that you? In my wagon?" Riodan's voice cracked. He grabbed Tucker's shoulders looking at him as if he were a ghost.

"Mister Dan, I meant no harm, please don't send me back!"

Del intervened with the men surrounding them. "It's okay. He's with us. I brought him here. Thanks for looking out for us." He hoped they would just go away.

Riodan added his own thanks as the men wandered away. He took a hard look at Del. "You brought him here? Is this what you wanted to show me?" asked Riodan stunned. "Tucker, I never thought I'd see you again." Daniel took him by the hand and shook it in wonder. "I can't believe it. How in the world did you get way out here? Were you looking for me? How did you escape the Conlons?"

"Yes, I run off, and I've got a good deal to tell you too!" said Tucker, smiling. "Look at him, Daniel." Tucker pointed toward Del. "He's got your build, your face and Rebecca's hair. Doesn't he look familiar?"

Riodan got very quiet and looked curiously at Del, then to Tucker and back again.

"Yes, sir—er, Pa. Father. It's me. It's Delaino. I didn't know how to tell you ... Until you got to know me a little first." Digging into the back of the wagon, Del emerged and handed to his father, Rebecca's picture and the packet of his father's letters.

"Is it really you, Delaino?" Daniel whispered hoarsely, staring at his wife's picture, then looking at Del, his face a mask of confusion.

"Yeah, I guess so. I wanted to know what kind of man you were. Get to know you some and for you to know me. I only had heard things about you from the Conlons."

Riodan was silent for a long time, just looking at his son, examining his every feature, studying Rebecca's picture and the old letters. Fighting his emotions, tears welled in his eyes. He walked over to Del, picked him up and swung him around, taking the breath from Del. "I, I was told you and Becky were dead from fever. Things have been clicking in my head since you appeared, but I put it off to wishful thinking. Something you would say or the way you moved or held your head, would jog a memory loose again. When you told me your age, I felt more confused. You'd be eighteen, I guess by now, not twenty?"

"Yep, eighteen last February. I forgot my birthday myself. Didn't realize how old I was till I got here. I've been lying about my age so much, I forgot how old I really was."

"And Tucker? How on earth did you get here, old friend?" Daniel hugged Tucker, again. "Whew, it has been quite a night. Do you mind?" Daniel pulled out a bottle from his wagon. "I feel very sober right now, but I need a drink to settle me down. I think I'm going to cry! Del, my son... My son...." He sat down hard on a log staring at the two of them. "You're like ghosts come back to life. The both of you, all at one time! He offered the bottle to Tucker. "Tuck, do you want one?"

"Well, if it's all right. I could sure use one, Mister Daniel."

"Okay, okay, no more of this Mister Daniel stuff. Did you come with Del and Raj?"

"Oh, no, sir, I hitched a ride with da Mormons after Del raised a ruckus at the Conlons. He laid a poker handle across Beaux's face, cut him something awful, then he took off on Raj. After he ran off, I got whipped for helpin' him and locked in da smoke house. Weren't nothing to break out of there. De never thought I'd be brave enough to leave. Gathered a few important things and stole out of dat house forever. No telling what Beaux or the Major would do to me for running. The Major had bad news the night you left Del, some problems at da bank. They were head-to-head in the library da night you left, drinkin' and arguin'. They didn't have a Merry Christmas none, either."

Riodan handed Tucker the bottle. "Here's to you, Tucker. You're a free man now, and I'll fight anybody who says different. Delaino, you've showed yourself to be a man. You came all that way from Baltimore. You and Raj alone. I can't believe it. I've dreamed of this... you and your mother, so many times, I thought I'd go crazy. I'm a little bewildered still. Er—Del, a drink? This is as good a time for a drink as any I could imagine."

Del took the offered bottle.

Riodan said, "I think a toast is in order. To Oregon! Oregon, who brought my family back to me, God bless her!"

They drank solemnly, each taking a pull from the bottle, avoiding eye contact for fear the magnitude of the moment would overwhelm them. The three men talked long into the night. Del and Tucker fell asleep with their heads propped up against the logs they had been sitting on, their new hats cushioning their heads. The fire sparkled and crackled long after they dozed off. Daniel sat looking at his son and friend, lying by the log next to him, the bottle still held in both hands, fire reflecting off his face. He covered Del with a blanket and put one over Tucker as well. Sitting on the ground next to Del, occasionally running his hand over his son's hair. He was not quite sure if he believed his son was really there until sleep overtook him and he crumbled down next to the boy, his arm around his son's shoulders. He remembered the letter he had written more than ten years before.

Dear Becky and little Delaino.

How much I have missed you both. Our new house is nearing completion. Becky, the window seat you wanted looks over the White River where you can see the red bud and dogwood trees blooming.

My work goes well. Mr. L'Enfant is an excellent architect. Indianapolis is to be laid out in a grid similar to Washington D.C., much like the European style.

How is Del? I am missing those times when he is learning so much. He is such a bright little fellow. I miss and love you both more than I can express. Come home soon to me and our new home. I have enclosed a bank draft for your passage, for when you return on a steamship. There is enough to bring Tucker as well. I know he misses his forest. Please kiss Del for me, and I wish you were here, so I could kiss your sweet face which I miss every day.

Your faithful and loving husband.

11

"WELL, I THOUGHT YOU BOYS would be up with the chickens this morning!" Ben spoke from the back of his horse. "That log must be right comfortable. You don't even got any coffee on and it's bright daylight! Well, get up! There's things to do even if I have to do them." Ben dismounted, gave the three lumps a push with his foot. "Now who's this? He new? I don't think I know him!"

Tucker showed his face.

"Holy tarnation! A Negro! Where'd you come from? If you're a runaway, Nightingale will have you back to the marshal in town by noon!"

"It's all right, Ben. He's with us," Riodan said.

"He came with Del, and he's a free man." Riodan hoped his lie would not be discovered until no one could do anything about it. Besides, he had come with Del separately, and he had belonged to Del. Del was Conlon family, so Del was responsible for his being here. They had told Tucker at least twenty times last night to stop calling Del and Daniel master, but a lifetime of conditioning was hard to break.

"Well, okay, if'n you say so, but if he's coming with us, he's got to sign Nightingale's register and to mind the rules of the wagonmaster."

The term, wagonmaster, brought everyone up short. Tucker grinned and said, "Yes, sir. I can shore do that." Riodan and Del laughed at him.

Ben took a long studious look at Riodan and Del, like he didn't get the joke.

"He's your responsibility. He's with your wagons."

A fire was soon blazing strong. "I need some dag-blamed coffee. You're going to need it, too, young fella. That is, if I can talk you into scouting with me for a couple days. Ya said you would go."

Del jumped. "We're leaving now? But where are we going?"

"Nightingale wants me to scout ahead to see how the grass and water is. We'll be gone about two days, I guess. It'll give us a jump on that big train. All their wagons ain't showed up yet. I heard they are expecting to have over a hundred wagons. That's a lot of mouths eating lots of grass, raising dust, leaving the water muddy and fouled for the rest of us. I thought I'd see if you wanted to ride with me. Show you the countryside, teach you how to live on the trail and what you need to know to survive out there."

"How about it Riodan, er, Pa. Can I go?"

"Hell, son. Son? You know, Del, that sounded sweet to my ears. You made it here without me telling you what to do."

"Son? Pa?" asked Ben. "I'd better keep my mouth shut." He continued to make the coffee, keeping his head down, looking up several times to peek from under his hat. They did favor each other, but he didn't want to intrude.

"Yeah, I did, but I hired on with your wagons. You're the boss as far as I'm concerned. I'm sure Tuck feels the same way.

"I sure do." Tuck's voice trailed away. He wasn't used to being asked his opinion. "Man, oh man, I sure do. I work for you, Daniel. We have a lot to talk about. Don't we, Dan?"

"Yes, we do, Tuck. All right, Del, you ride with Ben. I'll show Tucker the ropes around here. An extra hand is always welcome. As I recall, you were good with traps and snares, weren't you, Tuck? You'll be right useful in keeping some meat on the fire. Do you still cook?"

"Yes, I do." He took a sip of Ben's coffee and immediately spit it out. "Lord, you could float a horseshoe in this stuff!" Then immediately apologized. "Sorry, Mr. Ben, I didn't mean no unkind words."

"None taken, and its Ben. Seems, you're breakin' some old habits," Ben said and extended his hand, "Ben Grubbs, nice to meet ya."

"A great pleasure to meet you, Ben Grubbs. I'm Tucker. Tuck to my friends."

"That's prairie coffee, and it will wake you up in the morning. You better drink it, 'cause, if you leave it in your cup, it'll eat a hole in it and ruin it, shore enough. Can you make better?"

"I am surely going to try, Ben Grubbs. I am surely going to try." Tucker grinned into his hat.

They laughed and Riodan and Del filled their cups.

Ben and Del rode from the waking train heading for Westport, a small-town west of them. This little town was abuzz and growing as well. More and more trains were stocking up closer to the river and the mercantile stores and livestock pens were crowded. A few drunks staggered on the street. A barber shop had a crowd of men around it. Del saw what was drawing the crowd. A sign said they had ladies exclusively, to shave the men. Ben remarked that he needed a shave himself, pretty bad. He'd have to look into that shop when they got back.

Beyond the little town, they crossed the Kansas River and headed for the open prairies. If the grass and water were good, they would alert the ferrymen to prepare for their crossing. They headed northwest. Riding Raj again agreed with both the boy and horse. The trail was level. Green grass and yellow candelions stretched for the sun and blue sky, everywhere they looked.

"The Indians call them dandylines white men's footprints, 'cause the white man brought them over from the old country to plant in their gardens for food. They's spread from ocean to ocean. Most Indians refuse to eat them. I like them, myself, with some bacon and vinegar. Makes a tasty green.

"We're looking for the Big Blue River. We follow that until it branches north. Then we follow the Little Blue until it peters out. After that, we head north until we hit the Platte River at Grand Isle. That's when we turn the train west. We'll follow the Platte, until she splits into a branch going south. Bein' as we're going to Oregon, we take the northern branch. The trail to Utah goes south from there. Everyone going to Oregon or California takes the north trail.

You and me is only going to where the Little Blue branches off. The grass is looking pretty good here about. Later on, as we head west, I can take you with me scouting on ahead of the train, if your duties with Daniel's, er, your pa's wagons, don't come first. Wanna let me in on the secret?"

Del explained briefly. He told him that Tucker had practically raised him and of some of the trouble he had had with the Conlons.

Ben listened without comment.

"That's about it, Ben. Here we are—me and my pa, father and son, and friend, Tucker. We got a lot of catching up to do, but mainly, we're going to make a life as a family. Something the Conlons tried to take away from us. This trip is important to all of us. I gave Tucker his freedom. Out here in the west, he'll be his own man. He'll be a partner in whatever we do."

"Yes, sir, he will if those Conlons don't catch up to you all. Oregon is a good place to start a new life. The best place I've seen. You can bet on that. I guess all three of you deserve one," Ben said with serious eyes.

"You're the first person we've told on the train. I'd be beholding to you if you didn't mention Tucker's story to anyone. I suppose you'll have to tell Captain Nightingale. We'll let the rest know soon enough. I want them to get to know Tuck as a man first and not think of him as an ex-slave. Our past is unimportant. About the scouting, let me talk to Pa about going with you. He wants me to experience as much as I can. I would love to go. I love it out here, and I want to learn the ways of the west. I'll be glad to go with you when I can."

Del let Raj set his own pace. Those days on pasture had been restful, but he was used to traveling, and ready to stretch his legs. Del could feel the big fellow's strength. It was good to be on the trail again. This was pretty country, some rocky outcroppings, but mainly miles of undulating new grass. The prairie reminded Del of a breathing body spread out before him as alive as anything he had ever seen. He could feel her breath in his face and hair. Honeysuckle, columbine, and wisteria perfumed the air. Both men and horses breathed deeply.

Ben had checked their gear before leaving. They had grub and ammunition enough. "Enough is enough if you don't use it all," Ben said. "Not enough is when you run out. Same way with grub."

They approached the Big Blue River by that afternoon. "Grass looks like it is coming along. I'll tell Nightingale. It'll be a good time to leave. If'n we get behind that other train, there won't be enough grass to feed a scrawny milk cow. Rivers is full of water, but they're not flooding. We won't have to cross much going this way, just a few feeder streams to the main rivers. Keep your head on a swivel, boy. The grass is coming up. In a few weeks, it'll be tall enough to hide In-juns, cats, wolves, and worst of all, sinkholes. I had a buffalo surprise me coming out of the tall grass t'once. Scared us both so bad we took off running in the same direction. I could see his eyeball staring me down as we ran. I guess he couldn't figure out what the devil I was. An outcropping split us up. Never saw that buffalo again. He might still be running for all I know or lost in a sinkhole."

"How much grass do we need?" asked Del, sitting his saddle and surveying the land around them.

"Same answer. Is enough, enough? That dry stuff don't look like much. Its bluestem grass. Cures on the stem late in the year. It's not as nutritious as early on, but it'll help keep the cattle from bloating mixed with the fresh green stuff. Everything look's good here. The further west we go, the younger it gets. We're going to follow the seasons, so to speak. The eastern side grasses green up. Then the western side greens up. If we figure it right, we should have fresh grass clear to Idaho, before we get into the big mountains. That depends on rain, flood, cyclones, Indians, sickness and accidents. If we're at Independence rock sometime by the early to middle part of July, we will be fine."

"Are the Rockies as big as the Appalachians?" asked Del.

Ben looked at Del matter of factly. "Del Rio, the Rockies make those eastern mountains look like God was just using them for practice before he finished his master work. The Rockies stretch clear up into Canada and south below the Mexican border. I guess they stretch all the way to South America. They are so high that you can see the tops from hundreds of miles away. You'll have to see them for yourself as mere words just ain't enough to describe them."

They rode for two days. Ben was a never-ending font of information, wisdom, yarns, good humor and an occasional outright lie. They did meet a small group of Indians headed east. They pulled a travois with a sick old man on it. Del traded them some bacon and sugar for a buckskin shirt and a pair of moccasins.

"Good trade, boy! They needed the meat. Indians is damned fond of sugar. They don't have much sweet, 'cept for honey and such. They'll remember you. Shirt and moccasins is always handy. They fit natural. Moccasins is quiet, not like boots you can hear a mile off. They wear out after a while, but easy to make and quiet."

They made camp the second night. Ben had shot a prairie chicken and gathered some dandelion greens. They had those along with some biscuits and Ben's black coffee. All in all, a fine meal. It had been an interesting trip. They had found what they needed to know. The grass and water were good clear up to the Little Blue River. They set off in the morning, before dawn broke, to take the good news back to the train.

They reported to Captain Nightingale as he was finishing his noon meal. "Thanks, Ben, that's the news I wanted to hear. I don't think we should wait any longer. Call out up and down the lines to gather after the evening meal. Tell them to get their wagons ready. We leave in the morning. Good lad, Del. Stick to ol' Ben. He'll teach you a lot. Probably save your skin a time or two. What he can learn you can't be found in a book."

Del spent the afternoon with Daniel and Tucker getting the wagons ready.

Riodan showed them everything he had brought and how he had stowed it between the two wagons. There was flour, coffee, beans, salt, sugar, bacon, dried fruit, dry portable soup, and dried vegetables. They had the stock of blacksmith tools and fittings for the mills. He had corn meal, jerky, salted meat, lard, trading goods, shot and powder in kegs. He had provisioned well, as they had no furniture. The load should grow lighter as they ate their way to Oregon. There were the chickens, and the Kincaids had Flossy tied to their wagon. They, at least, would have eggs and milk.

"I laid in what I thought I'd need to start a new life. No furniture or frills. We'll sleep on pallets in our bed rolls. I've heard of families losing everything due to carrying too much. I chose oxen, because well, first of all, they were cheaper, but they're stronger than horses or mules. They'll eat what a horse or mule will starve on. I've got the two bulls pulling at the back of Del's team. They'll be fine after a few weeks. The experienced oxen will teach them to pull, without breaking them down. They will get stronger as we pull over the grasslands and be ready by the time we make the mountains.

"We have ourselves and our horses. We'll find a horse for Tucker along the trail. We've got good breeding stock. I've planned as best I could, Del. I don't make any guarantees we'll make it. Oh, since we're talking... anything happens to me, it all goes to you. This is your outfit. I expect you to keep going. Tucker, Del will make you a partner, just as I offered you a partnership in the mills. It'll be hard work, but you'll be working for yourself and your family. I want Tucker with me on the front wagon, so he can learn how to handle the team and maintain the wagon. Del seems to be comfortable handling his team. We'll all improve as we travel and learn from our mistakes. Tucker, would you grease all the wheels? There's a bucket of grease hanging from the rear axle of each wagon. Del, make a thorough inspection of all harnesses and straps. Repair them as needed. If anything is broke, fix it right then. Make that your practice, to fix it then. I'm going to double check the loads in the wagons to see that all freight is properly balanced and secure. If anyone needs help, just yell out.

"Oh, something else you both need to know. My wagons are big, but they are not overloaded. I carry extra casks of water, four to a wagon. I heard a lot of sickness on the trail comes from bad water. I've learned a trick from a fellow I knew in Indianapolis who had traveled all over the world. The trick to good water is to filter it through charred wood to take out the sickness and foulness. Oh, yeah, he also told me to keep several silver coins in the bottom of each barrel. He says it keeps the water fresh. I've been following this fella's advice. He had never been sick on a voyage when he followed these precautions. It's worked for me this far. When you clean the barrels, don't lose the silver coins. I've got a filter of charcoal made up and a funnel to fill the barrels. We'll fill the barrels after we're finished with everything else first. Remember, no water directly from a stream into the barrels. Filter it first. As far as drinking from any water, stream or lake, check for dead animals further up the stream. Make sure it is fast moving water. Most water will be safe to drink when it's clear. No drinking from water in a beaver pond. Seems it gives you the diarrhea or dysentery or some such sickness. I don't know myself. It's just what I've heard. Del, you might ask Ben about it, when you get a chance. Alright, let's get to work, men. It'll be a long day and a longer one tomorrow."

All that day, the men made final preparations. The entire camp was enlivened with renewed activity, becoming a living breathing flurry of excitement. Oregon! They were finally going to Oregon!

By that evening, all was in readiness. Animals and stores had been checked and double checked. They had water, clean and cold in the barrels, everything tied down and secure. A sense of excitement rose in Del's gut that made him feel he was going to burst. He turned to speak to Tucker, but paused, seeing the man's face. "What is it, Tuck? You look terrible. You sick?"

"No, no, M— Del. I, I, I've just never had no feeling like this before. I've seldom ever got to think of a future. Here I am, a part of something big. Something that includes me. I keep looking west and my heart grows so big and shining it about chokes me. When I look east, I'm afeared of what may be coming. I can't wait to leave, and yet, I'm afraid of what may catch up to us. I keep punching myself that I'm really here with the sky over my head, a part of history, moving west. I think on that. Yes, sir, I do. I'm a part of history right here and now. Thanks to you and Dan Riodan. Bless you both. That last whipping changed my life. It made me make up my mind and get away from the Conlons to here. I keep thinking, if I'm dreaming, I don't want to ever stop."

A fiddle started playing in the night's stillness. A clear voice lifted to sing the Scottish song, "Coulter's Candy."

"Well, Tucker... You just keep looking west, we'll deal with whatever comes. The three of us will. You can count on that. I, too, fear the Conlons may someday catch up to us, but damn them. We're men here, and I'll die fighting for that, for you, for Pa, for me, for this here damn train!" Del spit in his hand, "You've got my hand on that, Tuck." He held out his hand. Tucker spit in his hand and reached out.

"Whoa, whoa here, what's going on? I've been listening to you dreamers." Dan Riodan came over. "If any pacts or solemn oaths are to be made, I am in on it too!" He spat in his hand. All three joined hands like the hub of a strong wheel, the three stood united in purpose and commitment.

A shot fired in the air.

"Captain Nightingale wants everyone to gather in the center of camp at the fire. Everybody gather up." Calls came from all over the camp, as the word passed.

Torches and fires lit the faces of the gathered men, women and children, flickering over serious eyes and determined countenances of the souls surrounding Captain Nightingale, who commanded attention as he stood on a barrel.

"I don't have to tell you. You all know. We leave at first light." The crowd broke into a loud cheer. "The ferry will be ready for us. We've thirty-two wagons, so it won't be a long crossing, as such, about half a day if all goes well. Those that cross first will wait for the rest. Ben will show you. We will be ahead of that big train. Ben says the grass will be good. There won't be any if we follow them. Listen to your division leaders. Each leader is in charge of five wagons. These leaders report directly to me or Ben Grubbs. Dan Riodan, you've got the biggest wagons, I want you to ferry over first and wait. I want your division to break trail for the others. Each morning a new division will lead. That way we all eat the same dust."

Laughter broke from the crowd

"I know you've all brought your hopes and dreams with you. I can't promise you all of us will make it. This, I can promise you... me and Ben will do our utmost to see that you do make it. I don't know what will come. There hasn't been much trouble from the Indians. It's accidents and fever that takes the greatest toll. Every day will be different. We'll face wind, rain, and dry spells. You're going to walk till you feel like falling down, then you'll get up and walk some more. If you break down, we'll all pitch in to get you right and rolling. If it's a major breakdown, we'll have to move on and wait for you at camp.

If you don't show up by next day, we'll leave you. Sorry, but we must be at Independence Rock early in July, or we don't make the passes through the mountains before the snows. You all know this. If you break down, we must leave you. If you can't make repairs in a few hours, it's on you to catch up to us.

"Be prepared, be wary and be alert! Keep your spacing. We should leave by noon tomorrow, after everyone is ferried across. Circle up by six for supper. Keep your guns close to hand. There shouldn't be much trouble traveling until we reach Grand Isle. Then the way becomes rougher. That's where we turn west. You've heard the stories about where we're going. Land of milk and honey and such. Yes, it's a good place, this Oregon, but you will think you're in hell before we get there, and you'll work for it every step. Good luck to us all. I've asked Reverend Blaine to offer a blessing."

"If you'll all bow your heads?" asked Reverend Blaine. "May the good Lord bless and keep each of us. May he grant us fair winds, good grass, and crystal rain. Keep our hearts open with a determination that won't quit, dear Lord, and our powder dry, if the time arises."

"God bless you all. Peace to all we meet! Wake up trumpet at five. We roll at six," Nightingale said.

12

THE FIRST DAY STARTED SMOOTHLY enough. Anxious to be off, everyone got up and ready before the time to pull out. Crossing the river took most of the morning, but they experienced no accidents or losses. Where before, the women and men had looked to the West in wonder and hope, they now looked East with anguish in their hearts for the loved families left behind. Remembering homes long lost, memories of loved ones' faces, and fading places never to be seen again filled them with a guilty reverence.

Once all the wagons had gathered after the crossing, a tension gripped the pilgrims with a palpable pulse that touched each man and woman, as if they were all connected to the electrical earth by an overwhelming magnetic pull, none of them could resist.

"Mister Riodan, if you will, sir. Lead them out! Wagons, *Ho!*" said Captain Nightingale for the first time. Dan Riodan, flicking the whip over the head of his oxen, led the train that first day. His wagons, though heavier than normal prairie schooners, had been fitted with wider wheels so they could move over the prairies instead of cutting through the sod.

One by one, the pilgrims' wagons creaked into formation accompanied by shouts of "Haw! Gee! Get up there now, boys, we're off. We're off." Tears of joy, remorse, regret, anger, hope, and dreams ran unashamedly down their faces. But now, their eyes turned determinedly West, unwavering in their decision to trust to the western horizons. With hearts yearning for the unseen mountains and homes waiting to be built, these early heroes began their voyage through a sea of green.

Del's oxen had been enjoying unlimited pasture for the last few weeks. They had been worked for a few hours each week, but now it was work dawn to dusk. The first few hours the morning of the first day were unremarkable. The team seemed to pull to a rhythm orchestrated by creaking wagons, cracking whips, sharp whistles of the men, and the slap of leather above the flanks of the straining beasts as they pulled along, bells around their necks, clanking a cadence with each step. They didn't understand the trail yet, or that each day for the next six months they would wake to pull these wagons again. That morning, all went well.

After their dinner of left-over biscuits and bacon from breakfast, word was again sent down from Captain Nightingale, "Mister Riodan! Would you lead them out again, sir? I'll give the call shortly."

Dan, Tucker and Del quickly broke camp. They had watered the teams, and let them graze. The oxen enjoyed the tender grass and were reluctant to return to the toil of pulling the big wagons. They wanted to find a shady spot and chew their cud uninterrupted. Del had to pull on their yokes and flick his whip over their heads to move them off the new grass.

Tucker laughed to Del, as he lifted the pot of beans he was cooking from the fire and put them in a padded box. "They should stay hot, done to perfection by supper time. Yes sir, Del Rio, I can make a pot of good Baltimore beans. Some's calls dem Boston beans, but I knows my beans and these is Baltimore beans long before they ever saw Boston! They should be sweet and tender by supper time tonight."

"Wagons, Ho." The call drifted back from up ahead.

"Get up there, Big. We're going west. You can eat when we stop for supper. Up, Black. Let's go, Jefferson. You boy, Blood, get in line there." Del cracked the whip over his team's heads and shouted. "Get up, now! Stay in line! That's it, follow your noses. Follow Mr. Riodan there who is a-leading this fine company. Yahoo!" At those words, Dan smiled and waved back at his son.

Captain Nightingale rode at the head of the train along with Ben Grubbs. This part of the trail had already been scouted by Ben and Del a few days ago, so Ben stuck close to the train.

Ben fell back to talk to Del. "We're going to make camp at that stream we crossed before we met those Indians we traded with. There should be good water and grass for tonight. Cap doesn't want to push too hard on the first day. Need to get them pilgrims toughened to the trail first. Don't want too many sore feet and sore backs or sore heads in the morning. You're doing good yourself, pilgrim. Keep those oxen moving, they'll learn. See ya!" He galloped off to the next wagon.

They made eight miles the first full day over flat grassland despite the river crossing. Fields of spring beauties carpeted the mild, green, rolling hills off to Del's left. On his right, where the woods bordered the river, Indian paintbrush in brilliant reds stood out next to the fancy pants, pink and white Dutchmen's breeches. Spring was showing off. The smell of earth erupting into new life wafted across his nose carried there by gentle breezes. Del Rio walked along as carefree as he had ever been in his life.

Fading light found the Riodan camp finishing off the Baltimore baked beans, biscuits, and fried meat for supper. Tucker had stewed some prunes and raisins as well. He winked at Dan as he spooned some of the fruit onto Del's plate. "This'll keep you regular on the trail, Del!"

Del looked puzzled and shrugged, "Okay, Tuck, whatever you say. They taste pretty good. I needed something sweet. I'm not as tired as I thought I'd be. Who's watching the stock tonight, Pa?"

"I guess the fourth division has watch tonight. I think Captain Nightingale is pleased with our progress. Grass is pretty good and going to get better. The way we're going, we don't cross any major rivers until we reach Grand Isle. We'll follow the Platte and, soon after, take the North Fork. Hope the weather holds. This part of the country is known for its cyclones and icy storms this time of year. Sky looks good so far." Daniel scraped his plate into the fire and dropped it in the wash bucket. They set about their camp duties.

Del helped Tucker clean up after supper. His chores were taking care of the chickens, checking the wagons and harness for wear and to repair as needed. Tucker took care of the larger stock and saw that all provisions and water were secure and ready to travel. Dan was their division leader. He inspected each wagon in his group, answered questions on direction of travel, settled disputes, and helped everyone who needed it. He relayed communications from Captain Nightingale back to the heads of the individual wagons. None took their responsibilities lightly. Each man was ready for sleep when he crawled into his blankets under the wagons after a hard first day. A light breeze blew across their faces, smelling of fire, broken grass and animals. Soon, they slept.

Each day was a repeat of the day before. Get up, eat, gather the stock, set out, walk, eat, walk some more, eat that night, sleep, then do it all again the next day. They forded streams and followed trails. They had to cut logs and brush out of the way, but Kansas was flat with a few rolling hills. The sod, thick from thousands of years of growing grasses, built a thick turf of roots that burrowed into the virgin sod as much as ten feet or more. Each train followed a general trail, led by the wagon master and scout, but no specific trail existed. The pilgrims had been lucky so far. After a few weeks, there had been only one accident. A musket discharged as it was pulled out of a wagon. The owner had suffered a burnt face from the powder blast. The embarrassment of the incident was amounted to nothing compared to what blowing off his head could've been. So far, they had been lucky, very lucky.

Tucker enjoyed his new freedom. Every day, he shed more of the slave mentality. He pitched in with the work as every other man on the train, and he earned their respect. His personal respect for himself grew as well. He voiced his opinion freely in the camp meetings. Most of the men of the train travelled west for personal freedom, so they sympathized with him. Daniel and Del told the folks on the train that Tucker was a freedman and treated him like one. Seeing no reason to do otherwise, people accepted Tucker. He learned to let his own thoughts guide his life, trust to his own opinions and not to be ruled over by the commands of others.

It would take a while to change a lifetime of subservience, of suppressing his own thoughts and actions, of servility to another. He was shedding his old skin for a new one. Each day brought its own joy. When he was sought out for advice or his opinion on a matter, or when he put his back to work like the rest of the men, he was aware of their acceptance, and he stood a little taller. He dared to cast his eyes to the west and dream of a new life there in the unknown abyss of this territory called Oregon. He had stopped pinching himself, hoping he was not dreaming. Hard work and sore muscles convinced him he was not. Each shining grand day and the steps he took west were steps further and further from Baltimore.

"You know, Del, I tried counting my steps yesterday. I lost count at about ten thousand when I stepped in a hole and tripped. It doesn't make any difference, I guess. Each step keeps me going on and on. I'd keep walking forever if need be. It's a mind-altering experience. If I had been freed back in Baltimore, I don't think I would have handled it well. I've learned freedom is something you have to put on and wear for a while. You know what I mean? It doesn't come naturally to a person who hasn't been born to it. I like to put it on every now and then, get the feel of it. Out here is so big, and freedom feels even bigger.

"Why, yesterday I spoke to Miz Barlow. I looked her right in the eye and told her my recipe for biscuits. Her biscuits come out flat. Why, Miz Barlow, I said, if your leavening is a little old, it needs a boost. So, I gave her some of ours and told her to add a touch of vinegar to her milk or water when she was making them. She came and thanked me 'cause her biscuits were mighty plump and delicious this morning. Mister Barlow tipped his hat to me as their wagon moved into line today. He tipped his hat to me! Can you imagine? Just like I was somebody!"

"Well, Tuck," replied Del, "you're a biscuit-baking man. You are somebody! Now, everybody will know, and Pa and I are going to have to live with your big head, ain't we? You'll be known as the biscuit man from Independence to Oregon and Dan and I are going to be tripping over all the people coming to you for biscuit advice. It'll be a damn nuisance. We won't be able to get any work done. Dan'll have to charge a nickel a head to pay for what a bother it'll be. Did you ever think of that?"

Tucker stood blank faced.

Del burst into a roar of laughter and pushed Tucker back over a log causing him to spill the bucket of water he was bringing to the fire. Tucker started laughing and threw the rest of the water at Del.

Dan turned and smiled as he watched the two wet, whooping men playing in the mud.

13

SO DID THEY TRAVEL, WALK, eat, laugh, and walk some more. It was hard work. Captain Nightingale kept them on the trail dawn to dusk. They headed for Grand Isle and the turn to the west. The grass was good and getting better. Streams were high, but manageable. The first big river they would cross after the Kansas would be the Platte. The Little Blue River ran off to their right, and they followed it as it crossed over into the territory folks called Nebraska. The going was still mostly flat, but with more and more rounded sloping hills. Occasionally, a wagon would have to be hauled out of a muddy hole or extra oxen or mules hooked up to pull it up an embankment. Day by day, they moved ever onward. Feet got tougher, backs became stronger as rhythm and routine became their new life.

Del grew stronger too. He could do the work of any of the men. "He could handle his freight," the other men said. Del was proud to be a part of this family of strangers. The three men sat by the fire at night telling the stories of themselves, entwining the tendrils of their past lives into a firm bond of friendship and understanding. Del learned who this man Riodan was. His stories filled in Del's empty childhood. Those nights by the campfire, became Del's baptism into the lives of his parents. Daniel told of his falling in love with Becky and their life in Indiana. Tucker and he fished, hunted and learned from the Indians. He related how Becky, Tuck and their infant son had left, vowing to be together by the end of the year. Daniel remembered kissing Del goodbye on the steamboat. He remembered how Rebecca's hair looked and the smell of lilacs on her lips when they last kissed. The stories filled in the blank parts and corrected the assumptions and misgivings Del had conjured up in his mind over the years. Of all the men Del had known, Dan Riodan was the man Del would be most proud to be. Through these fireside talks, Dan taught him the life skills he would need in their new home. The first lesson was honesty, integrity, and that a man's word was a sacred bond. Out here, sometimes, that was all you had, and it might save your life.

Under his father's strong hand, he learned to heat a horseshoe and form it to fit the hoof and how to hot weld broken pieces of metal together in the heat only hard black coal could produce. Most of all, Daniel continued Del's shooting lessons. Youthful reflexes and a good eye were his best assets. He could hit a two-inch circle at fifty feet with his handgun and drop an antelope at two hundred yards with his rifle. All three men hunted. Tucker was the most successful at bringing in meat. He would disappear into the brush before supper, setting snare lines in likely places. They enjoyed rabbit, coon, possum, an occasional muskrat and beaver roasted over their fires as they rolled further along. Anything extra they shared with the Kincaids and other wagons in the train, as was all meat the men brought in. Large game was cut up and dried in the sun, or in the wagons, so the heat and wind could dry it to preserve it for later. They spent little time in camp but to eat and sleep. Time and schedule became the masters on the trail.

Del scouted ahead with Ben when the old scout wanted an extra set of eyes on his scouting forays. Tucker became proficient in handling Del's wagon. The train had crossed the north branch of the Little Blue, now a wide stream, and they headed due north to Grand Isle.

Del and Ben had been scouting the area ahead of the train a few days out and were heading back to report to Captain Nightingale. It was a grey still day with not much wind moving. There was a different feel to the day, and their animals were nervous and anxious for

some unseen reason. Raj's ears were up. He had been restless, nervously side stepping and blowing through his nose. Ben kept watching the south and west. Dark, ugly, yellow-tinged clouds formed on
the horizon. Ben urged Del to move on. He wanted to get back to the
train as fast as possible. The weather was changing quickly.

"Don't like it, Del. Too damn still. Feels like we're inside a well. No
air moving, no nothing. Listen, you hear anything?"

"No," Del said.

"Dang right, no! No animals are moving. No insects in the air. No
dew on the grass this morning. No breezes like we've had. It sets my
hackles on edge. That horizon is moving toward us fast. In this country, the weather can change in a minute. We've had it too darned good
so far. I've seen cyclones that ripped a path through a prairie, looked
like a plow done went through it. There! Do you feel it?"

Del could feel it. The temperature had dropped several degrees
as they talked.

"I hope this don't mean what I think it means. C'mon boy, we've
got to burn leather to that train. That weather is a-comin'!" With
that, both men galloped away, whipping their horses' flanks with
their hats, desperate to reach the train before the weather hit them
in full force.

Dan's wagon led the train with Captain Nightingale alongside,
when they saw the two scouts riding in waving their hats.

"Captain! Weather's turning bad. Better light a shuck, head 'em
out, and batten down everything we got. It's gonna get ugly. We
passed a line of small cliffs about a mile ahead. I'd head there for
protection. I'll ride on ahead to organize the wagons as they come
in. Stay out of the trees! It's getting colder." A brief gust of wind
flapped Ben's hat and he had to grab it. "Not good, Captain! Go,
Dan, get 'em moving."

"I'll pass the word." Captain Nightingale yelled and waved his hat
at the next line of wagons. They were moving six divisions abreast
on the broad plain.

"Del! Grab these reins and let me have Raj. I don't have time to
saddle up and I need to ride back and get my division moving. Watch
yourself, son. See you at the cliffs!" Raj hesitated for a brief moment

before deciding Daniel on his back was all right with him, and then he tore off toward the nearest wagons.

Captain Nightingale and Daniel raced down the lines urging everyone to get moving. Seeing and hearing the yelling and waving men, gesturing frantically toward the cliffs, the train gradually sensed the urgency and quickened their pace. Now, it became a race. Each face could see the mounting storm gathering strength. Cold wind blew in abrupt bursts, chilling bodies, tearing eyes, and biting cheeks. Reins and whips snapped over the backs of the cattle and mules urging them to move faster. Rumbling distant thunder sent vibrations through the ground.

Shockwaves from the wind buffeted Del's face, blowing his hair, and ripping at his clothes with icy fingers. "Get up there, Blood. Pull, Fire! You've had it easy. Time to earn your keep! Get up there, you bull!" He screamed and snapped the whip over their heads urging them to feel as driven as he did.

The shouting men's voices, and the creaking, swaying joints of the wagons were hollow, suppressed sounds that did not carry as they chewed up the ground, heading for the cliffs. There was an almost unperceivable mounting wail, underlying their flight to the safety of the cliffs, promising terror and destruction as the storm rolled over the far prairie toward them.

Del led the way. His oxen couldn't run fast, but they sensed the storm and moved with mounting anxiety. Cold gusts and the coming rain fairly tingled in the air and on their backs as the air charged with energy with each windy push that blew in. Billowing canvas tops became kites, catching the blustery wind and rocking the wagons side to side on their wheels.

The color of the westward sky turned ominously vivid purple and black. Deep into the coming storm, bright blue and silver bolts of lightning struck the plains leaving glowing bursts of light reflected on the swirling clouds above. Thunderheads trembled with explosions that shot into and shattered the ground below. It was a beautiful, frightful thing to see , but the shaking earth and swirling winds left Del deeply troubled. He had seen storms like this offshore, but not this close on land. The maelstrom rotated the sky to the left. The powerful intensity in the growing strength of the wind blasts urged him to move more quickly.

He waved to Tucker whose face was creased with worry. Tuck waved back that he was fine. They cast worried looks at the gathering melee and cracked their whips for greater speed from animals already pulling at their limit.

Dan rode up and down the train lending a hand where needed. People ran alongside their wagons, some stumbling and falling. Women grabbed their children, tossing them into the back of the wagons.

Dan stopped and helped close the back of a wagon that had broken open as its owner tossed the few items that had fallen out into the back. "Thanks, Dan," he said, looking at the horizon. He closed the latch and called to his team. "Get up now. Let's go, get up! Brownie! Bessie! Pull, you mules!"

The low cliffs Ben had sent them to ran north and south. They were a low-cut bank, about twenty-five feet in height. The train sought refuge on the lee side of the cliffs. Ben ordered the drivers to line up their wagons, parallel to the cliff face, and unhitch their teams. They moved their animals into any protected area they could find. Ben didn't want any frightened teams pulling a wagon into the wrath of the storm. Oxen put their backs to the wind and lowed apprehensively. Horses bunched protectively together, backs to the wind with their heads low to the ground.

The wind howled and became a whistling, blustering bully shaking the wagons to and fro with every gust. Women held onto their men to keep from being blown down. Families gathered their children to them, tying down their canvas tops, crawling under their wagons, embracing each other, and waiting for what was to come. Big splats of rain hit them and a deep blast of frigid air rocked the wagons in the tiny shelter of the ridge. Wet, fat hail splattered the rocks, changing to stinging pellets, then into fist-sized hard ice that pummeled the stock and sent them running. Sharp, hard hail ripped into the wagons, drumming on board and battens, threatening to strip the canvas from the wagon's ribs.

Dan, Tucker, and Del pulled the wagons close together, tying them together with ropes, then spreading a tarp over one side for shelter from the wind and rain. They grabbed rain slickers and took cover under the wagons.

The shrieking rain picked up. Just when they thought it had reached its worst, a pressure wave beat them down again. The wind roared, increasing in volume and intensity. Wagons shook on their wheels. Canvas was stripped off and the contents sucked up into the whirlwind. Then it quit.

The storm roared on to their northeast. The wind died. A light steady rain continued and then stopped.

The land lay silent, cold, desolate... waiting.

A child's cry broke the silence, hushed by a soft voice.

The men and women huddled under their wagons, staring blank-faced at each other.

Soaked to the skin, people crept out of hiding and surveyed the surroundings with white faces, trembling with cold, trying to make sense of the landscape. They blinked in disbelief. Moving around to the windward side of the cliffs, they saw where once had been green, growing trees and waving luscious grass, had turned into an unbelievable wasteland. The windward side of the cliffs was barren scoured ground as far to the north as they could see with the storm's debris flung to the sides. It was cold and quiet as Death's heart.

"Reminds me of a burnt battlefield," said Captain Nightingale.

Tucker said to Daniel, "It looks like somebody sheared it like a sheep." The prairie had been stripped, trees whipped about and some uprooted, grasses and bushes lay flat. In the wake of the storm, no trees or bushes over three feet remained. Whips of stripped saplings feebly pointed to the sky. Little to no grass remained upright. It was unbelievable.

"All right everybody, let's get organized. Not much light left." Captain Nightingale took charge of their recovery.

"Mrs. Blair, please start some food for everyone. Maybe some soup. It's going to be cold tonight. Let's start some coffee boiling. Ben, take some men and round up the stock, if you can find them. Get 'em gathered. You don't have to drive them in tonight. Let 'em calm down some and rest. Graze 'em if you can find it. Dan, check with the other divisions and see what needs to be repaired and see that each division leader understands what needs to be done. If one division is in better shape than another, everybody get to it and help those that need assistance. We've lost a lot of canvas."

"Have the older children pick up what they can find once the women get the fires started." Under his breath he said, "If we can get a fire started in all this mess." It remained cold. A fire had become paramount for warmth and morale. "Keep warm as best you can. Damn, I want a cup of coffee!" Captain Nightingale rode to the other end of their refuge to see what needed to be done there.

They were cold and wet. Most of what had been in the wagons had been flung over miles of prairie, and much of it would never be seen again—clothes, house linens and sheets of canvas. The women somehow managed to start some fires. Limbs and debris lay under and around the wagons blown to the leeward side by the wind. Using coal oil, Sarah Turnbull coaxed a flame into bravely licking tongues of fire. They dried wood by the fire as they started other fires from the coals. Molly Blair brought coffee pots to hang on the fires alongside simmering pots of soup made from whatever could be found quickly in the wagons. Soon, they had ten different fires sending steamy plumes of vapor rising over a ghostly scene of frenzied work and repair. People bundled up in whatever they could find, gathered their belongings and drifted in and out of those clouds of steam and smoke backlit by struggling fires. While some cooked, others started sewing canvas back together. The children gathered clothing and anything they could find and brought it to a central fire.

"Mary Mae, would you sort this stuff out so's folks can come by and find their belongings?" Captain Nightingale asked and gratefully accepted the welcome cup of coffee she offered.

Ben took Del, Marshall Whitfield, and five teenage boys to look for the stock. Each rode whatever animal he could find. They were a ragged group.

Raj had not run off. Del hugged his horse and got into the saddle.

Ben observed the Roberts boys, barebacked and barefooted. "Get some clothes on boys and something on your feet! It's a getting colder!" They scrambled off their horses, gathering what they could find to wear. Some had little more than rags wrapped around them for protection from the cold and wet. The scruffy little party, shod in whatever they could find, rode off in search of stock.

The oxen had stuck pretty much together in one spot. Most were still yoked. They found them at the bottom of a protected declivity, confused with exhaustion and exposure. The horses were spooked and skittish. The damn mules refused to go anywhere near the wagons, which they probably now associated with the hell they had been through. They dug in their hooves and wouldn't move until one of the boys found a sucker in his pocket. His mule liked suckers and greedily followed. Del laughed. The boys enticed each mule they found with that sucker. They gathered stock until dusk overtook them and the sucker disappeared. They made a camp within sight of the wagons, still sheltering against the cliff face.

Ben got a fire started and the women sent over a pot of soup. "Boys, it's going to be a cold, wet, miserable night. Bundle up and ride around the stock singing sweet and they'll settle down right enough. Wrap up in whatever you got. Tommy, drop a line over here and make a lean-to from this other sheet of canvas I found. Bed down on this canvas here with your feet to the fire. It'll reflect the fire's heat. Stay warm, boys. Eat that soup. There's biscuits, jam, and hot coffee on the fire, just like home. I'll take the first watch tonight, Walt next, then Sam over there, and Marshall next. Del, you got the last watch. Now, get to it fellas. Hopefully, we'll get out of this place in a few days."

They spent a miserable cold night on the bare wet ground. The canvas lean-to was some help, adding a little warmth, dryness, and protection to the shivering sleepers.

Slowly, the sun rose in the east bringing light to a barren plain, filling the sky with brightness on a breezy cold day. Del rode into camp after his turn on watch as the sun sent tendrils of pink and orange breaking the bleakness of the night. Nothing moved. Even the hungriest of wolves stayed tucked away in their dens. The cliff ridge still gave some protection from the wind. Del climbed off his horse and warmed his hands by the fire.

"Here's some coffee, Del. One hell of a night. One of the Roberts' kids almost froze his feet off. No socks, wet boots, no laces. I found him shivering. Got him warmed up with some blankets and fed him soup and coffee. He'll be all right, I think." Ben filled Del's cup with steaming blackness and passed it over to him "That'll grow hair on ya, boy. Whew."

"Makes my teeth hurt, this stuff. But, by jolly, I'm awake!" Del said. Ben took pride in his coffee.

It took the train two days to put itself back together. A few people had bumps and bruises. The Roberts' boy lost a toe.

Realization of what had befallen them and how alone they were began to show on the women's faces. Frightened, the vastness of the countryside caused them to feel small and vulnerable to whatever nature dealt them next. The men, too, were aware of how much they needed to depend on each other. The little community pulled itself up, dusted itself off, and found faith in themselves.

They repaired the canvas as best as could be. Patches of bold calicos and old curtains decorated the once cottony white tops. One of the wagons had an old quilt sewn into its side with a coiled snake beneath a familiar saying. It was the old Gadsden flag. Don't tread on me! Del read as it bounced by. He chuckled. "That'll confuse any Indian that sees that!"

He caught up to Ben.

"Did you see the look of 'em?" Ben asked. "This train just matured five years in two days. Most of them have never been so on their own before. It's not so much fun now. Del, we lost some stock, lost some clothes, and food. But we didn't lose anybody. We were lucky. We need to get out of this cyclone alley we're crossing. Let's you and me go find out where it ends and where the grass is standing again. I think water is going to be the least of our worries for a while, but grass? Grass is where you find it under these conditions. My daddy used to say that."

The cyclone alley was a little more than a half mile wide. They stood and looked back at the swath it cut in its path of destruction. They could see a half-mile wide chunk torn through forests and fields as neatly as if cut with scissors. The silhouette of the sharp cut boundaries of the forest astounded them. The stark realization of what could have been, if they had been in the direct path of the twister, made them feel queasy in their stomachs.

"Worstest storm I ever saw," said Ben. "Those cliffs saved us, sure!"

Repairs were completed, lost items found, sorted, and repacked. Many family papers, books, and letters would never be seen again.

A few head of stock either drowned or got lost in a mud hole somewhere. One horse had to be shot. It had gotten so far out in the mud that the men couldn't get to it.

Ruined food stuffs—flour, sugar, cornmeal, coffee had to be dumped or burned. They had no time for drying out the supplies. Chances were good they would only spoil later, anyway.

Somberly moving on, the train left behind evidence of several burning fires in its wake. Captain Nightingale drove them on, forcing them to the trail again. They needed fresh grass and a fresh start. Only smoke lingered against those obscure lifesaving cliffs as a fading reminder. Spoiled food, ruined clothing and bedding, trash that no one could use anymore had all been left behind or consumed by the flames and eventually turned to dust. Left behind as well, was Tommy Joe Robert's little toe, buried at the base of those cliffs. His daddy placed a small marker. His mama said a small prayer.

14

BEAUX GOT OFF THE STEAMSHIP in Independence. It had been a long journey. His father had died of pneumonia shortly after returning from the congressional investigations in Washington, D.C. The Major's trip back had been in a cold rain. He had taken a chill, retiring to his bed immediately, never to rise again. The Major returned a broken man. He knew federal indictments were being processed against him as he was leaving Washington. His bank had seized his assets. They could not touch the estate. It had belonged to Rebecca's family and had been left to her and her heirs. Del was the sole heir. Beaux was furious. He had been left penniless by his father, except for the small amount of cash he found in the Major's safe. Selling the slaves and horses, Beaux liquidated anything with the Conlon name he could sell for money. The court had forced him out of the house until the heir, Delaino Daniel Riodan, could be found.

A search for Del ensued. His name was not on any ship's registry. Only rumors had led them to the docks. Beaux's detectives found a trace here and there of a boy and a horse travelling west. He had been seen in Indianapolis and reportedly headed for Independence in search of his father. Independence was the gateway to the west. Tucker had been easier to follow. He was traced to some of the Mormon wagons headed west. There weren't many black slaves among them. That meant he was going to Independence or St. Joseph where most of the Mormon trains began their epic treks to the Great Salt Lake.

Not being able to pay his detectives any further, Beaux took up the chase with a white-hot passion of vengeance and malice. His sole goal was to find Del and see that he disappeared, thereby remaining the next likely heir to the estate. He intended to find Tucker and finish the beating he had started, then sell him back into slavery for the money and the satisfaction of seeing him in chains. Beaux could not stand the stain to his reputation from this slave who had defied him by running away. That vexed him to his very core. He was an unforgiving man. Beaux needed to go west to Independence. All the reports indicated Del and Tucker were headed west. Steamboats had not been able to successfully navigate much farther than St. Joseph, Missouri. Independence would be the first stop where he could get a lead on Delaino or Tucker. Most of the wagon trains organized there. Then, he would determine who to hunt first. If he found nothing there, his next stop would be St. Jo.

He pursued this goal with a zeal that was new to him. He had been lazy and spoiled at home. For the first time in his life, he became enthralled with the chase. Finding them was his only goal, or else he would be destitute.

Independence surprised Beaux with its hustle and bustle. He expected a sleepy, dirty collection of shacks and stupid people having had no idea of what the western emigration had generated. An outsider here, from his reproachful attitude to his shiny boots, Beaux stuck out.

He took rooms at the cheapest hotel, but because of his pride, he dined at night in the fancier restaurants. His inquiries were subdued at first. There had been so many people passing through Independence, that faces were forgotten quickly by the townsfolk, as there was always another to replace them. Inquiries about Tucker or Del met with little to no interest at all. After three days and with his patience running low, Beaux considered giving up. Perhaps he should go on to St. Jo. He had found nothing here.

To save the cost of steamboat fare, Beaux decided to travel to St. Jo on his own. He bought a horse and looked to the saddler for an outfit. He was not going back to Baltimore to face shame and ruin. The shop was busy. Saddles, new and used hung on display. Beaux headed to the back of the shop where the "little used tack" was displayed. An English saddle immediately caught his eye. It was familiar, too familiar. Looking under the skirts of the saddle, he found what he was looking for, the Conlon mark, a British crown surrounded by a large C. It was unmistakable. Del had been here. This was the saddle that Raj had worn.

Beaux rudely interrupted the owner and a customer.

"Hold it, mister, you'll get your turn," the customer said as Beaux tried to insert himself between them.

"But I—" Beaux started to reply.

"You'll wait your turn, mister!" The tall stranger pushed him away and went back to his business.

"Do not touch me in such a way, you foul-smelling horse turd!" Beaux shouted at the man.

Two of the stranger's friends turned to face him, watching with steady eyes.

The tall man stared at Beaux. "You're new to these parts, mister. We don't care who you think you are or what you might have been. I'm going to finish my business here and not cause a ruckus, because Otis is a friend of mine. If I see you on the street after this, however, this horse turd is going to teach you some manners." He turned back to Otis. The other men moved themselves between Beaux and the tall rancher. One of them intentionally stepped on Beaux's freshly polished boots.

Beaux winced and started to protest but looking at the two men with guns about their waists and dusty boots, he realized he was outnumbered. He elected to step back.

Otis looked at him as the rancher and his men left carrying a new saddle. "Well, mister, what in hell is so damn important that you interrupt a sale to my best customer? You're not carrying a gun, I see. I suggest you get one. That fella is Sam Shepherd, a rancher here about. Stay out of his way. Now, what do you want?"

Beaux asked about the saddle. Otis remembered Del distinctly. "Yeah, he was a young kid. Paid with gold sovereigns. His horse was a trick horse with good breeding, a real handsome stallion. He joined up with Dan Riodan. They were with the Nightingale train getting ready to head for Oregon. I traded that saddle in for a Mexican style outfit and some cash. I saw them in town a few times. That horse was hard to miss. Had a black fella with them once when they were buying provisions."

Tucker? Delaino? Daniel Riodan, too? The three men he hated the most in the world, all in one place. He couldn't believe his good luck. His trail suddenly seemed very clear.

Beaux apologized for his behavior and bought the livery suggested by Otis as to what he would need on the trail. At the stable, he asked about joining up with any trains leaving for Oregon.

The hostler told him, "They're all going west some place, mister. Them on the trains is headed for Oregon, California, or Santa Fe. The Army trains are heading for Mexico. Seems, we got us a war brewing. Try the saloons or the hotels. Somebody is sure to know in one of them."

Beaux hadn't felt so jubilant in days. Dressed in his best clothes, he dined that evening in the finest hotel in town. A celebration for tracking down his prey. Finishing his meal, he smoked a slim cheroot dipped in his final brandy, very satisfied with how fortune was turning for him.

Strolling into a saloon after his fine meal, he intended to make inquiries about any train leaving for Oregon. Beaux practically beamed. He had asked at his hotel earlier in the day about trains heading for Oregon, but everyone was going to Santa Fe or Texas. He still needed to find a way to Oregon.

Stepping up to the bar, Beaux ordered a brandy, the best they had. He turned his back to the counter with his elbows on the bar, surveying the room. A satisfied look of contentment enveloped him as cheroot smoke wafted across his face and joined the smoky cloud that hung just above everyone's head. A piano played jubilantly on a stage to his right. Games of chance were noisily being played to his left. The balcony above him was decorated with beautifully gowned women, flirting with their gentlemen companions. Beaux's world was turning right for a change.

Dark eyes followed him from a table near the back of the room. Tossing his cards to the center of the table, Dave Roberts pushed through the crowd toward the bar. He moved next to Beaux without the dandy paying him any notice at all and ordered a whiskey.

Dave worked for Sam Sheppard. He was a good hand and he liked working for Sam, but what Dave liked best was fighting. He was stout with strong bones—not very tall, but muscular and athletic. Being lightning fast with his left-hand, had earned him the nickname, Lefty.

Facing the mirror on the back of the bar, Dave studied the greenhorn. He let the whiskey roll across his tongue before swallowing and ordered another.

Piano music played and Beaux tapped his foot. Someone performed magic tricks on the stage, and a girl on the balcony above giggled. Beaux tapped his fingertips on the bar in time to the music.

Dave finished his drink. "You insulted Sam this afternoon in the saddler's. You should apologize for calling Sam a horse turd." He talked to Beaux's image in the mirror.

Beaux turned and stared down his nose at the short little man, his mood broken. "Are you addressing me?"

"No. I'm telling you that you should apologize for insulting the boss." He still talked to the image in the mirror.

"Oh, I recognize you now. You were with the rancher, weren't you? I believe you stepped on my toes."

"Oh, did I?"

Dave turned to face Beaux, right hand holding his drink. His left was closest to Beaux's chin. It rested easily in place on the bar. Dave's hairy fist, opening and closing slowly.

"Why, yes, you did. I think you owe me an apology for deliberately stepping on my boots."

Several of the men near Dave grinned at each other as they moved their drinks further down the bar. Dave appeared not to have heard Beaux. He saluted a red-haired woman in the balcony with his glass, his left arm resting on the bar top, already shifting his weight to his right foot.

"I said...," Beaux said much more loudly.

Dave caught him smack in the nose with his left. His right followed, creating a shower of blood and whiskey that stained Beaux's starched white shirt front.

Beaux collapsed to his knees in shock. His hands covered his bleeding face. He looked up, as Dave leaned over him. "If you carried a gun, greenhorn, I would have called you out for calling Sam Shepard a horse turd. But, since you're a gentleman, I'm just going to beat you black and blue!" He lifted Beaux up by his lapels, smiled and slapped Beaux's face twice with his right hand.

"How dare you!" Beaux jerked back struggling to breathe through the pain of his broken nose.

Dave slapped him twice more with his left hand. "Next time, wear a gun!"

"I have a gun, you jackass!" Beaux shrieked, as he lifted his right arm revealing his cocked hide out gun. He shot Dave Roberts in the forehead with a .36 caliber lead ball that blew the back of Dave's head off, splattering the smiling faces of the patrons enjoying the fight with brains, blood, and bone. Dave Roberts never knew he was dead.

Stunned silence filled the room, until the moment of comprehension set in. The red-haired woman upstairs screamed. Pandemonium broke loose!

Beaux ran to the batwing doors waving his double-barreled derringer at anyone who dared try to stop him.

One fellow came through the doors demanding to know, "What's going on in here?" Beaux shot him and pushed the bleeding man into the crowd.

Running for the stable, Beaux's mind went blank. He operated on animal instinct. Anyone who might have gotten in his way would have been killed. Throwing his saddle on his new horse, they raced through the town's main street kicking up dirt in all directions. They crossed the Missouri river several miles north of town. Foam speckled his horse's neck in thick clots as Beaux fled, whipping his horse all night toward St. Jo until the poor beast collapsed from a bursting heart.

Dawn found him, hunkered beneath a fallen cottonwood tree. His horse lay dead in the sand. Its heart had exploded, much like

Dave Roberts' head. Three had died that night. Beaux Conlon became a killer without remorse and a price on his head.

Back in Independence, Sam Sheppard offered reward money and ordered the sheriff to track down Dave Roberts' murderer.

Beaux sat up, assessing his situation. Most of his money and belongings were still in his hotel room. He had nothing but a few items in his saddlebags and what he had on him. Dried blood covered the front of his shirt. Tired, dirty and disheveled, he sat under the cottonwood staring at the river and considering his options. He wished he had a smoke.

———————

DOLAN AND MYRTLE OSTERN WERE EXCITED to have left their home early that morning in happy expectation of visiting their daughter and new grandchild in St. Jo.

Myrtle pulled closer to Dolan and laid her head on his shoulder. They were still very much in love.

Dolan stopped the buggy, puzzled, staring at the dead horse blocking the road.

"Whoa there, what in mercy…?" Dolan's words died in his throat. Beaux stepped from behind their buggy and shot him in the head. Myrtle, he shot in the face, her scream muffled by gunsmoke.

Beaux thought no more of these murders than he did the others. They had a horse. He needed a horse. He took theirs.

Releasing the horse from the buggy, Beaux saddled it. Helping himself to the dead man's clothes, he counted what money the man had.

Not much, but more than what I had. He sampled the picnic basket. Without another thought, he dragged the bodies under the cottonwood tree covering them with brush.

Chewing on a chicken leg, he pushed the buggy into the river, where it tumbled over and over breaking apart on the stones as the current rolled it, until only the Spanish moss stuffed seat was left floating on the current.

15

DEL RIO AWOKE, WIPING THE sleep from his eyes. The routine of the days blended into each other so much, he wondered what day of the week it was. Snuggling down into his blankets, Del closed his eyes again and sighed. Something smelled good. Was that coffee?

"Well! Ain't cha ever gonna get up! We got some scoutin' ta do. Captain wants us to go to Grand Isle and look around. 'Course you could just lie there dreamin' of little fairies in your head, if'n you want to." Ben threw a stick at him.

Del jumped up at once. A chance to scout ahead to Grand Isle with Ben was just what he had been dreaming of. The wily scout had a fire blazing, coffee boiling, and was grinning at Del when he rolled out from under his wagon. They would be gone several days. Orders were to find a campsite close to water yet protected enough that the cattle could be easily guarded. Water was important. The grass had been good. Water had been scarce these last few weeks since the storm.

The May sun beat down from the robin's egg blue sky with white puffy clouds and a brisk dry breeze. The sun's heat was relentless, and by midafternoon, left Del hot, tired and sweaty. A wispy breeze blew over the grass hinting at a promise of coolness, but there was none. They had had no rain since the storm. Water barrels were low. People's tempers had flared with the heat. Cool water would be a relief to everyone on the train.

"Unusual for it to be this hot so early in the year," Ben said over supper that evening. He flipped over a rabbit he had spread on a flat hot stone, sprinkling it with salt. "Turn over them taters, will you, Del? Everything will be done soon."

Using two sticks, Del turned the potatoes in the ashes.

"I'm a-hoping to reach the Platte by late morning tomorrow. It'll be nice to have some fresh water. My canteen is tasting brackish." Ben rinsed his mouth and spat the rest on the ground. "Makes my coffee taste bad."

Despite the heat, Del enjoyed himself. He preferred the loneliness of the trail, often alone with his own thoughts. His mind, his eyes and his ears grew sharper here.

Ben did most of the talking for both of them, anyway. He rarely needed an answer to anything said. "That was a good shot you made on that rabbit. I didn't see him at all. He was hid from me in that brush."

"His ears twitched," replied Del.

"Still, a good shot from horseback. I seen worse."

"Tomorrow, I want you to keep alert. A lot of trains pass at this place we're a-goin'. Ain't nothing but an island in the middle of the river. The French named it Grand Isle. It don't sound the same in English—Big Island. Does it? Anyways, we don't want to take the leavings of anybody else. People get sick drinking water downstream of another train. Indians know that. They graze their horses downstream of their teepees. Water carries the waste. White people don't think things through is all. They've been too long living in cities."

––––––––––––––––

THEY RODE OUT EARLY MORNING. Ben whistled when they spotted the river. "Well, look-a-here. They's no other trains about, and the Platte is running clear. Must be from the spring melt further north." Sure enough, the Platte was lively and clear. So inviting they had to jump in.

"That's mighty fine. Yes, sir." Ben pushed Del's head under water. Del didn't try to fight back. He enjoyed the clear water and spit a stream from between his teeth at Ben. The cold water lifted their spirits.

"All right, let's get to work." Ben climbed out of the water, wrung out his clothes and shook them out on some rocks to dry. Del did the same and changed into dry clothes.

"You like this, don't you, Raj!" Del patted his horse. Raj stood knee-deep in the water cooling off. After letting him drink, Del led the horse up the bank. He didn't want him to drink too much of the cold water.

"Saddle up and be ready," Ben said. "You take the south side. I'll ride the north. Look for manure and old fires. We'll set our camp upstream of anything we find. Fire your gun if you get into trouble. We'll meet up in an hour."

Del walked Raj along the stream. He found no trace of any recent camp. Nightingale's train must be the first of the season. There were old fire rings, but they looked over a year old. Pieces of broken wheels, bits of china, an old iron pot with a hole in it, showed evidence of people leaving their refuse behind them. It was easy to track white folk by the junk they left behind, Del learned. Indians seemed to melt away, leaving nothing.

"Looks like a camp had been here two, three weeks ago over on the other side," Ben said when he crossed the river back to Del. "We'll bivouac the train west of there about a mile, on the south side of the river. There's three graves dug over there with markers. No sense in letting the women see that. You go back to the train and lead them to me. Turn west at Grand Isle. I'll be five miles or so along on the south side. I'm going to build some fires and mark the grazing ground. Keep your hair! I'll see you all in a day or two." Waving, he loped away.

Del turned back toward the train.

He put Raj into an easy trot. This was Raj's type of ground, level and flat. He could eat up miles. They made good time back to the train. Del noted some tracks of unshod ponies heading east. He figured about ten ponies. Probably a hunting party. They were moving casually in a direct line. Some of the prints were extra deep.

Ponies loaded with fresh meat.

CAPTAIN NIGHTINGALE HALTED THE TRAIN when he spotted Del coming in at an easy lope.

Reporting to Captain Nightingale, Del told him. "Water at the Platte is good, Captain. It's fresh and clear. Ben is staking out a campsite about five miles west of Grand Isle on the south side of the river. Good grass and cover there, and we're beyond old camp sites."

"Good job, Del, take a break. I'll call on you when we're a few miles out from the Platte. We should be there by evening tomorrow."

Tucker whistled to him as Del found their wagons.

Daniel waved him in. "Good to see you, son. Glad you're back. Feel like walking a while? Tucker could use a break."

"Sure, Pa. Want to ride Raj, Tuck? He still has some spunk in him. He never seems tired. I won't mind walking with the wagons for a change. Let me have that whip."

Raj had grown accustomed to all three men as riders by now, and he was still ready to run. Tuck eagerly climbed aboard and kicked his heels in Raj's flank. He was ready for a run himself. His feet hurt and his back was sore from handling the big whip. Waving his hat with a shout, they were off.

At camp that evening, the Riodans had been invited by the Kincaids for supper. They often did this to bring variety to their meals, but most happily, a change of conversation. The Kincaid boys, Bart and Nate, were lively, peppering the three men with questions about the oxen, and the lands they passed through. They were curious about Tucker, asking where he had come from and about his home back east.

"Doesn't it hurt when you cut yourself?" asked Nate.

"Why, Nate!" replied Thomas. "Of course, Mister Tucker hurts when he cuts himself! That's silly talk. Now go help your mama. Mister Tucker has had a hard day and wants to rest while he eats his supper.

"Sorry, Tuck. Young boys ask what comes to mind."

"That's alright, Thomas. They're good boys and only wanting to know about what is strange to them. They'll see I'm like everyone else, the more they get to know me. It s all right.

"Miz Kincaid, that was some good beans tonight. It's mighty appreciated, tasting someone else's cooking. Especially yours! Those flat corn cakes we used to call hoe cakes back home, 'cause we cooked 'em on a flattened-out hoe. Doused 'em with molasses. These was mighty good. Reminded me of home, long ago!"

"Why thank you, Tucker. You're always welcome here. Having Daniel and Del and you in the train as our friends has helped us a lot. It seems so long ago we left Independence. Once we crossed the River at Westport, it felt like we left civilization behind. The rest of the trip is almost like being born again. I feel like we're being created and reformed by this new land we're traveling to, and we'll be delivered in Oregon. We'll be new and fresh, just like a new baby, looking at life for the first time."

"I think the same way, Miz Kincaid. I do feel like this journey is making a new man of me. I suppose being delivered into a new land of Oregon would be a kind of metaphor. Yes, a good accurate metaphor," replied Tucker. "I know I think differently about myself." He gave a wink to Del and Daniel. Both smiled. "My turn at watch. Guess I'll get to it!"

"I'm on after you, Tucker," said Thomas. "Holler at me and I'll spell you. I'll be sleeping under the wagon, so I don't disturb Nancy and the boys. I'll be close to that shotgun over there, leaning up against that back wheel. I'm all set to go. Supposed to be a full moon. Hope them critters ain't nervous. I want a quiet night."

"I'll call you, Thomas," said Tucker as he got up to assume the duty of night watch.

"He's a good man, Daniel," said Thomas looking after Tucker, as he left.

"Yes. Yes, he is," replied Daniel. "I have known him a long time. Taught him about living in the open when he was a young man.

That seems long ago. So many memories, make me sad a little. On a clearer note, we've been seeing greener grass. I spotted a few buffalo today as well. Ben says there's rivers of 'em further west. That'll be something to see.

"Thanks for supper, Miz Kincaid. We enjoyed it. Boys. We'll see you all in the morning."

Daniel and Del walked back to their own wagons rubbing their bellies and yawning, looking forward to their beds.

Del said, "I find it hard for me to imagine that you taught Tucker to live in the forest. That was while I was still a baby."

"And he's the one that taught you." Daniel laughed. "Life's funny, isn't it. Yes, I taught him when you were still in diapers. As you know, Tucker was your mama's slave. He stayed with her when Major Conlon went back east. It was the first time for him to be in the forests. Southern Indiana is a beautiful land. I had a job surveying Corydon, which was about to be the new state capital. That's how I met your ma. Major Conlon had come to Corydon to purchase bonds being sold to finance the new capitol and a bridge over the Ohio into Kentucky. They were investments for his bank. Rebecca, your ma, and I danced together at the ball celebrating the opening of the new state capitol. We fell in love, married, and settled down. Your ma was a looker! I fell in love the moment I first saw her. I see glimpses of her when I look at you sometimes. We were happy.

"Several years later, I received a request from L'Enfant, the architect of Washington D.C. He had been hired to design and build a new capital, in Indianapolis. He needed surveyors. I had been recommended because of the work I did in Corydon. I eagerly took the job. I guess you were close to five at the time. Frontier life was wearing thin on your ma. She missed the big city. So, she decided to take you back to Baltimore to visit your grandfather. He hadn't seen you yet. She took you and Tucker with her. I kissed you and her good-bye at the boat docks that summer day. Both of you were pink cheeked and glowing. She was so proud of you.

"Tucker had been his own man. He was comfortable in the forests. He got along with the local Indians, and they taught him as well. The Indians were curious of his dark skin and curly hair. They accepted him easily. He could have run away then, but he was loyal to Rebecca and to you as well. We had become friends and were all looking forward to a grand reunion later in the year. I never saw Rebecca or you again. I sent letters and money so you and Becky could return. I had had a house built in Indianapolis. Major Conlon wrote that you had both died.

"I showed up unannounced in Baltimore. Beaux and the Major were rude and insisted I leave. I knew those guns of yours looked familiar. I have stared down those barrels before. They get your attention. Your grandfather called the magistrate and had me locked up. Three toughs from the docks escorted me out of town with promises to toss me in the sea if I was ever seen in Baltimore again. They beat me up and left me bleeding on the cobbles of the National Road. I never saw Becky's grave or yours. Major Conlon blamed me for Becky's death, telling me she would be alive today if she hadn't married me. Saying all I was interested in was his money.

"So, I came home, convinced both of you had died of a fever. I continued working, surveying and running the mills. I lived in the house I had built for Becky and our baby, haunted by your memories. I kept busy. It kept my mind focused on the present. It was easier that way. After a few years, memories fade. I got on with my life. Never fell in love again.

"One day I simply knew I was ready to leave. I had read of California and the Oregon territories in the newspapers. The government offered free land if you stayed on it and built a house or farmed it. They had been encouraging people to move west to occupy Texas, California, and now, Oregon. The government wanted to drive the British and Mexicans out. The Astor Company in Oregon was making a lot of money buying from the trappers and selling furs to Europe. They spread the word of what a great land of opportunity it was. I had been hearing about it for years.

"Three hundred twenty acres is a lot of land. Lots of water, grass and forests to be had for the taking. You just had to get there. It began to sound better and better to me. Business in Indianapolis was good. I had a reputation as a reliable surveyor. I was always busy, but I became restless. I was lonely, looking for something else. Oregon

sounded wonderful to me. I sold out, had wagons built to my specifications, hired a teamster, Adonis, and here we are. Oregon reminded
me of the frontier as it had been in southern Indiana." They talked
long into the night, even after Tucker came back to the fire, before
they turned in.

A shot boomed in the middle of the night waking everyone.
Excited, alarmed voices started calling from the pasture, where the
stock was being guarded.

"Daniel! Come quick! Thomas has been shot!"

Off the three men went, running up to a grisly sight. They found
Thomas with a gunshot wound in his left groin, rapidly losing blood.
Daniel used his hands to put pressure on Thomas's leg but could not
get enough pressure or leverage to stop the flowing blood.

Ellen McCarthy, who had been a nurse in a hospital in Boston,
tried to fasten a tourniquet to stop the bleeding as well. Her face
was stricken.

"It's bad, Daniel. The wound is too high for the tourniquet to
work. He's lost a lot of blood." She spoke through pursed lips and
blurry eyes.

Nancy held Thomas's head in her lap. Their eyes locked together.
Their faces were both pallid and drawn. "Tripped over my own shotgun. Happened so fast. Plumb stupid of me." Nancy had to bend over
so she could hear him. "Let me look at you. Love you, Nance! Love
the boys," he said softly, and Thomas Kincaid passed from this life.

It's a hard thing to lose someone close—someone you had laughed
with during supper that very night. Watched as he kissed his children good night. Everyone in the train depended on one another.
They were a small moving village. Each loss was a crippling blow to
all. It was personal to them. Del stood in shock, not knowing what to
do. There was nothing anyone could do.

Nancy Kincaid gently closed Thomas's eyes, tenderly kissing each
one, then a lingering kiss to his mouth. The rising flood of fear and
loss, nearly overwhelming her as she clung to her husband. A husband, who could no longer hug her back.

"There, child," said Ellen. "Hold him tight. Say your good-byes.
We'll leave you to your grief." Several women stayed by Nancy, pro-

tectively ringed around her with enough distance to give her some private moments. The rest moved back to the wagons in silence. Many shed tears that night. The Riodans looked in on Bart and Nate and told them their mama would be coming soon.

Sensing bad news and knowing that, somehow, their father was involved, the boys sat in silence with the men around the fire. Neighbors walked by and touched their shoulders or patted their hair. Bart looked up at Del, eyes wide and frightened, holding Nate's hand.

Bart asked, "What's going on, Del?"

Del said, "Your ma will be here soon. It's not our news to tell. Sit quiet. We'll be here by the fire."

After the men took Thomas away, Ellen hovered close by, knowing she would be needed. Nancy sat silently, until remorse sent terrifying fear washing over her body in uncontrolled, sobbing spasms. Ellen took her in her arms holding her until her grief ran its course. Thomas had been her rock. Now, he was gone. She mourned until there were no tears left. Her strength came back to her when she remembered Nate and Bart. Nancy stood looking toward the camp, "My boys. I've got to go to my boys." She started running back to camp.

Ellen stopped her. "Whoa! Girl, don't go running back to your kids like a wild-eyed colt. There, smooth your dress." Bessie fussed with Nancy's hair. "Take a deep breath, Nancy Kincaid. Let me wipe your face. That's it. Take another one, a deep, long, spine-straightening breath. Those boys need you, and you need them. You need to look strong to reassure them. I know you don't feel strong right now, but you will soon enough. Go, comfort your sons. We'll see to Thomas."

Nancy walked into the firelight from the darkness, looking for Bart and Nate. She nodded to the three men and gathered her boys around her skirts with her arms about their shoulders. "Come into the wagon with me, boys. I have … I have sad news."

Daniel, Tucker, and Del bent their heads and wiped their eyes with their handkerchiefs when the cries from the wagon began. There was nothing else to be done.

Daniel stayed by the fire until the cries stopped. He found Nancy in the wagon with the boys' heads in her lap. She stared listlessly.

"My tears are gone, Daniel."

"I know, Miz Kincaid. We'll be by the fire if you need us. Thomas was a fine man and my friend. I'm sorry, so very sorry. I wish there was more I could do."

He returned to the fire feeling empty and helpless and sat next to Del and Tucker. "We lost a damn fine man tonight. Makes no sense sometimes, this life.... No sense at all."

Dawn slowly seeped over the eastern edges of the horizon. Grey light crept over the prairie followed by pink and yellow tendrils of promise, bursting to a white-hot yellow that burnt away the dawn and dew and shadows. The only remnants of yesterday's events were Thomas Kincaid's blood stains, darkening in the sand.

They buried Thomas on a small rise overlooking the river. Sunshine blessed the event, showing off stark vivid greens and the yellow colors of the ripening prairie, sending caressing breezes against the somber figures of the sad gathering. The lone widow dressed in black. Tucker had fashioned a headboard with Thomas's name, his birth, and the date of his death burnt into the cottonwood boards. Reverend Blaine spoke comforting words from the Methodist bible. Echoes of "Nearer My God to Thee," resounded across the valley. There wasn't a dry eye in the group. Nancy and her boys were given their moments for grief. The community gave death its proper respect, did what needed to be done, gave sympathy to the loved ones with tears and embraces, and then, they moved on.

"I'm sorry for your loss, Miz Kincaid. Thomas was one of the best men I've known, but we must move on. I hope you understand. We have to move on." Captain Nightingale stood quietly, until Nancy spoke.

"You're right, of course, Captain. We must keep going. Thomas would have wanted it that way." She turned to the grave site with her young sons. "Remember where we are, Eart and Nate. Maybe one of these days, you can return and lay some flowers by the marker for your pa. He would like that." They turned and walked back to their wagon.

The Riodan wagons lagged back to travel with the Kincaid wagon. Del drove their team of mules, while Tucker drove Del's team. Nancy and the boys rode. No one spoke. There was no need. Each heart could read the heart of the other. Del could hear the boys crying now and then. It was a long day. No one had had any sleep the night before.

The three wagons caught up to the train by the noon meal. Nightingale rode up to Riodan's camp looking for Daniel and inquiring about Mrs. Kincaid.

"I know you are all exhausted, but we must keep going. We'll stop a bit early tonight, so everyone can get some rest. How's Miz Kincaid?"

"She and the boys are holding up good as could be expected. They haven't gotten out of their wagon since we left Thomas. Tucker is taking over some food and coffee. They'll be fine in time. They're frightened now, but they'll make it."

"Let me know if they need anything, Daniel. The only thing I can't give them is time." Nightingale loped away.

"They ate a little, Dan," said Tucker. "It's something."

Later that day, as the dust of the train drifted off to the north, the sun hot on his face and shoulders, Del felt a tug at his shirt.

It was Bart. "Give me the whip, Del. I'll do it." Silently, Del passed the whip to Bart and fell into step, just off his whip hand and behind him. "Get up there! C'mon, that's it!" Bart took command, cracking the whip over the team's head.

Later, Nate slipped out of the wagon and fell in line behind Del.

Before too long, Del stood off, watching Bart drive the team. Nancy and Nate followed behind, tossing buffalo chips into a bucket hanging from the rear of the wagon.

Routine can be as healing as the most unctuous salve. Step by dusty step, the young family walked. The promise of new life before them. The heartbroken memories of the old left behind, drifting away from them as the dust of the prairie vanishes into the wind.

16

B EAUX CONLON BECAME A LOBO wolf on the vast expanse of the Kansas prairie. He had never developed any of the skills required for living on his own, nor any skill at all that would have helped him survive in these wild lands of the west. Wolf-like, he simply took from those who had provided for themselves in advance.

Following the many trails that emigrants were breaking as they headed west. Beaux would watch unobserved under cover of the tree line or in the rocks until he found a straggler or a broken-down wagon. Approaching them, he offered his help, then dispatched the trusting pilgrim quickly by gun or garrote. Sometimes, after disposing of the original owners, he would stay with a wagon or cart until someone else offered to help him, then Beaux killed his rescuer. He had no regrets. Acquiring clothes, money, guns, horses, Beaux took what he wanted and left what was used up. In this way, he emigrated his way across the country.

More than a month had gone by since his killing of Dave Roberts. Beaux avoided towns and other people. He lived a feral life and thrived.

Why did I think I needed anyone? A cold, cunning spirit, that had lain dormant in the society of laws and rules, now emerged from within the soul of Beaux Conlon brought on by the freedom of the vast land around him. His scarred face and broken nose closely mirrored his truer inner spirit.

The law was non-existent on the Kansas prairie. Beaux had, so far, avoided Indians and organized wagon trains out of fear or luck. The sick and lame were his meat.

Sharp bursts of gunfire drew his attention one morning, as Beaux poured his coffee. He wore new clothes today. A new horse and saddle were gifts from their previous owners. A few coins jingled in his pockets. His wallet was stuffed with bills. Biscuits and bacon filled his belly. All from the largess of departed emigrants. The only remnant from his former life was the hat he had had custom made in Baltimore with his name in gold letters embossed in the sweat band.

His curiosity piqued, Beaux saddled up and rode toward the sound of the battle taking place over the crest of a forested ridge, west of his camp. Maybe, if they killed each other, he would find easy pickings.

Riding cautiously through the leafy cover, Beaux stopped behind a large boulder. In the declivity below, he spied four men desperately fighting off ten warriors, using an arrow riddled prairie schooner for cover. Two of the Indians lay dead or bleeding on the rocks. One of the defenders had a bandana wrapped around his right thigh. As the Indians circled, the men continuously moved around under the wagon, so the Indians couldn't fire at their backs.

Beaux dismounted. Shielded by the boulder, he was transfixed by the sight before him. A determined charge would have finished the besieged men easily, but it seemed the Indians were toying with them. The white men constantly changed positions for cover and a chance shot at the fast-riding, painted warriors. Then three of the Indians fell from their horses.

Lucky shot! Wait! There were no shots! From his vantage point, he watched two of the fallen Indians start to creep forward under cover of the low brush. Sneaky bastards. It was a trick he would not forget. Rushing back to his horse, he pulled his rifle from the scabbard and returned to his protected rock.

For some reason known only to himself, Beaux decided to take sides in this one-sided battle. He didn't think of it like that, however.

It was the opportunity for an easy kill that got his blood hot. Sighting carefully, he dropped the first warrior who rose to shoot just as the white men had turned their backs to fire at the yelping Indians to their front. In the cacophony of the gun battle, no one noticed a third party had joined in. Quickly reloading, he sighted in on the second fallen Indian as he was about to attack one of the defenders from behind. Beaux fired and the knife dropped from the brave's dead hand, blood spurting from his throat as he fell. Startled by unexpected assistance, the white men's eyes grew large and questioning as they stared up into the forest line searching for the shooter. A pall of smoke drifted over the rock from where he'd fired. He reloaded. He was enjoying this. Out here, no one cared if he killed these damn injuns. The blood lust churned in his gut. Killing with no consequences almost drove him to ecstasy.

Beaux started singing "Camptown Races" as he sighted in on one of the attackers. His next shot took a dark warrior in the chest.

The defenders now became the attackers opening fire at the stationary targets, who had turned to watch their comrade fall from his horse. They dropped two more of the puzzled Indians, before they could react.

Shrieking war cries, the remaining four warriors charged the hill. Beaux's head popped up from behind his rock. His triumphant smile quickly changed to a look of terror and dismay. The screaming, yipping warriors were hell bent on getting up the hill and were coming right for him.

Dashing for his horse, Beaux found a terrified animal. His horse shied and stomped his feet, fighting the bit. Its eyes were large and white as he tried to get away from something concealed in the brush.

"What's wrong with you? Hold, damn you. Hold, I say!" Beaux had his left foot in the stirrup and was hopping on the other foot trying to get in the saddle. He grabbed the horn and pulled himself into his seat as a momma grizzly, snarling with fury, followed by two whining cubs burst out of the underbrush. A huge paw raked the unlucky horse's right hind leg. In blind terror, the lineback dun bolted down the side of the hill straight for the attacking Indians. Beaux was an excellent equestrian, but the sudden turn of events had him barely holding on to the reins. His right stirrup flapped with each bound of the frightened horse. He couldn't get his right foot in the stirrup, and his leg flailed in the attempt. The angle of the hill, as the horse stampeded down, caused Beaux to bounce in the saddle with stomach churning nausea.

They charged past the astonished Indians with Beaux bouncing and screaming for his horse to stop. "Whoa, boy. Whoa, horse. Whoa, damn you, stop. Stop!" If not for the western style horn on his saddle, on which Beaux had a death grip with both hands, he would have fallen under the feet of the Indian's horses.

Looking back at the crazy white man and his wild-eyed beast, the Indians rode right into the enraged grizzly. Fighting their rearing and bucking horses, one of the warriors fell off onto the back of the mama bear. Snarls and curses ensued in the fight that resulted in the death of the hapless warrior, as the others scrambled away. The three survivors fought their ponies to a stop and turned. The dying screams of the warrior echoed in the forest, and the defeated war party gave up and rode away from the snarling mother bear.

At the bottom of the hill, Beaux finally got both hands full of his horse's mane.

"Stop! Whoa, boy, whoa!" Viciously he pulled the horse's mane until the terrified horse sat back on his haunches, skidding to a stop in the gravel at the bottom of the basin. It had been a long time since morning coffee.

Wheezing for breath, the poor horse stood turning to look behind him blowing through his nose. Beaux rode him in a circle, allowing his animal to regain his senses. The men at the wagon called to him. Checking his guns first, Beaux approached cautiously.

"Hello, stranger! Where did you come from? You surely saved our bacon! That was some fine shooting." Their words congratulated him, but Beaux sensed something peculiar about this group. There was something in the way they looked, the way they wore their guns, their clothes. These men weren't the typical pilgrims he had seen in the past.

"Get down. Get down! You sure saved us!"

"Hey, mister. You'd better see to your horse. His hind leg has been hurt purty bad. What was it? It looks like he was raked by a bear. See! You can trace the claw marks in his hide. Too big for a cat."

Beaux got off to look. No wonder his horse had been terrified. "Yeah, I was attacked by a mama grizzly with cubs up there on the ridge. Just got away in time before she ate us both. I don't know where she came from. Those Indians rode right into her. They didn't have any good fortune this day, that's for sure." Beaux examined the claw marks. The hide was torn, but not so deep the wounds would be fatal.

"Ah, don't feel sorry for them scoundrel Injuns. They attacked us out of no place. We were eating our breakfast by the fire when they showed up. Waylon there, got grazed in the leg with their first shots. We all dove for cover under the wagon. Here, have some coffee, mister. What's your name, anyhow?"

Beaux thought for a second, studying them. "I'm Conlon."

"Well, sit, Conlon. You going far?"

"I'm working my way west, mister." Beaux realized they hadn't offered their names, other than naming the wounded Waylon.

The four men sat on the opposite edge of the fire making small talk and watching him. Beaux's back was to the wagon. He drank his coffee, then stood and stretched his arms and set his cup on the back gate of the wagon.

"Mind if I look in your wagon for some salve or poultice for my horse?" Beaux turned and pulled up the canvas flap at the back of the schooner. Inside lay a dead man and woman. The contents of the wagon had been broken into and scattered. The bodies had not been dead for very long. Beaux knew the look and signs of violent death. He turned back to the men with a question on his lips. That odd feeling, he had had earlier about these men, now flamed into realization. "Did those Indians do this?" He already knew the truth.

The four were standing silent, their guns drawn and threatening. Beaux smiled, recognizing his pack. "Well, boys, it looks like I'm among brothers." He lit a cheroot.

17

B EN GALLOPED INTO THE CAMP, purple mountains looming up behind him, fresh dust forming a hazy cloud in the still air. Waving his hat, he called to the wagons, "Close it up! Riders comin' in. Indians seeking a parley. Keep sharp! Close it up." Dismounting, he crossed over to Captain Nightingale, pointing off to the north.

Men reached into the back of their wagons for their guns and shotguns. Women coiled their whips, prepared to strike, if need be. All were alert, eyes watching Captain Nightingale's next move. The train closed up quickly.

Riders had come into the camp before, usually to trade or travel with the train for a few days for protection. It was fairly common. But Ben had urgency in his voice that day that was noticed immediately by the train in his insistence of keeping the wagons closed up. All watched as Captain Nightingale ordered the wagons to circle up into a defensive ring. They drove the stock to the middle of the camp and posted guards. All eyes remained alert and watchful.

"Del Rio!" said Ben. "Get your horse. I want you in on this. You need to witness a parley. And I want you to watch my back. Keep an eyeball on these young bucks and give me your thoughts on what you see and feel about 'em. Mostly, I want you to watch and learn. Keep your mouth shut."

Del looked over the prairie as he saddled Raj. Four mounted ponies had cut straight for the circled wagons, bursts of dust erupting
from their hooves. Dark eyes examined every aspect of the camp.
They stopped a few hundred yards from the wagons and waited.

Del rode to catch up to Captain Nightingale and Ben who had
already started forward. He followed several paces behind as they
rode up to the parley party. Del's eyes searched every bush, rock, and
tree in the near proximity of the meeting place. The braves seemed
to be alone. No one took anything for granted. This was Indian land.
Ben had taught him, "The white man is the intruder. Be polite, learn
their ways. Strike fast when you have to."

Ben approached the group and made sign then translated to Captain Nightingale what the braves said.

Studying each of the braves, Del could tell which one was the
actual leader. Like Captain Nightingale, he held back telling the in-
terpreting brave what to say. The Indians weren't painted for war.
Del deduced it was a hunting party or scouts for a larger group hid
out in the hills behind them.

The leader rode an impressive black and white spotted horse.
Her spots were very distinctive. She stood about sixteen hands high.
She was as large as Raj, unusual for an Indian horse. Wearing yellow
and red handprints on her flanks with feathers woven into her mane,
she was an impressive mount. All the Indians had rifles and carried
knives in their belts. The feathered sticks they carried, had hanks of
hair fastened to them. The dark leader carried six scalps, the others
less. The scalps were signs of bravery and prowess as a warrior. Having the Howdahs close by, primed and ready, made Del much more
comfortable. He carried the .36 caliber pistol in his belt.

Ben's voice rose and the two translators seemed to be arguing
back and forth. Captain Nightingale countered their demands and Ben
translated. Seemingly tired of the banter, their leader rode forward
gesturing with his feathered staff.

He was a finely built fellow, stern faced and demanding that he
get his way. It seemed that he wanted to know who they were and
what they were doing here. The leader kept nudging into Ben's horse
seemingly to drive him back. The warriors who had stayed in the

background studied the train intently, as the leader carried his argument, arguing loudly and ignoring his translator.

Were they looking for any weakness?

As the leader nudged his pony forward, Ben backed his horse. Del and Captain Nightingale did the same. The dark Indian, shouting now, slowly drove this party of whites back toward their train. Not knowing how many Indians were actually out there, Ben backed his horse each time the young chief pushed forward. Ben wasn't going to start a fight here.

"They asked about our women," Ben said suddenly. "They want to know if we have women to trade or sell."

Captain Nightingale put a stop to that immediately. He cocked his rifle and laid it across his saddle with the barrel pointed directly at Stern Face's bellybutton. The young chief stopped his horse and looked at Captain Nightingale with new respect.

Ben made cutting signs to their insistence about the women. Even Del could tell a distinct no when he saw it.

The Indians became friendly. Stern Face smiled and quickly reached a deal with Ben. The braves would settle for flour, bacon, sugar, and coffee. They also wanted a pot to boil the coffee in and cups. No horses, no cattle, no women. The Indians would leave them in peace.

Del had studied the warriors closely. He could identify the Indians and the ponies they rode if he ever saw them again. Ben had taught him well. Del was an apt student absorbing the lessons of this land and people. While Captain Nightingale stayed with the Indians, Del and Ben rode back to the wagons and gathered up what Ben described as "presents," but they were really a bribe.

Mrs. Kincaid and her two sons waved to them as they rode up to the train. "Can we help with anything, Ben?" she asked.

"With all due respect, Miz Kincaid, you should move back inside the circle. You don't want them braves to see you don't have no man about." Ben pointed the way with his rifle, for them to cross ahead of him between the wagons.

"Ben, we got more than enough in Pa's wagon being as we don't carry no furniture and such. I don't think he'd mind if you got your presents from us. We can make it up " Some of the other wagons volunteered to donate as well and soon the bribes were gathered.

They rode out to the parley where a determined Nightingale had been waiting with the braves. He had refused to back up more, as Del could see the Indian ponies bunched tightly in front of him.

"Captain Nightingale is trying to keep them Injuns from getting too close to the train. Let's hope this sends them on their way," Ben said as they rode up.

Stern Face gestured emphatically toward the wagons and began talking and signing something.

Ben spoke very sharply and again made a large cutting sign, saying "No" to the demand.

This silenced the Indians at last. They gathered their presents and rode away. Stern Face turned and looked back at the wagons. Kicking his heels into the flanks of his mare, he rode away into the dust from which they first appeared.

"On about women again!" said Ben. "Captain that's no durn good, them wanting any extra women we might have. I told him we don't have any women to trade. They all have men to hunt for them. I don't know what they believed, or what I thought they believed, but we're going to have to take extra precautions these next few days. Indians think altogether different than us. We don't want to lose any horses, cattle, or women. Hopefully, they'll be satisfied and go on with their hunt."

Back at camp, Nightingale called his division leaders together and explained what had taken place with Stern Face and his warriors. "We need to keep the wagons close together on the trail. No stragglers. Keep your stock close by and a gun to hand at all times. Women are to stay with their wagons. Everybody is to sound the alert if they see any Indians. We circle tightly with each wagon's tongue under the wagon in front of them. Stock, we'll keep in the circle at night. Double the guards and keep the cattle in a group when we're grazing and watering the stock in the evening before we bring them in. Any questions? All right, get to it."

That night, they bunched the wagons tightly. Cattle and horses moved within the circle. Everyone was low keyed, bright-eyed, and big-eared that evening. These were the first Indians that had made such demands. Trading for women was something most had never dreamed of.

"Makes 'em think, don't it," said Tucker. "Where I come from, your mother or your sister could be sold or traded, and you'd never see them again. I was took away from my mama at ten, before we come to Indiana. Miz Becky tried to stop Beaux from selling her, but he wouldn't listen. I've never seen her since."

Daniel and Del sat staring at the ground. Nothing they knew to say seemed good enough to soothe any of Tucker's feelings. Though they had had no part of any slave trade, they felt embarrassed. It was outside their experience.

The Indians had scared and mystified them at the same time. Most of the camp was from the north. Trading in human flesh was known in their lives, but most had never owned anyone. That their country practiced human trading and selling hadn't really crossed their minds, until now. Women looked at Tucker with a new respect.

So far, not many wagon trains had been attacked. Indians mainly traded for goods they couldn't make themselves—tools, knives, axes, sugar, flour, coffee, and bacon were favorite items. These "presents" were offered to urge them to leave, forget about the train and never come back.

Two nights later, after the wagons had circled for the night, their attention had waned. Men grew exhausted by constant alertness. The wagons weren't circled as tightly as they had been the previous nights.

Ben said to Daniel, "I wish they had attacked. Everybody is jumpy and tired. It makes for mistakes, I tell you. Look at them wagons. You could drive a whole team between 'em. They ain't listening to me or Cap'n Nightingale like they should."

"I know, Ben," Daniel replied, "I've got three men on two wagons, and we're cross with each other, too. Tension is in the air. I jumped when a stick popped in the fire last night. Del Rio is out bringing the stock in. All the men are on edge. Here they come."

Several men and Del Rio returned after bunching the stock on grass outside the circle of wagons. There wasn't enough grass within the circle to feed the animals that had been on sparse rations for two nights. All looked tired and uneasy. Everyone needed sleep.

"What's for supper, Tuck?" Del took off his gloves and slapped them against his thigh. "Sure smells good."

"Same as always, stew."

"Well, it's always good stew. Let's try it." Del sat on a fallen log and dove in.

A shrill shot ricocheted off a wash tub hanging on a wagon across from them. More shots followed. All the men grabbed their guns and ran to return fire. There only seemed to be a few shooters hidden in the rocks out of sight, but they couldn't tell how many there were. Someone yelled that they were hit. Tucker took off to see if he could help with the doctoring. Del and Daniel lay under a wagon next to each other.

"What do you think they're doing, Pa?"

"Not sure. They seem to have us pinned down. They're hid pretty good. I can't see well enough to take a shot. We're backlit by our campfires. They can see us, but we can't see them." A shot splintered the frame of the wagon just over their heads. Splinters flew in their faces.

Someone pulled on Del's boot. "Mister Del, Mister Del, come quick!" It was Bart, Nancy Kincaid's oldest son. Del scrambled out from under the wagon.

"What is it, Bart?"

"They took her, Del. The Indians took her!"

"Took who, Bart?"

"My mama!"

"Nancy?"

"Yes, sir. I couldn't do anything. He just grabbed her and rode off. I came up to see how the fighting was going, and when I got back, I could see them riding away. He cut through the canvas. It wasn't my fault. There was nothing I could do, Mister Rio!" Bart sobbed. "He took her. It wasn't my fault."

"Here. Stop now, that's it. No, it wasn't your fault. It's okay, I'll go find her. I promise I'll bring her back. Okay? Now, stop crying." Del wiped the young boy's face and hugged him. "I'll bring her back, Bart. Understand? They're Indians. They don't know any better.

"Now, go tell my Pa and Tucker I'm going after her. Tell them, not to worry. Me and Raj will track them down. You're the man of your wagon. Be strong for your little brother. Okay? Be strong for your ma. Go! Scoot! Tell Riodan, I can travel faster and quieter alone."

Del had about an hour of dim daylight left. He quickly picked up the tracks of the unshod pony. Its heavy tracks sank deeply into the earth indicating two riders.

He set off with his eyes glued to the trail. The shadows fell at a bad angle for him to make out the tracks due to the setting of the sun. He lost the track several times but was always able to pick it up again. It cost him time he didn't have. A blue tatter of cloth on some thick brush lifted his spirits when he found it. The Indian wasn't making it easy. They seemed to be making for some distant cliffs, but the tracks kept changing direction.

Nightfall found Del on his hands and knees in the tall grass using his fingertips to search for tracks. It was rough. He was tired. The sharp grass cut his arms. Sometimes, he wasn't sure if he was on the track or not, blindly feeling for the pressure ridges the hooves made when they pressed into the earth. He lost them several times. It was frustrating. His pants were torn. He had cactus spines in his fingers. He crept along on the ground, and the pony, with Nancy Kincaid, got farther and farther away.

He cried out in anguish. He couldn't let them get away. He was tired and lonely and doubting himself, but Del Rio had a stubborn streak a mile wide, and he wasn't going to quit.

"I wish I had Ben with me."

He lost the track about midnight in a stream bed. He went down one side then up the other but couldn't find any pony tracks coming out of the stream no matter how far along the bank he searched. Exhausted, scared, and anxious for Mrs. Kincaid, Del felt he would have to wait until dawn and good light before he could pick up a definite track again. He was new at tracking and didn't want to become more confused. That would lose even more time. Standing dejectedly next to Raj, he bent his head in defeat. He'd have to find it in the morning. It seemed his only choice.

Hidden in a willow thicket, he was pulling Raj's saddle off when he heard a horse snort in the night. "Whoa, big fella." Del covered Raj's nose. "Shhh" Another horse nickered in the darkness. Peering out, he saw three braves sitting their ponies as they drank from the stream. He recognized them immediately. One rode the black and white he had admired. The braves talked to each other in low voices as they sat their horses silhouetted by the moon. A wolf bayed from an unseen hilltop. Del felt very alone right now. The braves looked around but didn't act like they were afraid of pursuit. Grunting, the braves kicked their ponies up the far bank and sped away.

They should lead me to Mrs. Kincaid. He felt a grudging admiration for Stern Face's planning of the kidnapping—creating a diversion to the front and stealing a white woman away, from the rear. Pretty smart of those Indians. Bet, they're going to be surprised to see me!

Quickly, he re-saddled Raj. "Come on, old boy. We're going to follow them"

In the moonlight, he could see a plain trail made by the three ponies. Cautiously he followed, making sure to keep to the shadows and tall grasses, not allowing himself to be backlit against the full moon.

The braves moved confidently. They were not in flight, but sure of their destination and comfortable in the knowledge they were not being followed. The Indians figured the whites would not leave the safety of their wagons until morning, because they would be fearful of another attack. It was only one woman. The train had a lot of women. She would not be missed until morning. The braves made their way up into the surrounding ridges, stopping occasionally to check their back trail then moving up into the rocks.

Del watched as the Indians moved into the hills. The hooves of their ponies clattered on the brittle rock as they climbed higher. He guessed the kidnapper was hiding out in a prearranged camp, waiting for his friends.

Del feared for Mrs. Kincaid. Ben had told him how braves tortured women prisoners, unless one of the braves wanted her for a squaw. All four of them would have at her and when they had had what they wanted... Del shuddered. It wasn't a pretty thing to behold. Del needed surprise to defeat these Indians by moving stealthily and surely. Removing a roll of rawhide from his saddle bag, he cut it into large pieces and covered Raj's hooves to muffle his iron shoes. He needed surprise if he had any hope of defeating so many warriors.

The camp must be close by. All of a sudden, he wasn't tired anymore. A determined, angry resolve built in his gut, and it felt right.

MRS. KINCAID WAS TERRIBLY FRIGHTENED at first. A cloth sack had been pulled over her head after she had been yanked from her wagon by her hair and sat on a pony. Someone hissed into her ear and a knife pressed to her throat. She did not know what was said, but she got the message loud and clear. She immediately fought a surge of fear as it welled up. Clinging to the pony's mane, she let anger build courage and strength. She would not be a shrinking violet to these savages' attempts to scare her into some quaking, cowardly, white woman. Bart and Nate would be waiting. Nancy held on and stayed alert. She waited.

At last, they reached wherever her captor was taking her, and he knocked her to the ground. She stood up and defiantly faced him before he pulled off her hood. She didn't run. There was no place to go. There was only here and now. He saw her look of defiance and started to slap her. Thinking better of it, he grabbed her arm and twisted it brutally until she screamed in submission. He made a quick fire that illuminated a steep-walled cleft in the rock face. They camped in a small alcove of rocks with steep sides. There was only one way in or out. He had her sitting on a rock at the back of the declivity facing the fire. Only one horse at a time could pass through that narrow entrance. All that was between her and escape to freedom was the brave and the fire. He sat expectantly watching and waiting. He had not tied her hands. There was no doubt in his mind. She was not going anywhere.

Nancy decided that he was waiting for someone. She didn't know what to expect after that. She had heard the horror stories of female captives. All were gruesome. If the women lived, they were never the same. Never the same to themselves, to their families, or to a white society. Many were driven mad or took their own lives. Society could be cruel to these women. It was cruel on both sides of the red and white lines. Indian women who took up with whites or were despoiled by raiders were often ostracized from their tribes and families as well. She looked around for a stick or rock she could use. None were close.

Her guardian only shifted his steadfast gaze to her when she made any movement. He ignored her questions and sat as if he had turned to rock. Only his eyes moved. The fire crackled and popped sending up streams of sparks to disappear in the void of blackness overhead. Weird shadows of black and light worked a strange dance against the rocks and the face of her watcher creating a scene she could only equate with visions of hell as preached by her minister back home. Home? Would she ever have someplace to call home again? She had no hope for herself. No one had seen the abduction. Her fate lay in whomever the watcher waited for, be they saint or devil. There were no saints among these savages. Not able to fight away her imaginings of the inevitable, Nancy's bravado failed. She began screaming at her captor. Impulsively, she rushed to the fire scaring her guard into a startled wide-eyed jerk. Using her apron, Nancy dug her hands into the fire and flung the embers and burning logs over onto the chest of the perplexed man who never expected this white woman to do anything but cower.

He screamed as the hot coals burnt his bare eyes, face and chest. Pounding at the flames with his bare hands, he rolled in the dust trying to put out the burning live coals on his chest and smoldering hair, crying incoherently in a language Nancy didn't need to translate into English.

She dashed for freedom as fast as her tired legs would take her, ignoring her own burning flesh. His screams spurred her movement, and safety beckoned only a few feet away.

Dark mounted forms filled her escape route. Somber faces lit by the dancing play of light and shadow stared mercilessly as they gathered and viewed the chaotic scene before them.

Nancy collapsed at the feet of the leader's spotted horse. Gasping insanely and tearing at her hair with blistered, burned fingers, she sobbed into the dust. All hope had been snatched from her in an instant. She had no vitality left to fight the swelling wave of terror that took her mind and sprang from depths totally unexperienced before. Her mind knew hell, a hell as vivid and present as any she had been taught by a caring and loving church. No benevolent savior was coming to pluck her from certain torture at the hands of the tormentors who scowled down upon her. She gave way and crossed the thin line from reality into madness.

Uncontrollably, words of condemnation and mumbling nonsense spewed from her lips. She stared manically at her captors. She could hear her own wails but was uncertain where they came from. They blended into this surreal vision of hell confronting her. She grinned at them and began ripping at her hair and clothes, flinging the remnants at the astonished Indians. Chanting screams, mixed with laughter, Nancy leaped to the leader's horse and began pounding on the bewildered beast's side.

Stern Face slid off, staring confusedly at her. He gestured for one of the braves to attend to the other man thrashing around in the dust. He grabbed Nancy by her shoulders and hair, shaking her violently and ordering her to shut up. His words were as much gibberish to her ears as the ones emitting from her own throat.

He slapped her hard across the face. Nancy didn't feel it. She spat at him. He grasped her by the throat and proceeded to slap her again. As he hit her, a boom deafened them all to silence. The shock waves reverberated off the stony walls, straining their ear drums to almost bursting.

A crimson hole, as big as a ripe apple burst out the chest of the brave who was still sitting astride his horse. He fell as if poleaxed into the deep dust. Turning to face the assailant, Stern Face screamed a war cry and leapt forward. With the next step, his head exploded, and he collapsed in a bloody foam.

Del tossed the Howdah in his right hand away and shifted the other from his left to his right. He intently walked up to the remaining two braves who stared transfixed by the fire and shot the one attending to the burns of the man Nancy had set on fire, exploding his chest in bloody shards. The burned man began to chant, knowing he was seeing death in the eyes of a grim Del Rio. The chant died in his throat when Del discharged the big gun into his face.

All this violence erupted in the time of only a few moments. Del had not had time to think. Taking advantage of surprise, he had been able to dispatch all four men in less than a minute. He dropped his gun and walked slowly over to Nancy. She stared, trembling, dumbfounded by what had just happened and trying to decipher hell's myth from reality. Her universe had inverted from rescue to horror and horror back to rescue so quickly she couldn't get the reality of it focused in her mind. She stared unseeingly at him, then at the scattered, smoking, bleeding bodies. She collapsed into a squatting sit and stared into space.

"Nancy? Miz Kincaid? It's me, Del Rio. Nancy? Did they hurt you?" Softly, he kept his voice low as he moved toward her with a gentle pleading look on his face. "Nancy? It's me, Del Rio. You're safe. You're safe. They're gone."

Gently, he put his jacket about her shoulders and sat her by the fire. "Would you like something to drink?" He found a peppermint drop in his pocket, then gave her a drink of water and placed the peppermint between her lips. Gently, he embraced her and began to rock. The words to his mother's favorite lullaby came instantly to his lips. The only one he remembered. He sang and hummed and rocked her, stroking her hair, touching her face, and kissing her forehead. He lost track of time. Nancy never let him go. He sang, rocked and held her until the pinkish twinges of a new dawn sent creeping tendrils of promise brightening the mountains and valleys. A cool breeze wafted into their solitude.

Nancy inhaled sharply of the crisp air and looked into Del's face. Reason and sanity resided in her eyes again. "Del? Del! Is that really you? Oh, my word, Del, I've had the most awful dream. Why are you here at my wagon?" She looked around. "Wait... Where are we?"

Del gave her some water and another peppermint. He helped her up.

She began to take in the carnage around her. Del had not left her side. He wished now that he had dragged the bodies behind a rock so she would not see.

"It wasn't a dream, was it? It was real. I was so scared. I've never been so frightened in my entire life. I think I lost myself for a while in this dream... but it wasn't a dream at all, was it? It was this... this madness, that awful madness, in this awful place."

"Keep talking, Nancy. Keep talking. That's it. Talk it out. That's right. Here, sit by the fire. That's it. Look out there. The sun is coming up. Smell that wonderful breeze? Remember your boys, your family. They're waiting for you, just like before. You're going back to them, back to the wagon train going to Oregon and all your friends who love you."

Del led her through the cleft in the rocks into the awakening dawn. He sat her facing the rising sun and the morning palette of color brightening in the valley below. "Look at the sun and the dawning day, Nancy. Watch the morning unfold. Smell that? That's honeysuckle and sage on the morning breeze. I'll clean up about the camp and make you some coffee. That'll be nice, won't it? Stay here now. I'll be back in a few minutes. There you are. Good girl. That's it." She seemed mesmerized by the unfolding colors of promise spread out before her.

Del got some coffee on the fire. He pulled some biscuits and jerky out of his saddle bags. He always kept these things in case he had to leave with Ben.

Del drug the bodies out of sight and hid any trace of the Indians at all. He kicked dirt over the blood stains in the dirt and rock. Retrieving his pistols, he wiped and loaded them before placing them back in their saddle holsters.

He took a cup of coffee to Nancy and some pieces of dried meat he had warmed and put in a biscuit. "Here, Miz Kincaid, try this. I bet you're hungry, aren't you? I know I am. Sorry, I don't have any sugar for your coffee. I know you like it that way. Here, put some of this jerky and biscuit in your mouth. My pa makes about the best jerky I ever did eat. Them's Tucker's biscuits, too. You know how proud he is of those biscuits. There you go. That's better. Here eat, we'll have to go soon. Hey! What happened to your hands? Did those savages burn you? Oh, Lord, look at them!"

Del bathed her hands with water from his canteen. He gently applied some bear grease to them. "Ben always said bear grease was good for everything. You can even eat it if you need to!" Carefully, he applied the ointment and wrapped her hands in strips of cloth from her petticoat. "I imagine that is going to hurt some. Keep those bandages clean, will you?"

Nancy smiled weakly.

"Okay now. You rest. I gotta figure a way out of here pronto. I don't know if the train will wait or not. After an attack, I guess they'll move off from there if they can. There may be someone out looking for us, but I doubt it. They probably can't spare anybody. I think we're on our own." He went back to the fire for some coffee for himself. He sat and pondered what would be the best way to proceed. He would take all the weapons and horses. This might slow them down some. He couldn't go as fast as he'd like anyway, because he wasn't sure how Nancy would do with her hands burned as bad as they looked. He did not want the Indian ponies showing back up at their old camp and alerting any other Indians to come looking. They would be back trailed for sure.

Del knew these Indians were the trading party that had been interested in trading for women in the first place. He had recognized the leader by his horse in the dark. Stern Face was the Indian who had been choking Nancy. "I hope they were on their own. We don't need to get chased by no gang of Indians in the shape we're in."

The sobbing began softly at first. Nancy stood in the opening staring at the camp. Del moved to comfort her. "No, Del. Let it be. I'm all right. I just need to cry this out. Go on. I'll be okay." She leaned against a rock slab, covered her face and let herself have a good cry.

Helpless, he didn't know what else to do except get ready to start back. Casting furtive glances her way, every now and then, he gathered the horses and weapons. Collapsing a rocky clay filled bank over the bodies of the Indians, he knew they would eventually be found, but it seemed like the right thing to do. Besides, he didn't have a shovel.

"I'm ready. Let's get away from this awful place." She shied away from the Indian mounts as he tried to help her up on an Indian pony, so he put her up on Raj and took one of the ponies for himself. He'd do better riding bareback than she would anyway.

Del took the lead with the other ponies tied together behind him. They never looked back.

It was close to midday when they stopped. All he had were a few more sticks of jerky, a few biscuits, and some coffee—trail food for him and Ben. It was all they had and better than nothing. The color started to come back into Mrs. Kincaid's face. Her eyes were alert and took interest in the territory they travelled through. She asked questions about animals and how soon they would get back to the train.

This reassured him. She had started putting her ordeal behind her and looking to the future. Del hoped that was a good sign. He watched for Indians everywhere. He did not follow his trail from before but kept a good distance off it. Ben had told him to never follow the same trail both coming and going. He knew the five horses would leave tracks, but he couldn't help it. They traveled up creeks and stayed in the tree lines when they could. Switching ponies often, he scouted ahead to check the way before him, then rode back to check their back trail. Feeling more certain no one was on their trail, he headed straight south and east back to the wagon trail. He expected it to take at least two to three days to catch up unless the wagons had waited for them. They would not. They could not send men out when the train needed their protection.

Del left the trail they were on and followed a faint stream up a hillside about a half of a mile before they made camp that night. They ate the last of their jerky and biscuits, leaving only a little coffee for the morning.

Over the flickering campfire, he looked at the fatigue on Nancy's face. "You did great today, Miz. Kincaid. How are you doing?"

"I thought you were calling me Nancy, Del. I like it when you do. Thank you. Forgive me. I'm just now thanking you for saving my life. I hadn't thought of it before. I guess we're far enough away, I feel safe again. Thank you, Del. Thank you so much. You really are a fine man. Finer than most men I've ever met. Not many would have had the courage to do what you did—come after a woman who wasn't your own."

"Shoot, Miz—er, Nancy. I don't think it took courage. I just knew it had to be done. Pa says that's what distinguishes a man is just doing that... what needs to get done. Like shooting those men back there. I didn't think. I was too scared. I just gave in to instinct and did what I needed to do. I was lucky. In a stand-up fight, I'd be resting back there, not here. Just luck.

"Ben says, we haven't grown much past living in caves anyway. We are still mostly animals just learning to be civilized. I let the animal in me out and became an animal like those Indians back there. They live by their instincts mostly. That's how they survive out here. Take what you can to survive. Kill to live. Kill to feed your family and your tribe. That's what matters. I guess you and me are part of the same tribe, so to speak. I was just lucky. Nothing more."

"I think you were brave, and you were kind. I was so frightened. I had given up all hope in God or salvation. I have been lonely since Thomas died, always showing a strong front for my boys. Del, I need something else from you. I hope you'll understand. I... I need your arms around me and your body close tonight. Please? I know it's much to ask, and I'll not ask it of you again or make any demands on you after. I have been so afraid. I promise never to speak of it after, if only you'd hold me tonight."

She kissed his forehead lightly, kneeling to embrace him. She kissed his cheeks and mouth. "Oh! This is new to you, isn't it? It's okay, dear. I'll teach you." She unbuttoned his shirt, then the top of her dress.

Del hesitated, then kissed her face, then her mouth. She kissed him back, drawing him closer to her. They embraced and rolled into their blankets, hot flames from the fire heating Del's bare back and their own body heat blazing from within. They quenched her need to feel someone alive and living next to her in the dark coolness of the night.

18

MiDMORNING THE NEXT DAY FOUND them on the trail again. The last few days were a galvanizing experience for the two of them—only occurring when extreme conditions drive people to act together unselfishly for their own survival. A rare event, experienced at the very fringes of life and death culminated into a lifelong friendship between Del and Nancy.

Nancy's hands healed quickly with the clean air and fresh water. Wounds heal more quickly in the higher regions. Bear grease had softened her skin, soothing the inflammation, although it did have its own special pungent odor. Del melted bear fat and added some fresh pine needles, making a fresh preparation of the healing ointment and strained it through some muslin from Nancy's dress the way Tucker had taught him. The pine made the bear grease smell more pleasant at least, and she found it soothing. He bound her hands in strips of muslin from her torn petticoats, making her some awkward-looking riding gloves. They gave enough protection that she could grip the reins.

By that afternoon, they found where the wagon train had been attacked. Cold campfire rings and trampled grass marked the spot. They explored to see what they could find. There were no burial markers.

"Looks like everyone made it out," said Del. "Unless they've hidden a body somewhere so Indians and animals won't find it!"

"I don't see a bone from a meal, or anything left on the ground," said Nancy. "They left in a hurry after the attack, probably early the next morning. They're a day or two ahead of us."

"You're right. We should be able to catch up to them sometime before noon tomorrow, if we ride late tonight and get a good early start in the morning. You game?"

"Game? After what I have been through, I feel I could live through anything now and lick my way through wildcats. I miss my boys. It's time to go home!"

Mounting up, they rode on. Del held back every now and again, always checking the skyline and backtrail. He had seen nothing so far except a few far-off buffalo and magpies flitting about the pine trees. He didn't want to get complacent, though.

They rode quickly. Raj was a stayer. He could keep to the trail all day. Nancy's weight was no trouble for him. Del still rode back and forth checking the trail. The ponies were good mountain stock. He changed mounts often, preferring the black and white paint, who seemed to like him, as well. That afternoon when they stopped for a break, Del led the ponies to a stream, pulled the feathers and ornaments from their manes and washed the paint from their sides.

"I don't want trouble when we get back to the train. This way it won't remind people of the attack." He was thinking of Nancy, of course, but didn't want to say it. "If you don't mind, I'd like to give one of the ponies to each of your boys, one to Tucker and I'll keep the paint for myself. I've taken quite a liking to her. I know Bart and Nate will each need a horse. They're growing up. They've pulled their weight, and a pony will be mighty handy for them and for you. That is, if it won't disturb you any, Nancy."

"Why, that would be fine. What are you going to name your pony?"

"Been thinking about that. Gonna call her Star. You know, for the star on her forehead."

"I like that just fine. You know, no one back home would understand what it takes to live out here. What they wouldn't understand is how big life out here can be and what it means to be living so close to death, not just getting along. I feel very much alive. I can thank you for that... and for being able to go back to my sons."

"Much obliged, ma'am. I feel near to bursting myself!" With a quick laugh, he galloped off to check the trail ahead.

Nancy sat on Raj with flushed cheeks and a startled grin on her face as well. She laughed out loud just for the thrill of it. Covering her mouth quickly, she smothered her laugh. She had to be quiet.

Later that day, they topped out on a bluff when they saw below them spread out over the plain an enormous herd of buffalo. It seemed to stretch from the north forever. The black undulating mass, moved like a large flock of birds, crossing a river which had a high bank on the north side. The black swarm flowed across the river, churning the water into a muddy soup. Nancy and Del held their breath at the sight, feeling the earth shake from thousands of thundering hooves.

Hand to her breast, Nancy gasped. "I can't count them all! I would not believe it if I hadn't seen it with my own eyes."

They both spoke in whispers, in reverence to something that was beyond them.

"Well," he said, after a long wait, "we might as well sit and let the horses graze. We won't be crossing that river for a while. We're going to be here for a few hours, is my guess. That'll delay us getting to the train. Closer to noon tomorrow, I figure. Wish we had some coffee."

They had nothing to eat and only water to drink. They tethered the horses and made themselves comfortable watching the spectacle before them.

The black flow slowed and then waned to identifiable individuals as they slid down the greasy bank into the frothing river and moved on to their grazing feast on the green plain beyond. Del decided it was safe to go on. The river would clear soon, and the horses could drink.

Churned ground made walking difficult for the horses, so they took their time. They discovered a calf by itself above the bank, afraid to cross and bawling for its mama. Del lassoed it and helped it across the river. He smacked its little rump and yelled, "Go find your mama, little fella!"

"He wouldn't have made it across the river, I don't think."

"I don't think so, either. He's lucky we found him," Nancy replied.

"The animals out here are so different than back east. No pens, no harnesses. Man is not the master out here it seems. Don't you think?"

"I think you're right in that, Nan—err... I'm going to start saying Miz Kincaid again, if you don't mind. so I'll be used to it when we get back to the train. Don't want to ruffle some old hen's suspicions."

"Yes, I think we have to be proper... but I'll miss it!" She rode on.

They rode hard throughout the rest of the afternoon.

Cresting a rise, they were startled by several riders charging over the same hill right at them.

"Del! Del Rio! Miz Kincaid? Is that you?"

It was Daniel and Ben and several others from the train. "Miz Kincaid? I never thought to see you again, ma'am," Ben said. "After you went after her, Del, Cap'n Nightingale wouldn't let anybody else go after you, until the wagons were safe. We got overrun by a buffalo herd not too far back. Did you see them?"

Ben saw Mrs. Kincaid's bandaged hands. "Are you hurt, ma'am? Did those savages hurt you?"

"I'm doing okay now, Ben, thanks. Del saved my life, probably more than once in the last few days. You sure should be proud of your son, Daniel. He proved to be quite a man. I would have been dead, if not for him. Is the train far ahead of us?"

"I am proud of him, Nancy. He took off on his own and brought you back alive. I couldn't ask more of any man. We can catch up tomorrow morning or there about, ma'am? Are you hungry? Have you eaten anything? Do you have water? Lord, you surprised us so, I have forgotten about my manners. Can you ride okay?"

"Yes, I can ride. We are hungry, but we can eat when we make camp this evening. I miss my boys so much. Are they alright? Were they frightened? Who's taking care of my boys? Tucker?" She looked at each of them for a reassuring answer.

"There, there, those boys are fine, Miz Kincaid. Between me and Tucker and Ben, we took good care of them boys. Fine boys they are too. They've been scared silly for you, but they didn't want to show it. They pitched in like everybody else, and I almost had to hog tie the oldest one to keep him to his wagon and not come with us. Wanted to take one of your mules, he did. They've been worried plenty. They will be happy to see you. That's for sure. Ben, let's get riding. We'll make camp by those rocks where we crossed that gulley a little while ago."

"Sounds good to me. Let's go, men!!"

They headed back. Nancy, with a look of relief in her eyes, and Del, with the weight of responsibility taken from his shoulders. Let the other men lead the way. That night, Del and Nancy were waited on by the other men.

"Did you have enough beans, Miz Kincaid?"

"Would you like some more bacon, Del?"

"How's your coffee, Mrs. Kincaid? I know the Missus will have a peach pie waiting when we get back to the wagons. I'll make a present of it to you and your boys."

"Can I get you a blanket, Miz Kincaid?"

"Are you warm enough?"

"Okay, okay, everyone. Thank you. Del and I are fine. You're spoiling us, and I appreciate it, but I'm fine."

"I'm good, too! Fellas," Del said, feeling left out. "I couldn't eat another bite."

No one asked about their ordeal. That would be saved till they made the train. Right now, they would settle in and get an early start in the morning.

Nancy was just closing her eyes, lying by the campfire, when she noticed how the flames seemed so innocent and warm. She put her head down to rest, comforted by friends and a good meal and protected by this friendly fire, so unlike the one she had known in a terrifying nightmare, so many nights ago. She drifted off to restful, dreamless slumber.

19

DRY, DUSTY DAYS FOLLOWED HARD work and sweat. They crawled across the prairie walking, pushing, and pulling their heavy wagons steadily west under a relentless sun and clear sky. It seemed as if they were alone in the world with nothing but that straggling line of wagons, snapping whips, whistles and calls to keep moving ever moving along the tumbling Platte.

The train was always hungry. They had shot some buffalo, and shared everything among the wagons. Lately, as the grass thinned, there were more and more antelope. They were not considered as good a meat as buffalo but welcomed as provisions grew low. The more they could hunt and live off the land, the longer their provisions would last. They did not expect to get re-supplied until Fort John on the Laramie River in Wyoming. They did see wagons on the south side of the Platte. These were usually Mormon carts or trains headed for California or the Great Salt Basin. Once, some Mormons had floated a raft over to their side of the Platte to trade for flour and meat. What everyone wanted most was information. The Mormon train had lost cattle and horses ten nights ago and sent a party in pursuit. One of the men had been wounded in the ensuing battle with the Indians and had died a few days after.

It was good to see other travelers and to share stories of the trail. It seemed to lessen the feeling of aloneness in the vast expanse of the west when others had experienced the same trials and tribulations. Tucker made inquiries about Mary Beth and Brother James, the Mormon party he had traveled with to Independence, but no one had any news. They might have taken a more northern route. All were headed to Ft. John, to re-provision. From there, the southern trails split off and the Oregon bound trains would head more north. These Mormons would take the south fork of the Platte, hoping to reach California before the snows came.

Nightingale's train came to the north fork of the Platte, as the river split into another branch going south. They would make their turn to the north and follow the northern fork toward Oregon, keeping to the right of the stream. A few wagons crossed to the south side bound for California. The crossing took a few hours, hitching and unhitching the teams to pull the cumbersome wagons over the rocks and snags. Daniel, Tucker, and Del seemed everywhere, lending a hand and a strong back where it was needed. They wished teary farewells as the wagons parted ways. The train camped ten miles north of the crossing, on the East side of the Platte.

Del headed to the river for a much-needed bath. This main fork of the Platte had clearer water as it caught more snow melt off the mountains. It looked inviting and Del intended to take it up on that invitation. He ambled down a path toward the river when he was stopped by a loud challenge.

"Where are you going, mister?"

It was Ellen McCarthy, the nurse who had tried to help Thomas Kincaid. She was carrying a shotgun.

"Why, Miz McCarthy, I'm just headed to the river to wash the sweat and dust off me." Del smiled. "It's been a long hot day!"

"Well, you go off to the path to the left, young man. We women are bathing on this side of the river. We get hot and dirty, too! Now off with you, and you keep your nose to the river. We're guarding this path." They didn't seem any too friendly, and Del backed away politely. He didn't want the women of the camp mad at him.

"Yes, ma'am.... The top of the evening to all of you. I'll just go off here to the left. Good night!" He reached for his hat to tip it and realized he wasn't wearing one.

After a refreshing wash, Del, in a cheerful mood, looked forward to a pleasant evening. Whistling a happy tune, he remembered, he was looking forward to a good supper. Tucker was a great trail cook. His food was tasty, hot, and plenty of it. Del looked forward to a good meal and a long sleep to rest his sore muscles. He had grown over the last months. Muscles rippled across his arms and shoulders. He was about six feet tall, still growing hard and lean as sinew and toughened to this frontier life.

Someone hollered up ahead where the women stood guard. A shotgun boomed and yells shouted for someone to stop. "Who is that? Get away from here! Stop! I know I burned him!" The next thing he knew, Del was knocked back into the brush and hit his head on a rock. That was the last thing he remembered that night. He didn't get his supper, but he had a long sleep.

To his surprise, he woke to the morning light with a wet towel on his face and an egg size bump on the side of his head. Oh, Lordy, what happened now? He tenderly touched the painful lump on his head and sat up.

Tucker stood nearby. "Well, wakey wakey, my boy. Don't move till you're sure of your balance. We don't want you to hit your head again. You've got a doozy of a bump on your noggin. I don't envy you a lick for it. Drink some coffee. Sit. Rest. I'll get you a plate of food. Remember anything?"

"No, nothing. Just some big ol' thing bursting out of the bushes after that shotgun went off. I never saw who or what it was. Do you know what hit me?"

"The women say they caught someone sneaking through the brush above where they were bathing. Miz McCarthy yelled at them to stop, and when they didn't, she let go with that gun of hers. A ten-gauge loaded with tacks and nails. Sounded like a cannon going off. Whoever it was, must have been hit. That blast shredded the bushes and trees so, it looked like a tunnel had been cut through them. They thought it was you, when they first found you, because of the blood on your shirt. Then they found that lump on your head. We figured you'd been in the way of whoever they shot at. He knocked you off the path at least ten feet. Must have been a big man to do that. He left blood on your shirt. I washed it out for you. It's drying on the seat of the wagon. Your pa went for Cap'n Nightingale. He's coming to ask you some questions. So far, there's no body, and everyone is account-ed for. A big to do, that's for sure. The whole camp is riled up. Eat! There comes Cap and your pa now."

Del looked up at the serious faces approaching. He could see Mrs. McCarthy among the group. Daniel looked relieved to see him.

"Morning, Cap'n. I guess it's morning. What time of day is it, anyway?" He looked from face to face. They weren't friendly, but they weren't ugly, either. They were almighty grim, Del decided.

"It's about ten in the morning, Del. We've had to stop and sort this ruckus out, while waiting for you to come around. We won't tolerate that sort of behavior. You doing all right?"

Del held his head and nodded he was fine.

"So, tell me your story. Besides Miz McCarthy here, you were the only other person to encounter whoever it was. What happened?"

"Well, Cap'n, it was getting along after dusk. I was whistling and looking forward to supper when I heard that ten gauge go off and someone holler. I was just stepping up from the bank onto the path to see what had happened, when a big ol' bear or buffalo burst through the brush knocking me tail over teacup. The next thing I know, I was here. What did you see, Miz McCarthy?"

"I saw the big brute sneaking through the bushes. I hollered at him, and he took off. He was below me and I could only see his sil-houette as he passed. I let go with ol' Zeke and gave him a taste of nails. I didn't miss either. The last I saw of him, he was headed to the river. Found you when we followed after him."

"How did you know it wasn't me?" Del asked.

"I knew it wasn't you, 'cause he was twice as big as you. I also watched you when you went to the river. You were too far off to be him. Besides, you had blood on the front of your shirt. I shot him on his left side and back. Other than that knot on your head, you didn't have a scratch on you. I know. I checked you all over."

Del blushed. "All over?"

"I also heard you whistling as you came out of the river before I saw him and let go with ol' Zeke. I couldn't have missed—not with that spread of nails and such. No, I marked him. I just didn't put him down. How are you doing, anyways?"

"Oh, I'm okay, I guess. A bit confused is all. Sorry I wasn't much help. What else can I do, Cap'n? That's all I know, honest."

"I believe you and most importantly, Miz McCarthy believes you, and that's good enough for me."

"Ben, line up all the men and boys. We're going to have an inspection and get to the bottom of this. Oh, tell them to take their shirts off, will you."

"Okay, Cap'n," said Ben. "Men, let's get this done. Line up over here and file past me. Pull off your shirt when it's your turn. I know Mitchell was with me last night, pulling guard duty. I know we didn't do it, but we'll both stand the inspection as well." Ben and Mitchell shrugged off their shirts, showing they didn't have a scratch on their bony white hides. Both were embarrassed as they put their clothes back on, but they were taking the lead for the rest of the men. "Line up over here, you fellas. Del, you've been checked by Miz McCarthy, so you get a pass. Daniel and Tucker, you're next."

One by one, all the men, from Captain Nightingale all the way down to the youngest boy, stripped his shirt and were inspected. No one showed any wounds.

"We didn't find a thing, Cap'n Nightingale. Do you think it was some pilgrim traveling by?" Mitchell asked Ben after the last man had passed.

"I don't know, Mitchell. Someone is missing. Who is it?"

"Where's Captain Nightingale?" a voice asked. "I know who it was!" Bessie Martin and her husband, Luke, came through the crowd. "Captain Nightingale, it was Adonis!" Luke said. "We were on the way here for the inspection, when Adonis said he had to go about his business. He headed for the latrine pits and never came back. I went to get him just now and Bessie told me Adonis had come back to the wagon, got his gear and horse and skedaddled in a hurry! Thought he acted strange last night. Wore his plaid jacket all day too, as hot as it was. Bessie said he grabbed some beans, bacon, some onions, and off he went. She could see he changed his shirt and the old one was bloody on the back and left shoulder. I got it right here." Luke held up the bloody tattered shirt. "You shorely burnt him, Ellen He was putting some of Bessie's salve on his shoulder when she saw him."

"Is that right, Bessie?"

"Oh, yes, Captain. I startled him, and he scowled at me fierce! He buttoned up his shirt, took food and his tote sack. Oh, he took a jug of whiskey, too."

"Well, Cap'n," asked Ben, "should we go after him?"

"No, Ben. No, I think not. We've lost a day to this foolishness. Frankly, I'm glad to see him gone. No one was harmed. No one's honor was besmirched, as far as we can tell. Ladies, with your permission, I think we should go. Adonis will find it hard out there alone without the protection of the wagon train."

Mrs. McCarthy threw up her hands, "All right, Captain. I do hope that skunk gets his due. Let's go on. We still got Fort John to make."

"Thank you, ma'am. Ladies." He tipped his hat. "One more thing, Ben. If Adonis returns, shoot on sight. He's proven he's not to be trusted. I don't want him back. All right, make ready to move out in one hour.

"Ben, will you scout ahead? I want to go with the Martins' wagon, make sure they can handle it by themselves. All right! Get on with it. Get those fires out. Harness your teams. Let's get back to the trail!"

20

I T WAS TEN DAYS INTO June by Del's calculations, when they came up to the vast plain, surrounded by low bluffs upon which Ft. John was built. The fort was backed by the Laramie River and faced the Platte, which was over a mile away to the east. Open plains lay off to the north. The trading post commanded a large presence over the surrounding plains. This was a busy place, owned by the American Fur Company. It was named for John Sarpy, one of the owners of the company who had bought it in 1836. Earlier, it had been called Ft. William.

This was the only fort Del had seen during the trip. The adobe brick walls standing on top of a deep clay embankment that was fifteen feet high by itself, made the high walls a pretty impressive sight. The fort formed a quadrangle with large bastions placed at the angles so they could cover all sides of the fort. A single bastion was placed directly over Ft. Johns' main entrance. Anyone passing through this main gate had to be daunted by the fort's defenses. There were many other trains camped about, resting, grazing their stock and resupplying, before moving southwest over the Mormon trail or California trail. The Oregon Trail followed north on the Platte, before turning west on the Sweetwater River. Then it turned south, down the Green River to Bridger's fort, then north again up the Snake River into Oregon. Once there, they could either go overland along the

Columbia gorge to the south, or disassemble their wagons, build a raft to float the currents and rapids to Ft. Astoria or Vancouver on the coast. Overland was the longer way, avoiding the mountains, but much safer and there was less chance of losing everything you had in the treacherous waters of the Columbia River.

A village of Sioux Indians covered a portion of the plains at Fort John. Their village must have had about a hundred lodges in an orderly fashion. Smoke from their cook fires filled the air over the village.

Activity was everywhere they turned—riders on horses, men walking about talking to each other, women gathered in small groups tending children. The sounds of an axe echoed from the trees lining the river. Voices in many languages called back and forth. Laughter blended in a pleasant cohesive chorus. Del had seen pictures back home of the West, and here before him was a living bucolic rendition of the very thing.

"Those lodges look like corn shocks in a field back home, don't they, Del? All nice and neat." Tucker spoke in wonderment. They had not been among such a congregation of Indians before. Hundreds of ponies from the Sioux and the stock from the trains grazed on the vast plain with plenty of room left over.

That night, the train had been met by the man in charge of the fort, a Mr. Boudreaux. They circled the wagons and gathered quietly as Captain Nightingale addressed the people of the train.

"We have come a long way with relatively few casualties. We have been lucky. This fort has a blacksmith to fix anything you may need. They have dry goods, ammunition, food, and coffee. Mister Boudreaux says they recently received a resupply train. They haven't had much to sell to the wagon trains until a few days ago. Frankly, I'd like some fresh coffee. Ben has been roasting beans and wheat to make coffee and... well... anyway, I'm ready for some real coffee. You can trade with the other wagons and the Indians, of course. Sioux are peaceful, but they have their own ways. They do make items for trading. Be careful. They are savvy traders and know the value of what they trade. Mister Boudreaux says they may be here for months and then suddenly disappear. Like I said, they have their own ways.

"We'll be here for a week of rest and restocking. There are traders here who will buy your worn-out stock and sell you replacements for exorbitant prices, but that is the market. Make as good a trade as you can afford for sound stock. Grass is good and there is plenty of it. There had been a two-year drought. Luckily for us, it has rained in the last few weeks to freshen the grasses and the rivers. Our luck is holding good. Go about your business peaceably in the fort and with the other trains or Indians. Mister Boudreaux won't stand for drunkenness or rowdiness. All women are to be respected. He will deal with any transgressors harshly. There is no Indian trouble and hasn't been any for a while, and he means to keep it that way. Typically, the Sioux don't cause trouble here. Be wise, rest, and relax. Repair your wagons. Tighten bolts and axles. Fix worn or broken equipment. The next part of our journey is more difficult. We have been gradually climbing the last few days and will continue to do so. We are over four thousand feet at the fort. It will get steeper and rougher. Take notice of where you are at all times. We are on a timetable for Independence Rock by July fourth or fifth. That's good time. We should be grateful. A party got stuck in the Donner Pass, taking the Hastings Cutoff last year. They started too late, and the snows trapped them. Lost almost seventy-five percent of the party. After eating the cattle, then the mules, then the horses, then the hides, they had nothing to eat but their own dead."

The group fell silent.

"Reverend Blaine, would you lead us in a prayer of thanks and maybe a word for the poor souls of the Donner party?"

All heads bowed. The pastor prayed their thanks for their passage and sorrow for the souls that had passed on the trail. A few words for the Donner party and an "amen" was voiced by all. The news of the Donner party brought quiet and sober reflection to everyone present.

After supper, Daniel, Del, and Tucker set out to explore the fort and the Indian village. They were excited by the festival atmosphere the busy camp exuded. It was a welcome break from the everyday march of the wagon train.

At the busy trading post Daniel traded or bought coffee, bacon, flour, beans, rice, and molasses. He complained to Mr. Boudreaux

that one dollar a pint for flour was outrageous. Boudreaux replied
that it was expensive to ship into the wilderness. He should feel lucky,
as there were supplies to be bought, instead of the empty storehouse
of a few weeks ago. Del bought an apple, the first fresh fruit he had
eaten in weeks and found it delicious. Tucker and he wanted to trade
with the Indians for a buckskin shirt and leggin's. Riodan paid them
as he would any teamster, so both he and Tucker had money burning
in their pockets.

Tucker was delighted with the store, buying some peppermint
sticks, another hat and some boots. His old shoes were in terrible
shape. They had come three hundred and fifty miles from Grand Isle
to Ft. John walking almost every step. Ft. Bridger was the next place
to resupply and nearly four hundred miles through the mountains.
All of them would need new clothes.

They heard some fresh news. The fort had sent six hundred bales
of furs to Ft. Pierre. California was fighting with Mexico. California
wanted self-rule and there was much speculation over who would be
the new governor. There had been Indian trouble with other trains,
stock stolen, men shot. A lot of people from trains were sick with
headaches and nausea. They called it mountain fever.

More and more wagons were taking the south pass, then going
south down the Green River to Ft. Bridger. It was a longer route to
Oregon but offered better grass and water than the short cut which
traversed fifty miles of desert, cutting three to four days of travel but
without water. Some chose it. Many died or were bushwhacked. Most
went to Ft. Bridger.

The next morning dawned cold but clear. The air smelled fresh
when the men rolled out of their blankets. Tucker and Del went to
the Indian camp to see if they could trade for buckskins. Daniel had
brought knives, hatchets, mirrors, beads, hammers, and cooking
pots to trade. Del carried a dozen eggs he had been saving. They
came back with shirts, pants, jackets, beaded belts and several pair
of moccasins.

Repairs took up the next few days. They moved the stock to fresh
grass regularly. Daniel met with Captain Nightingale, along with the
scouts from the fort to decide which route they would be taking the

next few days. The land along the Platte was rough and irregular north of the fort. They needed to find a smoother, more manageable route, further to the west that was easier travel for the wagons and for the animals. Del and Tucker wanted to go hunting to lay in a store of dried meat for the journey.

Raj rolled in the dust contentedly taking it easy. Star came up and nuzzled Del's back, so he decided to take her. Tucker mounted his buckskin pony, Rocky. They decided on heading southwest across the Laramie River, in hopes of finding buffalo on the grasslands to the south. They did not expect to be gone for more than two or three days. It was to be a fast hunt because they wanted to keep to Nightingale's plan of starting again in five days, depending on repairs and the weather.

Both had hunted on the trip, bringing in whatever small game could be found. Neither had killed a buffalo. That would be meat for them and the Kincaids. As they rode away from the Laramie River, Tucker stopped and looked over his shoulder behind them, so he could remember landmarks.

"Uh-oh, looks like we got us a visitor."

Bart rode up on his pony, with a half-moon grin. "Ma said I should go with you 'cause I gotta learn, too. I've got a gun. It was Pa's." Bart held up his rifle. Del looked at Tucker, then back at the boy.

"You know, Bart, we should have thought to ask you earlier.... You got grub and blankets? A canteen?" He waved back at Nancy, who was standing by the river, hands pressed together in a silent prayer. She returned the wave and continued waving, until they were out of sight.

"Yup. I got 'em. Ma packed everything I would need. I can shoot, too."

"Okay. Here's the rules. You listen to me and Tucker when we're out here. Always stay to our side and behind or in front of the man you're riding with. Watch where your rifle is pointing. Don't ever get out of our sight unless we put you some place. Then stay put. We got to know where you are. All right? You savvy me?" Savvy was the new word they had picked up at the fort.

"All right. I savvy."

"Ride between us." Tucker moved his pony off to the right. "We'll ride fast, so keep up."

The three rode at a steady pace looking for buffalo, each carrying their rifles at the ready in front of them. They found no game of any size that day. When they camped for the night, Tucker shot a porcupine as it was starting to climb a pine tree. "I wonder if the Sioux would trade for the quills." Tucker said. "I saw they used them in their decorative work." He rolled the hide, skin side out and carefully placed it in a rawhide bag. Even then, he still got painfully sharp quills stuck in his fingers. "Porcupine is good meat but as dangerous as if it were alive," he said, grumbling as he sucked on his wounded fingers. They made a stew of porcupine, potatoes, and turnips for their supper. They camped on the ridge of a bluff above any trail that may have traversed the plains below. They found a spring pooled in a small coulee maybe four or five feet across and set up camp.

Bart returned after picketing the horses. "They seem happy. It is fresh out here and the grass is tender below the spring. Do you think we'll find buffalo tomorrow, Del?" Tucker offered him a plate of stew and a chunk of bannock.

"I don't know. Buffalo come and go a lot like Indians. We haven't cut any tracks and haven't seen any dust from a large herd, so all we can do is look. Tuck, you want first watch? Bart goes next, and I'll take the last. You'll be all right, Bart?"

"Sure, I take watch at camp. Took my pa's place on the watch list. I'm good. I'll wake you if I get sleepy," he replied looking up from his plate with his mouth full.

"Okay. See you in the morning." Del rolled over in his blankets.

Tucker found a quiet spot away from the fire, so the light wouldn't affect his vision. He could see around the camp, and he set himself listening to the regular sounds in the night. He woke Bart about one in the morning and showed him where to sit. "Come get us if you hear or see anything. Be quiet and alert."

A hand covered Del's mouth and shook his shoulder. Del woke looking into a wide-eyed Bart who had his finger to his mouth. "Shh! Something's after the horses."

Del rolled over to wake Tucker, but he was already quietly pulling on his boots. "Lead the way, Bart."

They crept close to where the horses were picketed. It was a clear night with a waxing moon.

Bart pointed toward the horses. They were agitated and straining against their tether pins.

"Stay here!" Del moved silently along the rocks. He could see a hand trying to release the nearest pin. Del whistled low. The face looked up. Del swung his rifle from the barrel and brought the butt up across the side of the surprised Indian's head. A rifle blasted from behind him. Soft clad feet raced away, dragging their fallen comrade with them.

"Paiute," muttered Tucker. "The Sioux said they were raiding in the vicinity. You never know where they is. Missed him too!" he said. "Everybody okay?"

"Yep," said Bart.

"I'm okay," replied Del, "but I gave somebody a headache. No more sleep for us. We have to move on."

They gathered the horses before breaking camp and kept close to the small fire Tucker had made to warm up the coffee pot. They ate some left-over bannock and the rest of the stew with their coffee then saddled up and moved on.

"It'll be dawn in a few hours," Tucker said. "Which way do you want to go, Del?"

"I think we go down and across the grass, skirting the trees, keeping to the shadows. We'll see them if they come after us. Bart, shoot if you have to. Make sure of your field of fire. Tuck, lead the way, my friend."

Tucker only smiled nervously. Bart's face was white and his hands a bit shaky. He hoped the other men couldn't hear his heart pounding.

Tucker stayed close to the treeline as they left their ridge walking the horses. They kept to the shadows in the dark of the predawn, making as little sound as possible. They heard no one following. Once they had moved over a rise heading west, they mounted and broke into a trot, pulling up in a copse of trees bordered by a loud babbling stream.

Tucker said, "We can't stay here. It's too noisy. We can't hear anything, but we can check our back trail, and if we keep to the stream, it will cover any noise we make."

They saw no one. Nothing appeared to be following them. They elected to turn upstream, hoping the water would clear away any tracks or silt stirred up by the horses. Indians expected the white man to go down stream. Ben had taught Del that, if the Indians had been on their trail, they would have gone downstream with the current.

Dawn found them stretched out on their stomachs, heads looking out over a high bank of the same winding stream as they checked their back trail. Their horses were well hidden, tied in some cottonwoods. The stream had broadened and snaked around cutting deeply through the prairie. Their little band faced directly downstream where they had a good field of vision. If the Indians were following, the men would see them.

If they were followed, Del intended to pick the field of battle. They must surprise them when they did not expect it. The bank was about eight feet tall, so they could move about unseen behind it. Del looked ahead. Tucker lay to his right. Bart was below, watching upstream. They spelled each other so two were watching and one resting. Bart had sharp eyes.

"Can you load quickly?" Del asked when it was time for Bart to spell him.

"I'm okay. I can load as good as anybody." He crawled up to where Del was lying and picked a stem of grass to chew on as he looked back the way they had come. Squinting his eyes, he shielded them with one hand before whispering, "Over there. Lord, is that Indians?"

About three hundred yards back, came riders on their ponies walking in the streambed with an Indian on each side of the stream searching for sign and leading their ponies. They advanced slowly. Del estimated it to be about ten o'clock. The sun was hot, though the earth of the bank still felt cool. Sweat began to glisten on his forehead. His pulse increased, throbbing in his temple. Tucker and Bart had never killed anyone in a gun battle. Neither had anyone shot back at them. He tried to remember what Ben had told him about a trick the Indians used.

There were three mounted ponies in the stream along with one on each bank, five warriors altogether.

"Bart, go get my pistols off my saddle. I want them for close up. Keep quiet." When Bart came back, Del said, "I remember Ben telling me that, as they get close, one will fall down and then another one jumps up. Then the first one on the ground jumps up, moving closer, making it confusing who to shoot at. So, let's do this, we all fire our rifles, the first round. Maybe we'll be lucky and get one or two. I'll cover you two with the Howdahs, while you load all three rifles. Next, Tucker and I will shoot, while Bart loads the Howdahs. Tucker, you watch where the first Indian falls and keep your aim on him. When the next Indian jumps up, I'll shoot at him. Only shoot when your Injun makes his move. Bart will cover us, as we reload. We also have our Patersons. We should keep them busy. What do you think?"

"Sounds good to me, if Ben says that's what they'll do," said Tucker.

"Me, too, I reckon," replied Bart.

"Here they come. Keep your barrels in the grass so they don't catch the sun. Tuck, give the word at a hundred yards."

"Will do." Tucker reached over and put his hand on Bart's back. It was soaked through with sweat. "You okay, boy? You're going to do fine. Just fire, duck and reload. It'll come to you. When the firing begins, stop thinking about the gunfire overhead and just do it."

"That's right." Del smiled at the boy. Maybe it was a mistake to have brought Bart. He did not want to tell Nancy she had lost a son, too!

"Okay, I got it. Fire, duck, reload, over and over again. I can do it."

"One more thing. Look at me, boy. If Tuck and I tell you to go, you go without question. Savvy? You hightail it! Grab Star and ride for the fort. She's the swiftest. You understand? A word from either one of us and you skedaddle. No question. Give me your word. Good. Take the Howdahs with you when you go. Give them to Pa for me. All right?"

"All right."

"But first, Bart, ole bean, we're going to dust us some horse-stealin' Injuns. Right?"

"Yes, sir." The boy gave him a nervous smile. "I got the one on the right bank."

"I got the one on the left," said Tucker.

"Why, gentlemen, you leave me with the ones in the middle, I suppose," said Del with a feigned lilt in his voice. "Here they come."

The men lay on the top of the bluff, shielded by grass. Their weapons were laid out before them as they sighted down the barrels. In the still air, the sun burnt the backs of their necks and shoulders. Sweat dripped down their temples and wetted their shirts. Time passed slowly.

"Center on their chests," whispered Del as they drew near.

Bart licked his lips, trying hard not to think about what was about to happen.

Tucker snugged the butt of the rifle into his shoulder. "Steady, steady.... *Fire!*"

Out of the first volley of fire, they felled two men. Time sped up. Tucker and Bart dropped to reload. Del fired two shots with the How-dahs, missing both shots. The rifles came back up. Indian ponies scattered off to their right side, out of sight. They waited. It was quiet. The wind rustled the grasses and blew their hair with a welcome breeze. It was a beautiful day, the sky a bright blue with skidding clouds. Sunbeams flashed in their eyes, and they had to shield them with one hand to focus. Then the Indians came at a full gallop to kill them, yipping and screaming, their faces contorted by paint and hate.

Del fired several shots with the Paterson. One Indian dropped off his pony.

Tucker took him. "I'm on him."

Del fired again.

"I'm on that one," said Bart.

Taking up his rifle, Del said, "I'll fire at the next one that moves, the others should jump up." He shot.

Two shots went off almost immediately.

"Mine went down," said Tucker.

"I'm not sure, but I think I nicked him," said Bart.

The Indians disappeared. Only one of the ponies kept coming along the stream bed between the steep banks. There was no rider.

"Maybe the pony was wounded. Reload. Reload," said Del. "I'll keep watch."

The pony continued coming, his hooves clomping like sharp metal in the dry rocks of the stream bed. Del could just see his head as he followed the winding stream. The pony's head went out of sight as it rounded the bank and only the sound of its hooves on the stones could be heard.

Del reloaded his pistol as he watched for the pony. He laid his Howdahs on the bank in front of him. His guts churned. He turned to face where he knew the pony would appear. A quail call sounded. Two Indians suddenly attacked on their right. Tucker and Bart fired. One horse went down. His rider was rescued by the other rider, pulled up across the front of his pony and they rode off.

The walking pony's head came around the bend. With a scream, a Paiute jumped from behind the pony and stabbed down at Del. He ducked under the blow, dropping his gun and the Indian somersaulted over Del's head. He started to turn as the Indian leaped up, swinging his knife low for Del's belly. Del blocked the knife with his arm and fell away. The Indian sprang on Del, raising his knife.

Boom!

Tucker stood transfixed, a Howdah smoking in his hand, and a look of surprise in his eyes, "I didn't know what else to do. I've never shot at anyone so close by."

It was over. The Indians disappeared and didn't return.

Tucker let out a long breath. "It's different when you can see the look on their face. A hundred yards away, they're just another target."

They left the dead warrior where he lay, feeling the others would come back for him. Del had a cut across his elbow that had sliced through his new buckskins. Tucker wrapped it tightly. "Let's get out of here before they decide to come back and bring more of their friends. I'll dress that better, once we're in camp." They rode toward Ft. John until they stopped for the night.

Tucker made a quick fire. He warmed some jerky and biscuits over the fire, boiled some water for coffee and for cleaning Del's wound. He covered the wound with fresh-crushed sage and bound it. When he finished with Del, they left that fire burning and moved their camp up in a dry wash over a mile away. They would sleep near their horses. Del had brought along the dead warrior's pony. He would use it to trade back at the fort, or maybe he would give it to his pa. It would be something to have from their failed hunt at least. They fell asleep exhausted. Del woke in the night, pulled on his boots and walked about checking the horses.

Tucker spoke out of the darkness. "I slept pretty good for a while, but I can't sleep a wink now."

"I know. Me, too. Bart made us proud of him today, didn't he?"

"Yes, he did. We all did. I've never killed anybody with a gun before today. I feel different. Did that happen to you?"

"Yes, I was different. I didn't want to kill those men, but they had Nancy, and I had no choice. I don't regret it. It made me confident knowing I would do the right thing when the time came. How about you?"

"Yeah, I think so, too. I know I can do what needs to be done when the time comes again to me. I'm okay, I think. Suppose every man wonders about it when it comes down to kill or be killed."

Without speaking any further, they sat on the rocks and watched the sunrise exploding over the horizon and burning the shadows away. A breeze blew up into the rocks, and the sun warmed the grassland below them.

Breaking camp, they looked forward to returning to their families. Bart was busting to tell of the battle. They rode with their rifles in front of them, sitting erect and alert in their saddles. Del's Howdahs nestled in their holsters. His Paterson revolver he kept tucked tight against his belly. The hard steel afforded a feeling of security that was comforting. Their eyes scanned everything in their field of vision with a new awareness they had not had at the beginning of their hunt.

They had just crested a rise close to the Laramie River, when Bart said, "I bet I can beat you all to the river!" He kicked the flanks of his painted pony.

"Bart, wait!" The men said loudly, both surprised.

Tucker grinned. "Well, you can't blame him for wanting to get back to his mama's cooking."

"You know, me, too," Del said. "I hope she cooks for all of us tonight. Apple pie sure sounds appetizing, don't it?" Bart had ridden out of sight.

A shot roared through the valley.

Del and Tucker looked at each other in fear.

"Oh, no. What now?" They took off at a full gallop.

They found Bart, bent over a cow elk near the river, knife in hand, getting ready to cut her neck to bleed her out.

"What's the matter with you fellas? Haven't you ever seen an elk before?" He grinned. "She was the last one in line, walking along the river heading toward the bluff. I took a shot at her. She fell with my first shot. See the others!" He pointed toward the ridge above the river, where a line of elk made their way up the bluffs to safety.

21

ACK AT CAMP, BOTH FAMILIES greeted them with happy welcomes. Tucker redressed Del's arm and saw it was healing unevenly. "It should be fine in a few days, but I want to put a few stitches in those deeper areas. Keep it clean. Don't use it much for a few days." Tucker threaded a needle with black thread. "Daniel, hold his arm, this is going to hurt."

Bart had become the hero, bringing in fresh meat for both camps. Building a drying rack, they worked quickly to dry and smoke the elk. Dan showed Bart how to scrape and tan the hide. They had to work quickly as Captain Nightingale was eager to get back on the trail in three days.

Del gave the Paiute pony to his surprised father. They all had dinner at the Kincaids' that night, broiling fresh elk steaks over the coals. Nancy had finally decided to leave some of her furniture. She couldn't find anyone on the train, who wanted her chifforobe or her mother's table. With much regret, but resigned, she watched Bart and Nate unload them. "They will be someone's campfire when we leave," she said. Others in the train were dumping their furniture as well. The women smiled at each other tearfully, touching a shoulder or a hand sympathetically as they moved past each other and went back to getting ready to make way.

Mr. Boudreaux took an interest in the table and bartered Nancy a bolt of blue linen and one of calico. "You know, after you leave and the Sioux pick out the items that interest them, we will have a huge bonfire. We have one two or three times a year to burn up the furniture everyone leaves." He left with the table and paid her for some fresh milk and butter. "I will have the butter on fresh bread tonight, mais oui! I have missed it. Lard is not the same, even with salt. *Merci!*"

Other trains moved in, mostly Mormon trains and militia. A lot of them had sickness with the mountain fever that many seemed to get when they started reaching the higher elevations. One of their leaders, a serious man by the name of Young, had spoken with Mr. Boudreaux and the masters of the other wagons. Boudreaux would not trade with them for some reason but remained friendly and shared news and information with Mr. Young on Indians and best routes to take. All safe roads going north still led through the South Pass.

Captain Nightingale called a camp meeting the second night, after the hunters had returned. He stood on a plank laid across two barrels. "We leave at first light. Make your preparations. We follow the Sweetwater to its headwaters and through the pass until we strike the Green River and then southwest toward Fort Bridger at Black Forks. Don't expect much. It is little more than a few shacks surrounded by a wall. Hopefully, they will have supplies. The water should be good there. We're in high desert country, so conserve your water. The Sweetwater usualy has good water. We'll camp one day there to refresh and give everyone a wash day. We will soon reach Mexican Hill. It is a steep decline. We'll have to hitch teams to the back of wagons to act as drags, as we lower them down the other side.

"At Fort Bridger, some of you will head south to California. The rest of us turn north to Oregon. If you haven't heard, John C. Fremont, the explorer, has just been appointed the governor of California. News came in this morning. It is four hundred miles from here to Fort Bridger. That's about how many miles we've come so far. We'll be at Independence Rock in a few weeks. The way from here is long, hard, and steep. We have no guarantee that Fort Bridger will be able to re-supply us. We'll send out hunting parties to hunt, as we've done in the past, but it's mountains we're in, so game will be scarce.

Be sparing with your supplies. Don't waste anything. Chew once and pass it along, so to speak. Be warned.

"You'll hear the bugle in the morning. Keep to your divisions. Make sure you have everyone. We're a party of thirty-two wagons, one hundred and forty-five people, over five hundred head of oxen, cattle, mules, horses, and a couple dozen chickens." The crowd laughed. "Stay together. Keep your eyes and ears open. The Indians have been raiding, as you have all heard. Keep your wits about you. Good luck on the trail. Reverend Blaine, will you say a few words of prayer?"

———————————

DANIEL'S DIVISION LED THEM OUT in the morning. "I'm sad to leave this place," he said to Del and Tucker over coffee in the morning. "I liked sleeping late." He smiled. "How's the arm, son?"

"Pretty good. Stiff when I use it, but Tucker's ointment is working. The stitches pull, but it didn't fester. I'll be good. I'll miss this place, too. It's the longest I've stayed anywhere since Independence."

"That's for sure. It's been good for the stock, too. From here to the Willamette Valley, it's mountains and high desert. It'll be dry. I hadn't thanked you for the pony. It's good to have two mounts. I'm thinking of calling him Laramie."

"I like that fine, Pa."

Captain Nightingale pulled up. "Daniel, you ready?"

"As ready as I can be, Cap'n." The three finished their coffee, dumped the remainder into the fire and tossed their cups into their nearest wagon.

"Okay, boys. Head 'em out! Wagons, ho! Wagons, ho." Captain Nightingale sent the word back. *Wagons, ho* echoed along the train. Twenty-seven wagons headed north. The rest joined the meandering line traveling south.

Whips snapped, wheels creaked, dogs ran barking at the heels of the oxen, excited to be moving again. Slowly, the fort on the Laramie vanished from sight.

They climbed higher still. They crossed rolling hills covered in grass, rushing deep-cut mountain streams instead of the lazy meandering creeks they had passed on the flat lands. This land boasted dryer air. Captain Nightingale stopped more often to water the stock. They traveled miles west of the Platte due to the steep hills and valleys of the Wyoming badlands that would make travel impossible.

At the fire that night, Daniel said, "I named my pony Laramie because of a story I heard at the fort. The Laramie River was named for a French trapper, Jacque La Ramie. He got lost from camp, and the rest of his party found him as part of a beaver dam the next spring. He was shot full of arrows. So, they called it La Ramie's River. Not the way I want people to remember me. After what happened back there, it seemed like a good name for the pony."

Mexican Hill should have been called Mexican Hell. This was a slope so steep they had to tie the wheel brakes tight and throw water on them to keep them from catching on fire. Ben ordered them to hitch two teams to the back of each wagon and walk them down the hill. It was slow heavy work repeated twenty-seven times that day, switching teams often. They lost a few wheels and broke an axle. Working all night, the men repaired the wagons and were ready to roll the next morning.

The hot, dry vistas stretched for miles. Rocks crunched under the iron rims sounding like flint. Men and women sweated and pushed their wagons up the inclines as their animals strained to pull each wagon over one hill and strained to keep from being run over as they went down another. The lush prairies of Missouri seemed far away. They turned west at the Sweetwater River, well named, for the water indeed, tasted fresh and sweet.

Del daydreamed, remembering all the sights they had seen thus far that had been named for some feature or where someone had died—Scott's Butte, Chimney Rock, Court House Rock, and Ft. Laramie. Independence Rock was probably the most famous of all. They would be there in a few days. Del had seen a blue haze on the horizon in the west one morning. He asked Ben if a storm was brewing.

"Them there is the Rocky Mountains I've been telling you about. They look like giant castles in the air. This is still eastern Wyoming, still mostly low bluffs and prairie. We're moving higher. The nights are colder. Grass is holding out pretty good still. You'll see the mountains in western Wyoming soon. Then you'll know why the South Pass is so important."

Del realized that these were not at all like the Appalachian Mountains. Not even remotely.

The train pulled into Independence Rock, Wyoming, on July 5, 1847. It was a welcome sight. A small camp had built up around the base of the rock. The Rock was just a big smooth granite rock sticking out of the desert, about one hundred feet high. It was carved with the names of the men and women who had passed here. For a fee, a man would chisel your name into the rock.

Ben came fuming into their camp. "Daniel! Do you have a snort of something? I need a drink of some liquor!"

"Why, Ben, what's wrong?"

"I was here with Fremont in the thirties well before this trail was much of a trail. He had carved a beautiful Maltese cross into the stone to commemorate our time getting there safely. Some idiot has blasted it off the face of the rock because they thought it was a pagan symbol and not Christian. Dad-blamed idiots!"

Daniel handed him a bottle. "That's a shame. People are pretty thoughtless at times."

"That's why I keep to the mountains. Some place that makes sense!" He took his drink and passed it back. "Thanks. I needed that. Just made me mad. Ignorance and stupidity is the downfall of all people, I guess. That and a swelled head." He mounted his horse and rode away.

Del and Tucker were not to be swayed. They wanted their names carved on the rock, too. They had to talk Daniel into letting them put his name up there with theirs. A surly fellow carved *Daniel Riodan, Delaino Riodan, and Tucker, 1847,* for the princely fee of five dollars each. They wanted it cut deep, so it would last.

"I'll come back this way sometime," said Tucker. "I want to see my name there, just like it is, now and forever."

They moved on the next day through the Devil's Gate and on to the South Pass before turning south to the Green River and Ft.

Bridger. The Rockies grew larger by the mile. Del stared in amazement at the ridges rising above the clouds. "You'd have to fly like a bird to get over them."

It grew still dryer. They had no rain, cold at night, hot and sweaty during the day. Del noticed that Tuck was losing weight, getting leaner. He must have lost thirty pounds so far. Daniel was the same. He didn't have the extra pounds Tucker had lost, but he grew leaner and stronger as well. They learned to put bear grease or axle grease on their lips to keep them from drying out and cracking.

Del had to cinch his pants much tighter the last few weeks. His shirts and his hat were roomier. I'll have to wear my long johns just to keep my pants up.

One of the wagons broke a wheel crossing a sharply cut bank. The train lost a day stopping to fix it. A party of hunters went out for meat. Daniel set up his forge to heat the iron hoop and put it back on the wheel.

Tucker rode with the hunting party. Daniel and Del were mounting the iron rim of the wheel back on the wagon when the hunting party returned. Tucker had shot a grizzly!

"Yes, sir, ol' Tuck saved my bacon." Olly Nordstrom said boastfully. "That bear charged out of the alders. My horse reared, and I fell off. I missed my shot, and I was standing there, nose to nose with Mister Grizzly with only my knife in my hand when Tucker trots up and shoots him right in the eye. Bears have mighty bad breath, by the way. Tuck, I'm going to help make a coat of that skin for you. Keep you warm this winter."

Riding up to check on the repairs, Ben eyed the meat the men had packed back in the grizzly skin.

"That'll be good meat for everybody. Them grizzly's is tough to kill. I remember once when I was younger by a few years, back on the Green River it was. Had a big ol' grizzly charge out of the rocks, spooked my horse who throwed me and run off. There I was, toe to toe with this here grizzly when he took wind of me. I'd been on the trail without no bath for about a month. Well, he took a big whiff of ol' Ben ... and he turned and run off. Guess I smelled worse than he did!"

Daniel and Tucker looked at each other in wonder and said in unison, "Well, I guess so!" Ben did a double take. "Ah, you fellas, always joshin' me!"

The men laughed. Finishing the repairs, they fitted the rim to the wheel, greased it up, turned the bolt on the axle and were ready to go.

Captain Nightingale said to the leaders, "Bridger's fort is about fifteen miles from here, so we're not going to stop until we reach it. Trail is wide, good water and grass is fair. None of those narrow passes we been dealing with. We'll rest there for a few days and then head north through the Idaho country and on into Oregon. We're getting closer. Finish up and keep moving."

22

A DONIS SAT ON A LOG roasting an onion on the end of a long stick over a dim and smokey fire. He looked up under the brim of his hat as a line of riders snaked out of the forest and rode around him and his fire. They were white. He stared at them, then turned his attention to the blistering of his onion. He cut off some of the outer layers of onion and stuffed it in his mouth huffing on it to cool it enough to swallow. "You boys lost? Hungry? I got more onions." He returned the stick to the fire and continued roasting his dinner.

"We're trying to figure out if you got anything we might want. Not partial to onions myself unless they's cooked in with some greens and some fatback." The talker stopped just short of Adonis's back. "Hey, I'm a-talkin' to you." He jabbed Adonis's back with his rifle.

With a great roar, Adonis rose and pulled the man from his horse, swirled him over his head and threw the screaming talker into the fire. Picking up the man's rifle, he struck the man a blow to the side of his head with the butt of the gun. He flipped it back into his hands and cocked the rifle, then stepped back so he could see across the fire, aiming it at the rest of the surprised riders. "Who's next? Any of you tinhorns got anything else you want to say? Where'd you come from, anyways? You're all Easterners. You smell like you're from the East. You ride like you're from the East. I heard you coming a mile away. Why ain't you boys dead? The Injuns will kill you soon enough if I don't do it first."

"Whoa, hold on there, fella. We was only playin'. Let us pull our man out of the fire there, and we'll give you some grub. We got coffee, too, and some canned peaches. How about it? Waylon, pull Benny out of the fire, 'fore he burns up. I think you knocked him colder than a codfish, mister. Mind if we light? Can't get into these saddlebags less'n we get off first."

"Damn greenhorns. Get your man, and you'd better have some coffee. I ain't had no coffee since I left the wagon train."

"Wagon train?" Beaux queried.

"Yeah, I got run off from a damn train for watching the women taking a bath in the river. Not like I hurt anybody. They never wanted me around."

"What was that like? Did ya or didn't ya watch the women?" Waylon drug Benny off to one side and used his hat to slap the embers from his coat, finally rolling him on the ground until he stopped smoking.

"I ain't saying one way or another. Got a rash of buckshot and nails in my shoulder, and I run off from the train before they could accuse me. Damn kid got in my way. I hope he smashed his head on a rock. Him and his damn horse."

"Kid with a horse, you say? Tell me about him." Beaux offered the man a cheroot and lit it for him by striking a match across his trousers.

"Him, his old man, and runaway slave has been making trouble for me ever since Independence. One of these days I'm going to get my hands around their necks, and I'm going to squeeze and squeeze until their eyes pop out of their heads. They'll be sorry they ever laid eyes on ol' Adonis."

"And you know where this wagon train is headed?" Beaux smiled and poured coffee into a pot of water. "How would you like to join us? We eat regular, and we have stayed shy of the Indians so far. Maybe you could show us greenhorns how to do better out in the west."

"Conlon, it ain't your place to say who gets to join up with us."

"I say it is, Marty. You been leading this band since Illinois. You didn't have anything to show for it until you met up with me, and I saved your scroungy hides. I showed you how to bushwhack those Mormons on the trail and play friendly to the lost and stranded, until we cut their throats and took their goods. You wouldn't be anywhere if not for me. I say he stays." Beaux pulled his gun and stared Marty down. "Any argument from anybody else?"

No one said a word.

"How about me?" Adonis asked. "Ain't I got a say in this after all? Who the hell are you in the first place?"

"I'm the kid's uncle and that slave used to belong to me. I'm wanting you to help me find them, and you can kill the daddy, but the kid and slave belong to me. I've been after them ever since Delaino stole that horse and ran away. I'm going to kill him and go back to living like a civilized man. You in or out?"

"I get Daniel Riodan all to myself?"

"I'll put him on a platter for you, any way you want."

"I'm in. Anybody want to say different?" He leveled his rifle at Marty. "How about you?"

No one spoke.

"Well then, I'm mighty hungry. Where's dem peaches. Anybody got any jerky? I ain't had no meat in three days. All I've had is onions."

23

SHIMMERING IN THE MOONLIGHT, THE Green River rolled swells over fallen trees and slipped over ancient worn rocks splashing its song as the train wound its way to Black Fork and Bridger's Fort to settle in for the night.

Daniel glared at his pocket watch. "If I'm correct, I make it to be about ten o'clock. We've been on the road a long time. You two take care of the wagons and stock. I gotta go with Nightingale and Ben to pay our respects to the fort."

They circled the wagons about a half mile above the fort. On the other side of the river was an Indian village. Fires and smoke hazily outlined the teepees against the distant black horizon and looming mountain range. Their dogs barked, warning the village of the intruders as the weary travelers circled their wagons, preparing for the night.

Tucker and Del put things in order at the camp, started a fire and put on the coffee pot.

Tucker moved a plate of day-old biscuits closer to the fire. "Grass don't look too good where we left the stock."

"Yeah, I saw that. Hope we can find better tomorrow, else we'll have to keep moving them every day. It's been hot and dry, that's for sure." Del spread some gooseberry jam on a biscuit. "Miz Wilson gave me this jam when I traded her some of that dried meat we had.

She said she had brought it all the way from New York. It's pretty good. Have some, Tuck. There's eggs, too."

"Don't mind if I do."

Daniel rode in. "Well, we're all set. They have some supplies, nothing fancy, just basic goods and such. They're expecting a mule train of supplies in another two weeks or so, Mister Bridger said. Cap'n wants to make up for lost time. He'll let the stock rest for three days and then we'll head north. So, we make repairs and hunt if we want. How's our provisions, Tuck?"

"We're pretty good. We're low on coffee, lard, and sugar. Though, we do have plenty of bear fat and dried meat. Not as nice smelling as lard, but it'll do in a pinch. I think we should top off the flour, salt and coffee. It'd be nice if they had some dried fruit to sell. Powder, lead, caps, we're in good shape there." He sipped at the coffee cup he held in both hands, studying their wagons. "Could use some grain for the stock. Harnesses and buckles, straps seem to be doing all right. Stock is tired and hungry. Grazing is dry and not much of it. There's bear meat and biscuits warming by the fire and Del has a few eggs he can throw in a skillet. Sit. Eat."

Morning grew light, cool, and clear. Accustomed to train time, everyone was up, breakfasted and starting the activities of a busy wagon train. The women concentrated on the washing of bodies and clothes. The men saw to their stock, moved them to a better meadow downstream, where the grass was sweet and tender, across the river from the large pony herd of the Shoshone.

Del walked down to the trading post to look around. He wanted to eavesdrop on any talk or gossip he might hear. News was always welcome.

Bridger's Fort wasn't much, just a long low-built cabin that served as store with stables and corrals. A stone wall looked like it was still under construction. Bridger kept good relations with the Indians, trading furs for pots, cups, knives, blankets, and other things the Indians wanted. They would come and camp, trade, and move on.

Some of the men sitting around the tables talked about playing baseball. It was a new game that had started back east and was starting to catch on across the country.

Del had seen a game once, back in Baltimore. It looked like fun, but he'd never played. He'd loved seeing the ball hit in a high arch into the outer fields with the players running the ball down and making impossible catches and throws. The banter between the players sparked excitement. His favorite part was when the managers ran onto the field to argue a call by the umpires, or when the teams batted the ball to the far outfield.

Arguing commenced between those at the tables over a discussion of the rules and how it should be played. Someone waved a book of baseball rules about and a fight almost ensued, until they decided to pick two teams and see who won. Somebody had a ball and a glove. A stout stick about two inches across and thirty inches long served as a bat.

A swell of excitement moved through the camp. A baseball game! Most of them had never seen a game, but had heard of it. The crowd grew, as men and boys wanted to join in. The women and kids sought a shady spot to sit and watch.

Two captains were chosen. Captain Nightingale was to umpire behind the base. Ben got elected to umpire at second base and call plays at the bases from there. They chose a level field, measured base paths and laid out the boundaries from a pamphlet of rules. Both Ben and Umpire Nightingale studied the rules intently.

The dimensions of the baseball diamond were laid out with care and arguing, until both captains were satisfied it was a proper field. The men chose sides of twelve players each. Men found rocks the size and weight of the rubber ball to practice catching and throwing to each other. Captain Nightingale kept the only ball and read the rules to each team.

"It's three strikes at the ball and you're an out," he said. "I decide if it's a strike or a ball, depending on whether the ball is thrown across the base or outside of it. If the pitcher throws four balls, the batter gets to proceed to first base. Ben calls outs on the field. If you're tagged with the ball before you get to your base, you're an out. You can't throw the ball at a man to make an out. The batsman tries to put the ball into play by hitting it into the playing field. The men on the bases, try to throw the batsman out before he reaches the next base.

The players in the field can get the batter out if they catch the ball in the air or on the first bounce."

"Ben, you understand how to call the plays in the field?"

"I think so, Cap'n. The man guarding the base must be touching it and have the ball in hand, if he tags a player running to that base. A batter can be tagged out on the baselines if the ball is in play. Otherwise, he must be touching his base. Right?"

"Right! I think so. He is out if tagged by a player who has control of the ball. We'll refer to this book on any disputes by the captains of the teams. All agreed?"

"Agreed." Both captains shook hands, and the teams sat on their assigned sides of the diamond.

There was so much enthusiasm for the game that Jim Bridger donated a keg of beer for the men and one of cider for the ladies. Families brought blankets and picnics to watch the game, most had never seen before. It was a welcome break from the everyday drudgery of the trail. They divided the teams between older men and younger men and traded friendly insults back and forth. Del was chosen to play with the younger men. He had only seen one game but was eager to try it, and the team captain assigned him to the right field because he could throw his rock the farthest. Each player in turn vigorously swung the stick around, imagining they were swinging at their precious hard rubber ball, hitting it high into the outfield. After this practice period, Umpire Nightingale finally produced the real thing.

Practicing with the actual ball now, the two teams faced each other and threw it back and forth to each other, until it was tossed from one end to the other and back again. Nightingale flipped a coin to see who the home team would be and who would defend the field. The other team was considered a visitor and was to bat first—a very polite game.

Del's team was the home team and would bat second. They were given their instructions by their captain, an Irishman by the name of Bobby O'Conner. He had seen the Knickerbockers play against the Boston Red Legs twice. The boys in his neighborhood played stickball in the streets instead of a field, so he was the most experienced person in the camp.

"If you can't catch it, at least knock the ball down and throw it to the fielder, who is standing ahead of the runner. Try to keep the ball in front of you. Before each batter hits, think where you want to throw the ball if it comes to you. Getting a man out at first is always a good option. You outfielders throw it to the closest basemen. I'll be yelling to you where to throw it next."

"Play ball, everyone!" Nightingale's voice boomed. "First batsman up! Stand over there, man, and watch where you're swinging that damn stick, will you?"

The catchers wore the only glove. Bobby pitched for Del's side. Del didn't know the other pitcher. He was one of the men from the fort who had been arguing about the game earlier, an older man with mutton chop whiskers down his cheeks. Women and children cheered for their husbands and sons. The Indians curiously watched from the third base side of the field. Del bent over intently watching the batter step up. What had they said at that ball game he had gone to? Oh, yeah! "Hey batsman, swing!" He yelled with the first pitch. That annoyed the other team when their batter swung at a ball thrown in the dirt.

They cast dirty looks Del's way.

"Boo! No fair, no fair!" They yelled. It delighted the rest of Del's team, though, who immediately took up the chant with each swing of the bat.

An agitated visiting team captain went out to talk to the umpire after his first three men swung at every ball, either over the base, over their heads, or bouncing across the plate. Neither umpire could find anything in the rule book against the other team shouting at the batsman to swing. So, it was allowed.

Bobby shot Del a grin, as Del trotted in from the field after the first three outs. "That's how to do it, me boy. Confuse 'em." He clapped Del across the shoulders. "Now, listen to me, all of you. It's hard to hit that ball. You keep your eye on the ball from the moment it leaves the pitcher's hand. Swing at anything about belly level, not over your head or on the ground. I bet we can walk some runs in. Swing fast and level. If you hit it, then run like the devil is after you to first base. Make sure you step on it and for God's sake, keep your foot on the base or they'll tag you out. Listen to me, and I'll yell what to do. I'll bat fourth. I'm the best hitter. If the pitcher hits you with the ball, turn and take your base. If it's deliberate, I'll hit one of their batters when I pitch next. It's only fair. They're going to yell their bloody heads off after that first inning. You can bet on that. Who wants to bat first?"

Lots of hands were raised. Bobby picked the youngest and shortest to bat the first two spots. Del next and Bobby fourth.

The visiting team had learned from the home team. They shouted and called for them to swing the bat and miss with every pitch.

"Miss it, stupid! Swing batter! Swing, you baby."

The first batter was ten-year-old Mickey Lambert. Biting his lip, he stared at the pitcher, not taking his eyes off the ball as it left the pitcher's hand. Poor Mickey was still staring at the ball as he stood there and the ball hit him squarely in the nose, right between his eyes.

Both sides erupted onto the field. The pitcher apologized to the bleeding boy, who stared triumphantly at the pitcher. A bright red lump forming on his forehead.

Bobby wiped Mickey's nose. "You be all right, Mick? Nothing broken. You're going to be all right but I think your mother just passed out on the sidelines over there!"

That brought a smile to Mickey's battered face.

"I'm okay, Bobby!"

When he was sure Mickey was all right, Nightingale whistled. "Batsman, take your base!"

Mickey ran to first and began sticking his tongue out at the pitcher each time he turned to look at first base. Everyone on the sidelines applauded as the little man stood his ground.

The Indians looked confused by the applause.

The visiting pitcher was afraid of hitting the next boy and he walked him on the first four pitches.

Home team had two men on base when Del came to bat. He was nervous and his hands sweated.

It can't be that hard, he thought as he watched the ball fly from the pitcher's hand.

"Strike one!"

Del couldn't believe it. He had barely enough time to get ready before the ball landed in the catcher's glove. The pitcher was not afraid of hitting him and went into his next delivery.

"Now!" He swung and hit it! The ball rolled back to the pitcher, and he promptly threw Del out. Crestfallen, he walked back to his side of the field. The little boys were now standing on second and third.

Bobby walked out to pick up the bat. He tripped and rolled over his ankle, falling to the turf. He grabbed his ankle, obviously in great pain. "Oh! Time, timeout."

"Timeout," said the umpire.

It seemed nothing was broken, so Bobby limped to the plate obviously in so much pain he could barely lift the bat, but he was going to tough it out.

The other team shifted as their captain shouted for them to move closer for a better play.

"Swing batsman! Swing!" The infielders chanted in unison. And swing he did. Bobby sent the ball over the outfielders' heads.

"Suckers!" He shouted gleefully as he rounded the bases, jumping on each one. His ankle had made a speedy recovery.

The little boys ran for home followed by an exhilarated Bobby O'Conner. The team boisterously congratulated their captain, their hero. Home team three, and visitors zero. The crowd applauded and shouted in the midday heat. Each team was inexperienced in the sport. Even Bobby had never pitched in a real game. Few could hit the ball. Sometimes a ball would soar into right field. Del would chase it down as it bounced around in the field before he could corral it and throw it back to the basemen. He didn't throw anyone out.

Indians on the side of the field ran down the line with him as he chased a ball, yelling encouragement and cheering all hits and plays for both sides.

One young Indian about Del's age ran faster than the others when they raced along the sidelines. He would stop and stare at Del quietly, arms crossed over his chest. Del nodded to him once after he had thrown the ball back to first. Nodding back, the young brave started clapping his hands joining the rest of the crowd on both sidelines.

Back and forth the game went. Most batters walked or were

hit by pitches. By the ninth inning, the players were tired, the keg was hot and close to empty, and the score was tied twenty-two to twenty-two.

Hitters were getting clever at hitting the ball as foul balls became more common. There were several hits an inning and a few balls had been thrown by the outfielders all the way to home plate. One throw had been called an out and the crowd had erupted into excited cheering. That bought the visitors' captain out to argue the call, but his argument was drowned in boos and catcalls from the onlookers.

Bobby was tired by the ninth inning and soon the bases were full.

Del had had a taste or two of the free hot beer. As he bent over in his stance, his shirt was soaked with sweat, his face red and his stomach churned. Wiping his face often to keep the stinging wetness out of his eyes, he was too tired to yell at the visiting team's batters.

Bases were still loaded with two outs when Tucker's turn at bat came up again. He had been hit, struck out twice and got on base when he hit a dauber in the dirt and outran the throw to first. Tucker batted left-handed. He swung the bat furiously back and forth and then stepped up to the plate, looking intently at Bobby. The crowd was still. They were hot and sweaty too. Only the Indians were moving about on the sidelines.

Crack! Tucker's level swing smacked the ball into right field. It surprised Del. He turned, stumbling over his own feet and fell on his face as the ball sailed over his head. A darting flash from the sidelines streaked onto the field and caught the ball in his bare hands. Yelling a war cry and waving the ball, the brave ran toward the bases and threw a lusty heave to home plate. His friends echoed the war cry, and the entire sideline of warriors erupted wildly dancing and whooping. The catcher caught the ball and tagged the runner out. The Indian section went wild again yelling and clapping, screaming defiant war cries and jumping around like crazy.

"You're *out!*" shouted the ump.

"*Safe!*" shouted Ben, as he raced to the home plate. Both teams erupted onto the field, shouting for their side. From ten-year-old Mickey to fifty-year-old Nightingale, the two teams argued back and forth.

Reaching out with his hand, the brave helped Del up.

Embarrassed, Del said, "Thank you. That was a good catch and throw." Then he attempted to make gestures to the brave, trying to explain what he had said. The boy obviously didn't speak English. He stared at Del with a passive look.

Boom!

Jim Bridger fired his shotgun into the air to get the attention of the still shouting throng.

Everyone turned to him.

"I declare this game a draw!" He pronounced and got up and marched back to his trading post.

"Well, I guess so!" said Ben.

That broke the anger and chaos. Shaking hands and pounding on each other's backs, the teams recounted the plays of the day and how each had been a hero in one inning or another.

"He was safe, you know. That Indian wasn't on a team!"

"Yeah, I know, but did you see that throw! What a beauty. What a catch!"

Joining their families on the sidelines, the teams went back to their tents and wagons, tired and strangely refreshed. Soon the field was empty, but for Del and the fleet footed, silent, Indian ball catcher.

Quietly, they walked back to home base. Del pointed to home base and made gestures like he was throwing and catching and pointing to the brave. He smiled and nodded, trying to convey to him what a good play he had made. Then his foot rolled on the bat lying on the ground. His feet flew up in the air and he landed flat on his back. He was humiliated for the second time in front of this Indian boy.

Reaching down to help this white boy to his feet once again, the brave broke into spasms of laughter, causing Del to laugh with him.

Del picked up the bat thinking to throw it away in anger, then thought better of it and presented it to the brave with a smile. Astonished, the young brave took it, staring at the bat in admiration. Del waved goodbye and ran off toward his wagons.

Del toweled off after cleaning up from the ball game by pouring a bucket of water over his head. His head was a little woozy still.

He swore he'd not drink hot beer ever again when Ben and Captain Nightingale rode up.

"What did you do?" queried Ben.

"Huh?"

"I asked what you did."

"You saw me. You was there. I just played baseball and drank some rank beer. Where were you?"

"I was there too, smarty pants. I mean after."

"Ben, I don't know what you're talking about. Did you drink that hot beer, too?" Del sat down in the shade of the wagon. "I think I need a nap."

"Well, get a good one. You've been asked to supper!"

"Would you mind saying what you're trying to say straight out? I'm tired and my brain is not following this conversation."

"He means," said Captain Nightingale, "that you've been invited to supper by one of the chiefs of the Shoshone. He's head shaman or their spiritual advisor. Big medicine in the tribe. This is an honor, Del."

"Well, holy cow. I didn't do anything."

"Did you give something to someone?"

"I gave that ol' bat to the fella that caught and threw that ball. It was a pretty throw. I did it kind of like a memento of the event. Something he could remember, sort of."

"That throw cost me a home run," Tucker grumbled. "And the game, for that matter."

"Well, boy. That young fella was the shaman's son," said Ben. "They felt you bestowed a great honor on their son."

"Ben, it was the stupid batting stick!"

"I know, but they'd never seen baseball before. Me, neither, come to think about it. They feel that bat and ball to be sacred elements of that game. They got caught up in it. Just like the white folks did."

"Look, Del," said Captain Nightingale, "to make a short story shorter, they considered what you did, giving the boy the batting stick, an honor. They want to thank you. So, they've invited you to their camp to be introduced. The chief is Standing Rock, and the son is Black Feather. Take a bath, wear clean clothes and try to look modest but not afraid. Be there about an hour before dark. I got all

of this from Jim Bridger who took the message himself from Standing Rock. Jim said this is a great privilege, and it's a chance to get to
know the Indians. Make friends with them. It's always good to be
introduced as a brother to the tribe. Black Feather is about your age."

"Okay, Cap'n. Do I take a gift or something to eat? Are there rules
I should know?" asked Del.

"You've already given a gift. Never give a gift so great the other
side could not reciprocate in like manner. It's rude to do so. They
may give you gifts tonight, so look pleased and honored. Oh, one
more thing... it's okay to belch after the meal. It shows you appreciated the food. I'll check with you tomorrow and see how you did.
Bridger will have heard as well. Good luck, son. Mind your manners.
Belch often. You'll be fine. See you tomorrow."

Ben turned to him and winked as they rode off.

"Well, if that don't beat all," said Del. "I'm to meet a real Indian
shaman. I *know* I need a nap now."

DEL APPROACHED THE CAMP SLOWLY with his eyes open
and his head on a swivel. He wasn't sure what he was getting into.
Torches and fires had been lit. A lot of activity bustled about the
camp as women and young girls prepared for the meal. Young boys
stared at him from small groups. People stepped to the side as he
rode through the midst of excitement and activity that permeated
the camp. He stopped in front of a group of serious-faced council
members. Unsure how to proceed, he simply sat, erect and alert. He
could see Black Feather standing behind this group. Del signaled Raj
to bow to the council.

This caused a stir among them as the men hesitated, talking
among themselves. Then Del backed Raj up and twirled him in a circle. He dismounted and smiled as he approached the group, nodding
to Black Feather, who smothered a smile in return.

One of the elders approached, his eyes searching the face of the young man before him. Then Raj shook his head with flowing mane and stepped forward to greet the elder. Surprised, the elder reached out and stroked the nose of this beautiful horse. Smiling, he said, "I am Standing Rock. You are welcome in our camp. We are honored you accepted our invitation. Our warriors wanted to meet you."

Del didn't know if he was supposed to shake hands or embrace this man in some way.

"It is I who am honored, Standing Rock. My name is Del Rio. The Shoshone are well known for their bravery and hospitality. This is Raj. He is my brother. We have traveled together from the great far eastern cities where the ocean meets the land. Black Feather showed how fleet of foot he is and how strong is his right arm. He deserved to have the baseball bat as a token of good will."

"Baseball bat? I did not know what to call it. Come, meet the elders of our tribe." He motioned for some of the braves to attend to Raj. "Don't worry, Raj has made a fine impression, as well. He will be well cared for."

Two small boys ran up and touched Del with a stick. Yelling their little war cries, they turned tail and ran back into the crowd who had gathered to meet him. Faint laughter erupted.

"Little Otter! Grey Owl! This is our guest. Mind your manners!" Standing Rock chided the children. "They are showing their bravery, Del. They just counted coup on you." He smiled.

Standing Rock introduced Del to the council and to his father, Grey Feather, who was chief. Black Feather approached and placed a necklace of bear claws around his neck.

"A token of friendship," said Black Feather with a serious face.

Del was astonished. "You speak English?"

"Of course. I have been around white eyes my whole life. I can speak French, too."

"So, why did I go through all of those ridiculous attempts at signing earlier today?"

"You had fallen down two times. I thought you were drunk." The two young men could not help but break out in laughter.

Standing Rock smiled at the two young men. "Come here, you two funny men. Let's eat." Standing Rock led the way to where the rest of the camp had gathered. Men sat in a ring around a large camp-fire. Del sat between Standing Rock and Black Feather. Grey Feather introduced Del Rio to everyone. Black Feather showed off his bat and Del praised the other boy for the good catch and throw.

Women began serving food to the men. A beautiful girl placed a bowl with roasted tongue and liver with a corn cake baked with acorns and onion in front of Del. She wore her hair braided in a thick braid and bound with a turquoise ribbon. She blushed, as Del couldn't take his eyes off her.

Black Feather nudged him."Stop staring, it's rude."

"Oh, sorry. I was just struck by that young girl. She's beautiful. Do you know her name?"

"Yes, I know her name. She is Shoshone. I know her."

"She's part of your tribe?"

"Yes. Eat! She gives you the choicest piece of buffalo, the tongue and the liver. Eat. Everyone is looking."

"Is this liver *raw?*"

"Yes, white man. Indian braves eat the liver raw. It is a sign of a warrior. Everyone is watching to see you eat it. It is an honor. Do not shame me. I told my father that we were brothers in age and in spirit."

"I would be honored to be considered your brother." Del picked up his strip of liver and gestured to the crowd, then to the chief and gulped down the liver in one bite. Yips of approval with mild clapping erupted from the circle of diners.

He wiped his mouth with the back of his hand. "Not too bad. Not too bad at all. Not what I'm used to, but I could get to like it."

He bit off a piece of his corn cake which was pretty good. A bowl of stewed greens passed and everyone dunked their corn cake into the green broth. The acorns were like pieces of nut that had been sweet-ened with honey. Skins of drink made the rounds. Del wasn't sure what it was, but it was pleasant. The tongue was his favorite. It had been broiled and cut up into pieces. The only thing he missed was salt.

Besides their own language, everyone spoke smatterings of En-glish, French, and Spanish. Del felt like a student, listening to all the dialects being spoken around him. He was definitely having a good time, though.

Soon, the bowls and serving dishes disappeared. Drums began a rhythmic beat. Lines of dancers formed. The women danced slow and rhythmic, swaying side to side, imploring to the crowd with their arms. The warrior dancers told of hunts and acts of bravery. The watchers voiced approval and shouts of encouragement as they sang or clapped to the swaying, leaping dancers and hypnotizing chant of the singers and drums.

Del realized the girl who had served him had stopped right in front of him, swaying to the sound of the chanting women as they gracefully side stepped around the circle of fire. Her eyes held a reflective luster from the fire. Her hair, undone, flowed across her back and shoulders swaying with a will of its own as the dancers moved to the right and then back. Despite all the dancer's movements around the circle, she seemed to always be in front of Del.

Standing Rock watched him. Black Feather appeared agitated.

"Black Feather, who is she?"

"She is Moon Star. She was born in the month when the moon carries a shining star with it as it travels across the night sky."

"Could you introduce me? Or is that acceptable? I don't want to get into any trouble here. I think she is trying to get my attention."

"Yes, she is. She is my sister!"

Now, Del felt Standing Rock's deep gaze boring into his neck. "Your sister?" He gulped, looking down into the dirt.

Del did his best to appear interested in anything that did not involve Standing Rock or Moon Star. But he did cast furtive looks at her when the dancing was over. That star must be Venus when it is so bright.

"Del Rio!" Standing Rock spoke from behind him. The hair on Del's neck stood up. He hoped he wasn't in some kind of trouble.

"Yes, sir. Yes, Standing Rock." Del slowly turned to face him. The crowd had grown quiet observing the two of them, both now facing each other.

"My son, Black Feather, said you told him it would be an honor to call him brother. Is that true?"

With much relief, Del nodded. "Yes, sir, I would be honored to call Black Feather of the Shoshone my brother."

"Black Feather, do you feel the same?"

"Yes, Father. I sense Del Rio and I share similar spirits. I feel we have been friends from the first moment we met."

"You feel this as well?" Standing Rock asked Del.

"Yes, I have, sir—err, Chief."

Standing Rock stood quietly as if he were assessing the spirits of both these young men and instructed them to stand. He placed his hands on their shoulders. Closing his eyes, he stood, face bent to the sky as if in silent prayer. The grip on Del's shoulder had the strength of iron, but he did not move or cry out.

Suddenly releasing them, Standing Rock, proclaimed, "I feel it is so myself with these two." He gestured to an old Indian behind him. He came forward with an obsidian knife with an elkhorn handle. Strips of soft leather lay across his arms.

"Stand before me. You have both spoken your wish for brotherhood. I feel the spirit in each of you is already a brother to the other. Hold out your left hand as this is the one closest to the heart."

Astonished, Del watched as the chief cut into Black Feather's palm, then moved to cut his palm as well. Standing Rock paused as if to say, "This is all right for you?"

Del nodded and did not flinch as the scalpel-sharp, stone knife sliced into his flesh. A dark ribbon of blood flowed across his palm.

Quickly, Standing Rock bound their palms together.

"Del Rio, Black Feather's blood now flows through your veins. Black Feather, Del Rio's blood now flows through your veins. May you forever live, as brothers. The spirits are pleased. I am pleased." He raised his arms to the night

———————————

DEL SLEPT LATE, ROLLED UP in his blankets. He had been up most of the night.

He stumbled over to a log next to the fire, sat and poured a tepid cup of coffee. "Tuck, is there anything to eat?"

"There's cold bacon and flapjacks. I think I have some stewed apples left, too. It's all over there beside the fire. I threw a deerskin over it to keep out the critters."

Daniel and Tucker watched expectantly as Del ate a bite.

"What are you looking at, Pa?"

"I'm looking at you, boy. You're the talk of the camp. We've been waiting all morning to hear what happened."

"C'mon, Del, tell us. I'm sitting here like I'm sitting on red ants. Tell us what happened. Ben will be here soon," said Tucker.

"Well, I think I just became a member of an Indian tribe!"

He held up his bandaged left palm. "I'm blood brother to the Shoshone nation."

24

ARLY THE NEXT EVENING THE Kincaid's had dinner with the Riodans. Relaxing after their meal and drinking coffee, Nancy asked about Del's bandaged hand. "How's the hand, Del? Is it healing? My hands healed up pretty fair. I will have some scars for a long time. I'm afraid I used to take pride in my hands. Now, I feel like they're tools to be used like a hoe or a shovel."

"It's okay, Miz Kincaid. Tucker fixed me up right good. It doesn't hurt, and the wound is knitting up fast. Thanks for asking."

"Do you feel different, now that you have Indian blood flowing in your body?" asked Nate.

"I feel like I can whip a bear!" Del tickled the young boy's ribs, to his delight, causing him to squeal with laughter.

Daniel looked over the rim of his cup. "So, Miz Kincaid, have you thought about what you're going to do once we get to Oregon City?"

"Daniel, I've lost sleep over that question. My boys are so young. I can't farm by myself, though I do plan on staking a claim. If I have property, I can eventually live on it and run some cattle. Maybe I can sell the timber. I can put up an old shanty and stay there every so often, so I can honestly claim I'm living there. I want Nate and Bart to go to school in town. Perhaps I can get a job in a store."

"That's good thinking. You could run some cattle and sell your timber. We are going to build a sawmill and, eventually, a grist mill.

If we all staked our claims close together, we could kind of look out for each other. I know Tucker and Del both want to file. You could sell your timber to us and work in town."

"You know, you're a fine baker, ma'am," said Tucker. "Have you considered a bakery or a restaurant? Everybody has got to eat, and no one makes a better pie than you. Not even me!" He laughed. "Men out here are crazy for bear sign. Donuts, if you will. You could get rich just selling bear sign. Cheap to make. Have some good hot coffee and good food. I'd say you couldn't help but be successful."

"That's a mighty good idea. I could have a nice place to eat for families. Men could drink some coffee and discuss their business around a table like civilized folk and eat a bite of pie. Maybe I could have a sitting room where folks could read books. That would make the ladies comfortable coming in. Oh, maybe I could serve tea in the afternoon. Let me think about it. I suppose there's already a place or two to eat in the town."

Daniel frowned. "Probably, but lots of folks are moving west. There's bound to be room for you. Lots of hungry folks moving through and some settling."

"We could help you get started," said Tucker. "It's going to be awhile before we start our mills. Can't do it until the spring breaks and the rains let up. Gotta let the lumber cure a while. You should be able to get plenty of supplies from Vancouver or Astoria, being they're close to the river."

"You're right there, Tuck. We have to look around for our piece of land. It needs to be close to a river. We can look for four sections all together if you like, Miz Kincaid. We have to fell the trees and let 'em sit to dry through the summer. I don't reckon we could start our construction until next fall, at the earliest. Del, what do you think?"

"Seems to me that you've all laid out a workable plan. I haven't given it much thought except how we are going to get there. I'd be glad to help Miz Kincaid until it's time to work on our own piece of land. Nate and Bart are like family to my thinking."

"Why, thank you, gentlemen. Let me think on it, and I'll talk with you about it later. Of course, that means you're eating for free. It's the only way I have to pay you back."

Daniel grinned. "Why, Miz Kincaid! That sounds like a good deal to me. How about you guys? Tuck, Del?"

"Why, sure," said Del. "We'll get tired of Tuck's cooking before too long, anyway!"

"You could do a lot worse than my cooking," replied Tucker. "I think that's a fine idea, ma'am. I also think young Mister Del Rio should start pulling some cooking duties as well. How about it, Daniel?"

"Okay with me, Tuck. But let's make sure what goes in the stew. We might just get poisoned like that Mormon family that ate that water hemlock and died. Killed all of 'em. Heard it at Bridger's Fort. Must've thought they was harvesting wild carrots or parsnips."

"Daniel Riodan? Mind if I approach the fire?"

"Who's there? Oh, it's you, Cap'n. Why sure. Come sit. We were just planning on what we want to do once we get to Oregon City. What's on your mind? Coffee?"

"Time for us to be off, gentlemen." Nancy shook out her skirts as she stood up. "Thank you for a lovely supper. Oh, and, Tuck, I *do* want some of your cooking secrets when we get to Oregon. Promise? Get up, boys. Wake up. It's time to go to bed."

"I surely do, Miz Kincaid." Tucker's appreciative face beamed. Then he glowered at Del. "There goes a proper gentlewoman."

Del laughed at Tucker and helped himself to more pie. "I guess you could teach me to cook biscuits or this here pie."

"What's on your mind, Cap'n?" Daniel poured some coffee in a cup and passed it to him.

"Well, Ben's gone with some friends of his he hasn't seen for a while. He's probably up in the hills swapping yarns and getting drunk. Can't say he isn't due his pastimes. He's worked hard getting us here. I was wondering if you'd go with me to Bridger's Fort. I've got a meeting with Jim so I can get the latest news and information on trails and the current disposition of the Indians. Two heads is better than one, and I'd like to get your opinion—your thinking on what you hear. You up for it?"

"Why sure. Del, Tuck, you want to go? You can look around and keep an ear out for any news circulating at the fort while we're confabbing with Bridger."

"Okay by me. How about you, Del?"

"I'm ready if you are."

"I could use a cold beer myself. Help me sleep tonight. You want another beer after yesterday's game?"

"If it's all the same to you, Tuck, I'll forego the beer. I had enough the other day to last me for a while. Birch beer or sarsaparilla sounds good though."

"Daniel, you go ahead with the Cap'n. Del and I will clean up here. We'll be along in just a little bit. Jump, boy! Go wash them dishes." Del jumped and Tucker laughed, "Got you!"

Tucker and Del took their time walking down to the fort. It was a cool night and dry. The two of them talked as they strolled along enjoying the night.

"Ah—Del, I was wondering... has your Pa mentioned anything to you about Mrs. Kincaid?"

"Why, no. He's not said anything other than normal. You know, we all watch out for her and her boys."

"I know, I was just thinking that both of them are alone. She needs a man. He's been alone for a long time. Seems they might just think about getting together is all. Seems natural. We're such good friends and all."

"What!" said Del, alarmed. "No! He hasn't said anything about that! Has he said anything to you?"

"No, he hasn't. Why are you so upset?"

"Why—err, you surprised me. I hadn't thought anything about it, is all."

"Just seems natural, don't it? Don't be surprised if it comes up. Men and women just seem to get together."

"Yeah, I guess, they do." Del wrestled with what to say next. "I just... can't think of her as my ma."

Tucker nodded. "I understand."

"You do?"

"Yeah, she's like having a big sister or something like that I guess."

"Uh-huh. I guess you're right." Troubled by the sudden turn in the conversation, Del cleared his throat. "Maybe I'll have that beer."

"Oh? What changed your mind? Thought it made you sick."

"It did, but the night is cool. Maybe I'll go half and half, ginger beer and beer. That sounds good. I'm dry."

"Okay, if that's what you want. I'm dry myself. Anything other than water and coffee sounds good to me."

Men moved about all through the fort going about their business. The many lanterns provided a bright light in the main store. Mostly men and Indians moved about. Most of the women stayed at their wagons this time of night unless they were out with their men.

Tucker stepped up to the bar in the back of the store. "I'd like a cold beer, please."

"It's cold all right. We keep it in a spring. That'll be five cents, mister. Hey, ain't you the feller that hit that long ball to end the game, the other day?" asked the barman.

"Yep. I was robbed of the only homerun I'll ever hit in my life."

"Too bad. It was a pretty hit. You were robbed all right. Those Indians did get excited, didn't they?"

"Yes, it was a nice throw. How about the beer?"

"Oh, yeah. Here you go. A nice hit, just the same."

"At least somebody remembers." Tucker smiled as he sipped his beer. "Ah, that tastes mighty good! Thank you."

A rough looking man bumped into Tuck from behind, as he moved to the bar.

"Excuse me," said Tucker.

"What?"

"I said excuse me. I must have been in your way."

"What do we have here, boys? A real genuine Negro!" the man said loudly.

Tucker nodded to the man and raised his mug to him.

Del had been nursing his beer and ginger beer next to Tucker, consumed by the wild thoughts and possibilities of his pa and Nancy Kincaid getting together going through his mind. His troubles just seemed to be starting. He wasn't paying attention to anyone, except his own troubles.

"Hey, nigger, what would you sell for, if I was to sell you here to one of these folks?"

That got Del's attention. Snapping out of his quandary, he

pushed past Tucker and stood face to face with the bemused mountain man.

"Mister, shut your mouth! Tucker's a free man, for your information. He's my friend and a better man than you'll ever be!"

"Better than me? Is that so! Listen, boy, get out of my face, or I'll grind you into little pieces and eat you on a cracker! I'm Big Tree Muldoon. I howl with the wolves and sleep with the wild cats. I can lick any ten men and twice as many Indians. I've never licked me a free nigger man before, but I am sure going to tonight. Now, sonny, stand out of my way!"

Big Tree picked Del up and moved him to the side as if he weighed as little as a pumpkin.

"Now, mister, I just came in here for a cold beer. Let me buy one for you. What do you say, Mister Tree?" said Tucker.

"*Mister* Tree? Why I'm insulted! I'm *Big* Tree. Understand me, free man! I'm calling you out!" Big Tree's chest bumped Tucker's arm, spilling his beer on the counter.

Tucker's jaw set tight, and he set his beer down on the counter lightly. Taking a deep breath, he said "I didn't come in here to fight, Big Tree. I don't even know you. What have you got against me?"

"Big Tree! I told you no fighting in here, last time you were here. You're always trouble. Do I have to throw you out again?" Jim Bridger stood at the door to his office, accompanied by Daniel and Captain Nightingale.

"Oh, Jim, he says he's a free man. I've never beat up a free nigger man. I'll only hit him a little."

"Hey, you!" Del pushed back against Big Tree again.

"Free man, get rid of this puppy. I eat young pups for supper. Boy, I wouldn't even work up a sweat with you. Now stand aside!" Big Tree pushed Del into the crowd.

"Tree! I'll not tell you again!" Jim said.

"Mister Bridger, I suppose it was bound to happen at some time. Some white cracker wanting my black skin. Now is as good as time as ever. Mister Tree, I'll fight you all right, here and now. Okay with you, Mister Bridger?"

"Well, all right. If it has to be, let it be here. I only hope he beats your brains in for you, Big Tree. I'll charge you for any damages since you pushed it. Tucker, watch yourself. He don't fight fair."

"That's fine by me." Tucker and threw his beer into Big Tree's astonished face.

"Tucker, you don't have to do this," called Daniel.

"Oh, yes, I do!" Tucker smashed Big Tree in the jaw as he wiped the beer out of his eyes. "Sure as hell!"

"Oh, yeah. I'm going to break you, free man!" Big Tree tilted his head back and howled like a wolf. "I'm going to eat you for breakfast!"

Moving quicker than seemed possible, Big Tree grabbed Tucker around the chest, picked him up and squeezed him, causing Tucker to bend backward over Big Tree's arms.

"I'm going to break your back, damn you!!" Big Tree jerked harder.

Tucker bent forward and clapped both hands over Big Tree's ears. Big Tree howled like a wolf and kept on squeezing. Tucker smashed both open palms against the big man's ears a second time much harder. This time Big Tree let go and grabbed for his ears, bending forward at the waist. Tucker stepped back and let go a haymaker right to the chin that spun Big Tree around and back into the crowd.

"Come on, come on. Get out of my way," he said, screaming as he pushed out of the crowd and charged Tucker.

Tucker was wise to Big Tree now, and wouldn't let him in close. Assuming a boxer's stance, he bare-knuckled Big Tree's face, as he danced around the mountain man, avoiding Big Tree's roundhouse swing. Someone tripped Tucker, causing him to fall against the crowd.

Jim Bridger shot his gun into the ceiling, "Who did that? It was you. I saw you!" Jim promptly laid the barrel of his gun across the offender's nose, knocking him to the ground. "I will personally shoot the next man that interferes in this fight. Is that clear? Resume the fight."

Big Tree shot a right into Tucker's ribs and Tucker moved to cover his side. Big Tree let go a left to his chin, turning Tucker away from him. Tucker retaliated by smashing a right back across Big Tree's face, followed by a solid left that had Big Tree spitting a bloody tooth on the floor. Again, Big Tree tried to grab Tucker into a bear hug, but Tucker backed away peppering Big Tree's face with short, jabbing, stinging, shots to his face and ears.

Big Tree was confused. He had never faced a fighter like Tucker, nor had he been hit so many times. He was used to grabbing and wrestling in close, banging away with both fists until his opponent gave up or was knocked silly and unconscious.

Tucker hit him in the jaw with a downward knuckle punch that threatened to dislocate his jaw. Big Tree shuddered and kicked Tucker in the stomach. Tucker moved away keeping his guard up. Encouraged, Big Tree kicked again. Tucker pushed the kick away with his left hand which brought Big Tree's face in for the right to land a stunning blow to his ear, knocking him down.

Down, but not out, Big Tree lunged for Tucker's knees rolling him to the floor where the two men rolled around grasping for a leverage hold in the dust, dirt, and tobacco juice that was the floor. Big Tree tried to gouge Tucker's eyes, but Tucker clamped onto his thumb with his teeth and bit fiercely.

Screaming, Big Tree jerked away and stumbled to his feet. Cautiously, the men circled. Sweat dripped into the dust and dirt. Puffs of dust swirled about their feet as they kicked up the loose dirt and stains on the floor. Swells of heat wavered over their sweaty bodies, their faces, puffy and swollen.

Calls of encouragement rang out from around the gathered circle for their favorite. Daniel and Del looked at each other in wonder. Neither knew Tucker could fight.

Bull rushing Tucker, Big Tree knocked his arms down and banged Tucker into a post in the middle of the room. He barraged hard short blows to Tucker's midsection then followed with a left to the face, which Tucker ducked, causing Big Tree's fist to smash into the edge of the square post. Big Tree yowled in pain and sucked at his fist, then backed off, glaring at Tucker.

"You're a hard man to put down, free man," Big Tree said with some respect.

"I'm your breakfast that's going to turn your stomach inside out, cracker! I'm only getting started."

Several quick stiff jabs, rattled Big Tree's chin. A right to the jaw sent lightning bolts of pain into Big Tree's brain. A left cross clipped his nose. Big Tree backed away, blinking in pain. His brain wouldn't think clearly, his vision was blurred, and blood ran from his nose, but he wasn't done. He was Big Tree Muldoon, the wolf howler, and he wasn't beaten yet.

With a wild yell, he rushed Tucker, knocking him off balance. Big Tree slipped behind Tucker and wrapped his arms around his chest, squeezing and lifting the smaller man off the ground until Tucker's back arched over his body. Big Tree squeezed so Tucker couldn't breathe. He shook him like a bear would shake a coyote caught stealing his kill.

Grimacing in pain Tucker flexed his legs and torso causing Big Tree to bend forward, then when Tucker felt his feet on the floor, he rammed his head into Big Tree's face with a vicious shove, that sounded like a loud clunk when it contacted the big man's nose.

This rocked Big Tree back. Dropping Tucker, he staggered over against the post and grabbed onto it which saved him from falling over. Dazed from the blow, Big Tree blindly searched for Tucker in the crowd through red puffy eyes.

"Here I am, big man," Tucker landed two homeruns on each side of Big Tree's jaw causing him to jerk his head up and down into the solid wooden post again and again. Eyes crossing, Big Tree slumped to the floor.

"Yee-ha!" Del, jumped up and down and pounded his friend on the back. Pandemonium broke loose in cheers and hurrahs. "You did it, Tuck!"

Tucker stumbled to the bar for support. Everyone rushed around and congratulated him.

"What a fight!"

"Never thought I'd see that."

"Big Tree never had a chance!"

"Way to go, my friend. Way to go. Buy him a beer on me, Ralphie!"

The bartender placed a dripping cold mug in front of Tucker. "That, me boy, was a fight to remember. Never saw Big Tree get pounded so much. It made me poor heart quiver in joy! You're drinking on the house tonight, Mr. Tucker, sir!"

Jim Bridger pushed through the crowd. Pumping his hand in congratulations, he said "I put ten dollars on you. I wanted someone to take it to Big Tree, and you did. My, my, that was something. Congratulations, Tucker. You proved yourself tonight."

"Tucker, I had no idea you could fight so well. That was splendid. No one could have done any better. You knocked his brains out. Look, he's still balmy, laying there on the floor." Del jumped, pounding Tucker's back and pointing to the lump of Tree covered in tobacco-stained dust.

Someone threw a bucket of cold water on Big Tree, who woke up shaking his head. He blinked and held his head trying to re-focus his eyes. His friends helped him to his feet.

Taking a deep breath, Tucker took two beers with him as he approached Big Tree.

"Buy you a cold beer, Mister Big Tree?"

The man stared at him sullenly, then he grimaced and rubbed his jaw. "Well... I... guess so." He stammered.

Del, Daniel, and Tucker gasped, looked at each other and burst into laughter.

"What's so damn funny?" Big Tree demanded.

"Come with me, big man, and I'll tell you," said Tucker. He put his arm around Big Tree's shoulders and helped him to the bar.

"Well, Big Tree, you met your match. What do you got to say for yourself?" asked Jim Bridger as he motioned for Ralphie to bring a round.

"What do I owe you for damages, Jim? I shore brought it on myself tonight. I swear to never fight again. At least not here! To Jim Bridger, everyone!" He raised his beer as he toasted.

"What did you say your name was, mister?" Big Tree asked Tucker.

"I didn't. You can call me Tucker. That's what everybody calls me. And I haven't howled with the wolves until tonight, neither. Normally, I make biscuits."

"Shore enough?" asked Big Tree. "I got whipped by a biscuit maker? Damn. Hey, listen, Tucker, I was trying to pull your leg before. I didn't mean any of it. I been up there in the mountains trapping. I come here to sell my furs and let off some steam. Just to show there's no hard feelings, would you take this knife of mine as a gift? It's my favorite, but by thunder, you deserve it."

Big Tree went over to his bundle of furs and brought out a Bowie knife with an elk bone handle. The sheath was hand stitched leather and decorated with bead work. "Here. I'd take it kindly if you'd take this."

"Whoa! That's a fine knife. Are you sure? It was just a little fight."

"A little fight? I swear, there's something about you I like. It would make me proud to give you this knife and call you friend. What do you say?"

"Okay, friend Big Tree. Thank you. I shall take good care of it."

"Look at that blade. It's as black as your hide, black like the sky at night. Blade is heavy, isn't it? Had it made from a chuck of metal I saw drop from the sky."

"You don't say. It is heavy now that you mention it." mused Tucker.

"Holds a sharp edge too!" said Big Tree. "One of the best knives I've ever owned." The two men shook hands. "Hey, by the way, how did you learn to fight, Biscuit Man?"

"See, Tuck, I told you people would be coming out of the bushes for that biscuit recipe!" Del said.

"Yeah, I'd like to know how you fought so well. I didn't know you could," asked Daniel.

"It's a long story," Tucker said. "Do you want to hear it tonight? It's late."

"I think we're all interested, Tucker," said Captain Nightingale. "We don't leave until day after tomorrow. So's, I got all night."

"Me, too!" said Del.

"I'd sure like to hear it," said Jim Bridger.

"Well?"

"Daniel, it includes Rebecca and what happened when we got back to Baltimore. How about you, Del? You won't remember any of this."

"Now I know I need to hear it," said Daniel rather soberly.

"Yeah, me, too," said Del

"Who's Rebecca?" Big Tree looked from face to face.

"Daniel's wife and Del's mother," replied Tucker.

"A wife? How does she fit into all of this?" Big Tree still didn't seem to comprehend the gravity of the story that Tucker was beginning to tell.

Tucker frowned "I was her slave, Big Tree."

"Well, I'll be damned."

"We arrived back in Baltimore. Rebecca was beside herself with joy to be home again. She had been raised in that house, Daniel, if you didn't know. Her mother left it to Rebecca when she passed. It did not pass to Major Conlon, Rebecca's father. The estate had been in the wife's family. It was all left to Rebecca and to her heirs, namely Delaino. Major Conlon acted happy to see us at first. Beaux Conlon was polite but kept to himself. It was not to last. Soon, the Major resorted to his old ways, telling Rebecca she had married beneath her class. He became disdainful of her and Delaino over the marriage.

"Rebecca knew this to be ridiculous, but old lifelong dislikes are slow to change. She was broken hearted at her father's and Beaux's petulant behavior, especially toward Del.

"She sought out her old friends and went to all the social events, taking Del wherever she went. She loved you very much, boy.

"She tired quickly of the city and especially her father. She began making plans to go home to Indianapolis. That's when one of her best friends got sick. Rebecca went to nurse her one morning.

"That's how she got sick. When she realized she was sick with what Vicki had, she gave you to me, Del, and told me to take care of you no matter what. She made me swear. Daniel, I swore an oath to Rebecca to take care of Del, as best I could.

"Before Rebecca passed, she summoned me to her bedside. She told me she trusted me. Forced some papers into my hand. It was the deed for her estate and her will, Del. The house belongs to you when the Major dies. I have saved all the papers. You own it all. The Major gets to live there until he dies. Beaux gets nothing."

Del stood quietly, very pensive. He had never imagined he would own the estate. It was a big mind switch he would have to talk to his pa and Tucker about, later.

"How about the fighting? Don't mean to rush your story, but this was supposed to be about how you learned to fight." Big Tree looked around the room, searching for faces that agreed with him.

"Sorry, Big Tree, but that needed to be told, so Del and Daniel knew what happened to Rebecca. I told you all of that, so I could tell you this.

"After Rebecca's funeral, Beaux started going to private clubs that would stage fights. Slave versus slave. Sometimes bare-knuckle fights, sometimes to the death. No rules, no holds barred."

Everyone was silent, listening intently.

"He got the idea to have me trained to fight. He hired a professional trainer. I had no choice. Beaux brought in fighters that could fight according to the Marquis of Queensberry rules and wharf rats who could wrestle, kick and gouge with the best. I sparred and learned to box and wrestle. I was naturally fast, and my trainer urged Beaux to use me in the boxing ring instead of brawls to the death. The white gentlemen staged these fights in their private clubs. They bet freely and took it out hard on their fighters when they lost. I fought five bouts. One fight lasted twenty rounds. We were both bloody. I won all five fights. My fifth fight was my last. I killed that young boy with a floor to ceiling upper cut that broke that kid's neck. By then, the city of Baltimore stepped in, stopping all the fights. Too many had died. They threw young society Toms in jail and published their names. That, of course, was too much to risk socially, so the fights stopped. Beaux was afraid of me by then. I had grown too strong and skillful, but he couldn't sell me. I wasn't his. I was Rebecca's. Later, I belonged to Del. Now, I belong to me."

"You know I freed you, when we met up in Independence, Tuck. I never considered or treated you like a slave."

"I know, and I'm grateful. So, Big Tree, when you started talking of selling me, you got my hackles up. I took a lot of frustration out on you tonight. You're the first I've fought since those mean times. I hope I didn't hurt you too much."

"You just about broke my jaw!" Big Tree said. "Guess I had it coming. That's some story, my friend."

25

"NEXT STOP FOR NIGHTINGALE'S TRAIN is Fort Hall on the Snake and then we'll follow the Snake River north into Oregon territory before turning west to the Columbia River Gorge." Daniel had explained to Tucker, Del, and Mrs. Kincaid the afternoon before they planned to set off. "We cross over the Snake to the north side a few miles above Ft. Hall. There aren't many crossings after that. Most of the way along the Snake is on high banks well above the river making water hard to get to. Ft. Boise will be our next layover and resupply."

Ben had been impressed that Del became a blood brother to Black Feather. "The Shoshone have been here a long time. Their land is the valley of the Snake River. They are called Snakes sometimes. As I recall from what I read about Lewis and Clark, Sacagawea was Shoshone. They've been friendly to the whites for quite a while now. I hope all these folks moving in don't change that. Most white folks don't respect the ways of the Indians. Something will clash sooner or later. I hope it's later."

Del made a trip to see Black Feather and his family, before the train left Ft. Bridger. He hoped to catch a glimpse of Moon Star as well. Secretly, seeing Moon Star again was the main reason for his visit. Ben told him to take some tobacco and sugar to give to Standing Rock and Blue Deer. It was good to see Black Feather again, and they greeted each other warmly. Standing Rock expressed interest in their journey to Ft. Hall. It would be a difficult trip. The rimrock of the Snake River would be easier travel for the wagons than along the river, but it would be dry and difficult to get down to the water in the river due to the steep banks.

"I will come back some day to my Shoshone family after I have made a home in Oregon. If you travel there, be sure to look for me. You will always be welcome."

He made his goodbyes sadly. The Shoshone tribe had opened Del's eyes. These people were little different than his own. Only customs and language were different. Hearts and minds functioned the same for all people. Moon Star had made a brief appearance and had gifted Del with a smile meant just for him.

IT WAS ABOUT ONE HUNDRED and fifty miles to Ft. Hall. The train made it in eleven days, despite a broken wheel, two babies being born, and losing a newborn calf to wolves.

Del rode Star most of the way. He was growing fond of this beautiful horse. Born in these mountains, her instincts were uncanny. She had warned Del of a lion attack just as the big cat rose to leap at horse and rider. Del had drawn his .36 Paterson and fired before the catamount could finish his jump.

"What a racket that cat made, Pa. He jumped and bit at himself thrashing on the ground like he was crazy after I shot him. Then, he just finished dying. I never would have believed it if I hadn't seen it. That cat was crazy mean."

"I've heard about that. Cats get crazy and more dangerous when they're wounded. Make some good steaks, though, Tucker broiled 'em up just right."

The second night out, Black Feather rode up to their camp. "I have decided to ride with you along the Snake Valley. Standing Rock wishes it as well. I would like to see how the white man lives in his teepees on wheels. It is Shoshone land. I know it well." Del was surprised but delighted. He introduced Daniel and Tucker.

"That's good of you, Black Feather. I think you know Captain Nightingale and Ben, our scout. I'll take you to them in the morning. I'm sure they'll appreciate any advice you can offer."

Daniel indicated a seat by the fire. "How did you get in here without being seen is what I'd like to know? We've got guards out all around."

"They are white. I am Shoshone." Black Feather cut off a piece of lion meat and ate it. "Good. Good meat. Lion is my favorite. I teach you to move in the shadows, Del Rio. You Shoshone now. I will teach you Shoshone ways, as I learn the white ways. Standing Rock wants you to know the ways of the Shoshone to make you wise and brave. Moon Star sent this as a token of friendship, as well." Black Feather tied a turquoise ribbon around Del's arm, refusing to meet Del's eyes in the process.

They crossed the Snake River about five miles north of Ft. Hall. The weather grew cooler at night, dry and hot during the day. The black flies came up out of the river and got into everything. They drove the poor animals wild, as they were covered black with the thieving blood suckers. At night they brought the stock into the circle and kept fires smoking in as effort to ward off the beastly critters.

When Tucker, Del, and Black Feather rode out to bring in the teams for the evening, they discovered that two of Daniel's prized Linebacks were missing.

"Damn. I guess we gotta go look for them. I bet the bugs drove 'em off."

"We'll go, too, Tuck. Between the three of us, we'll find 'em faster. You ready, Black Feather? Raj is needing a run."

"We had better find them before night falls. There are wolves and lions in these mountains."

Leaving Daniel at the camp, they headed for the river, searching for but not finding any tracks.

"They'll stay close to water, won't they?"

Tucker shrugged. "It would seem like it, but they're oxen. Maybe they're holed up in the rocks for the night. Those Linebacks have never run off before. They'll even come when you call them. Both the teams usually stick together."

"Here." Black Feather pointed to the ground. "These tracks are moving down the trail. They came out of the river and moved north. They're running. Something spooked them down by the river."

Black Feather led the way. As they topped the next hill, they stopped in surprise. A wagon lay on its side across the trail. Five riders had gathered around it. A man and woman talked with them. A little boy and girl watched quietly, behind their mama's skirts. Suddenly, the man and woman threw up their hands.

One of the riders had drawn his gun, and as he was about to fire, the man standing on the ground waved his arms in the air and jumped into the horse startling it, causing it to lurch back. The gun went off scattering the other riders, who quickly got their mounts under control and moved back to the upturned wagon.

"Looks like trouble!" Tucker fired his rifle, knocking one of the men's hats off. All three tore down the hill yelling like wild Indians and firing at the group of men. The frightened family dove behind the wagon. The startled gunmen returned a few shots as the three riders came charging down the hill shooting and hollering. The five bandits quickly gathered themselves and fled, leaving a black hat with a hole in it, lying in the dust.

"Hey! Are you all right? Anybody hurt? We're friendly," Tucker hollered, as he dismounted.

Black Feather and Del raced away in pursuit of the gang. They didn't pursue the riders very far, just enough to make sure they'd really run them off. Outnumbered and outgunned, Del didn't want to fall into an ambush.

"That's good enough. They've gone. Let's go back and find out what happened." He patted Raj. "Good boy. We ran 'em off." Good thing he'd switched to the big stallion so he could stretch his legs and run some.

Back at the wagon, Tucker introduced himself. "I'm Tucker. Those are my two friends, Del Rio and Black Feather over there, running those renegades off. What happened here? You folks look like you're in a fix?"

"Tom Dearborn, Mister Tucker. My wife, Alice, and my boy and girl, little Tom and Emma. We're all right. Those men appeared friendly at first. Thought they were going to help us, but then it got ugly. I thought for sure they were going to kill us all. My wagon rolled up on a rock and overturned. I had just unhitched the mules and picketed them on some grass. I tried leveraging the wagon back up, but I wasn't strong enough. Glad you boys came along when you did. I'm obliged to all of you, even the Indian. I was actually glad to hear those war whoops. I think you scared those renegades, too! Their faces turned white when they heard you all a-coming."

"Well, let's see what we can do to get this wagon rolling again. Our wagons are back down the trail about five miles. I reckon we can get you upright and see you into camp tonight, Mister Dearborn. See if the kids and the missus can clear out any of your goods from the bed of your wagon. They can pile them up over there. We can reload it after we get you on your wheels."

The Dearborn family scrambled about clearing their supplies out of the wagon as quickly as they could. Tucker, Del, and Black Feather tied their ropes to the wagon along the side.

"Okay, fellas, slow and easy." The three lines tightened from the wagon's side to the pommels of their saddles, each horse moved forward digging in with their hooves, until the wagon crashed back on all four wheels again.

"That's a fine sight," said Alice. "Thanks very much, gentlemen. Tom, go get the mules. Here, Emma, little Tom, help me put this stuff back in the wagon. We'll repack it when we get to the camp tonight."

Del recoiled his rope and rode Raj over to some junipers to take him out of the heat. He saw the black hat lying in the dust and stopped to pick it up, laughing as he stuck his finger through the hole Tucker had made. He'd give it to his friend tonight as a souvenir.

"I TELL YOU IT WAS that same kid, from Ohio and Indiana," sputtered Waylon. "I recognized him and that horse. Where did they come from?"

"Ah, you're tetched in the head, Waylon. Why would that kid be all the way out here?"

"I recognized him, too." Adonis sipped his coffee, looking pensively into the fire. "No mistaking that horse. It was him. I tol' ya that wagon train would be through here. That black slave, Tucker, was with him. I never saw the Indian before."

"Damn him. That's the third time that brat has interfered in a job." Marty sat on a log and scowled. "We had those pilgrims dead to rights. That little woman would have been a good time. I could almost hear her screaming. Now, all I got is the four of you to look at. Hell, we must've run for ten miles before it seemed safe. Tonight, it'll be jerky and coffee. Jerky and coffee every night. I'm almighty sick of jerky and coffee."

"Are you sure? I admit that horse was familiar. We haven't seen many folks, 'ceptin' the ones we bushwhacked. It's been several months since we last saw him?"

"I know it was him," said Adonis. "That must mean that his pa is with them somewhere. We're a few days out from Fort Hall. I sure want to meet up with them two again. I owe them both a good beating. I'll get it done, too, but it'll be on my terms this time. No guns in my face. I want to grind Dan Riodan's face in the dust!"

"I didn't get a good look at them, that's all. We keep running into this kid and the slave. Don't seem natural is all."

Beaux swore out of the shadows. "It's them all right. I'd know them anywhere. Damn them."

"You say you know this kid and his slave, too?" asked Adonis in astonishment. "How you know them?"

"I know them! I've been telling you, that's why I'm out here in this god-forsaken place. I've been searching for them ever since I left Baltimore. That's why I joined up with you as you were headed west. I knew I'd find them someplace out here."

"You sure?"

"Yeah, I'm sure. I told you, I'm the kid's uncle. That slave belongs to me. I'm tired of coffee and jerky myself. Let's ride. I want to go to Fort Hall. Besides, I need a new hat."

———————

BY THE TIME THE MEN got the Dearborns settled for the night, it was past ten o'clock.

"Those two Linebacks showed up about an hour after you boys left. Came right into camp. I guess they figured the black fly situation was better here than in the bush. Anyway, they came in pretty as you please, just like they was supposed to be here. Went right over with the others, like they was glad to see 'em? More pie, Black Feather?" Daniel smiled as the young Indian dug into his third slab of pie. "Del?"

"I've had enough myself, Pa," Del said. "It was good pie, but I wouldn't deny Black Feather the last slice."

"The Dearborns are giving up. They lost two of their children to fever, and Alice's brother died of a snake bite. They've had it. They're headed back to Fort Hall in the morning. Me and Black Feather is going to escort them, so they don't miss the turn at the ford. Oh, I almost forgot." Del fetched the hat from his saddlebags and tossed it into Tucker's lap. "Here, Tuck. I brung you a souvenir! That was a pretty good shot, you know." He tossed the hat into Tucker's lap.

"Well, what do you know!" Tucker laughed "I was aiming for his gun, but Tom bolted the horses. Thanks, Del. This is a smart hat. Too bad it has a hole in it."

"Like that'll stop you from wearing it."

He molded the hat back into shape snapped the brim down, and placed it on his head. "Ah, it don't fit—too small."

The others laughed at the sight. Frowning, Tucker took it off and turned it upside down to check the size—and froze.

His gaze turned toward Daniel and Del Rio, looking as if he'd felt someone step on his grave.

"What is it, Tuck?"

Tucker passed him the hat. Dan looked at it. Without a word, he passed the hat to Del. *J.H. Beaux Conlon* was imprinted on the band in faded gold lettering.

Del gulped. "What do we do now?"

"We keep on going. We'll run into them again." Tucker's eyes studied the father and son across the fire. "God, I'd almost forgotten about him. I had him in my sights. This could've all been over with a single shot."

Dan cleared his throat. "Black Feather, we have an enemy who has caught up to us. Not that we were running, but this Beaux Conlon wants Tucker back in chains and Del and me dead."

Black Feather waved this tidbit away like so much smoke. "I have enemies, too, who want me dead. Every man who is strong has enemies. I make your enemy my enemy. You make my enemy your enemy. It is the way of things."

"Somehow that makes me feel better," said Tucker.

"It is the way of things out here. Something is always hunting something else. It is the way of all things."

"Thanks, Black Feather. That is the way to look at it."

"Give me that hat, Tuck." Del reached for it. Tucker gave it to him with a question in his eyes.

Del tossed the fine black hat into the fire. It started smoking quickly then erupted into flames emitting blue and yellow tendrils of fire, until it collapsed into the embers.

"Dust to dust, ashes to ashes. Damn your black heart, Beaux Conlon. We know you. Did you know it was us today?"

26

ORNINGS IN THE MOUNTAINS TOOK Del's breath away. Well up before daybreak, the men went about their camp chores. They had three chickens still. One had escaped and disappeared and the other two were cooked up with dumplings and tender young onions on two different Sundays. They got an egg or two every day now. "It will be sad if we eat these three. I've grown to look forward to seeing them in the morning."

After chores, he'd sit on Star or Raj, facing east, waiting for the light. Magically, shafts of light stole through the narrow valley illuminating the steep sides of ever higher cliffs a little at a time, turning the dark shadows from black to purple to golden brown until the entire valley was a shining reflection of light. The mountains ran north and south across this spine of America. As the mountains climbed higher, dawn came later and later, and nightfall was earlier for the same reasons.

Del and Black Feather rode with the Dearborns for a few miles to make sure they knew which fork took them back to the ford the train had crossed a few days ago.

"Good luck on your journey, Mister and Miz Dearborn. Fort Hall is just a few days ride, a few miles below the ford from here. Stay on the trail. You won't miss it. You'll probably meet other folks coming this way. God Bless!"

Del and Black Feather headed back toward camp, sometimes racing their horses to get the lead or take it away from each other. Black Feather rode a red spotted paint. A good horse, standing just a hand or so shorter than Star, who Del was riding.

"Where are your people from?"

"My people?" Del had not thought much of the ancestry of his people. "My grandfather was British. He came from a land clear across the ocean, past the east coast of this continent. He lived in Baltimore when he moved to America."

"I have heard of this land from the French trappers. They make war on the French, yes?"

"Uh, I guess so. The British seem to always be fighting somebody, the French or Spanish, Eastern Indians or even us, the United States. I guess that's how things get started, men fight, then they make peace and learn to live with each other. My pa is Irish, a country close to Britain. Tucker is from Africa, a country as big as this, halfway around the globe, probably the oldest land around. Who knows where everyone came from? I envy you, that your family has known this land for many lifetimes. My people came from many different lands, always looking for a better life and opportunity. That's why we're headed for Oregon, for a better life and to make homes for ourselves and our families."

Black Feather frowned. "It must be a hard thing to be forever looking for a home. I am always at home, no matter where I go. My people know all these mountains and rivers. We move to follow the game and grass and water. We fight our enemies, who come to take away what is ours. The white men first came as friends, now their numbers have been more and more. That is what Standing Rock wants me to learn. What is it the white men look for? When will they stop? Do you know?"

"I don't." Del sighed. This was not a pleasant subject. "I know that as long as men want something better for themselves and their families, they'll keep searching. The English, the French, and Spanish have many men who are without land, who are indebted to someone else and get a pittance to live on in return for their labor. Here is land and room to grow. I hope we can all learn to live together. Your people have been the most fortunate. God or the Great Spirit has granted you a beautiful land in which to live. All you've had to do was gather or hunt and all your needs were satisfied. I truly wish I could have been born into your tribe. It is a gift from the Great Spirit of all men."

"It is good that we be friends. Our people have much to learn from each other." Black Feather reined up for a moment and looked around. "The train has moved on by now. We're several hours behind them."

"Do you know another way we can catch up to them?"

"The train follows the river down in the gulch at this point of the trail. If we ride above on the canyon rim, we should be able to skirt many of the twists of the river and travel in a straighter line. We can meet them when they climb back up to the rim for easier travel tomorrow. It isn't called the Snake River for nothing, you know. We must go up on the canyon wall instead of going down toward the river the way we came out. Once we are on the top, it will be much drier. We may find a few streams draining into the Snake, but it is the dry season. I think we can make better time on the flatland on top. Do you want to try it?"

"Why not? We have full canteens and both horses were watered at that creek not too far back. I'll follow you to the top. Lead the way."

Looking back over his shoulder, Del wondered how the Dearborns were doing. He hoped they had a safe trip back to Fort Hall.

———————

EARLY AFTERNOON FOUND THEM TRAVELING quickly. It had been dry. There was no water in any of the streambeds. "Let's rest the horses over in that shade. I could use a blow, myself." Del pointed to a line of green trees still a way off ahead of them.

"Sounds good, brother," replied Black Feather. "We may find a seep that keeps those trees green. Nothing else is growing along this ridge."

They dismounted and pulled their saddles and blankets off their horses, when they had reached the green trees, but found no seep.

Both horses rolled and kicked their legs in relief. Del and Black Feather wiped the nostrils of the horses and gave them about a cup of water each.

Black Feather walked over to a bed of bull thistles and cut several off at the base. Gingerly, he picked them up and tossed several to Del. "Trim off leaves and outer skin, removing stickers. They make mouth sore if you eat them. Stalk is juicy, pleasant. Chew. Suck moisture. Spit the pulp. Relief for thirst. I use often on a dry trail."

Del found them surprisingly refreshing, reminding him of celery. Several of the trees were cottonwoods, but the ground was bone dry. He found he liked chewing the thistles. They held a surprising amount of water. So much so, that he gave Star the rest of the water in his canteen. He trimmed about a dozen thistle stalks and tucked them into his saddlebags for chewing later. They started to re-saddle, when Del spied what looked like a rooftop through the line of trees.

"Well, I'll be," he muttered. "Look. Does that look like a cabin rooftop to you?"

"It does. We go see what it is. Maybe they have well."

The roof and chimney poked out just above a small hill. The actual building sat down in a shallow declivity. It was well hidden because of its location. Riding cautiously, they approached the cabin spread out about ten feet apart to make a harder target. They weren't sure if these folks were friendly or not. Keeping their hands open and out, they attempted to show they were peaceful.

Del called out, "Hello the house! Hello! Can we come in? We're just looking for a taste of water for our horses if you have it. We're friendly. Hello the house!"

Dismounting, they walked their horses up to the front porch. It was a well-built cabin, just a few years old. There was a covered porch. The door fastened with a leather hinge that ran from top to bottom. The cabin had a front window with sturdy shutters.

Del looked through the window to see if there was anyone about. "Hello. Hello. Don't shoot, now. We're friendly. Do you have any water?"

Black Feather held up his hand for Del to be quiet. He listened to something. A rusty squeaking came from behind the house. Del could hear it now. Then it stopped. Both men stayed where they were, listening. It started up again, then it stopped.

Del knew what that sound was. He hadn't heard a rusty pump handle in several months. It started up again, a steady, busy earnest pumping, and this time it didn't stop.

TOM DEARBORN LOOKED AT HIS wife. "This should be the turn off that leads to the crossing, Alice. It has been tough on you and the kids. I miss your brother and our children as much as you. I guess what I'm a trying to say, Alice, is... I'm thinking better of going back. We have made it this far. There's as much danger going back as there is going ahead. Hell, we've got family buried here now."

"I know. I'm just tired of being scared and my loved ones dying every time something happens."

"I think on that too. I guess I would just like to stop and think on it a while. When we get to Fort Hall, we'll be safe. Let's rest up a while. Keep our thoughts to ourselves for a mite. Let our minds work on it, so to speak. Then we can talk about it. Maybe I can find a job at the fort. That would be a good thing to do, don't you think? Let things sorta sort themselves out. Then we can talk and decide what we really want to do in a week or so."

"I don't know. It's been so hard. I would like a rest. I guess Fort Hall will have enough provisions. We wouldn't have to worry none about that, and we could rest the stock. I know the children would like a settled place for a few days. We'll see, we'll see. I miss the company of other women. Women think and speak differently than men. I would like to be with some women to talk and sew and share recipes and talk of family. I miss that, Tom. I truly do."

"So, we'll stop at Fort Hall for a rest then. It'll be all right."

"Yes, it'll be all right. I'm tired of traveling and I'm tired and sore of riding in this wagon. Fort Hall will be a welcome stop."

DEL WALKED CAREFULLY AROUND THE house. He had motioned for Black Feather to stay behind him a few feet, so they wouldn't scare whoever was pumping the pump. Del didn't think it would be Indians. White folks dug wells and had pumps, not Indians.

He didn't understand what he was looking at, for a while. The scene didn't make sense. It was like a kaleidoscope he had looked at in Baltimore. All the pieces and colors were fuzzy, until you turned the tube properly and everything came into focus.

Three bodies lay on the ground. They had obviously been dead for several days judging by the smell alone. Del had a difficult time focusing in on them, because they were partly covered by thick mud. They lay face up, their mouths open. It was so macabre his mind wouldn't accept what he saw.

A little man about five feet tall, dressed in grey pants and an undershirt frantically pumped water into a tin cup. Barefooted, with mud splashed up to his chest, his pants were caked in mud. Mud that had dried, re-wet and dried again streaked his arms and face. He wore glasses so thick, his eyes appeared oddly out of proportion to the rest of his body. It seemed impossible that he could see out of them, they were so muddy.

He ran with his filled cup and poured it into the mouth of the adult female. She wore a yellow gingham dress that had become part of the muddy ground beneath her.

The man ran back to the pump and frantically filled his cup. He ran over to a young boy, maybe ten years old and poured it into the boy's open mouth.

Giggling and muttering to himself the little man said, "Water, water, give them water. That will cure the fever." He next poured his precious cup of water into the mouth of a young girl. Del guessed she would have been eight or nine. He couldn't tell from where he stood.

Quietly, Del and Black Feather watched the little man repeat his task over and over again. After about ten minutes of this without a break, Del stepped over to the man.

"Mister, Mister. Hello, Mister. What's your name? Is this your family?" Del could smell the decaying bodies in the heat. Flies were filling the eyes and noses of this unfortunate family. The heat and water had sped up the bodies' decomposition. By now the bodies more resembled the mud in which they lay than solid flesh and bone. It was all Del could do to keep from being sick. Luckily, he had not had anything to eat since breakfast.

Finally, in desperation, Del grabbed the man by his shoulders and guided him to a nearby cottonwood stump. "Hey! Hey, buddy. What's your name?" Del snapped his fingers in front of his face. The little man looked at Del with an uncomprehending look on his face. He sat very still, looking at Del, but not saying a word. Del didn't believe the little man could see him at all, his glasses were so caked with mud. Del guessed his clock had run down. It looked like he had been performing this ritual, caring for his family for many days. The little man simply stared at him from the stump on which Del had placed him. A muddy lump of a man sitting on a cottonwood stump in the backyard of a house he had built with his own hands.

Black Feather came from the barn with two shovels. He handed one to Del.

"Mister? We're going to bury your family. Is this your family? Sir? We're going to bury them for you. Sit tight, right there, Mister. It's all right." He was yelling so the man could hear him.

They couldn't move the bodies. The heat and wet and flies had done too much damage. Standing upwind from the little family, Del and Black Feather scooped up what dirt and gravel they could and covered the bodies in shallow graves. Pulling some boards from the barn, they laid them over the sad corpses and covered that with more rocks and gravel.

"Mister? What were their names? We could say some words, Mister. It would help if we knew their names." Del caught himself shouting again.

The little man simply sat and stared off toward the rim of the canyon. It was a big, wide space of gravel, cactus and sparse grass about a half a mile from the house.

The sun started to turn red on the far western horizon. A cooler breeze filtered through, cooling them, and their sweaty clothes felt cold and damp.

Del spoke a prayer he had heard at funerals. He was at a loss for other words. He didn't know these people, but he felt a deep responsibility to them as he had just buried them. It troubled his heart that he didn't know any names of the family, or the name of the little man, who now sat hugging himself on the stump rocking back and forth.

"Del, I go find a bucket and water horses. Spend night here. Maybe he come to his senses. Tell what happened."

"Yeah, the horses. Is there any pasture about or hay in the barn? Go look, would you? I've never seen anything like this. It's a nice house, tucked down in this little valley. It's been well taken care of. We were lucky to have seen it. I wonder what happened here."

"I don't know, but when a person is touched by spirits, we believe he has special insight into the spirit world. This little man has been touched by spirits. He is special, a holy one."

Del took the man's glasses off and wiped his face. "Hey, buddy, let me clean these glasses for you. Let's get you cleaned up. You'll feel better, don't you think?" He placed the cleaned glasses on the man's face.

The little man turned and looked at him.

"Thank you," he said, his voice barely above a whisper. He stood up and took off running so fast, it surprised them.

Del and Black Feather just stood stone-footed, aghast at the little man's speed.

He headed for the canyon's rim. Black Feather was the faster of the two, but he could not catch that determined little man. Del fell far behind, gasping for air, a pain in his side. It must have been half a mile to the canyon.

What gave this little man the energy to run?

Del caught up to Black Feather as he stood at the rim, looking out. He breathed deep, fighting for breath as well.

"He run off the rimrock! He just run off the edge. Never slowed down. Still running in the air when he fell. He never said one word. Not one word." They looked down, but could see nothing.

Shadows had crept in by the time they got back to the neat little house. Bloody footprints led to the canyon's rim behind them as they returned. The little man's feet must have been bloody stumps by the time he ran off into the canyon.

"I'll remember this day forever." Del shook his head. "I have never seen anybody act like that. Have you?"

"I have seen white men do things I don't understand. The country is so big and wide open. I have seen fear in many eyes. I think the country makes them feel small."

Puzzled and mystified, they looked about the cabin, but nothing looked out of place. Finding tea, corn meal, and a ham hanging in a back-store room, Del put together an impromptu meal. He was very careful. The place had an over-lying spirit about it that Del couldn't shake off. He neatly washed and replaced the dishes, cleaned the table and swept the floor. For some unexplained reason, he wanted the cabin to remain neat and clean.

"I can't sleep in here tonight, Black Feather. I think I'll put up in the barn."

"I feel same way. Too many confusing spirits in this place. Out in barn with the horses will be better."

Before they rode on the next morning, they packed up what food would spoil and be wasted. Del paused by the fresh graves. He had seen death on the trail before, but even Thomas Kincaid's death had not disturbed him as much as the deaths of the four people whose names he did not know. They had put markers on the graves. One for the mother and the date, one for each of the children marked *Brother* and *Sister.* This morning Del added one more marker. It read *Father died 1847.*

"You know, this little man built this house with his own hands, dug this well and raised a family here. I see why he chose it. It's a beautiful place. If we hadn't spotted the roof peak, we wouldn't have seen it at all."

They removed the bars from the pasture so the cattle could roam at will and the same with the pig sty. There was a plow horse and a mare for riding.

"I guess we'll take the horses and leave the rest. In a few years there may be a sizable herd hidden here in this valley. It'll be a thing to remember."

Black Feather closed the doors to the barn and fastened the latch-
es. They did the same at the house, all the beds made and cupboards
set right, Del felt like he was leaving the place as a tribute, to this
little family.

They didn't look back when they left. It was a new day. A thought
occurred to Del as he rode off. There are no promises! No guarantees
to any of us. He hadn't thought about that in a long time. It did not
bring any reassurance to his mind.

27

B Y THE NEXT AFTERNOON, THEY caught up to the train. It alarmed Del that they were still circled. It was past the nooning hour, and they should have been underway.

"What's doin', Pa?" asked Del as he and Black Feather rode in. "What's going on?"

A large crowd had gathered in the center of the camp. Loud ugly voices argued among themselves.

"We had a killin' last night, son. That trapper, Caleb Bourgeois, who's been riding with us for a couple of days, murdered young Russell Hardy. He was married to Cap'n Nightingale's niece, Alice. Caleb claims Alice flirted with him, and when he made advances, she screamed. Russell got killed when he came to rescue her. Caleb stuck his Bowie knife in him, and it took him all night to die. It was awful painful. His cries kept everybody awake. There was nothing we could do for him. Caleb had opened his stomach—terrible wound. He talked and screamed most of the night. Alice is beside herself with grief. Cap'n Nightingale is furious and set on hanging Caleb. They've picked a jury, and Nightingale has presented Russell and Alice's story. They've been going at it all morning. They buried Russell this morning. I think they're going to hear Caleb's side now. You got here just in time. Come on. We'll catch up later."

Caleb Bourgeois stood in front of the jury, twelve men of the camp sitting on chairs beneath a canvas sheet for shade. Captain Nightingale, as judge, sat behind two barrels with a board laid across it, his hands clasped together on top of the board, his face a stony façade.

Caleb sat with hands bound, his face scraped, bruised and bloody. It looked like it had taken four or five to subdue him. One eye had swollen shut, his lip was big, and his scalp shone pink and bloody in several patches where his hair had been pulled out.

"Me, I never meant her no harm, y'all. I've been alone in the mountains for many a year and had just left to go to rendezvous when's I joined up with y'all. The beaver is running bad dis year. All I ever had was beaver. It's been a lonely life after my family died. A fire back home in Louisiana burnt dem all up. I've been wandering these mountains since, lost and not caring. I never meant her no harm. First time I seen her, I thought she was pretty as a newborn filly. Our eyes met, and she invited me to supper. She and her man, Russell, was real good to me. She always smiled. Invited me to eat with 'em just like family. Her smile was so sweet. I knew she took to me, too! I been in these mountains for nigh onto fifteen years. First time a white woman was nice to me. I wouldn't have hurt her on purpose for nothing in the world. I seen she needed help with a big ol' iron pot. I could see her struggling wit' it. So's I went to help her put it back in the wagon. Her man wasn't around dat I could see. So's, I went to help her. She was so close I could smell her perfume. I'd not smelled anything like that in all des years since my Mamie had died. I don't rightly remember how it all happened. It went by so fast. I was just settin' dat pot down when I smelled that perfume. Next thing I know, I'm a tryin' to kiss her, and her dress was tore, and she was screamin'. I don't remember grabbin' on to her or nothin' like dat. But there she was, face white and cryin'. I don't recall about the dress. She was screamin, and I put my hand on her mouth to shut her up. You know, make her quiet so's I could explain. I didn't mean to harm her. Someone grabbed me by the shoulder and swung me aroun'. I been livin' with Injuns, for so long, I just naturally swung my old knife around and back. I didn't even have to think on it. It was an instinct thing for me to do. Don't ya see? I've been livin' with Injuns.

I didn't think. I just did it. Next thing I know, young Russell has got my Bowie stuck in his belly, and he's on the groun' screamin. Miz Alice is screaming so hard, no sound is comin' out of her mouth. She's about to turn blue. A pile of men jumped me and wrestled me to the ground, and somebody walloped me on da head with an axe handle."

"He knocked three of them unconscious, before they hit him with that hickory axe handle." Daniel whispered to Del.

"Anyways, I'm sorry. Those young people had been good to me. I know, I behaved poorly, but I shore don't know what come over me. I just was headed for rendezvous and to trade for a new rifle and some ammunition. I still got ten bales of plume that I saved for tradin' in these hard times. I'll just go back to my mountain and my Injun's. I hope to never see another white woman again. I guess I ain't fittin' to be living among decent folks. Miz Alice can have the pelts. They'll surely fetch a little something. I'll trow in my rifle. It's still a fine one and my pelts and half my ammunition to make up for da loss. Does that sound fittin' to you?"

Loud voices shouted him down, drowning him out.

Captain Nightingale pounded for order with a big rock. *"Quiet! Quiet down everybody! There now. I'd whip you till your skin came off in bloody strips, if it was up to me, Caleb Bourgeois. If it was up to me, but it ain't. I'm the Captain here, and we got a jury to decide this. I don't ever want it to be said I wasn't fair in these proceedings. I am the girl's uncle, so's it can't be up to me. What do you say, you men of the jury?"*

Briefly, the twelve men conferred. One man stood up and said, "Cap'n Nightingale, we've reached a verdict."

"What say you?" demanded Nightingale.

"Guilty, on all counts."

"Is it a unanimous decision, gentlemen?"

"Unanimous, sir."

"Guilty it is, then. Caleb Bourgeois, you'll face this court. I pronounce you guilty of capital murder. Of the attempted rape of a young woman who only tried to be kind to a lonely old man, I pronounce you guilty as well. I sentence you to be hung at the nearest tree large enough to suit the purpose. Punishment to be carried out immediately. I also pronounce, that your body will remain hanging, until the birds pick it clean. I will not grant you a Christian burial. A sign is to be attached to the tree declaring who you were and what you did and that this train meted out your sentence. Do you have anything to say, Bourgeois?"

"Hangin'? You're hangin' me? I tol' you it were an accident. I never meant to harm nobody. He just surprised me, that's all. I'm sorry I scared the young girl. I never meant to hurt her. I got more in my pack of goods, if dat'll make up for her loss. I'll give her everything I got. Shure enough. Den, I'll just go away and never come back." Caleb spoke imploringly, like he still didn't realize the magnitude of what he had done.

"You're going to hang, Bourgeois, and the birds will pick your bones clean. Do you hear me?" asked Nightingale.

"I've known Cap'n Nightingale for over ten years. I've never seen him so mad before," said Ben after he had spat on the ground. "Can't say as I blame him, I reckon. That was a senseless killin', if ever I saw one."

The jury put Caleb Bourgeois on a bareback horse and led him to a massive old oak growing from a crack in the great slabs of granite that topped the rimrock over the Snake River Valley. A rope tied with the sinister hangman's knot hung waiting.

A cool breeze ruffled Del's hair. He couldn't help but wonder why, in times of tragedy, when epic events touched him, like he was experiencing here, why did time seem to slow down? Vision seemed sharper. Noises became more distinct. Even colors seemed more vivid.

He had a picture of Caleb Bourgeois sitting on a horse in the shadowy cool of that mighty oak, from where he stood. The mountains framed this picture as if someone had painted it. Caleb's big eyes stared about him imploringly. They tied his big hands behind his back. Breezes blew his hair and ruffled the fringes on his greasy buckskins.

It could have been four to five hundred years old, that tree. A sentinel to what had grown and died here, observing thousands of creatures' lives and deaths. Now, the tree had a hand in this death, as did every man and woman living with this wagon train. Was this death any more significant than any of the other creatures who had come before now? Was the death of the little family he and Black Feather had buried more significant than Caleb Bourgeois and Alice and Russell? For Del Rio, the last two days would be forever frozen in his memory.

Caleb began to realize what was happening. Tears ran down his face as he spoke, "Tell Miz Alice, I was real—" Captain Nightingale didn't let him finish. He smacked the rump of the horse with a coil of rope. Caleb's last words choked in his throat as he swung at the end of a stout hemp rope, kicking and choking on his words. The stillness broken only by the creaking of a good rope as it strained to strangle the life out of Caleb Bourgeois.

Del was sick to his stomach and felt a bit dirty and guilty for some odd reason he didn't understand.

"No promises, Caleb Bourgeois. No promises, Russell Hardy. No guarantees, Alice Hardy. No promises of a future, Muddy Man," Del said softly to himself, as if in prayer.

They nailed a board sign to the big oak, as Caleb Bourgeois swung grotesquely serene in the fading breeze, which reported the trial and name of the condemned man. Flies buzzing around Caleb's face were the only life left after the men finished their task. Russell Hardy, they had buried on the other side of the oak, under a mound of rock and boulders, as there wasn't enough dirt to dig a grave. His marker was carved with his name and date of his birth and death. A long black ribbon fluttered plaintively in the sporadic starts of breeze, placed there by Alice. Several women had to draw her away and take her back to her wagon. Amid much crying and sorrow, everyone readied to leave this place.

The harsh rimrock over the valley of the Snake River was hot on those granite slabs of rock that burned through well-worn shoe leather and well-worn hoof. Wagons creaked and groaned as they left that place, echoing the heartaches left in the wake of dust on the trail and the groaning of the hangman's rope, twisting beneath the branches of the sentinel oak.

28

BLACK FEATHER NUDGED DEL WITH his elbow and nodded his head away, letting Del know he wanted to talk to him alone. They left the fireside conversation with Tucker and Daniel and went well beyond the perimeter of the camp. They counted fifty-four wagons now, others having joined at Ft. Hall. Others left, leaving Nightingale's trail to go another route with other wagons. The number always changed.

"I teach you Shoshone way now, my brother." They crept away from the wagons toward the men guarding the stock. "The men are tired from heat, and the French man's hanging is still on their mind." Black Feather lay on the rocks flat on his stomach, almost invisible to any casual eye.

Del remembered how he had tried to hide among the shadows on the trail to Indianapolis. He wanted to be as inconspicuous as he could. Black Feather taught him to be a shadow.

"See the horses in the *remuda?* See how well your men watch them? What horse do you want me to steal? The Shoshone can steal a horse from a white man while he still sits on it. Pick. Black Feather will bring the horse back to you on this spot."

"I don't see it, but how about that plow horse we brought back with us? Would that do?"

"Wait here. Watch your white brothers. See if they notice Black

Feather among the horses they guard so intently." A wolf called from a far distant valley. The sound echoed briefly, only to be returned by another, then another.

"The wolves seek each other this night, my brother. Watch. Learn. Shoshone are shadows within shadows." Black Feather slipped away.

Del climbed up on a boulder so he could see better. He kept to the shadows to not draw attention to himself. He did spy Black Feather as he slipped into the remuda right behind an alert guard.

He lost sight of his friend after that. He never saw the plow horse, either, though he searched the herd thoroughly. He settled down to wait... Wolves yipped and howled unseen in the night. Del felt shivers go up his back. They were close.

A rock slapped him in the back. "Wake up, brother. I have brought you the horse you asked for."

Del looked to his right. There stood a smiling Black Feather leading the plow horse they had talked about.

"How did you do that? I didn't hear or see a thing. You need to teach me that. I want to move in the shadows."

"I will. But first, more urgent needs press us. We must alert the camp and get the stock moved within the circle of wagons. Wolf packs hunt, and your stock will die if we leave them out here. Even the Shoshone can't stop a determined wolf pack from attacking." Snarls and bawling erupted out of their sightline. "It's already begun. They will kill quickly and come back for them later. Let's go."

Calls for help echoed throughout the gathered herd. Men with torches spread out from the camp. They had hundreds of horses, mules, and cattle and not enough men to guard them all.

Daniel and Tucker came to them out of the darkness. "I wondered where you two went off to. What have you seen, Black Feather?"

"Open up the wagon circle and drive your stock in. Keep lighted torches all around the perimeter of the camp."

Wolves yipped and howled nearby. There were many wolves, more than Del had ever heard. A large pack attacked, decimating their herd, out of sight in the dark of night—undaunted, unafraid, masters of the night, slicing throat and tendon at will. Men on horseback circled the herd, pushing them into the protection of the wagon's torch lit circle. It proved tight quarters, but better than being left to fang and claw.

Ben rushed up, his horse breathing heavily. "Looks like we lost about four or five head over yonder. Cattle mostly. We'll have to keep up a guard all night and keep those torches lit. I seen this before. Wolves killing calves and the mothers when they come to protect them, and just leaving the carcasses to rot! Seemed like they just did it for the joy of killing. You boys join the ones guarding this quarter of the circle. Good luck. It's been a bad day all around."

Del's first thought was for Raj and Star. He caught them up and led them into the camp. Tucker and Daniel saw to the cattle they could find. Black Feather helped with the horses.

Men carried torches round and round the camp all night. No one slept. The women made coffee and kept fresh torches available all night. Attacks could be heard in the night, followed by shouting and gunfire. Snarls of the wolves and the whimpering of their suffering victims made the hair on their backs stand up in alarm. Growls mingled with the sound of bones being crunched as the wolves fought each other over their kills. One attacked a guard, but he was able to fight it off with his flaming torch. His leg needed to be cleaned, bathed, and bandaged. Guards fired at the gleaming red eyes, highlighted by the flickering flames in the wall of darkness.

Daylight came as a welcome relief. The wolves drifted as the dawn crept forward.

"Let's go see what we lost!" Daniel pulled several wagon tongues aside. The field was a tattered carnage of death— fourteen cattle and four horses down. They found several half-consumed, and some still alive.

One of Daniel's prized Line Backs still alive, but torn up too badly to live. His bellows of anguish carried over the killing fields, until Daniel put a bullet in his head. "Sorry, old friend. I hope that was a blessing!"

Del found Blood and Red—his two Durham bulls—standing back-to-back, eyes white and nostrils spread and snorting. Blood and hair matted on their horns. A dead mangled muzzle of hair and bone lay wallowed into the dust. It was a dead wolf, but there wasn't much left to identify it. It took a while to get the bulls calmed down. They had been in combat all night. Once they realized who Del was, they eagerly nudged him like puppy dogs wanting to be petted. They followed him until they came into the protection of the wagons.

"Looks like we lost a lot!" muttered Captain Nightingale to the men and women who had gathered. "Ben, how many dead wolves did you count?"

"I say four, Cap'n!" Ben replied.

Del spoke up. "Our bulls counted for at least one! Maybe more than that."

"Okay, maybe we didn't do too badly, after all. I know several teams were shorted by this attack. We have to butcher what we can and keep moving. I know you're all exhausted, but we can't stay here. Butcher the meat, salt it, and spread it to dry in your wagons. We'll have fires tonight for roasting and smoking, as well. Get to it, folks. We need to get off this frying pan and out of this heat. Do your best. We head 'em out at noon. Graze 'em what you can until then. We have one wounded, but Micah is going to be all right, I'm told. Thank God for that."

Daniel supervised his family getting their stock together. The men gentled their animals, wiped out their noses with wet cloths and let them drink a little water from a bucket. They wanted more, but the precious water had to go a long way. No one had planned for this emergency. Once the animals had been seen to, the task of cutting out any useful meat began. In this heat, the flies and black gnats were relentless. It was an awful job, but it had to be done. The wolves would feast on what remained.

"I figure we got us about eighty pounds of useful meat. We've salted it and covered it with a canvas. That'll keep the flies off until we can cut it into strips to dry tonight. We'll have to rearrange it from time to time to keep it from spoiling, but it should keep, as it's well salted. Once we get the teams hitched up and wash this blood off, it'll be time to head out." Tucker sat down with his head down. "These bugs are worse than the heat!"

"Maybe we should wash up first, Tuck. We'll feel better and the oxen won't be so spooked by the smelly blood on us. Surely, we can all wash up with one bucket of water. That leaves us two barrels until we reach Three Islands."

True to his word, Captain Nightingale pushed them out on the trail shortly after noon. The stunning heat made Del glad he had his broad brimmed hat. He wore a wet bandana around his neck. They made a quick meal of biscuits, molasses, and dried beef.

"I'll sure miss that Line Back. They're good animals. It's a good thing we could hitch that plow horse in his place," Daniel said. "We were luckier still, considering what could have been if we hadn't moved the stock into the circled wagons. We have Black Feather to thank for that."

After a hot and treacherous day on the trail, everyone gladly stopped for the night. Daniel and Tucker went to check on Nancy's wagon and her boys. She and her boys had not lost any of their mules. They were glad to join the Riodan's for some of their roasted meat.

"I opened a jar of carrots I'd been saving. I grew them back east. It's my last jar." Nancy offered the precious gift to them.

"They'll be welcome, Miz Kincaid," Daniel said.

Nancy smiled at Del. He smiled back and blushed.

After supper, they all fell to work cutting the meat in strips and hanging it over a low smoky fire.

"I salted the meat well, so's it won't go bad," said Tucker. "I hope it keeps, once we've got it dried out. It's awful hot. I'd hate to lose so much meat. We got to keep a good smoke on it to keep away the flies."

Taking turns, the men kept the fires going through the night. By morning it was dry enough to finish drying in the wagon beds under the hot sun without fear of infestation by the flies.

No one had slept much in the heat. They couldn't get comfortable in their sweaty, stinky clothes that felt like they were slipping around inside them. It was better to be by the fire and doze off occasionally while they tended the meat. The smoke helped keep the bugs off them. Bart and Nate stayed with the men, and Nancy cleaned up after supper but went to her wagon to sleep if she could.

"We should be at Three Island Crossing in two to three days at the most!" Ben said the next morning. "We'll see American Falls by tomorrow. It's named on account of two Americans being swept over them a few years ago. Shame you got to die like them fellas and ol' Laramie to get your name on something. Later, we come to Shoshone Falls. We'll hear 'em first. It's eerie to hear something so far away before you see it. Shoshone Falls has got a whirlpool that could suck up a wagon." Ben turned to young Bart and Nate. "You'll be glad to be on the rimrock when you see them, I betcha."

He was right, of course. The train passed American Falls the next morning. They could see them from the rimrock but couldn't get to them.

The falls were still well beyond their ability to get to, and Nightingale was not in the mood to linger. "Look and keep going. We got almost three days to Three Island Crossing and water. Keep up there, you'll water in a few days people, keep going." Nightingale drove them on as if the devil was driving him.

"I think he feels guilty about what happened to Alice and Russell. You see, he introduced Caleb to them when Caleb first joined up. He feels responsible, being his niece and all. Cap'n and me is looking out for her. Several men in her division are helping her out as well. She's game. That's for sure, but I do hear her weeping in her wagon at night."

Ben came to get Del and Black Feather to scout ahead with him.

"I'll go see, if there's anything I can do," Nancy volunteered. "I know she needs a friend to look in on her. I'm sure other women are visiting, but we've both lost our men. We can be a comfort to each other."

"Ma! I want to go with Del, and Black Feather!" Bart said to his mother. "I know they'll take me. I need to learn how to get along. They are the only ones I can learn from. Ben, will you take me? I won't be any trouble. I promise. How about it, Del? Black Feather?"

"I was out with the men at his age. I think he needs to learn. It's the way of my tribe. I'd like to see him come."

"Okay, if his ma agrees to it," said Ben. "But she has to know there's danger. He'll have to keep his senses about him."

"I'm good. Bart's always held his own on any trail he's been with me. As long as Miz Kincaid says so," replied Del.

"Ma?"

"Okay, but you take care. If you get hurt, I don't know what I'd do. Probably take a switch to your britches. Take your pa's rifle."

"Aw, Ma, don't talk like that in front of Black Feather, would you?"

"All right, Bart, you're part of the party. We ride before sunup. Be ready. We won't wait for you." Ben spit in the fire as he left.

Nancy put her hands on her hips. "If you take up chewin' a chaw like Mister Ben, I will take a switch to you and to your backside, as well. Del, Black Feather, you mind me, now. I don't want my boy to have that vile habit. I'll hold you both responsible. Do you hear me?"

Both men nodded in unison, dumbfounded. "Yes, ma'am, we hear you."

"What was that about?" Black Feather asked Del.

"I don't have any idea," replied Del with a surprised grimace and gesture of defeat.

The quartet rode out of the camp the next morning. A faint dew had settled on the dry grass, a daily dose of moisture welcomed by every creature. It was almost cool. Bart was wide awake and doing his best to look a part of this group. He held each of these men in very high esteem. He wouldn't let them down.

By nooning time, a roar had begun that caused them to doubt their ears at first. It grew louder with each passing mile. The stock had had only sparse dry grazing since they topped the rimrock, with very little water. They hoped to find both water and grass.

Shoshone Falls lived up to its reputation—over two hundred feet high with multiple falls spilling over the rock in many places at different heights. They had to yell at each other to be heard.

"The falls are kinda dry now," Ben shouted. "You should see this in the spring when the snow melt comes."

They rode on north of the falls and made camp. The wagons would have to camp on the rimrock. It was a six-mile hike back down to the river, and wagons couldn't make it.

"I sure want a drink," said Ben, "but I'm not up for a twelve-mile ride just to wet my whistle and fill my canteen. Let's make camp here. We'll be at Three Island Crossing tomorrow."

TOM DEARBORN'S STOMACH LURCHED. THE men who had just come in were the same men who had tried to rob and kill his family. He pulled the green visor down further over his eyes and grabbed a pair of spectacles that sat on display on the counter and put them on quickly.

"Can you fill this order, mister?" The biggest one of the gang handed him a list.

"Sure thing, Mister....?"

"Just fill the list, clerk. You don't need a name."

"Just makes it easier to keep my orders straight, sir. Names come and go. I'll have Walker pull the order in the back from storage. That suit you?"

"Walker, huh? Yeah, I guess that's okay. My friend over there needs a hat."

I'll just bet he does, thought Tom. Reading the list, he turned and entered the storeroom.

"Little Tom, stop what you're doing." Tom whispered to his son. "I want you to go get Mister Keller. Tell him that the men who robbed us, are in the store. Tell him to bring some soldiers. There's five of them and they are all carrying guns. Out the back! You don't want them to see you. Go quick now. Run! Tell them to come to the backdoor."

"Okay, Pa. Pa, you look funny."

"Go," said Tom sternly.

What did they want? Tom reviewed the list. Dry soup, flour, lard, salt, beans, bacon, dried fruit and vegetables and, one blanket. Oh, and one hat. He gathered the pile and placed it neatly on the counter. Feeling confident in his disguise, he approached a man neatly shaved and dressed, trying on several hats.

"Did you find one you like, sir?" Tom asked.

Beaux Conlon looked dissatisfied. The rest of the men had stationed themselves around the store looking at goods with one eye and keeping an eye on the door and the others in the shop with their other.

There was an air of tension about the store Tom had never sensed before. Maybe it was his nerves, making him anxious, but the air was thick with it nonetheless.

"Do you have a smaller size in this model?" Beaux asked. He hadn't shopped in a store since he had fled from Independence. The likelihood that anyone knew him out here in the west seemed remote. He enjoyed the feeling of being waited on, even if the clerk looked odd in those highly magnified glasses that made his eyes so big.

"What size do you need, sir? I'll have to check in the storeroom for another size."

"Let's try a seven. These are all over that and too big."

Tom turned to go. "I'll be right back, sir."

"I'll be over here by the shirts."

Tom quickly hurried back to the storeroom. Mr. Keller was already there with the six armed men. Tom pointed out the five men who had attacked them.

"Four of you men go around to the front," Keller ordered. "Capture any who try to get away. Shoot if you must. There are innocent people in the store. I don't want anyone shot who don't need it."

"Tom, go wait on your man. Try to get him to turn his back to us, and as soon as you do, we'll come out and apprehend them. Do you have a gun?"

"Well, no. I don't carry a gun in the store when I work."

"Well, get the one under the counter. Put it in your trousers so's he won't see it. Be careful, Tom. They've already tried to kill you. If they're the gang I've been hearing about, they're all wanted killers. They kill for sport and hold no remorse."

Tom told Little Tom to be a good fellow and stay in the storeroom. "I'll come and get you when it's over. Good boy!" Tom picked the boy up and sat him on a barrel. "Now, stay here, son. I'll be back soon."

"Be careful!" Mr. Keller warned.

Tom put the hat box down on the counter, acted like he was reaching for something under the counter, and pushed the revolver that was kept there for emergencies into his pocket.

Clancy Albright, the other clerk, watched him with questioning eyes. Tom put his finger to his mouth and mouthed, "Be quiet!"

The other man backed off.

Standing erect now, Tom carried the hat box over to Beaux, who was holding up a blue and white striped shirt in front of him. He placed it back on the shelf in favor of a white shirt with a ruffled front and cuffs. It reminded him of when he had clothes of the best quality and could catch the eyes of the ladies when he entered a room. He sighed. He missed those good old days, when he didn't have a care except which cigar to choose and which brandy to have after dinner. He looked at the clerk as he approached. Suddenly, there was something familiar about that man that pricked Beaux's interest and held his attention as the clerk approached.

"I believe this is your size, sir," said Tom cheerfully, though he felt far from cheerful. He opened the box and lifted the hat, handing it to Beaux. "Look in the mirror, sir."

Tom handed him the hat. Beaux took it, looked at it, then at the clerk and put it on his head. The hat sank down over his ears. "Good God, man! What did you bring me? I'm not a giant! Look at the sweatband, it's seven and three-qaurters. Idiot! Look for yourself! Can't you see out of those glasses?"

Tom, of course, could *not* see due to the thick glasses. He turned the hat bottom-side up and peered inside.

"I don't know what to make of this, sir. Surely, the box said seven." Without thinking, he slid the glasses down off his nose and stared at the size tag. "Seven and three-quarters …."

He looked back at Beaux.

"I know you! You were that family back on the trail, before Delaino and Tucker showed up. Aren't you?" Beaux's eyes blazed hard and mean now.

The other four men, alerted, started for the door.

"Hold it right there, gents. The jig is up. We've got the door covered and the backdoor is blocked. Stay where you are and lay down your guns. Do it now! Round them up, men!" Mr. Keller ordered his men to close in to apprehend the fugitives.

Beaux instantly had Tom Dearborn by the neck and a pistol to his throat. "Oh no, fellas! *You!*" He pointed to Mr. Keller. "Tell them who's in charge, or by jingo, I'll blow this man's head off! I'll do it, too!" He held the clerk by the throat with his left hand. A pistol, cocked and ready to fire, jabbed into Tom's face.

Beaux slowly pulled Tom toward the door, past the hat counter. "You men there, make way. We're leaving. All of you get behind the counter or your boy here dies leaving a wide' and two kids! You have two kids, right, bucko?"

Unable to think of any other response, Tom nodded.

Mr. Keller and two of his men moved behind the counter.

"I thought so. Wait. Just so's this trip doesn't end up being a total loss.... Adonis! Clean out that cash box." Beaux reached over. "What's this?" He put a pearl grey fedora on his head. "Well, what do you know. It fits. I'll take it, clerk, and I do mean, *take* it."

Adonis shook a fist filled with bills and jingled a canvas bag of coins over his head, signaling he was done, before stuffing everything inside the bag.

"All right, everybody, stay where you are. Don't move. Waylon, get our goods, will you? No sense leaving with our hands only half full. That's better."

"You'll not get out of the fort, Mister. You can count on that."

"You've got guards outside then, don't you? Call them in or I swear this man and everyone here dies. We'll open fire and kill every man and woman in the place. We're damned already! We've got nothing to lose. How about you, Mister Big Mouth? Call your men to come in here. Do it!"

Keller started for the door.

"Oh, no, fatty, not you. Ask one of your other men to do it. You're my second shot, you know. Boys, pick out a target. If they don't come in, start shooting. Women, too!"

"Clancy, go call them in. All of them," Keller said in exasperation. "We have no choice."

The other clerk nervously crept to the door and looked out, "Come on in, boys. Put your guns down and come over here! Mister Keller's orders!"

"Keep those hands where I can see them, boys. That's it. Nice and high. Get over there behind Fatty. I want a clean shot if I have to take it."

Beaux was feeling foxy now. He had this hand won for sure. "Clerk, you got any cigars over there? My boys could use a nice cigar." He dragged Tom back to the counter. "Grab me a box of them cheroots, would you, clerk?" He pushed Tom behind the counter.

There was nothing to do but get the cigars. Tom still had the pistol in his front pocket. Oh, if only he had the chance to use it.

"Okay, men, it's time to leave. Thank you all very much. Now don't go making any noise or we'll start shooting. We're going to leave here nice and quiet like. No one come out that door for five minutes if you want to live."

"Clerk, if I see you again, I'll shoot you where you stand. Let's go!"

"Pa, are you all right? It's awful quiet back there!"

"Little Tom, no! Go back!"

The child's sudden outburst surprised Beaux, and he turned to shoot. He fired just over Little Tom's head. Tom pushed his son out of the way and, pulling his pistol, fired a shot in the direction of Beaux Conlon. Keller and the other men reached for their guns.

"Hold it!" Beaux ordered. He covered Keller and his men as his gang quickly, scrambled out the door.

"Your boy was lucky, clerk." He cracked the barrel of his pistol over Tom's head, stunning him. "Don't be so stupid next time." Covering the entire store, he backed out the door and blocked it with a wooden plank pulled from a stack nearby. The gang rode away shooting back at the door, sending any nearby spectators scrambling for cover.

Mr. Keller sent out search parties, but they came back that evening with nothing. They did find blood stains on the door frame and in the dirt of the floor. "You creased one of them, Tom, with that wild shot! We'll put the word out up and down the trail to be on the lookout for them snakes. Robbed us and rubbed our faces in it, I'd say. That don't settle well with me. Well... you drew first blood at least. Glad you're on board here, my boy. Glad you're on board. Let's get this place cleaned up and get back to business." Keller went around behind the counter. "Any idea how much was in the till, fellas?"

Four men came through the door, looking around at the confusion. "You the owner, mister? What goes on here?"

"We were just robbed! Who are you?"
"Name is Shepherd. Mind if I ask you a few questions?"

29

A BAND OF INDIANS, DRAGGING their travois behind them, snaked in a line headed for Three Island Crossing.

"They go to fish," said Black Feather.

A wagon train crossed at the ford as they rode down to the river. They led their horses to water, took off their saddles, and let them roll in the dusty grass.

"Well, looky there." Ben pointed. "The grass *is* greener on the other side of the river. Now don't that beat anything you ever saw? Let's set up camp over there."

From Del's point of view this should be an easy crossing. They watched as the other wagons began to cross. Indian boys eagerly rode or swam cattle and horses over the river. They loved this task and were welcome to it, as most of the white people didn't know how to swim. There were three small islands between the banks of the river, making it look deceptively like an easy crossing.

A wagon started cautiously across to the other side making the first island. Water only came about up to the bottom, just level with the axles. Starting back in again, the mules fell off into a hole. Floundering under the weight of harness, the mules tangled quickly and went under. The wagon floated briefly, until the struggling animals and current tipped it. It filled, weighted down with hundreds of pounds of supplies, and now, thousands of pounds of water. The wagon sank, caught in the grip of the current. It pulled everything under—mules and men, hopes and dreams, tumbling along the rocky bottom, soon to be flung over Shoshone Falls miles downstream.

It was a shock. It happened so fast. After that, Bart, Del and Black Feather pitched in to help the others. Swimming the teams over the treacherous water first, mounted by whooping Indian boys, men re-hitched the teams to lines still attached to the wagons on the other side. Driving the teams up the sloping trail, they pulled each wagon across the ford. Tiresome, slow work, but they didn't lose any more wagons.

"That's what we'll do, boys, when Nightingale comes," said Ben. "We'll move teams over first and pull the wagons through the currents. Maybe we can caulk the bottoms someway with grass and grease. These Indian boys will be a great help in getting our stock over the blamed river."

That night they bought a huge fish, red fleshed and oiley, from a Shoshone boy.

"This tastes like salmon, but it doesn't look like it. The jaw is too long." Del had once caught salmon on the Atlantic coast. "What kind of fish is it?" He called to the boy as he left. The boy had one of Ben's arm bands wrapped around his forehead in payment for helping the men in their work and for the fish.

"Trout," said the young boy. "Trout from the sea. They swim and migrate like the salmon."

"Must be one of them steelheads, we calls 'em, due to their color," said Ben. "Mighty fine eating. Some of the Chinamen eat it raw. I like mine roasted over a hot fire myself. Lordy, that is good eating. Don't you think so, Black Feather?"

"Been eating it all my life. Good dried and smoked, too."

"Since there's so many Indians about and they appear friendly, I'm leaving the two of you here, while I go find the train in the morning. We'll cross directly as soon as they get here. After breakfast, young'un," he said indicating Bart, "you can go with me!"

"Aw, Ben, I want to stay with Del and Black Feather. Can I?" Bart pleaded.

"Oh, all right, you stay, too! I'll leave in the morning. Del, stake us out a camp on the green side of the river. That other train will be gone in the morning. Set our camp upriver from them. I'm turning in. I never felt so full in days." Ben fell asleep in a few minutes, his head on his rolled-up saddle blanket. Peaceful snores soon filled the campsite.

Black Feather took his friends around to the Indian camp. He was well known and liked by the elders of the tribe. It was an honor to have Black Feather introduce them to other members of the Shoshone nation.

Del explained this all to Bart. "Black Feather's father is a religious leader for the Shoshone. He and his family are held in great esteem by the rest of the Shoshone nation. His introducing us as his friends is a great tribute. Remember names and this place. It may serve you or save your life one of these days."

Bart beamed, amazed, and pleased to be with Black Feather. "Wait'll I tell Ma and Nate what I seen tonight." By the time they returned to a snoring Ben, Bart sported a brand-new knife and a pair of knee-high moccasins.

Crossing the Snake proved a task of chaotic order. Little Shoshone boys, ten to sixteen years old helped swim the stock across the river first. Splashing and hooting, those boys went unafraid over the river several times driving horses and cattle. Starting upstream after crossing the first and second islands, they bypassed the third by swimming around its upstream point, drifting down river until they landed, and men on the other side drove the stock on to greener pastures. Those oxen ate blissfully of the grass on this side of the river. Then, racing each other, the boys swam back to the other side to do it again.

Ben advised everyone to caulk the sides and bottoms of their wagons. Using axle grease and long grass the men drove this in between the planks of their wagons with hammer and chisel to keep them buoyant.

"May not be tight enough for an ocean voyage, but it should keep em' floating crossing the Snake," Ben said.

There were fifty-four wagons, over six hundred cattle, oxen, horses, mules, and Del's three chickens to get across the river. They lost one wagon when its back gate broke free and filled with water.

Leaping into the river a soaked and grateful emigrant crawled to his feet on the other side. One mule broke a leg and had to be shot. This they offered to the tribe and who fully appreciated it. Many of the tribes favored mule meat.

That night, the train feasted on salmon and trout stuffed with fresh herbs such as wild onions and goosefoot gathered along the riverbanks. They drank, bathed, and refreshed from a long day.

Indian boys displayed and swapped the prizes they had earned with each other. They received mirrors, sugar, some pots, flour, metal knives, anything the emigrants offered that the Indians deemed proper payment for their death-defying deeds. The Indian boys had a proper sense of value and were sharp bargainers.

"Believe it or not, Daniel, it cost me a petticoat, a roll of red ribbon, and a pound of tea to get my wagon across," Nancy said, laughing that night at supper. "I'll probably miss the tea the most! Those little guys were fearless. I don't believe we could have crossed this river without them."

"They were a great help, plus they caught supper for us. I bought four salmon for a dollar. It was outrageous! But I admired the young lad dickering with me. That six-year-old boy probably could have had my entire wagon, if I wasn't careful. I'd grown tired of smoked and dried meat and beans. I hope Ft. Boise is well stocked. It's been there since the beginning of the beaver trapping days, back in the 20's. Beaver is not bringing the price it used to and is much scarcer. Just like Bourgeois said, 'Da beaver is about trapped out.'"

Finishing their meals, the men cleaned camp and completed their chores.

As Del and Black Feather tended to their horses, Black Feather said, "I return to my village tomorrow. They will be moving to winter camp. We must hunt and prepare for the cold winter. I will miss you, my brother. This time has been good. You will always be welcome in our village. You and your family."

Del told Daniel and Tucker that Black Feather was leaving. Daniel shook his hand and embraced him. "You are my second son, Black Feather. Please give your father and mother my well wishes and good luck in the hunt."

Tucker and Daniel made sure he had provisions for the journey back. They gave gifts of tobacco, meat, sugar, and coffee to Black Feather for his family.

"Moon Star thinks of you, Del Rio." These were the last words spoken between the two friends when they rolled into their blankets that night.

In the morning, Black Feather was gone.

30

D ANIEL DETERMINED TO KEEP HIS stock until they reached Oregon City. They had already lost one of the Lineback oxen to wolves, and the rest appeared worn and exhausted from poor grass along the trail. Now that they had crossed the Snake, the grass grew lush and green. Daniel made sure his animals got to the meadows and insisted Del and Tucker do the same for the Kincaids' animals.

He was glad he had taken the care he did, as the stock offered for sale at Ft. Boise were exhausted skeletal creatures. The fort had started to decline. Once the gem of the Rockies, a byway that offered exhausted travelers a taste of elegance and ambience had grown shabby elegant, fraying around the edges. Daniel bought grain and made sure each animal got at least one cup a day to keep them in shape. A few days of good grass, good rest at night, and a bait of grain in the morning helped maintain Riodan's stock, keeping them among the best conditioned of all the train's animals. Judging by the upkeep on the fort, the fur trade obviously declined.

Keeping to his schedule, Nightingale had them cross the Snake one last time north of Ft. Boise, then they headed for the Blue Mountains. "We'll be in Oregon soon, folks," he said the night before departure. "We are about seventeen hundred miles from Independence as the crow flies. There's been a lot of ups and downs, but we have persevered through drought, heat, flies, and death. The bad news is the worst isn't over. We're in the mountains with range after range of rocky, dry peaks with little grass. We're headed for the Blue Mountains. Some of you will pull out for the Whitman mission after we get to the Umatilla River. We've made good time. The passes should be clear. It'll be October soon, and then the weather can change in a few hours. I know you've been dumping your loads. Your animals are tired and worn out. Put yourself in their place. Do you want to live or keep your grandma's dresser? Your choice, but I'd strip my wagon down to the essentials so I could get through. Some of you have already done that and your stock is in better shape than others. Do what you think is best. If you lose your stock, you're afoot. You will not be able to keep up. We will move on. You know that."

Early fall weather made the Blues appear rocky and bleak. The trail was only a few years old, and before then, wagons couldn't get through. They took advantage of the few streams that drizzled down the mountains for watering their animals and cooking. Graze became scarce once they reached the midst of the Blues, but the scenery was breathtaking.

"Tucker, Ben says we still have the Cascades ahead of us. I hope they're as pretty as the Blues. We'll be through these passes in a few days. Pa hopes to let the stock rest and eat for a couple of days before we make for The Dalles. The Columbia is supposed to be a pretty treacherous river."

"It is pretty here, Del. Pretty dry as well. I just hope the trail to The Dalles has some green grass. We've only so much grain left and that's about all they're getting besides the dry stuff in what is supposed to be meadows along the trail."

"Walla Walla is the local tribe around here," Nightingale said at the meeting that night. "We have to keep a good lookout. They've been known to murder emigrants for their clothes and horses. Everybody keep together when going for water or looking for firewood. We'll be at the Umatilla soon. We'll stop for a day or so to water stock and let them graze. I hope there is grass. These mountains have been more dust than decent graze. We are on the west side of the mountains, so we're headed out of the Blues. Next stop, the Umatilla River."

As if on cue, the Walla Walla *did* attack that night. Shots rang out about midnight as the camp had gone into an exhausted sleep. The trail was too narrow to circle the wagons, so the stock had been gathered in a small meadow downhill from the main body of the train along a narrow creek that offered water and the only green grass they could find. A full harvest moon edged around the mountain as the men scrambled to fight off the attack.

"C'mon, boys, let's head 'em off. The Indians are pushing the stock downhill." Daniel toed Del who was still rolled up in his blankets. Tucker handed him his pants and hat. The older men sped off leaving Del to dress and follow.

Del's first thought was of Raj and Star. He needed to find them. They kept the horses separate from the cattle and down the hill to Del's right. He remembered this as he pulled on his boots, belted his gun, and grabbed his rifle. He spotted Tucker's knife hanging by its strap and slung it over his shoulder without thinking. Leaping over logs and dodging running men, as the camp prepared a counterattack, Del anxiously searched for the horses.

This is where he'd left them, by God. He whistled for Raj and heard a shrill whistle in return farther down the hill. He went at a dead run, hoping somebody didn't shoot him in the back for his trouble.

Shots rang out above him and to his left, back where the cattle had been gathered.

Raj had whistled instead of running back to him. That meant something or someone had him. Del's feet barely touched the ground.

Bursting into a clearing, he ducked just in time to avoid a tomahawk smashing into his face. He rolled and came up swinging his rifle and clubbing the nearest Walla Walla with it. In the dark, under the canopy of the forest it was difficult to see, so Del assumed everyone was an enemy. Pulling the black-bladed knife from its sheath with his right hand, he swung his rifle with his left and stabbed at anything that moved. He didn't have time to shoot, but he could see and hear a commotion in front of him.

Some brave held a rope around Raj's neck fighting to control what was now a flashing, biting, kicking demon in the open meadow. Backlit by moonlight, a ring of braves surrounded Raj as they tried to pull him to his knees. Screaming with rage, Raj lashed and kicked at anything that got near him. A very brave Walla Walla dropped down on Raj's back from an overhead limb. Shouting with triumph, he grabbed Raj's mane and held on for dear life.

"Raj!" Del shouted and was immediately swarmed by sweaty feral bodies smelling of smoke, sweat and the forest. They pulled Del down holding his arms and hands behind him, pummeling him with fists and feet. They don't know what they got hold of. Raj was a trained war horse and Del turned the great stallion loose.

Strong arms held him as he looked at Raj in that mirrored moonlight through swollen eyes. It was a sight he would always remember. Time slowed to distort his perception of the scene before him. He was oblivious to his attackers.

The night, black under the canopy, allowing the full moon to only illuminate the small clearing in ethereal silver. All else were black shadows performing in slow measured movements, and the muffled sounds were incomprehensible. Del's vision sharpened vividly, his peripheral vision widened, completing his total comprehension of the scene before him. Raj, silhouetted, stiff legged in agitation, a rope strangling his neck, as he fought back. Other flaying black shadows tried to leap on Raj's back to force him down. All of this played before Del, as a scene from some unknown opera, backgrounded by black forest and that huge luminous moon. Raj's maddened screams broke through the night, cracking Del's dream.

"Attack. Attack! Raj! Attack!" Del's screams matched Raj's in ferocity and anger. A fist smashed into Del's mouth, cracking his lip and blooding his face. The horse's ears pricked up at his voice. What had been a game to these Indians, a challenge to subdue this strong courageous animal, earning them bragging rights and status within their tribe, quickly turned into bloody death.

Raj stopped, dropping his head, blowing through his nose in great gasping bellows-like breaths heaving his sides. The Indians thought the game was over and crowded around congratulating the brave rider on the mount's back. Suddenly, screaming in fiery delight to have his enemies drawing so near, Raj began to buck and kick, lashing out in all directions.

Del had only watched Raj during training, but to see the effect of that training in action was heart stopping. What he saw, now, was beyond anything he had expected. A devil in horseflesh, gloved with iron hooves, went berserk.

Bodies flew in all directions, broken and bloodied. Raj leaped, kicked, turned and leaped again, kicking and stomping anything he could reach. Full grown men somersaulted into the brush. Others crumpled into piles of sodden, bloodied, broken-boned flesh, as ironclad hooves stomped and kicked. Screaming his war cry, Raj challenged his enemy to come to him and die. It reminded Del of the Norsemen berserkers he had read about. Finally, only two Indian braves remained. The one, who had held the rope, somehow escaped the flying hooves. The other lay prone on Raj's neck grasping his mane in clawed hands, and a mouthful of mane between his teeth. Raj came to a standstill, then suddenly rearing up and crashing over on his back. He crushed the once triumphant brave into the dust and pine needles of the forest floor. Shaking him off, he charged the befuddled rope holder who had never seen a horse act this way. Even the most vicious wild grizzlies they had captured were docile, compared to the evil spirit that lived within this horse.

Visibly trembling, the brave wet himself as Raj deliberately charged him. Throwing his quiver of arrows at Raj's face, he turned to run, but not before Raj had bitten a huge chunk of flesh from the man's backside stripping off his buckskin breeches, leaving him naked and bleeding, as he shrieked his way into the forest. Raj shook it as a dog shakes a rat and spat it out, then looked in Del's direction.

Del's assailants all stood silent, seemingly transfixed by what they had just witnessed.

"Raj, here, boy!" Del whistled again. The horse returned that whistle and charged straight for him. The Indians vanished so quickly, Del fell on his rear, landing on a sharp rock. He winced. "Ouch!"

Raj nuzzled him and Del hugged his neck. "Oh, Raj, you were a devil. They didn't know what they had gotten into when they threw a rope on you, did they? That was almighty something to see. Oh,

Raj, my big boy!" Del held his forehead to the horse's, tears coming to his eyes. "I thought you were gone. I would have died if I lost you." He looked up at the moon. "Oh, my gosh! They still have Star and the other horses. C'mon, boy. We've still got work to do!"

Snaking the rope off his friend's neck, Del coiled it. It might come in handy later. He sprang onto Raj's back, thankful they hadn't pulled the bridle off. "Let's go find 'em. *Yah!*"

He had no trouble following the churned-up ground left by the stolen horses. It led down the mountain. Not getting a broken leg by jumping over the many fallen logs in the forest or stepping into a hole in the dark was harder.

"Easy, boy, that's it. We'll take it nice and easy. They've left a track a blind man could follow. Let's not get you lame or a broken leg. We'll catch 'em. They've got to go to water, and they can't move too fast in this terrain. Too dangerous. Them Walla Walla didn't steal them horses to kill 'em. Well, maybe the mules. Indians usually like mule to eat."

All night, they trailed the stolen herd. Del had to lead Raj when the thick forest obscured the moon and they couldn't see. Del could feel the ground with his feet. It felt like it had just been plowed. He bumped his knees, stumbled over branches and slipped into unseen holes.

"I don't want to come up lame or break a leg, neither, you know." Del stopped so he could rub a barked shin. Raj kept nudging him forward with his nose.

"All right. I'm going. I bet you're thinking about Star, aren't you? Well, I am, too." He led his horse forward. "Watch this log. Step over it. That's it."

By dawn they came to a break in the forest, a tiny meadow of grass, watered by an equally tiny rivulet that had pooled, before it joined with other small seeps and flowed down the mountain in a growing stream. If Del had not followed the track, he would have missed it. The horses gathered on either side drinking and stealing a mouthful of grass where they could.

Ten Indians guarded the herd or gathered about the fire drinking coffee and talking. Two braves talked animatedly with each other. Del thought it looked like an argument. He recognized one of the men as one of the Indians who had held him until Raj charged to his rescue.

"I bet he's telling that fella about that demon horse last night, Raj. What do you think? That other fellow doesn't believe him. Yeah, he's laughing at the brave telling the story."

The storytelling Indian seemed very indignant. He embellished his story with words and gestures, but the other man was having none of it.

"He just don't believe his story, Raj," Del said. "Let's figure out what we're going to do. We're still on the west side of the mountain. If we drive the horses down the stream to the right, we might be lucky and pick up the main trail in a few miles, then follow it back to the wagons. There's Star. Somebody's riding her. She's used to the way Indians and white men smell, but she don't look happy. She's looking around for something. I hope it's us.'

Del pondered his situation. There were ten Walla Walla's guarding the herd. The horses and mules were in that small box cove so the Indians could keep them gathered, making them easier to guard. They must have been waiting for more men to continue their drive. They certainly weren't expecting a raid.

"Here's what we do, Raj. We're going to be an army of two. I'm going to make Black Feather proud by sneaking over there and knocking that Indian off Star without him seeing me. I'll yell, attack, attack, like before, and you go for the Indians at the fire. By then, I'll have the herd moving and you drive them from the rear. Do you understand your orders, Sergeant?" Del smiled at his own joke. He didn't know if Raj really understood his plan. As much as they had gone through together, he hoped he did. Del always talked to Raj as if the stallion understood every word. He did know Raj would charge the Indians, when he yelled attack, whether he led or followed would be up to the stallion. He would just have to figure it out when the time came. There are no guarantees!

"Okay, boy, I'm off. Wait here, till I yell." He patted Raj's big head and rubbed his ears, before slipping into the shadows.

Del made his sneak to the opposite side of the herd, where the guard sat mounted on Star. "Thank you, Black Feather," Del whispered to himself. He moved in the shadows and through the horses silently until he was under Star's belly. The Indian watched over the backs of the horses when Del tapped the guard's right knee, ducked under Star's belly and pulled him to the ground from the opposite side, where Del promptly knocked him out with the butt of his handgun.

"Whoa, girl! Easy." Del rubbed her nose, so she could smell him.

Star immediately nuzzled Del as if saying, "I've been waiting for you. Let's get out of here!"

Slipping up on her back, Del lay out flat, waiting to see if anyone noticed the missing guard. Del wore buckskins which were dark tanned like the Indians wore, but his hair was lighter than an Indian. Nonchalantly, he sat upright and began circling the herd so he'd be in the front when Raj charged the loafing Indians.

As Del drew near the front of the herd, the storyteller caught Del's eye and called a warning. Del whistled and screamed. "Raj! Attack! Attack!"

Immediately, Raj screamed his war cry and charged, scattering Indians in all directions. One lay unconscious by the fire. Raj had someone's shirt in his teeth shaking it back and forth. Del fired his pistol to stampede the herd.

Del hollered again. "Hurrah!! Hurrah," as he gripped Star's mane and kicked her flanks starting the herd along the stream. Hooves pounded the turf to plowed land again, running through the fire at full gallop. No Indian could have stood against that flood of horseflesh. Five crushed bodies lay in testament to that, as they streamed through the narrow canyon.

The only Indian Del saw was the storyteller heading into the forest pumping his arms and legs just as hard as he could. He only stopped when he reached the safety of the forest. Seeing he wasn't pursued by the demon horse, he fell back against a pine tree and slumped to the ground watching the herd they had worked so hard to steal vanish from sight. The legend of the devil horse would be told around campfires for many years to come.

"H'ya, h'ya!" Del slapped his rope on his leg and spanked any rump he could reach with it. "Move up there, jughead! C'mon, mule, get going!"

The herd followed Star out of the cove. The stream bank was not wide, so the horses easily followed it, hemmed in by the steep flanks of the mountain.

Del hoped they were going the right way. He didn't know where the stream led, but he'd have to follow it until the sides of the mountain gave way.

They did well for several miles. He wondered where Raj was— he didn't see the horse anywhere. He guessed they were leading two to three hundred horses and mules, a flowing stream of hoof, hide, and hair. Star crossed through the streambed to the other side and climbed the shallow bank as rocky boulders blocked their way.

"Good girl." Del patted and rubbed her neck. He let her have her head. She was an Indian horse, mountain bred, and he trusted her.

They must have ridden another five miles along that tiny stream. They rounded a hillside and came face to face with men on foot, guns leveled with determined looks on their faces. A shot whizzed over Del's head.

"Whoa, whoa, there! Don't shoot, men. It's Del Rio, and by God, he's got the horses and mules." Ben held up his arms to signal. "Don't shoot!" He stepped forward, a big coon-eating grin stretching from ear to ear across his face.

Del pulled up quickly, sliding Star to a stop. The horses behind them scrambled to stop and began milling around in confusion. For a few minutes, men and horses milled and danced around each other trying not to get trampled.

"We've been looking for these horses all night!" said Daniel. "Thank God you're safe! We were crossing this stream when we heard echoes of hoofbeats against the mountain. Couldn't figure it out. Sounded like thunder at first. We've been lined up waiting to ambush the thieving Walla Walla for ten minutes. It was that loud. You're lucky somebody didn't shoot."

"Somebody did, Pa! Lucky me, they missed."

"Sorry, Del! Glad I missed. You look and ride like an Injun!" One of the men waved at him from the back of a clay-colored horse.

Del waved back with a grin. "I don't know him, but I'm sure glad he's happy he missed."

Just then, a ruckus started at the end of the herd. Horses pushed their way forward crowding the ones in the front. Screams of rage sounded on the canyon walls as something continued to drive the horses forward.

"Raj!"

Bursting through the crowd of horses, Raj ran forward as if driven by demons. He still drove them forward, and he wasn't putting up with any arguments. Blood splattered his flanks from multiple battles. Del whistled a softer whistle this time.

"Come here." He dismounted and embraced his horse.

Daniel gave Del a slap to his shoulder, and then his eyes fell on Raj. "What happened? He looks like he's been in a war!"

"Pa, meet the rest of my army! Raj fought them Indians all off. Came and rescued me and was my wrangler keeping the horses moving from the rear! The real hero in this battle is the devil horse from Baltimore!" He hugged Raj's neck. "Thank you, big boy."

31

COMING DOWN OUT OF THE Blues, Nightingale's train followed McKay Creek until it reached the Umatilla three days later. They found the water and grazing good here. Nightingale ordered the train to stop, wash laundry, make repairs and rest up for a few days. Five wagons, who had joined along the trek, aimed to head for the famous Whitman mission near Walla Walla.

Mrs. Narcissa Whitman and Alice Spalding, back in 1836, were the first white women to cross the Rockies on horseback. The Whitmans started a mission trying to bring the word of God to the Cayuse Indians in southern Washington. All the wagons, except for the ones heading north to the Whitmans, crossed the Umatilla and camped on the other side.

"Whew, it feels good to be clean and wear clean clothes," said Tucker that night. "I was able to swap that old shirt I left Baltimore with, for a nice fish for supper. Indian was pleased to have it. I was glad for the fish and happy to get rid of it. Never wanted to wear it again in the first place. I got some onions and nettle greens, a few mussels, and some potatoes roasting in the coals. We're eating good tonight, friends."

"We head west, after this. The Dalles is our next major stop. Then we go by raft down the Columbia River, unless we follow the ridge of the Columbia gorge. It is a long way from there to Oregon

City going that way, another month at least. No other choice unless we want to be trapped by snow in the mountains. I don't like it. I'm not a river man or a seaman, like Del here. I like the earth under my feet. We'll have to see once we get there. Del, I'll let you take a look. I'd rather wait to be safe. Doesn't make sense to me, to come all this way, just to drown on a flimsy raft. I'd rather be bit by a snake or get scalped. So, you're going to have a heavy say in any decision we make, if we go by raft."

"I'll take a look, Pa. I don't fancy drowning any more than you do. How about it, Tuck?" Del laughed. "Rather be drowned or bit by a snake?"

"If it's all the same to you fellas, I'd rather eat a fish than be *eaten* by fishes." Tucker pulled his big fish off the fire. "Here come Nancy and the boys, just in time. Is that a pie she's carrying? I do believe she's my favorite woman in the whole wide world!"

"YES, MA'AM," SAID TUCKER AFTER he had finished his last bite of pie. "It would be a tolerable shame if you hid your cooking skills under a basket and not share them with the good folks of Oregon City, Nancy Kincaid."

"Why thank you, Tuck. Between your biscuits and my pies, I do think we could make a living in Oregon City."

"We is sure going to try, Miz Kincaid!"

"Oh, God. Don't say another word about that man's biscuits!" Del groaned. "I can feel his head swelling up across this campfire!"

"You've eaten my biscuits every day for months, Delaino Riodan! Here, catch!" Tucker flipped a hot ember at Del's chest.

"Oh, ouch, hot!" Del fell over backwards trying to get away from the coal, causing Nate and Bart to fall off their stumps laughing.

Del crawled back onto his log, slapping out sparks on his shirt. "And did I say, Mister Tucker, that they's fine biscuits? I wouldn't eat anybody else's. Miz Kincaid's excepted, of course!"

"Of course. Apology accepted." With a grin, he flipped the coal loaded on his spatula back into the fire.

THE NEXT DAY, THE WAGONS headed for the mission set out. The Riodans and Nancy went over to say goodbye and give presents. Tucker took his famous biscuits and Nancy took a pot of cooked porridge, mixed with molasses to be eaten on the trail or cooked over a fire as hoe cakes.

That night, the adults talked around the campfire. Ben joined them for supper.

"I have to tell you, Daniel, those wagons that left for the mission this morning disturbed me. Some of those children looked sick with fever to my eye," Nancy said. "Glad Bart and Nate didn't go with us."

"Maybe that's why they went to the mission," Daniel said. "Reverend Whitman is a doctor as well as a minister. Good man, I hear. Trying to do his best for the Indians. He and Miz Whitman married up just so they could do mission work. I guess he has a real calling."

"Don't be so sure. I visited that mission for a few days once. Appeared to me that Miz Whitman was pretty set in her ways. Didn't allow much for the ways of the Indians. The Cayuse couldn't understand why the Whitmans' God wanted them to plow a field. Their god, the Great Spirit, had already given them everything they needed. It didn't make sense to them, so they went for the presents and bartered for things they needed like knives and hatchets, but I never thought they believed in the Whitmans' version of God. They had a few quarrels, but have always remained tolerable friends, the Whitmans and the Cayuse. The Walla Walla never took to them Whitmans. They resent our crossing their land. That's why they're always attacking the white settlers' trains. The Walla can't figure out where we're all coming from."

"Just the same. I hope those poor children get help from the doctor. The thought of losing one of my boys to fever... I can't even think about it. I wouldn't—I don't know what I'd do. It would be so hard."

Daniel studied Nancy's face. Something in her tone alarmed him, but he shrugged it off to a mother's fear. "Those kids were happy and healthy just a few days ago. I saw them playing with each other around the campfire when the other wagon joined up with us. Everybody looked rosy cheeked and sounded happy. I'm sure they will be all right. Nate and Bart, as well. Would you like some more coffee?"

"Thanks. It just worries me, is all. Tucker, you saw them. I know you've been a sort of doctor to your own people and to the folks on this train. Did you find those children looked poorly?"

"Miz Kincaid, I've been giving that question a good bit of thought since this morning. Something has been hanging up in my brain. I just couldn't get it to come out. Did you notice I didn't shake their hands good-bye, and I rushed you all off so you couldn't either? Don't know why, but it came to me when you were talking just now."

All eyes turned toward him expectantly.

"I remember treating children with measles."

Nancy gasped. "Measles? Here?"

"An old woman I used to know taught me what to look for. Flushed, pallid, clammy skin, high fever right before a scarlet rash breaks out across your face, chest, and stomach. One other thing, there's a smell to measles. Some people can smell them. This old woman could smell measles from ten feet away. She taught me the smell. That's what has been hanging in my brain all day. Why, for some reason, I didn't want to shake the hands of those folks. I could smell measles as I approached the wagon. That's the memory that came to me as we were sitting here. The stench of measles."

"Oh, dear God, bless those poor people," said Nancy. "Tucker, I hope you're wrong."

"I do, too, Miz Kincaid. I do, too."

Ben stood up, looking seriously at them both.

"If what you two are saying is true, I've got to tell Cap'n Nightingale and quarantine anybody who may have had contact with those people. Do you have to touch them to be contagious or can you just be in the vicinity for you to catch the measles?"

"I don't really know, Ben." replied Nancy. "I always thought you had to be close by, at least. Do you know, Tucker?"

"It seems to me you have to make some type of personal contact. Either touching them or their belongings is how I've always seen it. We were the only ones who went across. Everybody else just waved goodbye from across the river. We didn't make any contact with them or their wagon."

"How long before you would know if you have measles or not, do you think?"

"My guess is about a week to ten days. You should see signs in a week I think."

"I'm quarantining these three wagons for ten days, starting now. You'll stay at the end of the train and not mix your stock or horses with anybody else. I'm sending a message to the captain, 'cause it appears, I'm quarantined with you!"

"Oh my, what now?" Nancy asked quietly and tossed her coffee into the fire.

"Maybe they don't have measles, and we'll be all right," said Ben.

"Yeah, maybe." Tucker shrugged, but he knew better.

32

NIGHTINGALE ACTED PROMPTLY UPON getting Ben's message. He arrived at their camp but did not dismount.

"Ben, I got your message. I'm sorry folks, but I must act for the safety of the entire train. I know you are only suspecting measles, but if there is even the slightest chance of exposure, I have to quarantine your wagons. This goes for you, too, Ben. You are to stay at least one hundred yards from any other wagon, person or animal on the train. You will travel at the rear of the train, keeping separate grazing and water to yourself. You will not hunt within one hundred yards of anyone who is a member of this expedition. Sorry, but I must isolate you for at least ten days, or I'll have a mutiny on my hands. We all hope we're wrong about this, but I have to act for safety. I'd do it to myself. Keep to your camp tonight, and wait until we pull out tomorrow to take your place at the rear.

"Ben, I'll miss you, but I'm pretty familiar with this part of the trail. We should be at the John Day River in about ten days. You'll return to regular duties then.

"If anyone gets sick, we'll leave you. If you break down, we'll leave you. Ben knows the way from here. He can guide you in those eventualities. I'm sorry to have to do this. Good luck to you all and stay well!" Captain Nightingale touched the brim of his hat and rode off.

They all sat in stunned silence.

"Well, by golly. I knew this would happen." Ben scratched the side of his face, sat down, and reached for his coffee.

"I guess it had to be done." Daniel kicked the dirt with his foot. "Del, how's our water holding out? Tuck, let's bring in our animals, so we can keep our distance from folks. Don't want anybody to shoot them in fear. I've seen epidemics like this in Indiana simply terrify a town. It's only ten days. I don't suppose any of us are sick. We're exiled to help other folks feel better and safer. Nancy, how's your water and provisions? We're going to be alone for a while, having to depend on each other. Ben, I guess you got the raw end of this deal. You'll just have to make the best of it like the rest of it. Though I will say, I'll appreciate your company."

"Just let me make the coffee!" said Tucker.

"I'll just lay up and let the rest of you take care of me, I guess." Ben put his hands behind his neck and leaned back against a log. "I always wanted to be waited on like a king. Wake me if you need me, peasants!"

The next morning, they took their place at the back of the train. A few families waved politely, but the look on their faces read like they were looking upon the condemned, and most never expected to see them again.

Tucker eyed the other wagons with distaste. "Do you see that, Daniel? They think we're dead already."

"Yeah, I seen it. I guess we can't expect anything else. Folks are scared. They've seen so much death and sickness on this trip. You must bury the dead and move on to live. They just haven't thrown any dirt over us yet. I think we'll prove them wrong. No one here is sick, thanks to you, Tuck."

Del hitched his team together, and the three wagons rode abreast of each other so as to lessen the amount of dust blanketing them.

Ben helped Nancy with her wagon. His stories entertained more than the boys. "Why, Nate, I once had a bear chase me up a tree! I was so scared when he climbed that tree after me, I started swayin' the top of the tree back and forth, back and forth and I leaped over to another tree. That ol' bear was plumb smart! He started swayin his tree back and forth to jump over after me. Why I must've jumped into seven trees that day! That jumpin' bear, a leapin' tree to tree after me."

"What happened, Mister Ben?"

"Well, that seventh tree was lucky for me. Not so lucky for the bear. The top broke just as he was a makin' his jump and he fell and broke his neck. Et him for breakfast, I did. Why, I had shore worked up an appetite. Slept in his bear skin that night. Right cozy it was. He had lost so much fat by jumpin' tree to tree. I just shook him out of his hide, didn't have to scrape it or nuthin'. Seven is lucky for me. I can always bet on seven."

Nancy waved over to Del, pointed to Ben and shrugged her shoulders. "He's got my boys bamboozled by his tales. They love it!"

It was a feeling of loneliness they had not experienced since joining the train. Somehow, they felt exposed, not having the people and presence of the wagons, animals, and the bustle of activity about them. They drew tighter together and more resolute.

Even Ben, who had spent much time alone in the mountains and prairies, felt it.

"Sometimes, I get the prickles up my back being out here. Like something is a-watching me. Don't like it. Don't like it a'tall. I feel almost plumb naked, like I'm a-walkin', breathin' target. It's throwed me off. This measles business, it's throwed me plumb off. It has."

Sometimes, someone would wave from the top of a hill back to them. It was hard to make out who it was mostly. They could tell if it were a man or woman, and then from their dress only.

"I think that's dear Alice waving up there," Nancy said one day, though it was hard to tell as the sun was setting and the figure was obscured. "She was waving a green bonnet, I think. Bless her for thinking of us."

Captain Nightingale brought a haunch of venison and hung it from a tree branch. He fired his pistol and waved to them, so they could see where it was.

"They aren't going to let us starve at least," Daniel said over supper. "Is it just me or are we drawing further and further away from the other wagons? It seems we're not keeping up with them."

"The more alone we are, the more independent we feel," said Nancy. "I think we could do all right by ourselves if it wasn't for the Indians and wolves. Del shot a wolf last night, didn't he? We've been doing okay. I do miss some of the other women. You have all been so good to me and my boys. I miss women folks." She covered her face with her hands and wept, wiping her face with a hanky, and then fanning herself. "I'm so ashamed. I was just declaring how independent I felt, and then I break down a-crying like a little girl.

"Don't look so alarmed, gentlemen! I'm just fine. Some sadness overtakes me once in a while, then I go on. We always go on. Don't we, boys?" She hugged her sons to her. "Close your mouth, Tucker, and pass me a biscuit. Put some of that cooked meat on it. Thank you."

The little band followed the trail, crossing the Umatilla several times before pointing due west. It was dry, high desert in this part of the country with long, low rounded hills of brown dry grass the animals seemed to take to. The game they saw, elk, antelope, deer, and rabbit, were healthy and well filled out. Nothing starved on these plains, despite the dry appearance of the grass. Nights got colder. Mornings were brisk. The days rolled by uneventfully, one after another.

They woke to frost for the first time. Clouds of steam blew from their lips over the coffee and pancakes Nancy dished up from a cheery fire.

"It's cold, but I like it. It makes me feel alive," she said. "Nate, eat those cakes. You'll need them to keep you warm. I wish I had some milk for you boys, but you know we had to dry Bessie off, to save her strength. We're lucky she made it this far. Maybe she'll calve in our new home. That would be nice, wouldn't it, boys? Nice fresh milk. I could make some cheese. Oh my, I want to get settled, I guess. Run on now and do your work. We'll be leaving soon. How much further to the John Day do you think, Ben? You know this territory."

"Well, we're approaching the Columbia Gorge Plateau, now. I figure two more days of travel, barring break downs or rain. We should be there then. I'm ready to get back to scouting. Nancy's cooking is getting me fat. I can barely fit into my buckskins."

Replenishing their water at Rock Creek, after the main train had passed, Daniel had them filling barrels and letting the stock graze. It took a few hours to get their water filtered and fill the barrels of both wagons. "We'll be at the John Day tomorrow," he said. "Exile will be over. Then we should be two days or so out from The Dalles. Train will be breaking up there one last time. Some going downriver, some staying. Nightingale had mentioned that a new trail opened last year called the Barlow Road. Don't know much about it, 'cept the name and route of travel. She goes through the Cascades around the base of Mt. Hood. Pretty country, but dry and little grass. More water on the western side of the mountain always due to rains, but it's a way. Much shorter route of travel, than following the Gorge."

"The Dalles!" Del said to himself. "So close! The beginning of the end of the journey." He could hardly believe it. He had come to love this wild country. Taking a deep breath, he looked around him drawing a vision of the countryside into his memory. The winds blew cold. Maple and oak started turning red. The alders glowed gold up the hillsides. The leaves rippled in waves as the breeze moved them like God was painting the hillsides above. Large flocks of geese in long fluttering V formations fought their way southward through the updrafts coming off the mountains. Ancient urges drew them toward some feral place to feed, mate, and start the cycle over again. So beautiful! Tears welled up in his eyes. He held still, simply absorbed by this surrounding beauty in sight, sound, and smell. He was a part of this, this West!

"Del, what ya doing?" Tucker came around the wagon.

"I'm just being here. I can't explain it more than that! I'm just being here. Look around you. It's simply magnificent, ain't it?"

Tucker looked around. He looked to the hills and the fading honking of the geese that floated to his ears from their cries up above. A breeze caught the brim of his hat pushing it back on his head, like someone was trying to get his attention. Amazed at the incredible beauty surrounding him, he grabbed his hat off his head before it went sailing into the brush and held it to his chest. "Yes," he said softly. "It is truly, almighty magnificent."

Late in the night, Captain Nightingale rode into camp. "You look healthy and alive to me! How do you feel?"

"We're all good, Cap'n," replied Daniel. "Nary a fever or rash among us."

"I thought so. I hope you understand this precaution. You can join the train tomorrow. I'd like your three wagons to head em' out and lead us into the John Day. It'll let folks know you're well, and I've

approved your coming back. Ben, grab your gear. I'm putting you
back to work before you can't ride your horse." Nightingale laughed.

"First laugh I've heard out of you since we hung that Frenchman."
Ben grinned. "Okay, Cap'n. They've kept me fed all right, but I'm
ready to hit the trail. I've been camp bound too long! See you folks...
and thanks."

With that, he mounted up and rode off.

"Glad that's over." Nancy cleared away the dishes. "Here, Nate,
wash this for me. Is it mean or does it feel good to have them eat our
dust for a little while tomorrow?"

"You know I hadn't thought about it." Daniel grinned. "But it will
sit well with me at that."

They rousted out early to a fine, misty rain just starting up and
drove their wagons past the campsite of the circled train. Daniel
stopped just past, where he figured Nightingale would have them start.

"Hey, why don't we let them know we're here?" said Daniel.
"Grab a pot or pan and a stick or a spoon. We'll give them a shivaree
they won't forget!"

Banging on a kettle, Daniel starting yelling. "Get up and get going. We're here. Let's get going."

Tucker, Del, and Nancy all began banging and yelling. Nate and
Bart called and banged.

A few bangs echoed back in return. Soon the entire camp was
banging and hollering in response to the old newcomers. Then the
rains hit in earnest turning the day grey and murky. The train moved
out in a long snaky row, splashing in the mud and sliding on the flat
rocks lining the trail.

The John Day River was their next stop.

33

IT RAINED ALL DAY, A steady cold rain, making the way slippery and wet. They crossed the John Day with little incident. Everyone got soaked and miserable, trembling with the cold, and without dry wood, they had no fires that night. Some had oilskins for protection, but all got soaked sooner or later as they left the John Day behind them.

Crossing the Deschutes River proved more complicated with high water from the constant raining drizzle. They fastened ropes to the wagons after they had swum the stock over to the far bank and pulled the wagons across. Swift currents washed a couple of mules downstream. They swam back to the same side of the river from where they started and had to be coaxed to try to re-swim what had nearly drowned them once already. The terrified mules fought re-entering the river. They left them on some grass for the night. Their owner waited with them, patiently talking to them and giving them lumps of sugar, stroking and rubbing their ears. These mules had come with him all the way from Independence. He wasn't leaving without them. The next morning, they still refused to go into the river.

In exasperation, he said to Captain Nightingale, "They ain't a-going over the river. So here I'll stay, me, my woman and my Missouri mules. Maybe I'll build a ferry. Go on. We're staying right here, with my stubborn mules."

The Riodans ate a cold supper of ship's biscuit, jerky, and parched corn washed down with water. There was nothing dry to make a fire out of.

"Some soup would taste good right about now." Tucker changed into a dry shirt. "My hands is shaking with cold, but no wood, no fire, no biscuits, no soup."

It rained all the next day. The bedraggled band of thirty wagons stopped at a place Ben designated. He rode up and down the wagons, "We is at The Dalles! Circle up on the lead wagon when we stop."

Daniel, Tucker, and Del set up a canvas tarp to keep the rain off as they struggled to make a fire and dry out.

"I know, I've got a can of coal oil left in here some where's. Here you go, boys." Daniel handed it over. "I've only got a gallon or so, but it should get this wet wood burning and we'll have to dry more, as we go." He sprinkled a cupful sparingly over the prepared wood.

"I found some fatwood over in the pines," Tucker said. "It'll burn good, too. We'll be able to dry out by morning."

The coal oil blazed with a hazy black smoke that covered everything in sticky soot. They soon had a smoky, but earnest little flame going, drying the wood as it smoked, then catching the fatwood which blazed brightly. They could smell the pine resin as it bubbled, blackened and burnt with blue and yellow flames.

Stringing ropes under the canvas, they hung their sodden clothes and placed a pot of soup laced with dried meat, corn, and potatoes hanging from a chain suspended by an iron tripod. A pot of coffee boiled and Tucker put a pot of biscuits off to the side covering the top and bottom with coals.

"Daniel, I've had to throw out half the flour and cornmeal. It was wet and molded. I hope they got stores to buy so we'll have something to eat the rest of the way. The fire feels good all right. A hot supper and a good night's sleep and I'll be right as rain! I guess that don't make much sense in this rain, now, does it?" He poured himself a cup of coffee.

"I think they have supplies, Tuck. I hope so. Here come Nancy and the boys. Throw a few more lines up. I see they've got wet clothes, too!"

"Thanks for sharing your fire, boys. I don't think we could have managed it by ourselves. Wet canvas is too heavy for me and the boys to lift. You're a lifesaver."

"Just hang up your things and start drying them out. Boys, get some soup in you. Miz Nancy, I have coffee, but it wouldn't be any trouble to boil water for tea." Tucker ladled soup for Nate and Bart.

"Tea? You have tea, Tuck? I would love some. If it isn't an inconvenience, I mean."

"No, ma'am, no trouble at all."

All night they nursed their fire, moving clothes and bedding from line to line, until they dried out smoky and stiff as boards. Del had to beat his shirts and pants against the side of the wagon to soften them up, so he could wear them.

By midnight, the skies cleared. The stars sparkled brightly, innocent of any misery the rains had brought. Clear skies were welcome, but they brought in the cold. The puddles rimmed with ice by morning. The ground was hard and frozen on top. It would turn sloppy again with the warming sun. The mountains prepared for winter.

Daniel sensed the weather change. They had to get down river to Oregon City soon or spend the winter on the windblown, snow swept plateau of the Columbia River. The roar of the river reached them even though they were camped a mile south of the gorge.

Ben showed up around breakfast time, his moustache touched with frost from his breath. "I knew you'd have coffee, Tuck. Got so's I miss your coffee. Danged if I don't say so myself."

"There's bacon in the pan, Ben, and biscuits in the Dutch oven. No butter or jam. Sorry, but help yourself."

Ben helped himself to the bacon and biscuits, breaking one with his fingers and pressing it into the bacon grease. He folded over a couple of bacon rashers, stuffed them in the biscuit and bit the whole sandwich in half, washed down with hot coffee. "Mighty good, Mister Tucker, mighty good. I brag about you and Miz Nancy's cooking."

"Daniel, why I came this morning. I think you should see a raft going down the river. You should all see it. Help you decide if that's what you want to do or go by way of that new Barlow Road that just opened or follow the Gorge rim. I heard three families was launching their rafts today. You should watch and decide for yourself. A Mr. Louviere on the river builds rafts, takes three days to a week to build, but you get down the river in a day. You land at Vancouver, or Astoria, put your wagon back together, load up and head out to wherever you want to go."

"I'd like to see that. You're right, Ben. Thanks!"

THE FALLS OF THE COLUMBIA River were churning froth as it bounced over rocks and fell to the depths below, stair-stepping down the river until the flow was broad and smooth. The water was high from the recent rains. A good thing most of the time, as the depth cleared the boulders below the placid surface, waiting to catch a corner of a raft unawares, tipping it enough to dump man, beast, and wagon into the silent grip of the swift current, never to be seen again. They arrived as one raft was preparing to leave.

"Stay to the right of the ripples on your left. They's rocks under the water there. Though it's been a-raining, there's not enough water to clear those rocks underneath. You'll be okay if you stay on the right when you shove off. Then avoid any turbulence you see as they mark where the rock is. Whirlpools form downstream of the big boulders. Avoid them at all costs! Mostly stay in the middle of the river." A man was unwrapping the mooring lines of a raft loaded with a deconstructed wagon and all the worldly goods of a young family, giving instructions as he did so to the young couple in front of him.

A cheery faced young man, with wife holding a baby in a basket looked down the river with hope lighting his eyes.

"Thank you, Mister Louviere! You've built a fine raft. I'll follow your advice. Come visit up in Vancouver. It's the end of a long journey to be sure." He earnestly shook Mr. Louviere's hand. "Let's go, Mattie. We'll be in Vancouver by nightfall."

They stepped onto a raft that held their wagon, free of its wheels, lashed to the bed of a wooden raft. The logs were still green and covered with bark. A long sweep tiller was built on the rear. All their worldly possessions, their trusting, their raft, and their love for each other floating on the seemingly docile surface of a swift moving river. Two other rafts were about to make way as well. All three families waved their good-byes and stepped aboard. The cheery faced young man stepped to the tiller and waved to the crowd.

Mr. Louviere walked down the wharf repeating his instructions. "Stay to the right." He gestured emphatically with his right arm. "Stay to the right of the ripples."

He rubbed his hands together nervously, obviously anxious that this little family got off safely.

All three rafts pushed off at the same time. Three families trusting fate on that wild untamed river, all three drifted placidly along. Their men worked the tillers to move them to the center of the river.

"So far, so good," said Ben. "I'd rather sit a horse, myself, as to trust to those flimsy things."

"They don't look flimsy," said Tucker. "Why do you think they're flimsy?"

"I seen this river snap logs twice that size into kindling wood, smashed against rocks, trapped in whirlpools and spit out in pieces as long as your arm is all. That's why, Tuck."

"Oh," Tucker said wide-eyed.

The second raft moved toward the center of the river. It got caught in a swift current, causing it to turn to its right. The man at the tiller desperately struggled to correct the rotation of his raft, but they were at the mercy of a strong rolling current, spinning the raft like a toy, pushing it toward the first raft. The cheery faced young man immediately tried to slow his raft as the other raft, spinning out of control, bore down upon the young family. The spinning raft caught the foremost corner of the first and locked into place. The weight of the rafts together plunged their corners below the surface catching the waiting boulders, tipping the rafts upon their edges, ripping their loads apart and plunging them below the surface. It was so sudden that, if the onlookers had glanced away, they would have missed it. Stunned silence gripped them all. Sobs and cries broke out next.

Mr. Louviere ran up and down the wharf crying! *"Non! Oh, mon Dieu! No!"*

The third raft fought its way down the river and out of sight. Louviere collapsed on the wharf, covering his face. His body wracked with tears and disbelief.

Daniel put his arms around his friends and family and moved them away from the wharf. His face was drained, and he spoke with much difficulty. "Del, I told you, it would be up to you if we went by raft, but I'm making that decision for you. There is no way in hell I'm getting on that river. I did not come all this way to die. Ben, how do we get to the Barlow Road? I hope I'm speaking for your family as well, Nancy."

"We go where you go, Daniel. Let's bow our heads and say a prayer for those poor people. They were so alive just minutes ago. I still can't believe I watched that awful scene. My heart breaks for those babies and mothers." She covered her face and wept. Del and Tucker put a hand on her shoulder, trying unsuccessfully to comfort her. Each felt hollow and remorseful for the lost families and helpless to comfort their friend.

That night around the campfire, they sat wrapped in coats and blankets. With supper over, they finished the chores for the day. Nate slept in his mother's lap bundled up in a sheepskin. Bart considered himself an adult now and fought to stay awake so he could hear what the adults decided to do.

Daniel smoked his pipe. This was something he did when he had serious thinking to do. He peered out through the smoke and spoke to Del.

"Ever since you came to me in Independence, I've never stopped thinking I would never lose you again. Not by any choices I made nor by any direct action I took. I've watched you grow, and in my prayers, I've told your mother what a handsome wonderful man you've become. She would be so proud of you. She was always proud of you. You've overcome hard work, thirst, hunger, Indians, and the damned measles. I'll not put our fortunes or our lives on the whims of a wild river and a damnable raft. I didn't like the looks of them the first moment I laid eyes on 'em.

"This Barlow Road was cut out of the forest by the Barlow family around Mt. Hood and down into Oregon City just last year. It's a toll road. They charge five dollars a wagon. Depending on weather and travel, it's five to ten days from here to Oregon City. It's pretty rough. Lots of stumps and rocks. It hasn't been traveled much yet, but more and more will start going this way. Here's what I propose to do. Mrs. Kincaid, we've been thinking of you as family, even when your husband, Thomas, my good friend, was with us. I hope you'll not take offense in that I've included you in my plans."

"Thank you, Daniel. You are all family to me. I'm in for a penny or a pound, whatever you decide to get us there. You're family to me and my sons, and I know Thomas is with us, as well."

"The Nightingale train breaks up here. Everyone will go their own way. So far, I haven't been approached to join with any other wagons on this road. We will probably meet other wagons on the road, but I'm not sure of even that. At best, we'll be on our own again. Thankfully, we're pretty good at being on our own.

"As you all know, our stock is worn out. I propose leaving my second wagon here, in storage with all the heavy equipment for the mills. We then divide up all the animals between our remaining wagon and Miz Kincaid's. We only take food, clothing, tools, and what we need to get us to Oregon City in our big wagon, emptying the Kincaid's wagon, except for bedding and their necessities. We leave everything else here. In the spring, when our stock has wintered well and they have fattened on good green grass, we drive a team back to The Dalles and retrieve our property. We can't build our mills until we've filed our claims, anyway. I don't know how long that takes. It will probably be sometime next summer before we can begin to cut lumber for homes and the mills. In the meantime, Tucker and I have discussed a plan to build a bakery or restaurant for you, Nancy. We should be able to have it finished by Christmas. It'll be rough, but you can start your life, get your boys in school and start to get settled. We can all pitch in and help you, until we return to The Dalles for the other wagon. I think this helps preserve our stock, so we don't lose them, and puts us on a timetable that's suitable for everyone. What do you all think of this plan?"

Excitedly, they all started talking at once. No one wanted to face the river. The Barlow Road, it was.

They took two days to rest the stock and re-supply the best they could. Daniel spoke to Mr. Louviere, who agreed, for a reasonable fee, to store the wagon and equipment.

Miraculously, the baby from the tragedy on the water had been found floating in his basket several miles downriver. He was hungry, but dry. The basket's tight weave and swaddled blankets had proven far more buoyant than the doomed raft. Louviere's wife claimed the baby and vowed to raise it as their own. Nothing was seen or known of the young parents. They decided to call the boy Moses.

Captain Nightingale and Ben rode into camp as the wagons moved out. Del looked at his almanac. It was October 5, 1847.

"Guess this is the end of the line. Me and Ben are headed to Mexico. The army is still needing scouts. Hope the war is still on by the time we get there. It was nice knowing you folks. Best of luck on the road. I'll look you up sometime when I'm in Oregon City."

Nancy waved and smiled. "Look for Nancy's Bakery, Captain! You'll be welcome anytime."

"Well, Del Rio, it was sure good getting to know you pard…" Ben shook Del's and Daniel's hands. "Tuck, I am going to miss your biscuits, but to tell you the truth, I'm still partial to my own coffee!"

"The hell you say." Tucker gave him a warm handshake.

"Miz Nancy, boys, I'll be at that bakery as soon as I can." Ben grinned, touched the brim of his hat, and loped off to catch up to Captain Nightingale.

"Pa, I learned a lot from that old man. I owe him."

"I think we all do. There's not many men like him and Nightingale. Miz Kincaid! Follow me to the Barlow Road."

At the Barlow gate, they paid their money, received a crude map, and were told the worst part of the road topped Laurel Hill.

"Laurel Hill doesn't sound too bad, mister," Nancy said.

"Laurel Hill is mainly the name, ma'am. The trees look like laurel, but they is really rhododendrons. It'll poison your stock if you let 'em eat the leaves. It's a steep hill."

"Oh, my. We'll take care. Thank you."

Barlow Road did not live up to its name. It wasn't a road at all. It was a narrow lane cut through the mountain forest leaving stumps and boulders. The wagons had to be careful to avoid breaking an axle. They made eight miles to the first creek and stopped for the night. There wasn't any grass, as they were still in deep forest. The oxen and mules had to browse the leaves off the low-lying shrubs.

"None of this looks like rhododendrons to me, Tucker. I hope there's nothing here that will poison them. They've got to eat. I wish we had grain to give them, but we don't. Got water, anyway." Daniel looked worried. It had been his decision to come this way. Responsibility rested on his shoulders.

For the next week, Daniel drove them on, through rain or sunshine. They were some of the first wagons to go this way. The trail was still new, filled with roots, holes and the never-ending stumps. Nancy's wagon overturned once when her wheels got lopsided into a deep mud puddle. They had to unhitch both teams to pull it upright and spent the rest of the morning putting everything back together.

"Didn't' break an axle, luckily," Daniel said.

That night they had to cut young maple trees and sycamores for their leaves to feed to the stock. It was all forest with little grass. The stock grew visibly thinner by the time they reached Laurel Hill. It was a long steep ridge, with a sharp drop off on the other side, but there was water at the bottom of the ridge. Getting there was the problem. They would have to lower the wagons one at a time down Laurel Hill.

Using ropes and hitching both teams together, they lowered the empty wagons, down the steep embankment to the floor below. They had wrapped their ropes around some trees as brakes to help take the strain off the ropes and their animals. It was nerveracking. Even at double strength the oxen and mules had a mighty struggle to keep everything from crashing to the ground. They lowered their clothes, supplies and what equipment they brought and reloaded. It required a full day. The men had to drive the oxen out of the rhododendrons several times. It was evident they were starving.

In the morning, they had lost three of their oxen. "I don't know if they ate the rhododendrons or if they died from starvation," Daniel said to Tucker. They had started with eight Linebacks. He had only four of the starving animals left.

"They're not the first," Tucker pointed to several dead oxen lying off to the side of the road. "We only noticed them now because the wind was right." The stench of death was overwhelming. "Let's get out of here."

Two days later, they came to a house along the road.

"A house? A house! Would you look there? A house!" Nancy said. She hadn't seen a regular house in almost eighteen hundred miles. Three miles further on, a second house. "Look, my boys. A real house! Do you remember houses? Daniel, we must be close."

The Barlow Road became a dirt road, lined with two wagon tracks with a grassy middle like all roads of its time. It was not gravel or stone, but merely worn by the repeated travels of brave men and women following one another in their stalwart wagons. The road disappeared down the hill, then reappeared on the floor of the valley winding through the grass to their destination. As they approached the crest of the hill, Oregon City took shape little by little until it finally revealed itself on the shining banks of the Willamette River a few miles ahead.

"Oh, I'm going to cry! We're here!" Nancy gathered her boys to her and hugged them tightly. "That's home."

The men stared out at the city.

"You did it, Daniel," Tucker said. "You got us here."

The two men embraced each other.

"We did it, Tucker! We all did it! Come here, boy, I want a hug!" Del actually picked his father up and gleefully set him down. He was an inch taller than Daniel, wider across the shoulders. Other than that, they looked amazingly alike.

"Well, Pa, what are you waiting for? Lead us into Oregon City." It had taken ten days exactly to get through the Barlow Road. They were home at last.

34

DRIVING THROUGH TOWN WAS A wonderment to the emigrants. They had returned to civilization and gazed in amazement at the modern city. The newcomers stared at the people on the street as they rode through town, until Nancy caught herself and admonished everyone else to mind their manners. Daniel stopped at the land office. When he came out, he told them they would camp at the end of town until they could get settled. There was, he had learned, feed and water available for their stock.

"Dan, there's a little café down the street almost to the corner. Let's eat there after we set up camp. I'd love to eat someone else's food. No offense, Tuck!"

"None taken, ma'am. I'd like that myself. See what town food tastes like with no ashes or flies in it."

"All right, Nancy. It seems fitting to celebrate a little. We'll do just that!" said Daniel.

They made camp and cleaned up as much as they could. Appearances, all of a sudden, became important to them. No one wanted to have the town folk think they were dirty or uncouth.

Nancy brushed her hair a hundred strokes.

"I'm so excited, boys. I used to brush my hair like this when your pa lived. He loved my hair, but I've not done it since he passed. Come here, Bart. Wet your hair and let me comb it."

"Aw, Ma!"

"Wet it and come here, Bart!"

The men had pulled the wagons close enough so they could tie a tarp over them forming a tent, giving them more living room than just a wagon bed. While Nancy and her boys were in their wagon getting ready, Tuck, Daniel, and Del Rio gathered around a basin of water and a piece of mirror between the wagons. They tried to shave, alternately bumping each one out of view of the mirror, taking a few swipes at their whiskers, before being bullied away and replaced by another half-shaven face.

"C'mon here, Delaino. Wet your hair and let me comb it!" said Daniel, laughing.

"Aw, Pa!"

"I can *hear* you, you know." Nancy's voice drifted from the wagon. "Stop fussing, Nate. There! All right, we're ready."

Walking to the café was an adventure. Lots of windows filled with dry goods, tools, and readymade clothes caught their eyes at each turn. Bart shepherded Nate, pushing him along if he lingered too long at any window.

"Gentlemen, today is my treat to you. You've been so much help. I can never repay you. I'll buy your first meal in Oregon City!"

Nate ran ahead and held the door for everyone.

"Why, Miz Kincaid, that's mighty nice, but you don't...."

"I must, Daniel. Sit down. I'm paying for the meal."

A nervous, anxious man thrust some menus into their hands. He kept looking out the door. "Have you heard? They found gold south of here. *Gold!*"

"We just pulled in, mister. Do you have a steak? I've had plenty of stews lately."

"We got pork chops. Lots of people leaving town going to the gold fields, you know."

Daniel licked his lips. "Pork chops sound good. I haven't had fresh pork this whole trip—'sides bacon."

"Hey, you're emigrants! New to town? Got a job? Gonna start a business?"

"Well, I thought about a bakery myself. Do you buy your baked goods from someone or do you do your own baking?" Nancy surveyed the menu. "I think I'll have the fried chicken dinner. Three fried chicken dinners please, sir!"

"Me, too," said Del. "With pie."

"Make mine the same," said Tucker. "With pie."

"I'll have the pork chop dinner with pie," said Daniel.

"Pie for me," said Nate.

"Me, too," said Bart.

Nancy couldn't help herself. "Pie sounds good to me, too. Make it lemon for me, please."

"A bakery, huh?" The waiter seemed to be ignoring everyone except Nancy, his gaze transfixed on her.

"How'd you like to buy a café, instead? All ready to go? Got a good kitchen in the back, a new stove. You could bake your heart out. I'll sell it reasonable."

"Where would you go, mister?"

"Lady, I got gold fever like nobody's business! I'm planning on leaving town just as soon as I can get a stake. All I own is in this place. I'd sell it for $150, cash on the line. I'd certify the deed at the Land Office right down the street. I own the corner lot next door as well. I'm asking $30 for it. What'll you say? Lock, stock, and barrel. I got a good cook, name of Clem, but he ain't no baker. How about it, mister? Want to buy this café for your wife?"

Daniel laughed. "She's not my wife. You'll have to make your deal with her, if she's willin'. What do you say, Nancy? You'll find she just came down the trail fighting Indians, floods, flies, and ornery mules. She can speak for herself. But if I was you, I'd be glad I'm bald, 'cause I think she'd have your scalp!"

Nancy looked about the café. A few people were eating. It wasn't very tidy and needed paint and a woman's touch. That was for sure. A touch of pink crept across her face. She nodded to the owner. "Let's eat first. I want to taste Clem's cooking. Have you entertained any other offers?"

"No, it just came on me to sell, right after you mentioned a bakery. I ain't even told Clem yet. I've been hearing about the gold, and I just want to be gone."

"We're hungry. Bring our food. I want to meet Clem and see the kitchen. Let me think on it, while we eat. You'll wait that long?"

"Oh, yes. Right away, miss."

"It's *Miz* Kincaid."

"Oh, yes. Right away, ma'am! Er—Miz Kincaid."

No one spoke during the meal. Nancy looked at each plate, as it was set before them. They were blue and white plates in a Dutch design she hadn't seen before. She observed people as they ate, paid, and left. A growing excitement welled up in her breast, and she fought to tamp it down.

After the meal, she gestured for the owner. "Send Clem out, would you, please? Then I want to see the kitchen."

Clem came out, wiping his dirty hands on his apron. "What is it?"

"Lady wants to meet you, Clem."

Clem wiped his hands off and shuffled his way to the table his boss pointed to.

"Your name is Clem?"

"Yes, ma'am?"

"How long have you been cooking, Clem?"

"Since I got here in Oregon City, ma'am."

"May I see your hands?"

"My hands? Why—er, sure." He held them out to her.

She inspected his nails and turned his hands over. "Thank you, Clem. Now, I'll see the kitchen."

"I'll leave you to your business, Nancy. I'm going to look at the lot next door. It interests me." Daniel and Tucker got up excusing themselves and walked outside.

After her inspection, Nancy sat and asked for a cup of coffee. Her boys sat next to her and Del across from them.

Daniel and Tucker came in and seated themselves.

"What do you think, Miz Kincaid?"

"Daniel, you've been in business. I've not. Tell me if what I think is off the mark. This town is going to continue to grow. This is a good location, and the building is well made. Clem cooks all right, but the kitchen is a sty. I think, if given a week, I could make it a pretty place to bring a family, and with much better food. I could make a go of it here, Daniel. I'll need some help to fix it up, but I do think I'll buy it. What do you see?"

"The building is like you say, well built. There's rooms upstairs for you and your boys. It's a good location. The blacksmith is across the street from this place. A mercantile store is across the street from the vacant lot. There will be plenty of traffic to those businesses. People can't help but notice this place. There isn't another restaurant that I see for many blocks. If you put up a pretty sign, it'll draw people in. There's not much color on the front to attract the eye, so paint the front, something catching. Give it a woman's touch. I like the corner lot. It faces two busy streets. I'll buy it if you're not interested. You could expand your business there if you need to in a few years. It's a place to grow, I think. It's your call, but it is what you were looking for."

Nancy made her offer. She held firm at $100.00 for the café, but offered the full price of $30.00 for the corner lot. The owner fumed and swore he was being cheated, but when Nancy placed the money on the table in front of him, he eagerly caved in. By that afternoon, she'd held a signed, certified deed to the café and the corner lot.

"I can always sell it later, if I need to," she told Daniel. Then she turned to the soon-to-be previous owner. "One last thing, before you rush off for the free land. You must fire Clem."

Nancy closed the café the next day and placed a sign out front.

Under new ownership.
Temporarily closed for renovation.

She would re-open in a week.

Nancy Kincaid became a general, marshalling her crew in cleaning, painting, and putting the stove and kitchen in good order. Daniel and Tucker painted the front a canary yellow with dark blue trim around the windows and doors. She ordered a new sign.

Nancy's Bakery and Home Cooking

She was scrubbing the floor in the kitchen when she spied Clem holding his hat and standing in the door.

"What can I do for you, Clem?"

"Well, ma'am, I got to thinking. If you'd give me a second chance, I would do things your way. Ol' Bob didn't care too much for the cleaning, so's I didn't either. I need a job. I cook pretty good, or so's I've been told. Would you give me another shot at it? I know I could do it."

"Hmm. Do you know the local vendors?"

"Vendors, ma'am?"

"Yes. Where the owner—Ol' Bob—used to supply the café with food and supplies."

"Oh, them. Yes, ma'am, I do. Most of them are locals."

"Come here."

Clem stepped forward.

"I'll tell you what... what did Ol' Bob pay you?"

"I got thirty dollars a month, ma'am, plus my meals."

"I believe in second chances, Clem. I've had them myself. You go home and bathe. Change into clean clothes and meet me back here at one o'clock. Don't be late, or just stay at home. You're going to introduce me to the vendors, and I want you to look like I expect my restaurant to look like. Get a haircut and shave clean. I'm hiring you back because your hands were clean. I want this kitchen and you to be clean at all times."

"Yes'm. Thank you. I will be here at one sharp." He turned to go. "You won't be sorry, ma'am!"

"I hope not. See you at one."

An hour or so later, Daniel hung a bright blue ribbon across the front door.

Grand Opening Monday

"Tucker, I tell you, that was a hard week. I don't know what was more difficult, getting across the mountains or keeping up with Nancy Kincaid. She's turned this place into a mighty pretty shop."

"I wouldn't let her hear you call her restaurant a shop, Daniel. It has been a hard week, all right, but mighty satisfying to finally start making dreams come true. Lots of dreams to be coming true in Oregon. I can't wait to start the mills and our home."

"We're going to look into that soon, I promise. We'll find out where the homesteading land is and go find someplace for our home. After we get Nancy's place open tomorrow, we'll see to it. Have you heard what the plan is, come Monday?"

"Me and Clem's doing the cooking. Nancy, the baking in the morning, and at the counter greeting folks, during the day. Bart and Nate are washing dishes, and Del's waiting tables. You're to fill in where needed. Nancy's going to be running her own place by spring. Let's go see what she wants us to do next. It will be a busy day tomorrow."

Opening day was a huge success. The mayor came, made a speech, kissed some babies, and and had quite the time eating Nancy's fresh-made doughnuts. The whole event would be in the local newspaper the next day. That evening, Nancy's crew sat slumped in chairs, exhausted from the busy day.

"Whew! What a day! You must have sold out of everything." Del's feet were up on a chair as he sat leaning back on two legs. "I made five dollars and some change today—most I've made since I started. I'm giving Bart and Nate a dollar apiece for helping me."

"The women loved the cakes. They liked not having to bake one at home. They said mine are as good as homemade, because they are. The ladies can say they made them. I'll have to double what we made today. Clem, you did well, today. Do you want to stay? If you do, I'll give you a five dollar raise, but you'll have to work twice as hard."

"I'll stick, Miz Kincaid. Your recipes are going to make people come back for more. It was hard, but the time passed quickly. Tucker is great in the kitchen. I'll miss him when he goes."

"If this keeps up, she'll be able to hire everyone she needs. I'm headed for my bed. Congratulations, Miz Kincaid. You're home." Daniel tipped his hat. Nancy turned out the lamps and locked her front door.

Nancy's business was good. Tucker worked in the kitchen with Clem, but Del and Daniel made themselves scarce as soon as they could. Finding good help was easy as there was a steady flow of emigrants coming in until the passes snowed over. The Barlow Road closed by the end of October. Goods and services flowed south from Vancouver and Astoria's busy harbors developing north of Oregon

City. Nancy had no problem with supplies except for fresh vegetables and fruits as the winter closed in. She made do with what could be grown locally and dry fruits when she could get them. Daniel and Del frequently left for several days at a time looking for land.

Tucker joined them when he could. His job provided a source of ready pocket money he depended on. Everyone settled into their own routine, much like being on the trail.

35

NANCY WAS PLACING A CHOCOLATE cake on display in the open pie safe one Sunday afternoon, when a stranger came in after the dinner hour.

"Howdy, ma'am." He tipped his hat and sat at the counter.

"That's a mighty delicious looking pastry you have there. Might I have a piece and some coffee?"

He turned to place his pearl grey hat on the stool beside him. His lace cuffs showing below his black coat sleeves, his broken nose and a vivid scar on his cheek, all caught her attention. A chill crept through her body, sending prickles up her spine. Something bothered her about this man.

"These cakes are sold whole if you want an entire cake. The slices over here are sold by the piece. There's chocolate and a Chantilly cake with almonds. I have one piece of pecan pie left as well."

"My mouth is set for the chocolate, if you don't mind."

"Good choice. Chocolate is my bestseller." She served the cake and poured him a cup of coffee. Nancy began straightening the shelves and wiping the counter in preparation for closing. She glanced at her customer occasionally, trying to understand what was troubling her.

"Nice café. Been here long?"

"Not really, just bought the restaurant a few weeks ago."

"You've turned it into a comfortable place. Reminds me of the cafés I knew in Baltimore."

The hair on her neck and arms stood up. Warning flashes sounded in her head. Baltimore?

"You've come a long way, haven't you? Do you have family?" She was trying to control the shrillness in her voice. She knew who this was. *Beaux Conlon!*

She had to warn Tucker.

"I *do* have family, actually. I'm looking for a man and a boy, name of Riodan. They're cousins of mine. They have a slave with them that belongs to me. I'm looking for them. I'll be staying at the Star Hotel down the street."

Nancy's stomach fluttered wildly. "No, I don't know them, I'm afraid. I've only been here a short time myself. Excuse me, I must check on my bread in the oven."

Beaux forked a piece of cake and placed it appreciatively in his mouth. "Good cake!"

Nancy closed the door to the kitchen. "Clem. *Clem! Oh, God.* Where's Tucker?"

"He's out back, bringing in wood for tomorrow. He'll be right back. What's wrong?"

Nancy put her fingers to her lips. "Shhh, go get him for me. Will you? And keep quiet."

"Okay, I'll get him. Anything wrong?"

"Just get him quickly, please!"

Nancy came back to the counter. "How was the cake? You'll have to dine with us tomorrow. We're about to close for the evening. It's Sunday."

"Fine cake, very fine, best I've had in months." Beaux paid his bill and left two bits on the counter. "If you see those fellers, I'd be appreciative if you'd leave a message at the Star. Have a pleasant evening, ma'am." Beaux turned and went out the door.

Nancy breathed a sigh of relief. Tucker came from the kitchen. "Clem said you wanted to see me? What is it?"

"Beaux Conlon was just in here. I recognized that scar Del told me about. He said he was from Baltimore. He's looking for you."

Tucker stood silently for a while. "We knew this time would come. We've been living in a fairy land thinking it might pass us by. Daniel and Del should be riding in soon. We'll figure out what to do then. Mind if I put on another pot of coffee?"

"No, go ahead. My stomach is so nervous. I think I'm going to be sick." Nancy wrung her hands. "Oh, Tucker, I've never been so scared. He's an evil looking man. Real polite, but that just makes him scarier."

Beaux Conlon watched all of this through a corner of the glass window, out front on the sidewalk. He had felt the woman was hiding something because of the nervousness in her voice. He couldn't hear what she told Tucker, but he knew she knew who he was.

He walked to the edge of the sidewalk and looked up and down the street. There wasn't anyone else around. The street was quiet.

Walking over to his horse, Beaux pulled a pair of manacles from his saddlebag and slid a double-barreled coach gun out of the scabbard. He moved quickly so that he would catch them unaware.

"Hell-o, Tucker!" he said in a low, slow voice, steppingback through the door. "I've chased you across the country, and now I have you. Ma'am, just step back out of the way if you don't want to get hurt. It matters not to me, I assure you, but I am taking Tucker with me. Get up, boy!"

Clem burst through the kitchen door with a stick of firewood in his hand. Beaux hit him across the nose with the butt of his gun, felling the big cook immediately.

Nancy screamed.

"Shut your mouth, woman. If I wanted the whole town to know, I'd have blown his head off. He was lucky I didn't." He pointed back at Tucker. "Come here! I've been saving these for just this day. Hold up your hands, boy."

Tucker just stared at him.

Beaux slapped him.

Tucker didn't blink.

Beaux slapped him again.

"That's both cheeks, Beaux. You forget I'm not a slave anymore. I'm a free man. Delaino gave me my freedom. Why don't you quit this madness and just be on your way?"

"Once an uppity slave, always an uppity slave, ain't you? Give me your hands, or I swear by all that's holy, I'll kill the woman and take you, anyway!"

Tucker raised his hands and Beaux clicked the manacles in place.

"Tucker! Oh, my God!" Nancy's voice was shrill with stress.

"I told you to *shut up,* woman! Sit down and keep still, or I'll kill him in this pretty café. It'll make a bloody mess for the fine folks of Oregon City."

Putting the barrels of the coach gun to Tucker's neck, he said, "You're coming with me. There's a blacksmith shop across the street. Let's see if he's got some leg shackles, that'll fit. I bet he's got some hot irons too. I think it's time to re-brand my property. You've forgotten who you really are, boy. Let's go!"

Jamming the gun deeper into Tucker's neck, he guided him out the door and across the street to the blacksmith shop and pulled the doors closed. The smith had gone home for the day. All was quiet. Coals in the cooling forge glowed against a backdrop of wagon rims, hammers and tongs. "Adonis and the rest of the boys should be here soon. Let's see if we can stoke a branding fire, while we wait."

He sat Tucker on a stump close by, still covering him with the coach gun. Beaux worked the bellows, until the coals were glowing cherry red.

"Stay still, Tucker. I'll blow off a foot if you run, but I won't kill you right off. You ran once! You vexed me by running, you know that? No slave escapes Beaux Conlon! Where's Delaino? He's the one I really want to kill—him and his daddy. Marrying my stepsister? Who did he think he was? I'm going to kill both of them and hide their bodies so no one will ever find them. I'll go back to Baltimore and claim my rightful estate! And as for *you,* Mister Tucker, I'm going to put you in shackles for the rest of your life and cut out your tongue so you can never tell the story! How do you like that, boy?"

Keeping a close cover on Tucker, Beaux carefully looked over the different irons the smithy kept for daily use. He found one with a large circle on its end.

"This'll have to do. I'll only burn in half of it, so's it makes a C. You know, for Conlon!"

Tucker watched Beaux like a snake watches a canary. He didn't feel anything. Beaux was poison mad, but it didn't matter. Tucker had already planned what he was going to do. He was going to kill the man. Nothing else for it now. Beaux wanted him scared, and Tucker refused to give him that kind of satisfaction. As the O-shaped brand in the fire pulsated with a white-hot heat, though, he knew he'd have to play along to get his opportunity.

So he would play into Beaux's ego... no matter how humiliating it might be.

"Oh, no, Mister Beaux! Please don't burn me, Master! I'se do anything you want. I'll go back to Baltimore willingly. I'll show you where Master Del and Mister Daniel live, so's you can kill them! Anything! Just don't burn me with that brand! Please, Mister Beaux. I didn't mean it. I's sorry I's run away!"

"Not *that's* more like it!" It was like music to Beaux's ears.He wanted Tucker to cower.

He drew the brand from the fire and approached the other man, who turned toward him, tears running down his face, hands clasped to his lips.

"Please, Mister Beaux, not the hot iron!"

"I've waited a long time to hear you scream, boy! Now, it's brandin' time!" He let the barrel of his gun drop as he thrust the iron at Tucker's bared chest.

Striking like lightning, Tucker kicked the coach gun with his foot, knocking it skittering across the floor. He bolted upright, clenched the shaft of the blazing iron, and tried to wrench it away from Beaux. Tucker's black manacled hands grasped the iron, just above Beaux's lace-cuffed, white ones. Tucker was taller than Beaux and this advantage slowly began to show as Tucker deliberately started bending the fiery O toward Beaux's chest.

"I'm stronger than you, *master*," Tucker said through gritted teeth. "You were always weak, letting others do your work for you. I came across the plains, driving horses and oxen, and fighting Indians. You're just not a match for me!" He pushed down, jamming the handle of the brand's rod behind Beaux's belt, giving him the leverage he needed. Now the master, he forced the glowing brand nearer and nearer to Beaux's chest. Using all his strength, he forced the glowing *O*, slowly, so slowly, until Beaux's clothes burst into flames.

Both men jumped at the sudden roar of ignition. Tucker lunged, thrusting the brand as deep into Beaux's chest as he could and held it there as the other man struggled, screaming tormented curses, his skin melting from the white-hot heat. They fell to the floor and Beaux kicked at Tucker like a crazed wildcat, the brand still stuck in his chest.

Shrieking insanely, Beaux knocked the brand from him, "I'll kill you!" He grabbed a pair of tongs off the anvil and threw them. Tucker raised his manacles to ward off the blow, but the tongs got caught in the links of chain, causing Tucker to drop his hands to shake the tongs from the manacles. Seizing a hammer, Beaux fiercely threw it at Tucker's head, knocking him to the floor.

DANIEL AND DEL BURST THROUGH the door of the restaurant, guns drawn, worry showing on their faces. A tall dark man followed behind them, seemingly drawn in by the excitement.

"Nancy, what's happened here?" Daniel asked. "Where's Tucker? Why are you crying? What's going on?"

Nancy looked up from wiping Clem's pale face. "I think he's going to be all right. Tucker's going to need help, though. They're in the stable across the street."

"Who's *they?*"

"He has him in manacles with a gun to his head. I'm afraid of what he will do."

"Who?"

"Beaux Conlon! I've seen him, Daniel. He's a crazy man!"

"*Beaux* has Tucker?"

"You must go carefully or he'll kill Tuck."

"Beaux Conlon?" The tall stranger stepped forward. "Is that what you said? Beaux Conlon took your friend?"

"Yes. Who are you, mister?"

"Name's Sam Shepherd, ma'am. I've been chasing that scum clear across the country. I thought he might have come in here, beings you're the only open door on the street. Beaux Conlon killed one of my hands, back in Independence."

"You're after Beaux, too, then?"

Shepherd nodded. "I've chased him from Independence. He's the vilest killer I've ever known. I've sworn to see him hang for what he has done."

"He said he was taking Tucker to the blacksmith's across the street to brand him. Hurry! I fear you'll be too late."

Shepherd stopped them. "Mind if I join you fellas? I've got a vested interest in all this too. I don't want to be denied, now the chase is this close."

"You're welcome, but we've got scores to settle with Beaux that happened long before your claim to him."

"I just want to see him dead."

The men stepped into the street. Del walked over to Raj and pulled his Howdahs from their saddle holsters He passed one of them over to his father. "We're going to need these."

Daniel turned and carefully examined his son's face. It was tight, his voice contorted with anger. "Lead the way, Del."

Making sure his Paterson was free in his holster, Del nodded and started toward the door to the blacksmith's shop.

That's when all hell broke loose.

Six horses suddenly came galloping up the street and turned into the yard of the blacksmith's.

Adonis leaped off his horse onto Daniel's shoulders. "I've got you at last, Riodan!"

Confusion erupted immediately. Del and Shepherd were knocked off their feet amid a melee' of fists and knuckles, elbows and teeth, screaming horses and hooves, all scrambling about in the dust so thick, you couldn't tell who was who.

Del looked up to find Waylon standing over him, an ugly grin creasing his face. Del recognized him immediately from from Ohio and Indiana.

"Bet you didn't think you'd see me again, did you? Still got your pop gun, I see, little boy."

"Hoped is more like it," Del said. Waylon raised his pistol, but not before Del let loose with both barrels of his Howdah. The blast nearly cut the robber in half, and he fell where he stood. "You'll find I ain't so little, either."

Turning, he banged the heavy barrels across the temple of the next man who came at him, knocking him senseless. He dropped the heavy gun and snatched the revolver from his holster.

Daniel in a bareknuckle brawl with Adonis—a fang and claw fight if ever he had seen one. Adonis outweighed Daniel by at least fifty pounds. He was taller and had arms like gnarled posts. Daniel was faster and a smarter fighter, though. He had wrestled with Indians and learned to fight at the Army post in Corydon, Indiana. His punches were sharp and cutting. Adonis was a pounder. He tried to hurt Daniel by sledge-hammering him with massive fists, until he drove him into the ground. Daniel would dart in with cutting jabs to his attacker's face, causing him to raise his arms, then Daniel would snap punches to the big man's ribs and solar plexus. Daniel leaped back when Adonis brought both hammy fists down about his shoulders, trying to knock his arms away. Adonis plodded on, swinging and missing. Daniel moved like a dancer, just out of reach, then diving in with lightening stabs to the face and belly.

A shot splintered the post by Del's face. Diving behind the water trough, he rolled over trying to see who had fired the shot. He was just close enough to the feet of the fighters to get a face full of dust and horse apples. Spitting to clear his mouth, he wondered what had happened to the stranger who had come with them. He heard shots over by the blacksmith's door but couldn't see him.

———————

ALERTED BY THE SOUND OF horses and gunfire in the smithy's yard, Beaux crawled to his feet.

"My boys showed up." He winced in pain as he sucked in painful breaths, leaning for support on the huge anvil. Tucker still lay prostrate on the dirt floor, eyes beginning to flutter. "Now, I'll finish you."

Staggering, Beaux limped over to retrieve the coach gun. His left hand covered his pulsing chest, forever marked with the blistered, bleeding O. Dragging the gun over to Tucker, he placed it on the black man's bleeding face. The fingers of his right hand felt for the triggers, and his thumb pulled the hammers back. "You'll never run again, Boy!"

The shot was a surprise to both.

It didn't come from Beaux's gun, though. A hole suddenly exploded in the center of Beaux's forehead, twisting his body from the impact. Sightless eyes glared at the door in shock.

Beaux Conlon fell dead in a heap, his clothes still smoldering from the hot iron.

Tucker looked up in amazement. "Whoever you are, I am thankful to see you." Raising a shaking hand, he felt for the throbbing gash in his head. He looked at the stranger and then back to Beaux's body. "Did you know him?"

"Yeah, I knew him. A meaner, more viscous bastard never lived. He deserved to die. I've been following him since he killed my man in Independence. How badly are you hurt? Your head is bleeding. He came pretty close to finishing you off. You're Tucker?"

"I'm Tucker."

"Sam Shepherd. Let's get you up."

"What's all the shooting?"

"Your friends are fighting off the rest of Conlon's gang. Sit here, I'd better go help."

DEL ROLLED BACK TO WHERE he had been and fired two shots from his Paterson at a dark form sneaking across the corral. His shots

were answered, blasting into the trough, wetting Del's face and par-
tially blinding him.

Shaking his head to clear his eyes, Del wiped at his face with his
sleeve. He fired back as a flash from the barn sent a bullet just over
his head.

Daniel began to tire. The big man just wouldn't go down. Adonis's
face bled from multiple cuts. Daniel knew he must have broken at
least two ribs on his left side. It felt mushy there, each time he hit the
big man, but Adonis kept coming.

The man in the dust who Del had knocked down with the Howdah, pushed himself to his knees, shaking his head to clear it. He
wasn't out of the fight yet and rose to his feet. Seeing Del behind the
trough, he snuck up behind him while Del looked the other way.

Del couldn't see where that last shot came from. He cried out
when someone attacked him, viciously kicking his ribs. Rolling
away, he fired off a quick shot. It tore through the man's thigh,
causing him to shriek and throw himself away from Del, scrambling into the barn.

A single shot came from the forge.

Adonis could tell Daniel was flagging. The big man's ribs ached,
his chest burned like fire, his mouth tasted dry as cotton, but he
would not give up. A hatred burned in his belly for the humiliation
he believed Daniel had inflicted upon him. Now, it was his turn.
Daniel moved in to pound Adonis's ribs, but he was ready for that,
bringing his arms down suddenly he trapped the smaller man's left
arm against his side, then began beating Daniel's face and shoulder
until the arm separated and Daniel screamed in pain and defiance.

Adonis paused and gestured toward the barn. "Come here, you
two! Hold him."

Holstering their guns, two burly men pinned Daniel's arms and
Adonis punched into his belly with powerful piston-driven punches.
He stopped, puzzled, because Daniel wouldn't fall. Seeing a singletree
hanging on the corral fence, Adonis's face contorted into a sneer.

"I'll knock you to your knees." He laughed. Grabbing the singletree, he smashed it on the fence for effect. "Now, I'm going to knock
your head off, Dan Riodan."

Del shot him through the shoulder, breaking the big man's arm, leaving it to dangle uselessly. Adonis grabbed his arm, collapsing in the yard, moaning and cursing.

Shepherd came up behind Del firing, burning the cheek of one of the men who held Daniel. They fled. Shepherd's hammer clicked on an empty chamber. Daniel fell in a heap, face to face with Adonis.

Adonis leaned over to Daniel and sneered with malice, "It ain't over, Daniel Riodan. Damn you. It ain't over. I'll be back for you. You'll never see me coming. I'm going to kill you sure as I'm still breathing." Holding his arm to his side, he barked an order to his men. "Let's ride!" The men mounted quickly and rode out of the yard, leaving the three men alone in the clouds of dust and gunpowder.

Going to Daniel, Del picked him up and laid him against the trough. Wiping his father's bloody face with water from the trough, he asked, "You hurt bad, Pa?"

"I think I'll live, boy. This shoulder is gonna need to be set by a doc. I think it's dislocated. Where's Tucker?"

"He's all right. A little dazed. He's by the forge, still in irons, but he's going to be fine, I think," Shepherd said.

"Where's Beaux?" Del and Daniel asked at once.

"Laying dead in the dirt. I shot the rabid wolf."

Sam searched Beaux's pockets for the keys to the manacles, as the rest of them watched. "I've been chasing Beaux Conlon forever it seems. I'm glad it's over." Quickly, he turned the key in their locks and the manacles fell off Tucker's wrists. Tucker shook his wrists in grateful appreciation. As they left, Tucker dropped them on Beaux's smoking corpse.

"Wear these in hell, Beaux. Heaven wants nothing to do with any part of you."

"Let's get you across the street. I'll bet that pretty lady has some coffee on the stove. She's the one who told us where you were you know." Shepherd slapped Tucker's shoulder.

Tucker looked at him, then at Del and Daniel, with wonder in his eyes. It was over. It was finally over. Beaux Conlon would never haunt them again.

Nancy stood in the door, watching as they crossed the street. She quickly washed Tucker's bloody face, sending Bart down the street to fetch the doctor for Daniel and for the Sheriff.

"SO THAT'S IT," SAM SHEPHERD said as he finished his story. "Beaux shot Dave Roberts in a saloon in Independence. I put up a reward, but no one could get a lead on him. Me and my boys have followed him from body to body, till finally at Ft. Hall, a shopkeeper identified him to us and put us on a fresh trail. As we came down out of the mountains, my boys spotted the gang, and we took off after them. Beaux split and made for the town. I followed him to the café. It was the only place that was open. I saw Daniel and Del come in with guns in their hands, and I followed them in."

"Wait, here's the Sheriff," Bart said. They looked up from their table as the Sheriff entered.

"You Sam Shepherd?" Sheriff Able Boyd knew the faces of Tucker, Del, and Daniel. "It looks like you fellas have been in a war here," he said. "I'd just rode back into town when this young fella comes tearing up to my office. Said there was a gunfight across the street at the blacksmith's."

"Bart, listen to me. Go see what's holding up the doc. Quickly now. Go," said Nancy.

"Yes, sir. I'm Sam Shepherd."

"I just came from across the street. I count two bodies and a lot of blood. Luckily, that hot brand didn't burn the smith down. We've had word on Beaux Conlon for several days. Is that him, lying dead, with a bullet in his brain? The other fella will have to be picked up in a basket. You boys hang around town for a few days. There will be an inquiry into all of this. You saved a man's life tonight, I think. You'll all have to testify about what happened and how this baffling story came about. Hate does a terrible thing to a man. It's like a disease that eats them up from within. I'll be around to let you know when the inquest will be held. Good night."

"Sam saved my life. Though, I was doing pretty good, until Beaux hit me with that hammer. Knocked me silly. Del, I got a brand on him! Branded him as he was trying to brand me. Sam Shepherd shot him right between the eyes as he was about to shoot me with a coach gun."

"That's how he shot Dave Roberts, right between the eyes. I owed Dave that much."

Doctor Orton burst through the door.

"Sorry, it took me so long. I was setting a broken leg when Bart came in. Who do you want me to look at first? I heard the gunshots." His sharp eyes settled on Daniel, and he took a seat next to him, tenderly lifting his arm.

Sam looked at Del. "Your name is Del?"

"Yes, sir. They call me Del Rio."

"Would that be short for Delaino, by chance? As in Delaino Daniel Riodan?"

"Yes, sir, it would. Daniel over there, is my Pa."

"When Beaux left Independence, he left his belongings at the hotel. I claimed them hoping it would lead me to Dave's killer. Funny, Beaux Conlon never killed anyone until he came west."

"I knew him, Sam. He was mean. He was cruel." Tucker shook his head. "Just hemmed in enough by law and social restraints to stay within the boundaries of law and sanity. Out here, those boundaries fell away. The man I saw tonight was crazy insane."

"I want to turn Beaux's possessions over to you, Delaino. There are several documents with your name on them. I think you'll find them important. I'll see you tomorrow. We're headed back to Missouri as soon as the passes clear and this thing is over. I've got to find out what happened to my men. Hope you're open for breakfast tomorrow, Mrs. Kincaid. I'm looking forward to it. Good night."

Several days later, the court held the inquest.

During the inquest, Shepherd swore he had tracked Beaux from murder to murder. There were more deaths after he joined up with his gang. "They were all a gang of vicious killers. I counted at least ten dead."

The judge reached a decision of justifiable homicide. No other charges were filed. Del was awarded Beaux's possessions. With his mother's will—the document Tucker had hidden all the way from Baltimore—the totality of the documents made Delaino Daniel Riodan sole heir of the Conlon estate.

"What do I do now?" Del asked Daniel. "I can't claim anything out here in Oregon. What do I do?"

"Why don't you write to that Mister Randazzo, the attorney you met in Indianapolis? His father's a prominent attorney in Boston. Maybe they can look into managing the property until you're able to return. You sounded like you had made a friend. I imagine he would help you in this matter."

"That's a good idea, Pa. I should have thought of it. I'll write today. Right now, while it's fresh in my mind. Would you look it over to see if I've covered everything when I've finished?"

"I'd be happy to. It will take some time to get word back and forth. We've got time."

Del sat at one of the tables in Nancy's restaurant, back out of the way so he wouldn't be disturbed to gather his thoughts.

Putting ink to paper he started writing....

December 13, 1847
Randolph Randazzo Esq.
Dear Mr. Randazzo,
My Friend, I'm writing to inform....

The doors of Nancy's restaurant burst open.

"They've massacred the Whitmans! The Indians have killed the Whitman missionaries!"

Nancy wiped her hands on a towel as she ran around the counter. "What happened? The Whitmans have been friends to the Indians."

"Measles, ma'am. The Cayuse killed 'em, because the Indian children all died from the measles, and the white kids didn't. The militia's being called up!"

Nancy looked up at Del and their gazes locked, dumbfounded with shock.

EPILOGUE

DANIEL LAY IN A BED above the café, his face bandaged, his left arm suspended in a sling. Tucker sat in a chair, a bandage wrapped around his head, watching him. Nancy had turned Nate's room into convalescent quarters.

"Daniel, I can't thank you and Del enough. It's been the hardest thing I have ever done, coming west, but it was worth every drop of blood I paid. This is such a beautiful country. Finally—at last—we're free of the specter of the Conlons hovering over us. We can live our lives without looking over our shoulders all the time."

"Enjoy it for a while, my friend," Daniel said with a solemn face. "You're the first one I've told this to. While we were eyeball-to-eyeball in the dust of that corral, Adonis swore he'd be back to kill me. So I'll just keep looking over my shoulder for the time being."

M ICHAEL LEE is a contributing roundtable correspondent for Western Writers of America's *Roundup* Magazine and *Saddlebag Dispatches.* His fresh voice paints detail and gives historical authenticity to a frontier-life coming of age saga. Del Rio's characters move off of the page in three-dimensional images fighting nature, human frailty, disease, Indians, and human greed on the Oregon Trail, growing bigger and stronger as they fight their way west. The past relentlessly pursues them, clashing in violence, until it ends in a bloody climax. To learn more about Del Rio and The Pacific Frontier series, find Michael Lee on Facebook and the web.